BLACK
TIE
ONLY

BLACK TIE ONLY

JULIA FENTON

CONTEMPORARY
BOOKS

CHICAGO

Library of Congress Cataloging-in-Publication Data

Fenton, Julia.
    Black tie only : a novel / Julia Fenton.
       p.   cm.
    ISBN 0-8092-4308-3 : $19.95
    I. Title.
  PS3556.E56B5   1990
  813'.54—dc20   89-77207
                                          CIP

Published by Contemporary Books, Inc.
180 North Michigan Avenue, Chicago, Illinois 60601
Manufactured in the United States of America
International Standard Book Number: 0-8092-4308-3

To the three most important women in my life . . .
Stella, Mary, and Dolly,
and the many others who have so generously and graciously
offered their hearts in friendship. Thank you.

And to brother Ed, who really helped pick me up when
it got sort of scary out there for a while.
And especially to Cynthia and Robbie, who have constantly
been towers of strength for me and will
always be a source of inspiration.

Also, to Jean and Will Haughey, who gave their love
through dark times and happy, and who
gave me a star to wish on;
to Michael and Andy, who made my life bright
and everything else worthwhile;
for Jean Haughey Temme, Bill Haughey, and Russ Haughey,
so loving always, with wish stars of their own;
and for "Jean Jean," my creative, vibrant grandmother,
who somewhere is watching with love.

Acknowledgments
and Author's Note

I would like to thank the people who helped me throw a wonderful party. My loveliest bouquet goes to Dolly Rotenberg and Charlotte Silverstone of The Party Planners, Birmingham, Michigan, who designed my "Charles and Di" party from favors to menu. Dolly, I hope you always invite me to your parties. They're fabulous!

I would also like to thank the late composer Sammy Fain, who helped me write the song "Easy Woman," and Kenneth Jay Lane, who offered advice and suggestions for Alexandra's necklace, the "Fitzgerald Fifty."

I am also very grateful to Ginny Borowski, Special Services, American Airlines at O'Hare International Airport, Chicago; LaDene Bowen, Butte–Silver City Chamber of Commerce; Mary Kathryn Boyer; Livio Capicchioni; Sheila Clifford; Peter Crociato; William Davidson; Margaret Duda; Phyllis Factor; Dr. Richard Feldman; Oscar Feldman; Peter and Annette Fink; Douglas Fraser; Ralph Gerson; John and Peter Ginopolis; Dr. Ken Gitlin; Patricia Locricchio Goff; Bonnie Sue Harris; Mike and Barbara Horowitz; the Alan M. Hurvitz family; Gary Kessler; Irv Kessler; George Killeen; the Joseph Kopicki family; Mickey and Joyce Lolich; Byron and Jojo MacGregor; Harvey Mackay; Nancy Mackechnie, Special Collections, Thompson Library, Vassar College; Robert Magill; Fred Manfra, ABC Radio, New York; J. P. and Judy McCarthy; Peter McInally,

Library of British Information Services, New York; Tillie Milgrom; Louis Rudolph; Dr. Herschel Sandberg; Catherine E. Schaffer, Account Manager, British Airways; Joe and Edna Slavik; Emmet E. Tracy, Jr.; Marilyn Turner; Karen Warner; and Larry Wilkinson.

I would also like to thank Al Zuckerman, of Writers House, and my dedicated and superb editor, Nancy Coffey, and her assistant, Rachel Henderson.

Very special thanks also go to Robert L. Fenton, entertainment attorney, Hollywood film producer, and most recently producer of the made-for-TV movie *Double Standard*, and to Julia Grice.

The characters in this book are all fictional—that is, they come out of my imagination. If they bear any resemblance to specific individuals, this is a matter of coincidence. It was not my intention. I have created fictional events that use the names of certain celebrities or very prominent people and I put them in places they were not, saying words they did not. The actions and motivations of the characters named after real people are entirely fictitious and should not be considered real or factual. Simply put, there is no connection between the characters in the novel and the people whose names I have used. If I have caused embarrassment to anyone in any manner, I wish, here and now, to apologize—openly and most sincerely. Without the "stars" and "princesses" of our world, we would all be much poorer.

Julia Fenton

December 1989

Now, imagine that a pale ivory vellum envelope has arrived with your name inscribed in a calligrapher's hand. You are invited . . .

BLACK TIE ONLY

Kenneth Jay Lane
and guest

In honor of Their Royal Highnesses
the Prince and Princess of Wales
Mr. & Mrs. Richard Fitzgerald Cox, Jr.,
request the pleasure of your company
at dinner
on Saturday, the ninth of September
at eight o'clock
at the Chicago Fitzgerald Hotel

R.s.v.p.
1450 North Michigan Avenue
Chicago, Illinois 60611   Black tie

Prologue

"Please hold for Her Highness, the Princess of Wales."

Faint, deep-sea static crackled over the wire as Alexandra Cox, taking the call in her lush penthouse office in Chicago's Fitzgerald Tower, gazed out of floor-to-ceiling windows at the endless panorama of Lake Michigan. On the photo-lined wall behind her desk, her platinum record for "Easy Woman" glowed in the mellowing sunlight.

"Alexandra? Is it you? Alexandra?"

"Diana! Yes, it's me. It's been forever! It's so good to hear your voice."

"Oh, and yours too," Diana's laugh was light. "I know you and Richard are fine—I'm reading about you everywhere. What's the news with Jette and Mary Lee? Have you seen them lately?"

"I saw Jette just last week. She was here in Chicago promoting her perfume."

"Oh, so our Jette even has her own perfume," interrupted Diana, amused.

"Yes, and of course it's named after her. And she's negotiating with NBC for a new series. Mary Lee's still on top. Every time I turn on the television there she is, interviewing another hot celebrity."

Diana sighed, "Oh, it's nice to talk with you, Alexandra. We never see each other anymore. Remember last time? Running around London in those awful sunglasses and wigs?''

The two women laughed, friends since school days at the West Heath School, in Kent, England, when Diana had been merely Diana Spencer, and Alexandra the lonely child of a wealthy, grieving widower.

"But how is everything, Diana? Are you and Charles going to be in Chicago on your tour? You know how Richard and I would love to show you the city."

"We *were* thinking of visiting. Actually, that's why I'm calling. Alexandra, I have an enormous favor to ask of you. Charles and Mrs. Thatcher would like you to give a party for us in September."

"A party?"

"Well, Charles would like an opportunity to talk informally with the CEOs of American Motors, Ford, and Chrysler. You know they have plans to establish plants in Europe, and Charles wants to lobby personally for some of them being built in England. We thought a party would be the ideal setting. Perhaps five hundred people?"

"My God, Diana!" Alexandra could feel her pulse quickening.

"I almost hesitate to say it," Diana went on, "but you know that if we're the guests of honor, everybody will come to gawk at the Royals. And you're the perfect choice, Alexandra. Everybody knows what a brilliant hostess you are, besides being a great songwriter. Between us, I just know we'd have a fabulous party. Please say you'll do it."

Alexandra stared out the window as Diana talked, oblivious to the magnificent view from sixty stories above Lake Shore Drive. Her imagination raced, and she was seeing towering arrangements of flowers, soaring candelabras, glittering jewels, a gala more glorious than Malcolm Forbes's seventieth-birthday bash in Morocco! She'd be the hostess of the year, and the publicity value for her husband's Fitzgerald Hotel chain would be incalculable. But more than that, it would be *fun*. A chance to put together one unforgettable night for a dear friend.

For one second Alexandra hung on the brink of what was part exhilaration, part trepidation, part awe. Could she organize a gala for five hundred people in only six weeks?

"May I send you our personal guest list?" Diana pressed. "It's only about thirty people."

Alexandra drew a short, nervous breath. "Yes," she said, a tremor of excitement in her voice.

"And Alexandra," Diana added.

"Yes?"

"Wear that spectacular necklace Richard gave you, because I have a new one. It's my ninth-anniversary gift from Charles, and I've been dying to show it off."

—— ◄► ——

Some received invitations, some did not.

—— ◄► ——

In Studio City, morning sunlight spilled across actress Darryl Boyer's bed, caressing one naked, perfectly contoured hip. She stirred, sighing, as she nudged the smoothly muscled side of her current lover, a twenty-one-year-old aerobics instructor, reaching across him for the *Los Angeles Times*, which her Mexican maid had just placed on the night table.

Darryl decided her time with him was finished. A man could have all the muscles in the world, but that didn't change the size of his cock or what he could do with it.

Idly she flipped through the pages, her eyes flicking from riot to drug conviction to senatorial scandal to tax hike, then focusing on a headline on the second front page: *Their Highnesses to Tour U.S., Royal Gala for 500 Slated.*

Darryl skimmed the article. Princess Diana always interested her, and she thought Charles might be a lot better in bed than anyone supposed. The *Los Angeles Times* estimated the budget for this particular party to exceed $3.75 million, and its guest list . . . Darryl narrowed her eyes and started reading every word . . . would include luminaries ranging from President Bush to Lee Iacocca.

The hostess . . . Darryl's eyes narrowed still further . . . was none other than Alexandra Cox, married to Darryl's own ex-husband, Richard.

So Dickey-bird was entertaining royalty, Darryl mused.

Since this was Los Angeles, the article devoted six or seven paragraphs to a list of Hollywood people who had received invitations, including Neil Diamond, Frank Sinatra, the Lew Wassermans, Sammy Davis, Jr., Steven Spielberg, Elizabeth Taylor, Paul Newman, Sigourney Weaver, the Aaron Spellings, Sidney Poitier, and the Louis Rudolphs. The list continued with Merv Griffin, Bruce Springsteen, Sidney B. Cohen . . .

Darryl gripped the paper with shaking fingers. She rolled over to sit up in bed, her heart racing. Sid Cohen! He was head of Omni Studios, which was now casting a fabulous new movie, *Indigo Nights*. Eight years ago, she would have been sent a script—they would have been after *her*. Now she might as well not exist.

Savagely she rolled up the *Times* and hurled it across the bedroom, where it smashed into an étagère, sending crystal vases, silk flowers, and framed photos smashing to the floor.

Darryl jumped out of bed and pulled on a champagne-colored satin robe, heedless of the pieces of broken glass. This party was her chance. She hadn't been able to get to Cohen— and Cohen was not returning her calls. But if she could get to that party, and spend just ten minutes with Cohen, ten lousy minutes in a dynamite dress that showed off her spectacular new breasts . . .

Yes.

Maybe Myron Orlando could help on this one. After using Darryl as a springboard to forming CAA years ago, he owed her plenty. Picking up her mint green telephone, she began dialing.

— ▶◀ —

In Hong Kong, the fragrance of exotic flower blossoms rose with the steam from the almond-shaped bath pool where David Kwan, millionaire businessman and Chinese movie mogul, was enjoying the erotic pleasures of an oriental bath.

A petite beauty scrubbed his back, using the circular movements he particularly liked. For an instant Kwan gave himself up to the sensuous luxury he had earned through a lifetime of working twenty-hour days.

At poolside, his secretary, a thin Chinese man with wire-rimmed glasses, was reading aloud from the day's papers, proffering to him only the tidbits he could use.

" 'Charles and Diana, Prince and Princess of Wales, will make an unexpected U.S. and Canadian tour next month, say U.S. sources, who speculate the trip may be related to British efforts to convince U.S. automakers to build four or five new plants in England,' " the secretary read in his dry monotone.

From the bathwater, Kwan grunted.

The secretary continued to read. " 'The couple will attend a party in Chicago, given by international hotelier Richard Fitzgerald Cox, Jr., and his wife, songwriter Alexandra Winthrop. Guests will include . . . " He droned on, listing names of celebrities and movie stars, several of whom Kwan had tried unsuccessfully to get for his latest karate picture.

The secretary came to the name of Sidney B. Cohen, and Kwan grunted again.

"Read me the mail now," he commanded, as the bath girl circled his back with her strong but delicate fingers. The secretary began sorting through the stack of letters. Kwan sighed, pushing away the girl, as he waded to the edge of the pool and reached for his towel. He had long been thinking of buying a U.S. film studio and had made advances to Omni Studios three times in the past two years. Cohen had summarily rejected his overtures. Foreign ownership was a controversial issue in the United States now.

But if he could talk to Cohen again—in person, in a party setting, where perhaps Cohen would have had a bit too much to drink . . .

"Read me all the invitations," he ordered his secretary.

He had done business with Richard Cox many times and knew he would be on the list.

— ►◄ —

In New York, Kenneth Jay Lane had one hand on his carotid artery as he anxiously checked his post-run pulse, sweat pouring down his face, soaking his bare chest and running shorts.

Jesus, his pulse was still 130.

He checked it again, feeling the heavy throbs in his neck that signaled he was a fiftyish, sedentary man trying to run like a twenty-three-year-old.

Panting, he loped through his Park Avenue apartment, grabbing for the *New York Times* his maid had left on the hall table. He scanned its closely spaced and dry-looking front page as he went into his bedroom to strip.

Donning a brocade bathrobe, he examined the headlines, his eyes drifting to a small one, front page, lower left, that began *Coxes to Host Royals*.

Six years ago, he'd designed a diamond necklace for Richard to give to Alexandra. The newspapers had had a field day with it, dubbing it the "Fitzgerald Fifty" for the fifty important South African diamonds it showcased, including five huge, rare pink diamonds. It had been sheer good luck for him. The publicity had brought him even more famous customers, everyone from Bianca to Liz and Jackie O. Now he was a celebrity, with his own following.

He skimmed the article, nodding, satisfied. Of course Alexandra would wear the necklace to a party of this magnitude. What else could she wear even half as stunning? But a party in Chicago. It wasn't his usual style.

He padded back to his hall table and retrieved the stack of mail Odelia had left on the sterling silver tray.

Yes, there it was.

The oversized envelope was stiff and cream-colored, made of heavy, watermarked, pure linen paper, addressed in perfectly wrought calligraphy. Hand-stamped, of course.

A nice touch.

He slit open the envelope. Beautifully engraved, the invitation bore his own name, hand-lettered. *Mr. & Mrs. Richard Fitzgerald Cox, Jr., request the pleasure of your company . . .*

He smiled. Undoubtedly his friends Sid and Mercedes Bass would be attending, and Al Taubman. He would not have to suffer a commercial airline flight, but could fly on one of their private planes.

For the Coxes, he'd even go to Chicago.

— ►◄ —

In London, at No. 10 Downing Street, Prime Minister Margaret Thatcher had also received an invitation by air mail. She was working late, so intent on her work that she had forgotten to draw the drapes against the soft gray rain that splattered against the panes.

She paused for a moment to rub her temples, where the beginning of a tension headache throbbed.

On her mahogany desk, the invitation lay opened, weighted down with a millefiori paperweight given her by the Italian ambassador some years ago.

She would not be able to attend, of course, because of the Saudi situation, and would send her regrets. Still, the sight of the invitation encouraged her.

The purpose of the Cox party was to bring difficult people together, and Alexandra Cox had been very carefully selected to accomplish the task. An experienced hostess and a well-known songwriter, she had organized political fundraisers for as many as fifteen hundred with little fuss.

Other women could give parties with equal brilliance, but Alexandra had been chosen for something far more important— her warmth. There was something special about her, their sources had been told over and over by those who knew the Cox woman. She possessed . . . what was the proper term for it? . . . a genius at projecting good will and happiness, so that those around her felt it and acted upon it.

Mrs. Thatcher turned the invitation over in her hands. Poor Charles! His existence had unkindly been called "a comfortable form of inherited imprisonment." Here he could be useful. They would have to count on the Americans' infatuation with any- thing royal, of course. She remembered the dinner party for Elizabeth and Philip on their U.S. tour in 1983, held in Holly- wood at Sound Stage 9 at Twentieth Century-Fox. Even sophis- ticated American movie stars had stood on tiptoes for a final look at Her Majesty as she left the dinner.

The prime minister just hoped it would work that way again.

— ►◄ —

And in a Georgetown apartment in Washington, a woman with disheveled blonde hair and burning eyes paced the same stretch of carpet over and over. She could smell her own sour- ness, an angry odor that no amount of perfume could camou- flage.

A copy of the *Washington Post* lay where she had tossed it, the article on the Cox party almost burning a hole in the newsprint.

As she walked, she passed a mirror that she kept for the deliberate purpose of reminding herself who she was and what had happened to her. She stopped in front of the glass, the familiar nausea returning as she forced herself to look at her reflection.

Hideous.

The scars . . .

Hatred consumed her. She had read *his* name in the article in the Style section, the man who had ruined her face and her life, caused the nightmares that still made her wake screaming at night . . .

His fault.

Using his staff as buffers, he had cleverly kept her away from him. But he would not prevent her from going to the Cox party, not if she was clever.

And she would be very clever.

She intended to kill him. She had been planning it for years. The knife would enter at about the navel. Then, striking hard, she would angle the blade downward. There would be the horrid friction of his internal organs, but she was strong. She would not stop until she had cut away every vestige of his manhood.

Gazing in the mirror, she parted her lips in a smile. It was a sweet smile, even a pretty smile—people still told her so. Some of them said that her face looked just as good as it always had, that the plastic surgeons had not failed. But they lied.

She knew better. She knew how scarred she was, how ugly.

And *he* was finally going to pay.

1

Alexandra
1989

Andre Burton, the doorman of the Fitzgerald Tower, at 1500 North Lake Shore Drive, was chief of a domain that consisted of about twenty square feet of curb, sidewalk, and revolving door trimmed in high-tech stainless steel. He had seen plenty in the 1,650 days he had stood on guard here. Elegant women hurrying inside with packages from stores and galleries along Chicago's Magnificent Mile—Bonwit Teller, Ralph Lauren, Gucci, Tiffany & Co., Jax, and Brittany Ltd. Powerful men who tipped him as they strode toward taxis and limousines.

The top fifty-five floors of the sixty-story Fitzgerald Tower were condos, selling for a minimum of $2.5 million each. Each condominium offered stupendous views on all four sides. City canyons extended gray to the limit of the eye, the Chicago River winding through like an iridescent scarf, and Lake Michigan as blue as any astronaut's vision.

Now a deliveryman approached, wheeling a cart holding a large box from I. Magnin. Andre waved him to the service entrance and turned as the Cox limousine pulled up, whispering to a stop in front of the building.

He hurried forward to pull open the rear door.

"Hello, Andre." The woman who stepped out of the limousine with graceful certainty was blonde and beautiful, with such a warm glow that Andre dropped his own professional smile and gave her a real one.

"Beautiful day, Mrs. Cox," he told her.

"Oh, yes."

Alexandra's shoulder-length mane of tousled hair was golden and sun-streaked. She had wide-spaced blue eyes the color of Wedgwood, and the high cheekbones and full lips that suggested a model.

"How's your daughter?" Alexandra asked him as he escorted her to the door.

"Oh, she's fine. Gettin' her leg out of the cast in two more weeks."

"Wonderful. Did she get the cassette tape I sent her?"

"Sure did. She loves it. She listens to your songs all the time; she says 'Easy Woman' is her favorite, but she likes 'Forgiving Woman,' too. Wants to write some music herself someday."

"Well, tell her all it takes is incredible persistence, much luck, and a bit of insanity." Alexandra gave Andre a little wave and disappeared into the building, leaving him to stare after her for an instant.

Alexandra greeted the security guard and strode through the magnificent lobby toward the express elevator. The building had been designed by a disciple of Mies van der Rohe, and except for the towering arrangements of flowers and foliage banked along one black Carrara marble wall, the lobby was extravagantly stark.

Waiting, Alexandra caught her reflection in the steel elevator door. In her white linen Ferré suit and alligator pumps, she was an image of understated elegance. She wore no jewelry except for pearl earrings and her Cartier watch.

She tapped her foot, reminding herself to call Dolly Rutledge, her party planner. Damn—that florist she'd interviewed just didn't have it. They'd have to find someone more inspired. That was the least of her worries, however. With so much to do, she realized now she was going to have to put the new song aside until fall.

The elevator arrived, and she stepped in, followed by the deliveryman. Alexandra glanced at him, thinking he shouldn't be in the express car. She pressed the button for the fifty-ninth floor and leaned against the back wall, pulling the *Chicago Tribune* out of her briefcase.

As the elevator sailed upward, she opened up the Style section. Another article about the gala. This one described her "impeccable Boston background," listing her three platinum and two gold records and her affiliation with Arista Records. The feature writer, Dana Chen, went on to speculate that Alexandra would wear the "Fitzgerald Fifty," a gift to her from her husband.

"Dripping with 45 white, five-carat diamonds and five rare, 10-carat pink diamonds, as well as hundreds of smaller stones, it is reputed to be one of the most expensive necklaces ever—"

The necklace. Symbol of the marriage she once had, the love that had somehow slipped away.

Richard had given it to her six years ago, upon the birth of their eldest. She had never seen anything like its blazing beauty, and she had been overcome with its glitter and her own love.

Richard, too, had been filled with emotion. "We had a whole jeweler's workshop in Paris working overtime," he'd told her, his voice breaking. "I'm not much with words, but . . . the diamonds stand for all the ways I love you. For so many kisses . . . "

In that moment, Alexandra thought with a pang of sadness, Richard had been almost poetic, and she adored him for it.

Then the real world came crashing in. Not all at once, but gradually there were more and more meetings, phone calls, and business trips to Europe, South America, the Orient. Mergers, acquisitions, leveraged buyouts.

They'd talked and then talked some more about their marriage, but Richard didn't see the problem.

The elevator stopped with a jerk.

"What . . . ?" she began in surprise.

Suddenly the deliveryman tore away the wrapping paper to reveal a television set with a VCR hooked up on top.

He pushed a button, and voices filled the elevator. There was a commercial for spaghetti sauce—a family gathered in a kitchen, a woman smiling into the camera.

"Very nice," Alexandra said, the tremor in her voice barely detectable. "But I'd like to get off at my floor."

He punched another button.

After a moment the static cleared, revealing a scene that stopped Alexandra's heart.

The scene was her children's playroom. The camera panned to show the three Cox children crouched around a dollhouse, intent on their play. Trip, a handsome six-year-old boy with the steady gaze of his father, was seated cross-legged on the floor sorting through a large box of miniature furniture. Lying on his stomach and reaching into the house was shy Andrew, the "me-too" boy of five. Stephanie, aged three, squatted beside her older brothers like a chubby frog.

And then the picture changed.

The outlines of the children suddenly became stylized, the movements jerky, and as the camera pulled back, a new figure entered the screen, holding an upraised knife.

It's been done by computer graphics, Alexandra thought wildly. *It's not real, it is not real.*

The cartoon villain crept toward her children, raising the computer-drawn knife higher. Then abruptly he vanished, and the video camera cut to the playroom again.

Alexandra bit her lip, realizing that the three dark, mutilated shapes on the floor were her children or, rather, computer-designed images representing her children, crumpled corpses soaked in bright red pools of blood. The tiniest figure, representing Stephanie, was closest to the camera. She had been depicted as a lifeless little china doll, eyelids closed, stylized circles of pink on her small, round cheeks.

Only the blood had been depicted realistically. Splashed all over the children, all over the room, covering the dollhouse in grisly spatters.

Alexandra wrenched her eyes away, so shaken she could not even scream.

The deliveryman was already covering the TV set. His eyes darted toward her.

"If your husband don't sign the union agreement," he began, the first words he had spoken. "If he don't sign, we're gonna strike, *and* we're gonna bust up your family . . . "

"What?"

"Just tell him," he whispered.

He released the stop button and quickly exited at the next floor, wheeling his cart in front of him. The whole incident had taken no more than two minutes.

My God, the union.

The elevator slid soundlessly to a stop, and with a shaking hand Alexandra used her floor key to unlock the door, which opened directly into the Coxes' apartment.

She ran frantically to the stairs and took them two steps at a time. If they had hurt her children . . .

The playroom door stood half open. She rushed in, breathless with fear, and stopped. In a rocking chair sat their British nanny, Elizabeth Clifford-Brown, placidly crocheting a sweater. Hanging over her shoulder, talking rapidly, was Trip, his eyes alight with a six-year-old's enthusiasm. Andy was crouched on the floor, dismembering a Transformer. Stephanie, her brow furrowed with concentration, had removed the furniture from the dollhouse and was trying to arrange it on the house's shingled roof.

"Brownie! Are they?—Oh! Oh, God!" Alexandra rushed to the children, not knowing which one to hug first, frantic to feel their small, warm bodies in her arms. She scooped up baby Stephanie and reached for the squirming Andy. Trip came to her on his own, and she engulfed him with both arms. She had all three of them together in her arms, burying her nose in their freshly shampooed hair.

"Oh! Oh, I love you guys! Do you know that? You are the nicest little guys in the whole world!"

Trip pulled away a little. "Mom," he said. "Why are you so huggy? You're hurting me, Mommy. We love you, too."

"Oh, sweetheart! I just felt like hugging and kissing some." She was laughing now, her relief making her slightly giddy.

"Is everything quite all right, Mrs. Cox?" asked the nanny, an attractive, forty-year-old woman who had once worked for Princess Michael.

"Oh, yes, yes . . . I only wanted to see my babies," Alexandra said, ruffling Trip's hair and looking into his intelligent eyes. "Are they having a good morning? Is Trip having his swimming class today at school?"

"Yes, at three o'clock."

"Are you going to swim a length of the pool today? Will you go all the way this time?"

"I did that last week, Mom."

"Mommy!" piped up little Stephanie, gripping Alexandra's legs and begging to be picked up.

Alexandra hoisted up her sturdy daughter and held her on one hip.

God, she loved her children.

— ◄► —

Richard Cox emerged from his private elevator at the sixtieth floor executive office of the Chicago Fitzgerald Hotel, walking through the private corridor toward the bank of superbly furnished offices that faced Lake Michigan.

A secretary greeted him with a respectful smile. Among his staffers, Richard was legendary. He was, as the *Wall Street Journal* once referred to him, "the hotel czar of America."

Several vice presidents spoke to him, but Richard only nodded and muttered a few words, continuing to his office suite at the end of the floor. At fifty-one, Richard looked fifteen years younger, a handsome man who could easily have gotten a role in the movie *Wall Street*. His compact body was in excellent shape from hours of working out, swimming, and sailing. A light heavyweight boxer at Syracuse University, he could still go a few rounds in a creditable performance, giving him a physical confidence some found intimidating.

His luxurious brown hair was only slightly grayed at the temples. His square face held a firm, straight nose, full lips, and light blue, piercing eyes. Richard had the confident jawline of a man accustomed to getting what he wants without fuss. But laugh lines around his eyes softened and humanized that appearance.

"Good morning, Mr. Cox," said Ingrid, his receptionist. He noticed that two men were seated in the plush waiting area.

He continued through a door and into a central area where his four personal secretaries, all multilingual, sat at their desks.

"Mr. Cox." One of the secretaries, Diane Rizzuto Crosby, hurried up to him, a list of messages in her hand. "The bankers have been waiting for fifteen minutes, and there are several messages for you from Lee Iacocca. It's the third time he's called. There's a call from Marvin Davis, and Mr. Green called twice. Congressman John Dingell wants you to call him right away, and the manager of the Rome Fitzgerald says you're to call him, too. It's urgent."

Richard nodded. "Tell the bankers I'll see them in just a few minutes. And place a return call to Iacocca. Anything else?"

"Nothing really urgent. I've put it all on your desk, along with the fax mail. There are quite a few transmissions today from Tokyo."

Richard entered his private office and closed the door. Floor-to-ceiling windows offered sweeping views of Lake Michigan harbors, marinas, and passing Great Lakes freighters. The carpeting was thick, cranberry red, with chairs and couches of supple, butter-soft black Italian leather. His huge, walnut partner's desk was an antique that had belonged to his father.

To his right was a conference and screening room. There,

behind a louvered cabinet, Richard kept his private computer, so that when he chose, he could crunch his own numbers. Some figures were too important or too private to leave to staffers.

There was a large bathroom with a shower, small steam room, and dressing room where he kept enough clothes and luggage so that in an emergency he could leave for anywhere in the world without going home first.

"All right," he said, buzzing Diane on the intercom. "Send in Mr. Wheeler and Mr. Greenwald."

The two bankers from First American Securities Trust entered the room and shook hands with Richard, their palms slightly sweaty. They tried not to look overly impressed with the trappings of power around them—pictures of Richard and his father, Richard F. Cox, Sr., taken with Presidents Roosevelt, Eisenhower, Kennedy, and Reagan. One photograph showed Reagan and Gorbachev with Richard in the middle, looking jovial and holding raised hands in celebration of the signing of a contract for the Moscow Fitzgerald Hotel, and another was of Richard and Alexandra with the just-married Prince and Princess of Wales. There was also a framed copy of his prospectus put out by Eastman Dillon for the successful sale of a $2 billion issue of convertible debentures.

"All right, gentlemen," Richard said to the two bankers. "I have thirty minutes on my schedule. Let's talk."

The bankers wanted to become Richard's prime investment banking house, and although they hinted that the Fitzgerald Corporation was a bit more "diluted" than they would like to see it, they were still anxious to establish a relationship. Each side assessed the other. Steven Greenwald and James Wheeler had just begun their presentation when Diane interrupted by buzzing Richard on his private line. "Mr. Cox, your wife is on line five; she says it's very urgent. And I have Mr. Iacocca on line six."

"All right, Diane. Pardon me, gentlemen," Richard said. He walked through the reception area to a staff room where he could use the telephone in privacy. "Lexy? What's up?"

"Come home," she said hoarsely.

"I'm in a meeting. I'm up to my ears in bankers. What's wrong?"

"I can't tell you over the phone. Please, Richard. It's . . . " Her voice caught. "I have to tell you in person. I have to talk to you—now."

◄►

"What is it, Lexy? Why the hell couldn't you tell me over the phone?" Richard entered Alexandra's study, his eyes dark.

"Something happened to me in the elevator, Richard." She forced the tremor out of her voice. "There was a deliveryman. He made me watch this video. It was . . . they'd done something on a computer . . . I don't know how they did it."

He stared at her. "What are you talking about? Someone approached you in the elevator?"

"Not just approached!" she cried. "He played a videotape that showed *our* home, *our* playroom, *our* kids. It had been doctored up to show . . . to show them dead," she finished in a whisper. Then, through tears, she repeated the threat uttered by the union man.

"Jesus!" Richard ran his fingers through his hair. "The bastards have even invaded the privacy of our home."

"But why?" she demanded. "Why would they do such a thing? Would they really—"

"Of course not." Richard took her in his arms, kissing her as he held her close. "It's only an attention-getting move, Lexy. They know where I'm vulnerable. They're smart, those rotten bastards. It was all planned. Now, please, darling," he added, "please don't worry anymore."

"Oh, God, Richard." She sank into a chintz-covered chair.

"Lexy, this is tough, but it's all part of the game as far as they are concerned, and the less we react to it, the better. I promise you, it will be all right."

She stared at him. "You're patronizing me, Richard. You almost enjoy this, don't you? It's just another challenge to you, isn't it? One more business adversary to conquer. You against the union, no holds barred, fight until the last breath."

"Alexandra—"

Her voice rose. "They're using the children to get to you!"

"Lexy, nothing is going to happen—not to the kids, I swear it on all that's holy."

"It better not!"

He went to her and started to knead her shoulders. His fingers were firm and strong.

"I'm sure," he said after a minute, stopping the kneading. "We're very near agreement. We should have it settled in the next week or so." His smile looked tired, as it did so often lately. His arms tightened around her. "I promise, Lexy," he whispered.

Richard walked down the hall to his study, which was equipped with two private telephone lines, an additional WATS outlet, a fax machine, another computer, and an outstanding collection of sailing-ship models, some dating from the 1700s.

He reached for the telephone and speed-dialed the number for Slattery, his chief of security. Busy. Outside the wall of windows, a jet was tunneling into the blue. He scowled at the spectacle, bitterly hearing his own voice so confident with reassurance.

He wasn't sure that he believed his own words. He was far more worried than he had admitted to his wife. He had never run up against a union more determined to have its demands met. The list was ball-breaking and would cost millions.

It was time for a new master contract with all the hotels in the country, and the Fitzgerald chain—biggest and newest— had been targeted for a possible strike. Such an event could make the Cox empire vulnerable to a hostile takeover, just as the airlines now had their problems with the Carl Icahns and T. Boone Pickenses of the world.

At the very thought, beads of sweat sprang up on his forehead. He had expanded a little too quickly, he knew, and some short-term financing was starting to come due. Three-year debentures at 9½ percent. Not that that was a problem—if things could just stay stable for a year or two.

He reached for the Rolodex, found Robbie Fraser's personal number, and quickly punched out the digits. Fraser was the only Teamster official he trusted—a rugged, stocky organizer who had started out as a cross-country truck driver and was now an international vice president of the Teamsters. He was also a director of the Midwest Conference, which gave Fraser plenty of muscle within the union. Fraser, a fiery orator, was popular with the rank and file, and it was generally known that he was honest.

The phone rang five times before Fraser answered.

"Yeah?"

"Richard Cox here. One of your men got cute with my wife in an elevator, showed her a doctored videotape of my kids. Fraser, I can't believe you would pull this kind of bullshit!"

"Slow down, man. What videotape?"

"My family is off-limits, Fraser. I want you to tell that to every hairy son of a bitch on your committee, and I want you to do it today."

"Hey—"

"Leave my family alone, goddamn your ass. Because if there is one more contact made with my wife, you can fucking well whistle for your contract."

"I don't know what the hell you're talking about."

"The hell you don't. You got into my house, you got right in with the kids, and I won't stand for it. You don't mess with my family, Fraser."

Richard could hear Fraser cursing under his breath. "Those dumb pricks . . . I swear I don't know anything about it, I give you my word, Cox. I'll find out. These guys—" Fraser expelled his breath harshly. "They've gotten a little hungry, that's all. And hunger makes people do crazy things."

"Save the talk for the union meeting," Richard snapped, hanging up.

— ►◄ —

Robbie Fraser listened to the click as the line went dead, then he slammed his fist on his desk. He jabbed the familiar phone number with a thick forefinger and sat listening to the rings, until finally a male voice picked up.

"Powerhouse Gym."

"Tank Marchek," Fraser snapped.

Fraser paced, narrowing his eyes at the framed, autographed pictures that hung on his wall, of George Meany, the former president of the AFL-CIO; Walter Reuther and Doug Fraser of the UAW; and his old friend, Jimmy Hoffa, with whom he'd fought the first union wars at Allied Trucking.

"Emil Marchek," finally came the voice of Local 296's president.

"Tank, what the fuck's going on? I'm hearing a shitload of rumors."

Tank chuckled. "Whaddaya hear?"

"You know damn well what I heard. Did you arrange that little scene with Mrs. Cox? The one with the fucking videotape?"

"Yeah. Cox is a tough hard-ass. I figured a little scare would soften him up."

"Your ass ought to be fried!" Fraser snapped. "You don't soften a man up by threatening his family. You've managed to unzip in one hour what's taken me three years to put together.

You keep your nose out of my negotiations, and you stay the fuck away from his family, do you hear me?"

━━━ ▶◀ ━━━

Richard scowled at the telephone. Robbie Fraser was supposed to be honest, and he'd denied everything. So what did that mean?

The light finally dawned. There were two factions in the union—and the faction led by Tank Marchek must have perpetrated that stellar bit of union intimidation. That figured. Marchek was under federal investigation for extortion and defrauding the union's pension benefits plan.

He dialed the number for Marchek's home and waited impatiently while the rings mounted. He hung up and found the number of the gym over in Germantown where Marchek pumped iron. Someone there said he had just left. Richard hung up, aware that he was too angry for rational decisions.

Alexandra . . . the kids . . . Tripper. Not even Alexandra knew how empty he'd be without them.

He leaned back, willing the tension out of himself. He fastened his eyes on the wall that held the square-rigger models. His latest acquisition was a model of the British clipper *Taeping,* designed and built by Robert Steele for the China tea trade. He loved the free feeling of sailing, and he focused on that, imagining a day of crashing whitecaps and fresh wind that smelled of salt water.

When he reached for the telephone to call Jack Slattery, he was coldly calm.

The security chief came on the line, and Richard told him what had happened.

"Shit!" Slattery exploded. "Excuse the language, boss." He was a former detective in the Chicago Police Department who had run his own successful security business. Richard had lured him away with a large salary, car, profit sharing, and a 401(k) plan.

"Yeah, right, so what do you recommend?"

"For starters, you'd better go over your household staff with a fine-tooth comb, boss. Any new servants? Anyone who's just come in in the past week or two?"

"No."

"Then it's got to be someone you already have, maybe

someone they paid to come in and take the video of your kids so they could run it through the computer. You'd better check them all, sir, and you're going to have to tell your staff about this, so they know not to let anyone near your children or your wife.

"Do you want me to send over a couple of men? We can add them to your staff for a week or so. Let them be butlers or something."

Richard smiled dryly at the idea of a pair of butlers in his household. Alexandra wouldn't stand for being guarded. She always wanted a certain amount of privacy—at least until now. "OK. I'll talk to her—we'll get the staff figured out."

"And the doorman of your building, the front-desk security guard, your building security. Where the hell were they? How the hell did the guy get in? Even more important, how did he get out? Did anyone see him? Did he leave with the TV set, or did he dump it somewhere in the building? Shit. I'll be there in ten minutes."

—— ▶◀ ——

But Alexandra, descending the stairs to the main level, was already making a mental list of the household staff, cataloging them by name, background, and length of employment. There was a betrayer in her home.

Mrs. Abbott, the housekeeper, had been with them for seven years. A plump, businesslike woman in her forties, Mary Abbott was a superb organizer, excellent with details, as faithful as any Victorian household retainer.

Judy Wallis, Alexandra's social secretary, four years. Judy, forty-eight, was a faded beauty with a Philadelphia social background. Now she was divorced and putting two children through college. No. Not Judy. And not Brownie, the nanny, either. The woman was scrupulously honest.

There were also three live-in domestics and a cook . . . all people she had trusted.

She sighed as she reached the bottom of the staircase. Which one of her staff had let the union people in?

As always, her home reached out to welcome her, the sensation almost physical. Warm grays and peaches, and fireplaces that in winter burned sweet applewood and pine. Beautiful things were a necessity to her, as important as the air she breathed. In the entrance, a warm pink-mushroom marble floor had been accented by a Kashmir rug in pale cream, peach, and gray. Above symmetrically arranged Chinese demilune tables were hung early-eighteenth-century mirrors in front of which glowed glorious bouquets of her favorite pale pink roses.

On the vast living room's white-oak floor lay another Chinese rug, this one patterned with muted flowers in peach and cream. Curved Palladian windows were trimmed in cream. Overstuffed chairs and sofas, upholstered in a soft, glowing floral pattern, were matched by elegantly flowing drapes. A white Steinway grand piano was one of two pianos in the house.

An intricately carved marble mantle held a pair of silver vases from Cartier, etched with delicate undersea patterns. These contained spiky, delicate irises. A long, nineteenth-century Japanese screen in pale, burnished copper was embellished with an exquisite pattern of white chrysanthemums.

Alexandra turned right, heading toward the wide hallway that led to the complex of rooms that formed the kitchen and household area. A golden pine trestle floor lent warmth and a French country flavor. The area smelled deliciously of the pear and raspberry tarts the cook was baking.

She went into the vacant housekeeping office and stood in front of the intercom. She stared at its control buttons and speaker panels, her heart feeling small and cramped. She dreaded the interviews that were going to follow, the tears and denial, the hurt feelings. These were people she trusted, people who trusted her.

She closed her eyes, wishing that she could think of something *before* she called them all in . . .

An idea hit her and, opening her eyes, she went to the two small filing cabinets Mrs. Abbott used for household receipts and employee records. Ten minutes later she had pulled all the employment applications her employees filled out when they hired on. She leafed through them, looking for some clue, although she was uncertain what it would be.

Then her eyes focused on a statement made by Corazon Morales, twenty-six, who had been their maid for three years. Printed in crooked pencil lines, it said, *Brother Ramon Morales work Chicago Fitzgerld Hotel.*

— ◄► —

Corazon Morales wept bitterly as she was being fired.

"I din' mean . . . Miz Cox, I din' mean . . . my brother, he give me the camera, just take the peectures and give to him . . . ''

Alexandra said sharply, "Didn't you know what they were going to be used for, Corazon? Didn't you even wonder?"

The girl rocked back and forth, sobbing. "No . . . no . . . I deedn't wonder."

"Don't give me that!" Alexandra cried. "You knew they were going to use it against us. You knew they wanted to scare us."

"Oh, Miz Cox . . . "

"If you had stolen from me, Corazon, if you had walked off with the silver, at least I could understand it. But this . . . Those were my *children*, Corazon. Those were my babies you put at risk." She gripped the edge of the file cabinet in order to steady herself. "Where was your loyalty, Corazon? Where was your *common human decency*?"

"Please, please," the maid began to babble. "I live here three years, I don't have no place to go . . . "

"I don't care," Alexandra said coldly. "I want you to go and pack. Be out of here in twenty minutes. I'll call Henry from downstairs, and he'll escort you."

"But . . . but Miz Cox . . . "

"You just received two weeks' pay yesterday, and I'll add two more weeks to it." She heard her voice crack. "Just *leave*, Corazon. Now. Go."

Alexandra walked slowly upstairs. The anger she'd expended on the maid had left her feeling ravaged, and she needed a few quiet minutes to herself. In the upper hall she passed her housekeeper, but the woman sensed her mood and only nodded silently.

Alexandra went into her own study and closed the door. She stood there shaking, her skin swept with a chill, her knees suddenly feeling rubbery.

The room was really her music room, her refuge, and she had designed it herself. There was a state-of-the-art stereo system, and a huge collection of compact discs, everything from Ella Fitzgerald to Big Band stars such as Kitty Kallen and Helen Forrest, from Helen Reddy to Olivia Newton-John, for whom she had written many songs.

And of course there was another Steinway grand piano, as well as her collection of antique sheet music and music memorabilia. On a low table, bouquets of roses were arranged in a collection of hand-painted ceramic cachepots.

She threw herself on a love seat, reaching for the nearby phone. A short conversation with Henry, the building security man, ensured he would escort Corazon to a taxicab and out of their lives.

She hung up, closing her eyes. Richard had said there was no danger, but she wondered whether he was telling her the truth.

No, Richard would not lie about something as important as their children, she thought, forcing herself to relax. If he expected a settlement, there would be a settlement.

She opened her eyes, her glance traveling to the far end of the room, where her cherrywood desk and matching table held stacks of papers, notes, lists, and campaign literature. On the wall a portrait of her older brother, Derek Winthrop, smiled down at her. Kennedy-handsome, Derek was the junior senator from Massachusetts and a ranking member of the Senate Foreign Relations Committee. Next to Derek's picture hung a large bulletin board.

The gala. Already she and her party planner, Dolly Rutledge, had posted a weekly schedule, which became a daily schedule as the party reached final countdown. The minutiae were staggering. Security coverage alone would require complex coordination among five agencies. Hundreds would come from out of town and would require overnight accommodations, airport limo pickups, hairdressers, makeup experts, and seamstresses available for emergency alterations of couturier gowns.

There would be other meals, hospitality rooms, even gift baskets in the rooms selected individually for each guest. To help with this, she and Dolly had prepared a loose-leaf notebook that listed the name and arrangements for each guest, one couple per page. After only four or five days, the notebook was already filled with details.

She decided to call Dolly and get it out of the way. Focusing on the party would calm her down, she decided, and besides, the work had to be done.

"So, OK," Dolly said, once they had made the usual greetings. "Now what about this guest list? I know we've been over and over it, but it isn't too late to add a few more, because we don't want to forget any important people. What about Detroit? You've got all the automakers coming. Have we got Max Fisher? Yes? How about the Taubmans, Richard Manoogians, and the Glancys?"

"They're all here." Alexandra became businesslike as she

got out her typed guest list and scrutinized the pages of names.

"The Emmet E. Tracys? Mr. and Mrs. Frank Stella? Harold and Barbara Beznos? Peter and Nicole Stroh?"

"Check."

"And we can't forget Judge and Mrs. Roman S. Gribbs, the Richard Kughns, and the Chick Fishers."

Slowly they moved from major city to city, double-checking to be sure that important people had not been forgotten. In Los Angeles the guests she had selected included Dorothy and Otis Chandler. Chandler owned the *Los Angeles Times*, and the Academy Awards ceremonies were held each spring in the Dorothy Chandler Pavilion. There was a liberal sprinkling of old-guard movie stars to add sparkle. These included the James Stewarts, Kirk Douglas, and Burt Lancaster, along with Mike Douglas and "The Boss"—Bruce Springsteen—a personal request from Princess Di.

And, of course, performers and record people, she couldn't forget them. Friends she'd made over the years, or performers she'd written songs for. These would include composer Sammy Fain, who, at age eighty-eight, was the composer of such songs as "I'll Be Seeing You" and "Love Is a Many-Splendoured Thing." Without Sammy, she never would have gotten started. Sammy had agreed to perform a medley of his songs for the guests and would be bringing Minnie Phillips, his long-term and charming friend.

There would be Donald and Ivana Trump from New York. Sir Run Run Shaw from Hong Kong, with his son, Harold. Gore Vidal and Estee Lauder. And more, a list of names that transcended society blue books, bestseller lists, and *USA Today*, to focus on people Alexandra thought Charles and Diana might genuinely enjoy meeting.

They added six more names. The guest list was already swollen to 650.

"OK," Dolly said at last. "That's done. We're saving a couple more invitations for last-minuters. Hopefully, there won't be many. We can always tell them the invitations got lost in the mail. Oh, my God, press! God forbid if we leave off some crusty old news gossip. Now, are we going to include TV personalities like Johnny Carson and Barbara Walters, or what? You know Barbara and Mary Lee have always clashed. What do you think, Alexandra?"

Forty minutes later, Alexandra hung up, thinking that she

would probably see more of Dolly in the next days than she would of her own husband.

She studied the pewter-framed photographs arranged on a small table nearby. Herself as a child, with her father at Hyannis. Herself and Richard on his sloop, *Lexy Lady*, taken the year she'd crewed with him in Australia for the America's Cup.

Sadness overcame her. When had their relationship changed? She couldn't think of a specific month or day; it just had. Now she was just the woman he hugged because he was supposed to. The one he called "Lexy" and "punkie," maybe because it was old habit.

Another, smaller, photo claimed her attention. It was just a snapshot, really. Four young girls posed beside a crumbling stone fence coated with moss, that looked—and was—several hundred years old. The blonde in the center was herself.

Alexandra examined her seventeen-year-old face. Had she really been that young? That long-legged and colty looking? She'd stared so fearlessly into the camera, unaware of all the things that were going to happen to her.

The picture was taken, she remembered, the day they'd been punished and made to shovel the school garden. She, Jette, and Mary Lee. Diana had come by to cheer them on. The four friends who'd stuck together through so much.

She reached out and touched the photo lightly, as if that touch might somehow connect her, taking her back eleven years to a night of terror and a secret pledge . . .

2

London
1978

Shrieks and calls of schoolgirls on the lacrosse field drifted through the opened window of Edwina Sloane, principal of the West Heath School, near Sevenoaks, in Kent, England. Also drifting in were the green and wet smells of April, a month that, she had found, usually brought some kind of trouble with the girls.

Edwina looked up, sighing, from the letter she was writing to one of the school's alumnae, the most famous of whom had been Princess May of Teck, who had gone on to become Princess of Wales and then Queen Mary. She turned her gaze on the three American girls who stood in a row before her. At seventeen their bodies looked awkward in the navy school uniforms designed for a younger girl's flat bosom. Black stockings gave them the legginess of half-grown fillies.

Their faces wore the familiar chastened, squelched look of all who were called into her office for reprimanding.

"I understand that you girls played a prank on Miss Dogwood," she began in the clipped voice she used for occasions such as this.

"Yes, ma'am," they responded almost in unison.

"You . . . how should I delicately put it? Packaged a natural product from a dog and boxed it in a wrapping of silver foil, leaving it as a 'surprise' on her bed."

"Yes, ma'am," they all said.

Americans. They had been admitted because Edwina's new theory was that exposure to girls from America might ward off any provincialism of their own girls, who tended to be a bit insular, many belonging to the approximately 150 families listed in *Debrett's Peerage*.

The experiment had not been an unqualified success. The three Americans before her were so . . . flamboyant, standing out among the red-cheeked, sometimes horsey British girls like poppies in a field of violets.

And they were enormously popular with the other girls. The three talked endlessly about American rock stars and used swear words seldom heard on the West Heath campus. All were accustomed to endless money on a scale scarcely imagined by most of the British girls in the school, whose families, although blue-blooded, were often impoverished. They received an inordinate amount of "tuck," food packages supposedly sent by parents, but which they actually ordered themselves from London with their parents' Visas and MasterCards.

Edwina's eyes fastened upon Brijette, who was nervously entwining a finger through a jet-black curl of an extraordinary mane of hair that refused to accept its required barrettes and rubber bands. Brijette, whom the girls called Jette, had been reared like a little Hollywood gypsy, alternately coddled and neglected by her movie-star mother, Claudia Michaud of the Michaud theatrical dynasty that dated back to silent-film days.

Most interested in lacrosse, rock music, and pranks, Jette had passed only two of the dreaded O-level tests that determined a student's future—and was merrily nonchalant about her performance.

Edwina pressed her lips together. She saw a promise of danger in the girl's voluptuous looks. At seventeen, Jette already possessed a woman's lush breasts and hips and an unusually tiny waistline. Even in her pleated skirt, the girl exuded an erotic aura.

Edwina's eyes traveled to Alexandra Winthrop. Here was another girl who would be disturbing to men. Alexandra resembled the finest type of British beauty, with her roses-and-cream complexion and smooth, blonde hair lustrous with shine and forbidden daily shampoos.

She was the daughter of Jay Leonard Winthrop, a Boston textile magnate who proudly claimed among his ancestors several U.S. Presidents and signers of the Declaration of Independence.

Alexandra was the most musically gifted girl in the school. Even Edwina was moved by the pure tone with which this seventeen-year-old could play the piano. Because she could sing, in a soft, husky voice, she was much sought after for impromptu dormitory sessions after dinner.

The girl's trouble was her independent nature. She was too forthright in her opinions and too stubborn in her resistance to certain school rules. She had balked at taking only three scheduled baths a week, insisting—to the shock of the floor prefect—that she wished to bathe daily. Of course, she could not be accommodated. With several hundred girls and limited tubs, one must take one's turn.

Edwina's eyes turned to the third girl, the one whose presence had caused the biggest and most unwelcome stir. Actually, the stir was caused not by the girl, but by her mother.

Mary Lee Wilde was the daughter of the notorious American novelist, Marietta Wilde, who had written a steamy blockbuster novel that made a Jackie Collins book look prim. Edwina had not read it, naturally, but had confiscated nine copies this semester, dog-eared from being passed around from girl to girl. In some of the copies, prurient passages were underlined and marked with comments like "I am mad keen for Brentwood!" and "Deep Kisses!"

Edwina remembered the day Marietta Wilde had sailed in, checkbook in hand, to register her daughter, more interested in berating her child than in speaking to school staff. The mother had given her own occupation as "widow," and Edwina had not realized her true profession until it was too late. She certainly would not have admitted the girl if she had known.

Now Mary Lee was standing at attention like a little soldier, as if she were accustomed to being abused by adults. She reminded one of a chubby little marmalade cat, with her soft titian hair and green, slanting eyes. Her nose was tiny and pug, like a kitten's. She had a voracious intelligence and had already passed eleven of her O-levels.

Edwina sighed, returning to the matter at hand. "Then you admit you are the ones who deposited this animal fecal matter in Miss Dogwood's room?"

"Yes."

"Are any other girls involved?"

They stared at her like a row of owls. "No, we're the guilty ones," chirped Jette.

"Are you very sure?"

"Oh, yes, yes!"

No doubt the entire school had known of the prank within five minutes of when it was committed.

"You have insulted a fine woman who has worked hard at this school for low pay, giving up a family life and living here in order to ensure that you young ladies receive the best education possible. Not only that—" Edwina made her voice exceptionally stern, "by your crudity, you have insulted the very name of West Heath, which stands for the highest principles."

Tremors from all three of them, and the evaporation of any remaining vestige of giggles. Edwina meted out one of the school's standard punishments: "You will prepare the kitchen garden," she decided. "The gardener is readying it for vegetable planting, and you will assist him. You will spend the entire day today working with rake and hoe, thinking upon the good educations you wish to receive."

They stared at her incredulously.

"You don't mean—we're to use a *hoe*?" Jette squeaked.

"I've never gardened," Alexandra said.

Mary Lee was silent.

"The gardener will instruct you in the use of the tools," Edwina said briskly . "Go along now, and do find him. Oh yes. There will be no afternoon tea."

—— ▶◀ ——

The three girls waited until they were safely outdoors and on the walk that led to Rose Hall, their dormitory, before bursting into a fit of giggles.

"Oh—oh!" Jette cried. "Did you see her *face*? She looked like she'd eaten a gallon of prunes for breakfast instead of those awful baked beans they serve here!"

" 'A natural product from a dog,' " Alexandra mimicked.

"Is it something like granola cereal?" Mary Lee questioned.

They laughed hysterically, staggering around on the ancient bricked walk on which Queen Mary had strolled.

"I thought she was going to expel us," Mary Lee said when most of the laughter had subsided.

"Why would she?" Jette demanded. "I bet we paid her double what all the other girls paid. My mother told me that she wrote a check big enough to buy a new Aston Martin. Can you believe it? *I* would rather have the Aston Martin."

They linked arms and walked toward the dormitory the

girls nicknamed Cowsheds, passing a class of younger girls being accompanied by their teacher to the nearby woods to catalog the first of the spring wildflowers. The little English girls were all fair-skinned, with naturally flushed cheeks that looked as if they had been colored with rouge.

Alexandra's eyes lingered on them, then she turned to her two friends. This school wasn't a family tradition for them as it was for the English girls, but an expedient. She was here because poor Papa was so grief-stricken after Mama's death that he was wandering around Europe trying to drown his sorrows by eating fine meals, drinking wine, and photographing an endless series of broken-down castles. Jette's mother was on location in Spain and involved with another lover, so she didn't have time to supervise Jette. Mary Lee's mother, who was researching another sexy novel in Hawaii, wanted Mary Lee to attend the most prestigious, distant, and repressive school she could think of. Mary Lee was lucky there hadn't been a very good school in Siberia.

Their laughter was sometimes very near tears. Alexandra swallowed back one of the waves of sadness that still washed over her after the death of her mother more than a year ago, from complications following surgery. When Mama was alive, life had seemed perpetually golden. She and her mother had played piano duets, and Mama had loved the songs Alexandra wrote by the dozens, insisting she had "definite, God-given talent." It was because of her mother that Alexandra had studied piano for twelve years and had received voice lessons from one of the country's top teachers.

Now suddenly it seemed she was on the other side of the ocean, exiled in a place where they served kippers and baked beans for breakfast and inspected your room every night to make certain you were in bed. Where you had to bathe in a huge, echoey bathroom in a tub soap-grimed by a procession of girls. Where you had to sneak into the lavatory after hours and bend your head under the sink to wash your hair.

But she had her music and her friends, Alexandra reminded herself, blinking back tears. Even hoeing in the garden was not really a punishment when you did it with friends.

— ►◄ —

Jette lifted her hoe and hacked solid brown English dirt, wincing as the tip of the hoe hit a stone with a ping. "Damn-shit-fuck!" she yelped. "Another stone! What is this, the rock pile at Sing Sing?"

"I think it's known as reflecting on your sins." With a sweaty hand, Mary Lee brushed back a hank of gold-red hair.

"I haven't got enough sins to reflect on, that's my problem," Jette fumed.

Various other girls had dropped by to commiserate and to tell them that the afternoon tea was going to consist of chocolate *gateaux* and five kinds of tinned biscuits. They groaned. There were only three methods of eating at West Heath. You had a permanent case of carbohydrate hunger, or you refused all food and became anorexic, or you put your finger down your throat to throw up after you had overindulged.

Diana Spencer trudged up with a schoolmate and a small Nikon camera. With a great deal of fuss, she made them drop their hoes and stand in a row with her beside the tumbledown garden fence.

"What is it you Americans say? Say 'cheese,' " Di Spencer said, giggling as her schoolmate pressed the button. Di was what Jette called a "soul sister." Like Jette, she had passed only two O-levels. She was dark blonde and smooth looking, "mad keen" about dancing. Her room was decorated with a portrait of Prince Charles, on whom she had a strong crush. To get out of certain school activities, Di would decorate her legs with eye shadow and then tell the teacher that the colored spots were bruises. Unfortunately, she was going to leave the school next week for the Institut Alpin Videmanette at Château d'Oex near Gstaad, Switzerland. After that she wasn't sure. Probably a job.

"I am *bored*," Jette exclaimed when Di had left. "I am tired of this place! I'm longing for the taste of *freedom!*"

"Yes," Alexandra agreed, "and London is only fifty miles away."

"London," Jette sighed.

They all echoed her, having tasted some of the treats of London on school trips to the ballet or symphony.

"The British Museum is in London," Mary Lee sighed.

"And I could make a long-distance call and talk to my father," Alexandra said.

"And we could see the Rolling Stones," Jette suddenly remarked. She smote her head and gazed at them all with as much triumph as if she had suddenly been able to import a Big Mac into the school cuisine. "We *could*. I know a girl—she's a groupie—she and a bunch of girls live in an apartment in

Mayfair. She *knows* Mick Jagger, she sleeps with people who know him. What do you say, huh? Spring hols are next week."

The others stared at her.

"We have credit cards," Alexandra said slowly. "I can drive. We could call and arrange for a rental car, pay to have it delivered to the school."

"Clothes," Jette said.

"We'll order by telephone."

"But we could get caught and kicked out," Mary Lee said nervously.

"So what?" Jette replied grandly. "If we do, at least we had some fun."

— ►◄ —

They first drove to Althorp, seventy-five miles northwest of London in the heart of Northamptonshire, in order to have tea with Di, who had invited them.

"Oh, it's such fun you motored here. So far to drive!" Di exclaimed.

"Far?" Alexandra was puzzled.

Diana giggled. "Oh, I forgot. You Americans drive three hundred miles in a day and think nothing of it."

They gazed around, awed, at the massive red-brick building that once had a moat around it and dated from the 1400s. A 115-foot gallery upstairs held a collection of ancestral portraits that Mary Lee, running along them excitedly, told them were by Sir Joshua Reynolds. "He's famous, so famous he's in all the art books," she exclaimed. "The art collection here is *formidable*. And did you see the porcelain collection downstairs? Jeez! My mother would die to see this place. She'd put it in one of her books."

Tea was stuffy, with Diana's stepmother, whom she and her sisters disliked, presiding over a beautiful sterling-silver tea service. There were delicious small cakes, tinned biscuits from Fortnum and Mason's, and a marmalade made from grapefruit.

"And your father is in trade?" Raine Spencer asked Alexandra in a tone that implied that being in business was definitely lower-class.

"Oh, yes," Alexandra replied. "Of course, now he is more interested in real estate. As a matter of fact, he has been looking at several properties in England." And she named a property they had seen on their drive—one that was larger and more imposing than Althorp.

"I see," Raine said, sipping her tea.

In Diana's bedroom was a collection of newspaper photographs she had clipped of Charles at Cambridge, being invested as Prince of Wales at Caernarvon, windsurfing, and dancing with a shapely, scantily clad black dancer in Rio de Janeiro.

The girls pored over the pictures. "He has a great build," Jette decided. "All those polo-playing muscles. And the way he dances . . ."

"Sexy," Diana breathed, flushing. "The press has written him up with so many women. Even one of my sisters. All he has to do is speak to one, and they have him married to her."

"You need to get him to speak to you," Alexandra said thoughtfully.

"Oh, I've spoken to him, but I was a baby then. All I did was babble."

"You're no baby now," Jette said.

◄ ►◄ —

By four o'clock the following afternoon, they were in London. Alexandra slowed the red Audi they had rented, proud of herself for managing with the driver's seat on the wrong side of the car. She had even conquered the London streets swarming with taxis and double-decker buses.

"Mother of God," Jette breathed.

"Well, I think this is it," Alexandra said, thrilled to be visiting a building in which one of the English poets she studied at school might have lived. She rolled down her window and inhaled the London air, tinged with petrol fumes and the tantalizing aroma of a nearby fish-and-chips shop.

"I think this building is early Victorian," Mary Lee remarked. "Queen Victoria was—"

"Who cares? We're *here*," Jette squealed. "We're really here! We're free, we're out of prison, we can break loose and do anything we want!"

"What do you have in mind?" Alexandra inquired dryly, driving down the street in search of a parking space.

"Oh, *I* don't know. Anything. I can't *wait* for tonight. Joti swore to me that the Stones would be there, and you know how hard it is to get into any party where they are. They have bodyguards that toss you out if you're not wanted. There're all kinds of girls who'll do anything to get in, Joti says. Like us." And Jette giggled.

In the backseat, Mary Lee excitedly called, "Look! There! Someone's pulling out of that parking place—take it! Hurry, Alexandra, turn around right here."

They were staying with two stewardesses from British Airways, Gwen Jeffries and Joti Sengal, to whom Jette had been introduced by her mother's business manager, Eric Catalan. According to Jette, these two women were in with the trendy crowd that circulated around the Stones.

To be at a party with rock stars . . . to actually *talk* to someone like Mick Jagger . . . Alexandra felt giddy. No girl she knew in Boston, including her best friend, Pims, had ever done anything even remotely like this.

She wondered what the Stones would be like. Of course, Mick was fabulously sexy.

They lugged their suitcases up to the building and climbed three flights of stairs to apartment 3C. They knew they were at the right place because the heavy rhythms of "Jumpin' Jack Flash" were thumping out from under the door, raw and aggressively sexual.

They pounded on the door, and finally it was opened by a young Indian woman with perfect golden skin and a small red jewel affixed between her elegantly arched eyebrows, wearing nothing but a black silk teddy.

"Come in, won't you? I'm Joti. Gwen's in the shower bath. We just got in from Paris, and we're beat. A lot of turbulence and some heavy-duty action with the bloody chuck-up bags. Not my idea of heaven."

The three girls entered what probably was a fairly decent flat underneath the litter of panty hose, bikini panties, stewardess uniforms, issues of *Rolling Stone, Elle,* and *Jours de France,* roach clips, cigarette papers, and empty bottles of Evian water.

"Pardon the clutter," Joti said. "You know how it is when one has the long haul. We're seldom here." She noticed Alexandra eyeing the walls, on which various pieces of clothing had been hung, as if on display.

"That's my collection," Joti explained proudly. She pointed to an embroidered lavender stretch top with rhinestones and gold metal, and a pair of black velvet stretch pants. "Those are Mick's. He wore them on his last U.S. tour. Aren't they smashing? They aren't even washed; they've still got his sweat in them. I like to smell them sometimes, when I get horny."

"Wow," Jette said.

"And this," Joti said, assuming the role of tour guide, "is

a scrap of rubber from a giant inflatable cock that Mick used on tour. It would be blown up, and he'd ride it. Isn't that fantastic?"

Alexandra stared, shocked and fascinated by the bit of pinkish plastic.

Joti showed them a square glass frame, in which had been carefully mounted three sets of male underpants.

"These are my real prizes," the stewardess told them. "I could sell them for a hundred pounds. The leopard-print bikini is Mick's, and they're not washed. John Lennon wore those Jockeys, and the jock strap belongs to Greg Brent. He wore it during the game in which he won the World Cup for England."

By this time Gwen was out of the shower, a petite redhead who did not bother to wrap a towel around herself.

"Are you Claudia Michaud's daughter?" she inquired of Jette.

"Yeah," Jette responded.

"Is it true your mother's slept with Richard Burton?"

"Probably," Jette said, shrugging.

"Has she slept with Vadim? I read in *Paris Match* that they were having an affair."

"Oh, that's finished. She's sleeping with Harry Belafonte right now," Jette lied, giving Gwen a defiant grin.

Alexandra and Jette would sleep in a small back bedroom, one on a twin bed, the other in a trundle that rolled out, while Mary Lee would sleep on the couch in the tiny sitting room. They were not to be surprised or worried, Joti warned, if either she or Gwen did not make it home that night.

"*You* know," Joti shrugged. "Oh, and one more thing. The bathroom is very tiny here, so please put on your makeup in the bedroom. And if you brought any . . . you know, any boxes or anything, you can leave them in the pantry."

"They're being sent tomorrow," Jette said.

"What's she talking about?" Alexandra asked Jette as soon as the three were alone in the little back bedroom, which looked out on a small garden. Although it was growing dusky, a few songbirds still warbled. "What boxes?"

"I told her we'd ordered a couple of boxes of groceries and two cases of wine," Jette explained. "They didn't *have* to invite us to their flat, you know. We're a little young for their crowd."

"But you're Claudia Michaud's daughter," Alexandra pointed out. "That's what they really like."

"So true," Jette said, with the blasé confidence of one who had grown up in Hollywood.

They had three hours until the party started, which was just enough time to walk down the street to the fish-and-chips shop. The girls wolfed down the lightly battered fish, spurning the vinegar supplied for sprinkling on the french fries. Then they walked back to begin the ritual of dressing.

Sexy was the byword, and Jette took charge, decreeing that she would wear a tight black jersey and a short leather skirt that showed off her curvy legs. Alexandra would capitalize on her tall, aristocratic blondness with a clingy white jersey. And Mary Lee . . . well, black was always sexy, and sequins would distract from any slight bulges, so she would be the one who glittered. All three of them would wear spike heels and all the makeup that Jette had been able to carry, most of it belonging to her mother.

"I'm going to be sick," Mary Lee said, sitting on the twin bed in her slip with her hands clutched together across her chest. "I'm so nervous, I'm going to be *sick*."

"No, you won't," Jette said.

"I will. No one's going to look at me. I'll just stand there, and I won't know what to say."

"You? Not know what to say? Come on, who wants to be first?" Jette asked, waving a makeup brush. "I've been making up my mother for years."

——— ◄► ———

Two hours later, they took turns admiring themselves in the small mirror in the bathroom.

They were going to be noticed, all right. Alexandra stared at her face in astonishment. Somehow her skin was as fair and pure as a white rose petal. Her eyes were huge, subtly lined with warm grays. Her full lips were tinted the most sensuous shade of deep pink—glossed and shiny. And the white jersey dress clung to her, emphasizing curves she had not even known she possessed.

"You're going to knock 'em dead," Jette pronounced. "And Mary Lee—you're a knockout, too."

The seventeen-year-old with her masses of golden-red hair had also been transformed. Clever application of matte makeup and peach blush erased her juvenile freckles and gave her a lush look. The black faille dress, dusted with bursts of sequinned flowers along the shoulders, was one of the funky little creations London "birds" loved, with side slits that revealed Mary Lee's pretty legs.

And Jette. Alexandra gazed at her friend, thinking her the sexiest one of them all. Her mane of curls tumbled and tangled around her small, beautiful face. Farrah Fawcett had made this look famous, but Jette made Farrah seem positively bland.

Pale skin and dark eyes emphasized by midnight blue eyeliner gave her the look of a gypsy. The wisp of black jersey top outlined every curve of Jette's full breasts, making it breathtakingly obvious she wore no bra. Jette's waist was tiny, her hips gloriously curved. But it was not only these attributes that made Jette sexy, Alexandra realized with a thrill that was part jealousy, part vicarious excitement. Jette exuded sensuousness as strong as a cloud of Joy perfume. She looked as if she craved sex, as if she had *created* sex.

"Well?" Jette's black eyes flamed with excitement. "Are we going to wow 'em or what? I hope there are some paparazzi at this party, because I want to get my picture in the paper! I'm *ready!*"

"Yeah!" echoed Mary Lee.

—— ►◄ ——

"Our hostess is someone named Tara Brown-Halduff," Jette explained as they pulled up in front of an elegant block of apartments in Kensington. "She's a clothing designer, very in right now."

As they entered the building, Alexandra noticed several uniformed security guards who stood inconspicuously in the lobby, and a doorman who was busily opening doors of Rolls-Royce limousines, various makes of long, British touring cars, and European sports cars.

The three girls tried not to gawk at the other guests they could see arriving. Was that tall, skinny blonde Twiggy? And there was Erwina, whose face they had seen on *Vogue* covers, arriving alone.

"She hasn't got an escort," Alexandra whispered to Jette.

"Maybe she doesn't want one." Jette shrugged.

"But—to come to a place like this alone . . ."

"She probably won't leave alone, silly. At this kind of party an escort would only cramp your style."

The building had an elegant, old-fashioned cage lift, with polished brass fixtures.

As the lift rose, so did the sound level. They arrived at the second floor, where the din spilled out into the hallway. Loud voices mingled with the rhythmic pound of bass guitars and the clink of glasses. Suddenly a young girl came stumbling out of the door, her face streaked with tears. A bouquet of daisies wrapped in green paper drooped from her hands. Following her was a thin, dissipated-looking man in a black leather vest and jeans.

"Sorry, luv. Gate-crashers ain't wanted here."

"I'm not a gate crasher!" the girl sobbed. "I was deliverin' these flowers, you freakin' wanker! Ring them up! Put it to 'em, Brompton Road Florists. Please! Just let me stay for a few minutes . . . please! I just want to meet Mick and Keith!"

"You're not meetin' anyone, dolly bird."

"Bloody layabout!" the girl screamed. "Bloody bastard!"

"Get on, before I call the coppers and yer bounced proper like."

As Alexandra, Jette, and Mary Lee made their way to the door, the girl pushed her way past, sobbing in frustration.

They stepped inside and were instantly swept into the pulsating beat of a party at full surge. At least two hundred people were packed inside a large, elegant apartment beautifully furnished with French antiques and Impressionist art. Knots of people crowded around a bar, where two white-uniformed bartenders were dispensing drinks, and another group was gathered about a low table on which rested a crystal bowl filled with a white, powdery substance.

Music pounded suggestively. Alexandra breathed in the acrid smoke of marijuana and English cigarettes mingled with clouds of expensive perfume, and shivered with forbidden excitement. She couldn't believe they were really here.

"What do we do now?" she asked Jette. The three stood there, unnoticed so far, trying to get acclimated to the crowd. A familiar face wandered past—Jean Shrimpton, escorted by a tall, dark, saturnine-looking man. Jean wore something embroidered and velvet. Her sister, Chrissie, Jette recalled, had been Mick's mistress before Bianca.

"We'll find Joti and Gwen. They said they'd be here." Jette began scanning the crowd, and suddenly Joti stood by them, dressed in a clinging gold lamé gown that emphasized her warm cinnamon complexion. She looked flushed, her eyes much brighter than when they saw her last.

"There you are," Joti said. "I'll give you a quick introduce. Then you're on your own."

She dragged them through the crowd, reeling out names and giving fast introductions. There was Roger Vadim, and a man named Prince Stanislaus Klossowski de Rola, known as Stash. Andy Warhol with Princess Lee Radziwill, Jackie's sister, thin and striking in a white Norman Norell. Carly Simon and Jerry Hall also were there.

David Kwan was a handsome forty-year-old Chinese, who, Joti said, made a fortune in producing kung fu movies and was in London on business.

"Do you film in London or Hong Kong?" Alexandra asked him politely.

Kwan's dark eyes flicked up and down her body.

"We film in Hong Kong mostly. You ever think about making a movie?" he inquired. On his arm hung an Asian woman wearing a red cheongsam that clung to her perfectly formed body.

"Me?" Alexandra laughed nervously. "Oh, no . . ."

"You look like, yes, Grace Kelly. Ah, yes. They like blondes in the Orient—you'd do very well if you'd make a movie with me. Many thousands of Hong Kong dollars. Ring me at my hotel," he added, handing Alexandra a business card.

"See?" Jette whispered after Kwan and his date blended into the crowd. "Are you glad you're wearing foundation now? I *told* you that outfit was dynamite!"

Alexandra quietly tucked the business card inside a house plant.

"Over there," Joti said. "Near the table. See those fuzzy young men? The tall one is Simon Heath-Cote; his father is Lord Heath-Cote. Filthy rich. They own an enormous estate in Cheshire; they're all down from Oxford for some fun."

A shorter youth, wearing a pair of John Lennon–style wire-rimmed glasses, was Viscount Peter Baldwin.

"Watch out for them," Joti warned. "They'll try to get into your knickers."

However, at the moment, the young aristocrats seemed more interested in the crystal bowl, and they were scooping up white powder with little gold-plated spoons.

"Oh!" Jette bubbled, looking away. "This is so great! Who

else is here, Joti? Is Mick Jagger here yet? And Bianca? And Keith Richards? When are they getting here?"

Joti pulled them aside. "In the first place, Mick might not get here till late, but Bianca is here. She's over there . . . in the red dress. Don't say anything to her about Mick, because they're not getting along too swimmingly—he's been seen with Jerry Hall. God, both Bianca and Jerry are here tonight. And Keith, he's up on drug charges right now; they say he might get kicked out of the group. So if he talks to you, don't mention it, and *don't* ask Bianca about her little girl, Jade, because she and Mick have been rowing about her, too."

Jette pursed her lips. "We'll talk about the weather, then. 'Oh, Bianca,'" she smirked, "'I just love all your London drizzle and fog. Where *do* you buy your umbrellas?'"

"Oh!" Mary Lee exclaimed. "Look at that lady over there—the one by that white bowl. What's she doing?"

They all swiveled their heads to stare.

Joti shrugged. "What do you think? That's coke."

Coke? Alexandra knew by her tone that it could not be Coca-Cola. The girls watched as an elaborately dressed woman of about thirty licked her forefinger, dipped it in the white powder, and then carefully rubbed the powder all over her gums. She then thrust her finger back in the white substance, and, holding the finger up, made a beeline for a hallway where there was a ladies' room.

"I don't understand," Alexandra said, puzzled. "Why's she heading for the ladies' room with that white stuff on her finger?"

Joti eyed Alexandra scornfully. "Oh, God," she said. "Where have you been anyway? Why do you *think* she's going to the powder room?"

"I don't know."

"Guess," Joti said sarcastically, and walked away, abandoning them in a swirl of people and noise.

Alexandra shook her head. "Am I missing something?"

Jette's smile was superior. "She's going to rub it on her pussy, you idiot. It's even a better toot than the gums."

"Oh . . ."

Stones music pounded around them, louder and more frenetic. A tall, weedy-looking young man in a tweed jacket and Eton tie left the group around the crystal bowl to approach Jette.

"Hello, luv."

"Hello," Jette chirped.

"Simon Heath-Cote. You're a raver, you are. A right little raver. Want to go to another party?"

The four young men had been huddling around the coke bowl, taking turns sniffing lines of first-rate white stuff with the gold-plated straws that the hostess had set out. Others were cutting new lines with utensils that resembled single-edged razor blades.

They had been drunk when they arrived. Now they were getting high as fast as they could, savoring the sweet jolts of energy, power, and control that flooded into them through the membrane lining of their nostrils.

Gerald Blenheim was nineteen; his father had been knighted by King George. Colin Downham's father was an oil tanker and shipping magnate comparable to Onassis and D. K. Ludwig. He was a weedy age twenty. Viscount Peter Baldwin, at nineteen, was fourth cousin once removed to the Queen herself. And Simon Heath-Cote's parents had recently been written up in *European Travel and Life* as "Britain's richest aristocrats."

Simon, always the rebel, had ridden from Oxford on his Harley "Hog," a motorcycle he had had shipped from California at an exorbitant price. The others had arrived in a shiny black Rolls-Royce limousine "borrowed" on a lark from the Downham chauffeur.

The Rolls-Royce, with its interior upholstered in chamois-soft black leather, was crucial to the plan they had evolved on the way over. Dolly birds. Crumpet. Getting a leg over. However one phrased it, they planned to get laid.

Crowding each other, fighting for turns at the bowl, they simultaneously scanned the room for suitable female prospects. The ideal prey would be unsophisticated women who might not attach a great deal of significance to their family backgrounds.

Groupies were perfect for the evening's anticipated entertainment. Luscious, young, eager ones, willing dolly birds who creamed their knickers within fourteen paces of any rock star and would do anything, absolutely anything whatsoever, for any rocker who crossed their path. Mick Jagger's leftovers were better than most other men's first choice.

"Look," Peter said, nudging Colin. "Look what I see over there, coming in through the door. And look at the pair of bristols on the dark one."

They all stared at Jette.

"Smashing! I fancy her!" Simon and Colin said simultaneously. Gerald, noticing Alexandra and Mary Lee, shook his head. "Coo-ee! The other two birds ain't bad either."

They put the finishing touches on the rough plan they had evolved on the way over—a plan that began with inviting the girls into the capacious, fully stocked Rolls-Royce.

"*I'll* go and chat up the little black-haired raver," Simon decided. "She's the one *I* fancy, and I know I can get her. We'll invite them to an after-party. Tell them Mick'll be there." All four of the young men guffawed. "They cream for rockers, so we'll tell 'em *we* play the guitar and sing, too. Right?" They all nudged each other. "It's going to be bloody easy!"

Someone found out Alexandra could play the piano, and she was soon playing for a group of people who gradually began to abandon their conversations to hear her bluesy style. She sang in a low, smoky voice—a variation on a Judy Collins song she liked.

"You're very good, do you know that?" Carly Simon said when she finished. "Your songs, I mean. Your unusual phrasing. In a crowd like this, to get people to actually listen . . . amazing."

Flushed with the compliment, a little high on champagne, Alexandra wandered back to her two friends.

"I suppose you want to meet Mick Jagger, eh? I suppose that's why you came here, luv, am I right?" Simon Heath-Cote was asking Jette, steadying himself.

Jette looked up at him, assessingly. "Why, do you know him?"

"You're freakin' right I know him. I've toured with him twice, me and my mates here." Heath-Cote gestured behind him to where his friends were now lounging, their eyes eagerly taking in the girls.

"I don't believe you," Jette said.

"What? You don't believe us?"

Simon called over Peter, who said, "It was in '76, right? At the Hague, Lyons, and Barcelona, right, mates? Then we went to Stuttgart and Zagreb, and after that to Los Angeles. What a blast. All the people hangin' on—half a BOAC planeload—all the equipment, my God."

Jette's eyes widened: "You were in Los Angeles? *I* live in Los Angeles."

"Then you might have seen us," Simon said grandly.

"Come on," he added, steering her back in the direction of the coke bowl. "Have you ever tried the white stuff? You've got to try this. It's pure as the driven snow; just a little bit is going to send you straight over the moon."

"Jette—" Alexandra said, catching her friend's wrist, "Jette, remember what Joti said—"

But Jette shook Alexandra away. "Go have your own fun," she hissed. "I *know* what I'm doing. All my mother's friends do coke; I know how it's done!"

"We should find someone to talk to, too," Alexandra said to Mary Lee as they watched Jette get swept up with the young aristocrats. "Look, let's go over to the bar and get a drink. People always stand around bars, and we can find someone to talk to there."

"Not necessary," a voice said. Greg Brent was suddenly standing in front of them holding two flutes of champagne. The soccer star smiled into Alexandra's eyes in a way that suddenly told her why Joti thought him so sexy. He thrust one glass into Alexandra's hand, the other into Mary Lee's.

"Here, you beautiful girls look thirsty. Are you with Bianca's crowd? Haven't I seen you at Pimlico?"

Alexandra took a big gulp of champagne; it was excellent and seemed injected directly into her veins, shimmering along her skin like satin.

"No, we're just here for a few days," she blurted. "I . . . own a shop in Boston."

"What sort of shop?"

"I sell musical instruments," she improvised.

Greg Brent edged closer, gazing into Alexandra's eyes. His eyes were as deeply blue as a Killarney sky. "Maybe I can give you some advice on what to buy for your shop. Or maybe I could just blarney you a little. You're beautiful enough to be Irish, did you know that? Irish women are among the most gorgeous in the world—if one is an Irishman . . ."

The party, six times louder than when they had arrived, was cycling to its peak. Keith Richards entered the room in a cloud of laughter and cigarette smoke. Immediately he became involved in a dispute with the hostess because he wanted to hang brightly embroidered scarves over all the lamps.

"Gives it atmosphere!" Alexandra heard the rocker shout over the din.

"You always want scarves over the lamps," Tara Brown-

Halduff said angrily. "Well, you are not going to have them tonight. I've gone to considerable effort in having this place look nice, and you are not going to spoil it."

"Slag!" Keith accused, stalking off toward the cocaine.

Alexandra left to find the ladies' room and walked in on a couple fornicating on the toilet seat, the woman straddling the man.

Alexandra froze in the doorway. The woman was a model they had seen in *Elle*. She had muscular haunches that thrust up and down, glistening with a sheen of perspiration. Alexandra caught a glimpse of a thick, pinkish-brown phallus, glistening with heavy, milky fluid.

"Sorry . . ." Alexandra choked.

"Get out of here, lovie," the man growled. "Unless you want to be next."

Alexandra slammed the door and leaned against the wall, her heart pounding sickly.

"Something wrong, sweet?" At her elbow was one of the young Britishers, she didn't remember which one.

"Oh—no . . . no . . ." Embarrassed, she pushed past him, fleeing down a hall. This was awful. She never should have come here. She needed a drink of water. A door at the end of the hall stood ajar, and she hurried inside, switching on the light.

She saw Gwen and Joti, totally naked, sensuously entwined. Joti lay with her legs apart, and between her thighs a man crouched, his head down as he licked the open lips of her vagina. He was naked, too, his erection huge. It was Greg Brent.

It seemed she stood there for a century, her eyes riveted on the writhing bodies, her ears taking in the sound of Joti's pleasured moans. While the Indian woman was still climaxing, the man moved upward along her prone form, kneeling astride her. Joti urgently arched herself toward him as he guided his cock into her.

Alexandra gasped and fled, leaving the door wide open in her haste to escape.

Down a second hallway, she found an unused bathroom. She rushed inside, bolted the door, and stood shaking, her mind flooded with afterimages of what she had just seen. She had never thought . . . never dreamed. . . . Then she realized that she was damp between her thighs.

Alexandra stared at herself in the small mirror. She barely recognized her own face, with its glossy pink lips and luminous skin, heavily accented with blush. That Chinese man, David Kwan, had said she looked like Grace Kelly. But Grace Kelly, Alexandra was sure, had never been this drunk.

She found a tissue and impulsively began scrubbing away the makeup until she looked like herself again. Then she picked up the champagne glass she had brought with her into the room and poured its contents into the sink. Pale bubbles vanished down the drain.

It was time they left.

"What do you mean, *leave*?" Jette demanded, her voice shrill. "We haven't even seen Mick, and they said he's definitely arriving. Any minute now. Are you going to throw away the chance to see Mick Jagger?"

Alexandra laughed bitterly. "What does it matter about Mick, for God's sake? Jette, didn't you hear me? I walked in the bathroom and found . . . a woman . . . and a man . . . *on the toilet seat*. And then I went in a bedroom, and I found . . . Joti and Gwen were . . ."

Jette wasn't listening. "*You* leave if you want," she scoffed. "Go on back to Joti's flat, and be a pooper, but you'll be the only one there, because nobody else is going home yet. It isn't even two o'clock!" Then Jette dug her fingernails into Alexandra's arm. "Listen! What's that? He's here, Alexandra! Holy shit." Jette looked as if she were going to explode. "*He's here*."

Mick Jagger wore black from head to toe, and expensive, hand-tooled boots. Some kind of a silver emblem hung around his neck. His hair was long, clean, and deliberately cut to look rough. His red, protruding "Jagger mouth" was just as Alexandra had seen it on all of his record albums. In spite of his slight frame, there was something electric about the star as he made his entrance. A visceral energy that caused the very air of the room to change.

A woman screamed. Then another. Then a female horde surged forward to surround him. Someone switched the stereo to another tape of "Jumpin' Jack Flash."

In the crowd was Mick's wife Bianca, whose high cheekbones and arrogant face marked her as the beauty once chosen by the star. Now Bianca was scowling, and Mick, too, appeared edgy as he approached his wife. Jette stood on a couch, denting the cushions with her spike heels, nearly falling as she strained to see.

Simon Heath-Cote steadied her. "Oh, you can't meet him

here," he urged slyly. "He's only stopping here for a few minutes. Then he's going on to another party in Belgravia. Prince Charles is going to be there with his new bird—my friends and I can get you in. Want to come? It'll be better people, what? And not so noisy. You can have a real chance to talk to him, not just mill about in all this crush."

— ►◄ —

It was a typical London night, the air soft, gray, and wet. Church bells chimed the hour, 2:00 A.M.

"I'm *going* to this other party," Jette slurred under her breath to Alexandra in the parking lot where they all stood. "*You* can go back alone if you want to, but I'm not going to miss this."

She broke away and began dancing and twirling, humming Stones lyrics, while Mary Lee giggled. Alexandra felt a flash of indecision. She could hardly leave her friends alone at this hour. They were all too high to drive anyway. And the boys had promised to drive them to the party in their Rolls, so they wouldn't get lost. Peter Baldwin swore he was sober enough to drive and they would be "safe as houses."

Anything sounded better than *this* party, and if Royalty were to be attending, surely it would be sedate and proper.

The young people veered through the long, narrow parking lot, the boys and girls straggling separately. The Rolls-Royce limousine was at the end of the car park, an annex set somewhat apart and partially shielded by a huge oak that cast enormous black shadows. A gleam reflected off the taillight of a Harley parked next to it.

"Want some bubbly?" Simon offered, turning as the girls approached. "We've got some in the Rolls—and some 'Ludes . . . ever try 'Ludes?"

The interior of the Rolls-Royce smelled of expensive leather and spilled gin. Simon popped open two bottles of champagne. Then—before Alexandra realized what was happening—he slipped a pill in her mouth, tilting back her chin until she was forced to swallow.

Almost instantaneously, she felt a glorious surge of power. Was that a 'Lude he had made her swallow? She felt as if she'd suddenly been lifted to the top of a Ferris wheel.

But the feeling soon proved illusory, as Alexandra found

herself struggling in the cramped backseat with Gerald and Colin.

Mary Lee, in the front seat, fought with Peter Baldwin, struggling to push away his groping hands.

Jette, the drunkest of them all, just lay there giggling while Simon poured champagne on her. Colin bent down and began lapping the bubbly liquid from Jette's cleavage, thrusting his tongue between her breasts as far as he could. He then moved down to her crotch, pushing aside her French-cut panties.

"Enough—!" Alexandra kept saying, but the Quaalude made her voice sound far away, as if it didn't belong to her. "Stop . . . Let us out of the car right now!"

"In a bit, lovie," Gerald moaned, his hands crushing her breasts.

She pushed him away, yanking at Jette. "Come *on*," she urged. "Jette—we have to go now—*please*—"

"I want Mick," Jette burbled, her eyes shut. "I want him!"

"You'll have him, baby doll," Simon crooned, pulling away Jette's panties. "I'm Mick, right? I'm Mick Jagger, baby. I'm Mick all the way."

He lifted his head and nodded at the three other boys, as if in signal. In a flash, they pushed Alexandra and Mary Lee out of the Rolls-Royce and scrambled into the front seat to give Heath-Cote more room.

"Jette!" Alexandra called anxiously, fighting the effects of the champagne. "Isn't Jette coming?"

"She's *coming*, all right!" wheezed Simon.

Inside the Rolls they could see the movements of Simon's head as he thrust up and down.

"Jette!" she screamed. "My God—*Jette!*"

Crying, Alexandra yanked open the door and jumped inside. Simon Heath-Cote was crouched over Jette, Colin and Gerald watching from the front seat with Peter. She slammed at Heath-Cote's nose with the side of her purse, and he immediately pulled off Jette, blood gushing from his nostrils.

"Come on!" Alexandra hissed at Mary Lee, grabbing Jette. "Help me carry her!"

Between them they managed to drag the half-conscious Jette to their nearby car and shove her into the backseat, thankful that Colin and Gerald were administering to Simon. Alexandra jumped in the front seat as a sobbing Mary Lee ran around to the passenger side.

"Bitch! Freakin' bloody bitch!" Heath-Cote came racing

after them, his face and shirt red with blood. Panicking, Alexandra jammed the key in the ignition, put the car in reverse, and backed up.

"Hurry!" Mary Lee screamed as the young aristocrat ran to the Harley-Davidson parked nearby and began to kick-start it. "Hurry, oh, hurry, Alexandra!"

The Englishman on the Harley-Davidson drove with devilish skill.

"Bitches! Assholes, all of you! Friggin' cunts!" Simon screamed, swerving the Harley toward the car. "Cock teasers, that's what you are. I'll get you!" he shrieked.

Alexandra squealed the Audi through the London streets, racing through stop signs in an attempt to escape the motorcycle and its driver.

"He's still following us," sobbed Mary Lee, peering out of the back window.

"I'm sick," Jette groaned. "God, I'm going to barf . . ."

"Well, don't," Alexandra said coldly, turning another corner with a screech of rubber. *Why* didn't he drop back? As blasted as he was, it was a miracle he had kept up as long as he had.

She veered left, into a narrow street that led into a mews, the Harley right on their tail, its motor roaring.

But she was slowed by a metal garbage bin that protruded into the narrow lane. Heath-Cote caught up with them, pulling up even with Alexandra's window as he fumbled behind him for something in the saddlebags. A magnum of champagne. Raising his left hand, Simon flung the oversized bottle at the Audi.

The window on Alexandra's side shattered in a blitz of tiny fragments. Caught off balance by the effort of his throw, Heath-Cote swerved and lost control of the motorcycle.

There was a frightening thump.

"Oh, God!" Mary Lee screamed. "Oh, God, Alexandra! He's crashed! He's fallen! He crashed into that wall!"

Alexandra put the car in reverse.

"What are you doing?" Mary Lee screamed.

"I have to go back," Alexandra said dully. "I think we've killed him."

"We didn't kill him, he just crashed. He lost control." Mary Lee clutched Alexandra, her fingernails digging into Alexandra's flesh. "Don't go back; I don't want to see. What if he *is* dead, Alexandra? What then?"

"Then we'll—I don't know!" Alexandra snapped, stopping the car. "I have to go and see."

By some miracle, no one in any of the flats had yet emerged to see what the noise was, but she expected it would happen any second. She opened the car door and went over to look at Simon, half-covered by his motorcycle.

"He's dead, isn't he?" Mary Lee sobbed from the car. "He's dead! He is, I know he is, I feel it, I can tell! I know he's dead. What are we going to do? We can't—"

Alexandra forced herself to look at the motionless form that lay sprawled on the old cobbled pavement. The head was turned at an awkward angle, eyes wide open and staring, blood pooling in them.

"Jesus . . . come on . . . come on, Alexandra . . ." She felt hands pulling at her, and realized they were Mary Lee's. "For God's sake, we have to go!" Mary Lee was weeping in fear. "Come on, will you? I mean it. We have to go now. It's the only way we can still save ourselves."

— ▶◀ —

They drove through London, all three of them crying intermittently. All three were beginning to realize the grim reality of their situation.

"Oh," Jette kept moaning.

Mary Lee took charge, directing Alexandra to drive to a working-class neighborhood where families hung their laundry on lines in the back gardens. Here they found a flat where the wash had been left out during the night. They parked the Audi and climbed over the fence to steal a pair of workmen's twill pants and a shirt.

In the backseat, Jette wept as they forced the clothes on her.

"We have to *hurry*," Mary Lee kept urging. "It's going to be dawn in a few hours. Oh, God, if the papers ever find out about this . . . Do you realize what would happen? Every tabloid in the *world* would be after us! The daughters of Claudia Michaud, Jay Leonard Winthrop, and Marietta Wilde."

Alexandra choked back a sob. "I don't care about that. He's dead, Mary Lee. He was only *twenty years old!*"

"Who cares? He raped Jette. You've never heard scandal until you've heard what'll happen once the world gets wind of this. Thank God they raped Jette. Thank God for that . . . because it means they won't dare tell anyone what really happened. They've got their reputations to protect, too."

Mary Lee's voice, coolly planning how they were to deceive everyone, chilled Alexandra. "This is wrong," she began.

"Is it? Do you want to go to a British prison, Alexandra? Do you want to have your reputation ruined in Boston? You're going to make your debut this year, aren't you? A coming-out party. Do you think that a convicted murderer gets to make a debut? Or to get into Vassar College? Or to marry someone from a good family? Are you crazy? We don't have any choice, Alexandra! We *have* to get ourselves out of this. We're talking about all of our futures."

They drove back to Joti and Gwen's flat, where they retrieved their luggage. The flat was empty, the "memorabilia" on the wall looking tawdry and obscene, and the place smelled cloyingly of bath talcum and perfume. They changed their clothes and stuffed the stolen workmen's clothes into the building's rubbish bin.

By this time Jette was beginning to sober up. "God," she wept. "Oh, Lord, it was awful. He . . . he just rammed himself into me! It hurt s-so bad . . ."

"Hush," Alexandra said, holding her. "You'll be fine in the morning."

"I won't, I won't be fine. He was . . . he . . ." Jette dissolved into more tears. "He r-raped me, Alexandra! I feel so *sick*," Jette said, leaning over to heave into a wastepaper basket stuffed with old panty hose and cigarette butts. "Oh," she groaned.

"You'll be OK," Alexandra said, stroking her friend's tangled mane of black curls.

"Ah . . . ah . . ." Violently Jette vomited. Then she lay back weakly. "I'll never be clean again," she said, shivering. "It—it was all my fault, wasn't it? I acted like a goddamned s-slut . . ."

"You didn't," Alexandra lied. "It wasn't your fault."

"It was, and you know it. It was all that coke . . . oh, God!" Jette tossed and turned, dry-heaving. Alexandra and Mary Lee finished packing and threw their bags into the trunk of the Audi.

They drove into the English countryside, the sun edging up along the eastern treeline. Pearly pink light flooded the hedgerows and the old stone cottages, where lights were now blinking on. The sky gradually flushed with salmon, with flocks of tiny, sheeplike clouds lit from behind by a golden fire.

Jette lay in the backseat, crying quietly. In the front seat, Mary Lee was silent. Alexandra stared ahead, dry-eyed. The morning was too beautiful, she thought. Almost scarily beautiful. A girl had been raped, a boy had died, and still the sunrise was full of golds and pinks and dusty blues.

They were only twenty minutes from the West Heath School. A little copse lay ahead, a small woods full of blackberry bushes and the season's first wildflowers. Alexandra pulled the Audi underneath the trees and switched off the motor.

"I—I'm not quite ready to go back yet," she said. "Let's just sit here for a minute."

They sat in silence, gazing at the dewy English morning in which birds already trilled, their calls liquid with April. Somewhere a dog barked. They instinctively huddled close together, Jette leaning forward from the backseat so that they all could touch. They had left the West Heath School as three careless schoolgirls on a lark; they were returning with their emotions in turmoil.

"I didn't mean for it to happen," Jette said in a choked voice. "I swear it . . . I swear!"

What was there to say? That spoiled Jette had insisted on everything, even the idea to go to London in the first place? Her punishment had been the severest of all.

"We believe you," Alexandra said after a time.

"What's going to happen now?" Mary Lee wailed. "Do we just go back to school?"

"I guess we'll have to." Alexandra spoke slowly. The story they had agreed upon before they left, about staying with Alexandra's Aunt Sarah, who was visiting London, now seemed fantastic and naive. "But I think we should swear a promise. A solemn promise. Let's link hands."

They clasped hands, squeezing each other's fingers tightly.

"We swear we'll never talk about last night with *anyone*," Alexandra said.

"Never, ever," said Mary Lee. "We can't talk about it, because if we do, our futures are shot to hell."

There was a little silence as each reflected on the truth of her words. Their futures were all laid out. Alexandra would return to Boston, make her debut, and then attend Vassar College. Mary Lee also planned to attend Vassar. Jette planned to return to Beverly Hills, where she wanted to be "a fabulous success at something." But if even one of those young men talked . . .

"And—and we'll always help each other, like you helped me last night," Jette added. "No matter where we go in life, no matter what we do or who we marry or what happens to us . . . all we have to do is ask, and we'll help each other!"

They were silent again, their hands connecting them.

"Solemn pledge?" Alexandra said finally, her voice cracking. "Do we all swear?"

"Wait a minute!" Jette said, recovering a bit of her old verve. "We can't just *say* we swear; we have to swear in blood! Does anyone have a pin?"

Mary Lee produced a pearl circlet pin, and they passed it around, each of them pricking the pad of her forefinger to draw a small dot of red. They pressed their fingers together, smearing the blood, feeling a bond of sisterhood that could last a lifetime.

"There," Jette said in satisfaction. "That means we've sworn—sworn forever!"

Then she burst into tears. After a minute, Alexandra began to cry, too. Mary Lee's face got very red, and she clenched their hands tightly. She alone did not cry.

3

Alexandra
1989

Friends, Alexandra thought, replacing the small photograph on the table. What would you do without them? How could you focus your life without their support? Your husband might seem distant and busy, your marriage might seem as if it were permanently on hold. But your friends were always there.

Even eleven years after the girls had made their vow, the memory of it warmed and strengthened her. She could depend on Jette and Mary Lee.

And Diana. Despite the years and a certain amount of drifting apart, Diana was still her dear friend.

Impulsively, Alexandra picked up the phone and dialed the private number Diana had given her. Because of the five-hour time difference between Chicago and England, it was nine o'clock in the evening in London.

"Hullo, this is Di," her voice came across the wires. Female laughter could be heard in the background.

"Diana? This is Alexandra."

"Alexandra," Diana said with obvious pleasure. "I was just thinking about you and our lovely party."

"I just had to call. Everything's coming together beautifully."

"Oh, wonderful," came the princess's soft, warm voice. "And, Alexandra, I can't wait to hear about the celebrities you're having. I do like Don Johnson and Melanie Griffith. I adored her in *Working Girl*. And Phil Collins, from Genesis. Oh, and Joan Collins. I always have her program taped," she raced on without a pause. "Don't you think she is fabulously glamorous? She uses Bruce Oldfield, too, don't you know, one of my designers. Please send her an invitation if you haven't already."

There was a bubbly warmth about Diana that Alexandra found tremendously appealing. Nothing, not relentless media scrutiny or tabloid gossip, not even numbing official dinners and ceremonies, had been able to dim her.

They spent some time discussing the various stars Diana wanted to see, and then Diana said, "Oh, Alexandra, it's just *so* good to talk with you! It's been so long since we've seen each other. Couldn't you and Richard fly over to spend a long weekend with us at Highgrove? Weekends, you know, we escape from all that tedium and boredom at Kensington—Charles hates London. It's so pretty at Highgrove at this time of the year. And there's Royal Ascot, you know. Do bring a hat for that; it's the one thing you can't forget."

Alexandra caught her breath. But no, she wouldn't leave her children now. It was unthinkable.

"Do bring the children, too. Wills and Harry will love having them to play with. They can have a nursery party. Alexandra, we'll have such great fun."

Diana instructed Alexandra to have her secretary call her lady-in-waiting the next day to finalize arrangements and let her know how many staff she planned to bring. The stay would be five or six days.

Alexandra hung up with a bemused expression. Dear heavens, she would actually meet the Queen. What should she wear? Would she do as Nancy Reagan had done, and forgo a curtsy?

She realized the invitation could not have come at a better time. The children would be out of the country, away from any threat, and by the time they all returned, security measures would be in place.

Leaving her office, she walked down the corridor to the playroom. She had to admit it, she'd allowed her fantasies to run wild when she decorated that big room. It was bright and carpeted in leaf green, its walls painted with jungle and animal murals.

"Mama, I'm drawing a alien!" six-year-old Trip exclaimed excitedly as Alexandra entered the room. "He's so big he takes up the whole page, an' he's got evil wings."

Alexandra admired her son's splashy effort, his inspiration derived from Saturday-morning TV cartoons.

"I draw a alien, too," Andrew chimed in.

"*I* draw a li'l girl," Stephanie pointed out with dignity.

"Yes, Mrs. Cox?" Elizabeth Clifford-Brown was attractive in a dignified way, with fair skin and light brown hair that she wore short. She had impeccable credentials. A registered nurse, she had trained at St. Bartholomew's Hospital in central London. For several years she had worked as an assistant nanny for Princess Michael of Kent, helping the Princess with her two children, Lord Frederick and Lady Gabriella.

"Brownie, I have wonderful news—we're going to London, all of us, including you and the children."

"Really, Mrs. Cox?" The woman's cheeks flushed with pleasure.

"Your airfare and lodging, of course, will be provided, and I want to give you a little bonus, to do with as you wish." Alexandra named a sum that caused the Englishwoman's cheeks to redden even further. "Also, I'd like you to take an additional two weeks in London, so you can visit your mother. I know you haven't seen her in several years."

"Oh, no, Mrs. Cox, not two weeks. I couldn't do that. The children are accustomed to me."

"Then I'll arrange for you to see her during the time we're at Highgrove." Actually, Alexandra was relieved Brownie hadn't accepted. She was right; the children did need her. They discussed security arrangements, and then the nanny cleared her throat discreetly.

"You don't think, ma'am . . . that is, you don't think that I might have been lax in my duty? I certainly have done everything that I could, and I never would have allowed strangers in to photograph them. If you think . . . if you . . ." For an instant the woman's composure broke. "If you think that I was derelict, I could give my notice, if you desire it."

"Your notice?" Alexandra was touched. "Of course not, Brownie, don't be silly. You didn't know what was going on. None of us did. I know how much you love my children. Please, don't distress yourself."

"Very well then," the nanny said, seeming relieved.

"I'll let you know our traveling dates," Alexandra promised.

⊷

She spent the next day conferring with her staff and interviewing several hotel security personnel she had reluctantly
agreed to add to her household.

"But only temporarily," she specified to Richard, whom she
met for a quick lunch at his office. "I don't want the children
frightened. I mean this."

Lines around Richard's mouth were drawn tight, but he
relaxed them to smile at her. "Lexy, it'll all be over in a week,
I promise." Richard smiled at her, the tension leaving his face.

She searched his eyes for reassurance.

"A week, babe, I promise."

She nodded. "Anyway, I do have other wonderful news,
darling. Diana's invited us to Highgrove for a week! We need to
get away from all this for a few days, and I want the children out
of the city until all the security arrangements are completed."

Something in his eyes flickered. "I know it's important for
you and the children, but I've got other problems here in town."

"You mean . . . you might not be coming? Richard, we
need some time together!"

"Punkie, I know, and I will try." Just then the phone rang,
pulling Richard away for a conference call he had placed to
David Kwan in Hong Kong. Alexandra excused herself and left.
She'd lost his attention anyway.

That night, Alexandra soaked in a long, hot bath, trying to
release the tension of the day. She leaned back, forcing her
muscles to relax. As always, the bathroom itself had a calming
effect on her. It was done in pink-veined gray marble, with
banks of tropical plants and fragile orchids from white to deepest purple. The Jacuzzi area had been softened by deeply swag-
gered mauve drapes that cast their pink light on the bather and
at the same time gave coziness to an environment that might
otherwise be overwhelming. More than once she and Richard
had frolicked in the Jacuzzi before retiring to the largest of the
fluffy sheepskin rugs to make long, slow, delicious love.

Sighing, she stepped out of the Jacuzzi and dried herself,
then walked naked into her adjoining dressing room and drew
on a white satin Scaasi negligee with a deep spill of lace across
the bodice.

She had been reading a biography of Ella Fitzgerald;
however, after scanning ten pages without absorbing a word, she
put the book aside.

Where was Richard? He hadn't eaten dinner with them, but had closeted himself with Blackjack Slattery, his security man. Even the children had sensed the uneasiness in the house, and Stephanie had wept piteously before being put to bed.

Damn, she needed him tonight. Sometimes she felt such loneliness that she ached. She drifted into restless sleep.

Some time later she was awakened by the sound of the bedroom door closing as Richard entered. Drowsily she listened to the familiar sounds as he undressed, laying out the contents of his pockets on a table in his dressing room, as he had done every night of the seven years they had been married. Billfold. Money clip. Bits of change. Like any other husband getting ready for bed.

She stirred, murmuring sleepily, "Richard, darling. What time is it?"

"After three."

"Three?"

"I had to call London and Hong Kong," he told her. "You know how hard that makes it with the different time zones. And Slattery was here until two."

She said nothing, waiting until he crawled into their king-size bed, then settled into a position near the center of the mattress.

"Mmmmm," he said, touching her hair. "You smell good, punkie. I love the way you smell when you've been sleeping."

"Not sleeping," she mumbled, trying to wake up. The anger she had felt toward him seemed to have mostly vanished, and she curled her body into his.

"Like magnolias," he whispered. "Or roses. Yes, I think roses. So pretty. Mmmm. Yes." He began running his hands along the lace bodice of the sumptuous negligee, slipping his fingers underneath the half-transparent triangles that covered her breasts.

The touch fully awakened her. Slowly, caressingly, he pulled down the narrow satin straps, revealing her bare, full breasts. He bent his head and began licking and kissing her nipples, bringing them to exquisite life.

She felt his tongue stroke her sensitive tissue, sending little thrills of involuntary sensation through her. Oh, yes, he was trying to melt her reserve.

Their sex life had always been wonderful. Sometimes too wonderful, she thought, seducing her into complying with his ways. Even now, she felt herself weaken. His kisses explored the softness of her breasts, familiar with every crevice, every warm curve.

As he kissed her breasts, his hands caressed her flanks, cupping her buttocks, gradually extending their range to the area where her vagina met those other curves. Involuntarily, she moaned.

"I never get tired of you," he whispered. "Never." His hands sought her pleasure, nurturing it, delicately spreading her open like a rosebud blooming. His breath was deep and ragged with desire.

She sighed, moving against him, responding to the virility hundreds of other women could only envy. It scared her how much she loved him. How addicted her body was to his.

"Richard," she whispered, caught now in the throes of passion.

"My Lexy," he groaned against her breast. "My darling, darling."

——— ▶◀ ———

At breakfast, sun slanted in the windows, touching the Waterford crystal glasses Alexandra used for orange juice because she loved the way they refracted the light. Last night's passionate lovemaking seemed to have vanished into the steam that rose from their coffee.

The children ate cheerfully, then ran off to be escorted to the park by Brownie. Richard seemed preoccupied, but Alexandra decided they had to talk.

She began, "Rich, what about England?"

"Lexy," he said gently. "You're not planning on me going, are you? You know I can't."

Disappointed, she asked, "You mean you really can't go?" She was ashamed of the shakiness in her voice.

"I can't, punkie. Didn't you listen to me? I've got to get this union thing taken care of and the contract settled. So you won't have to worry about anything," he added persuasively.

"Oh . . . " was all she could say.

"Lexy, honey, I'm doing this for you and the kids. Anyway," he continued, "I do have some good news for you. One of my calls yesterday was from McDonnell Douglas. They've finally got our bird ready. You and the kids and Brownie can fly to

London in that, and there will be plenty of room for the kids to move around and play."

Alexandra nodded, gazing out at the sun rising over Lake Michigan. McDonnell Douglas specialized in re-outfitting MD-80s, successors to the DC-9 aircraft, to be made into company jets. Luxury was their byword. Richard had paid $27 million for theirs, with another $16 million on refurbishment. They had been waiting eagerly to take the ship on its maiden flight. Now she really didn't care.

"The first flight, with just me?" she said, her voice cracking. "Richard . . . it was going to be *us*."

"Babe, I know we were going to fly in it together on the first time out, but I'll make it up to you."

She met his eyes, refusing to cry. "Planes aren't important. *We* are," she said quietly.

—— ►◄ ——

Alexandra, the three children, and Brownie walked through the boarding ramp into the *Fitz II*.

"Is this our plane? Our very own plane, *ours*?" demanded Trip. He wriggled out of Brownie's grip to race into the large central lounge of the plane, lavishly appointed with dove gray leather, deep rose carpeting, and pale suede walls.

"Ours! Ours!" echoed Andrew, running after him.

"Me, too," squeaked little Stephanie, clinging to Brownie's hand and looking around wide-eyed. "Do they got toys here?"

"All kinds of toys," a pretty flight attendant promised.

Brownie shepherded her charges to their seats, where they would be served glasses of fruit juice and oatmeal cookies.

Thank heavens for Brownie, Alexandra sighed, walking around the interior of the plane. It seated only twenty, in sheer stretch-out luxury. Every seat was upholstered in chamois-soft leather. Ample as a single bed, each could at the push of a button assume more than five positions, from fully upright to completely flat. Alexandra had had the seat belts and cushions custom woven in a graduated-shade, rose flamestitch pattern. A large wet bar stood available to serve anything from soda to champagne, and there were two conference rooms with IBM computers, fax machines, and inflight telephones—everything needed to conduct business in midair.

Of the two large staterooms, the master room, decorated in

blues and grays, had small dressing rooms for Richard and herself, a bath with bidet, a wet steam room, Jacuzzi, and sauna. There were reading lamps, a TV set with VCR, an extensive library of videotapes, and bestsellers that would be updated every month.

Walking into the master stateroom, Alexandra caught her breath at the sight of a gigantic bouquet of her favorite, frilly pink roses, almost overwhelming the room with their fragrance. She went over and read the card.

You're the most wonderful and understanding woman in the world. Thank you for sharing your life with me. Forever, your Rich.

Her eyes watered, and she tucked the card in her purse, snapping its clasp shut. Flowers. Promises. Easy to give, and much more difficult to keep. He had done it all for her—even this plane had been planned to her specifications—yet part of her longed for him to say, "I'm going to throw everything to the winds and come with you because I love you so much I can't let you go even for a long weekend."

"Mommy!" Trip came running in to her. "Can I go up and talk to the pilot and get a pilot's hat, like Brownie said? Can I steer the plane? I want to steer!"

Alexandra laughed. "Of course, you can all go and meet the crew. As for steering, I'm not sure. We'll have to ask the pilot."

"*I'm* going to be a pilot, too," Trip crowed. "I'm going to go up and down," he demonstrated.

"Darling, let's go and meet him now," Alexandra said, taking her son's hand. "Andrew, too. And Steffie. We'll all go and visit the cockpit."

Later, the attendant lowered the movie screen, and they ran *Cinderella*, the children's selection, while Alexandra sat sipping a wine spritzer, lost in thought.

The trip was going to be wonderful.

But without Richard, nothing was really one-hundred-percent wonderful.

Over the Atlantic, Alexandra leaned back in her seat, closed her eyes, and began thinking over some of the protocol she needed to check on in England.

Dolly had already been on the telephone several times to Kensington Palace—"KP" as Diana jokingly referred to it. She had talked at length with Diana's chief lady-in-waiting, Anne Beckwith-Smith, who assisted Diana with official engagements, and the Waleses' private secretary, Sir John Riddell. But Alexandra had many more questions.

Food likes and dislikes and other preferences of the Prince and Princess of Wales must be taken into consideration. She knew Charles liked Bollinger champagne, disliked chocolate, and was an ardent nonsmoker. Diana drank gin with lots of tonic water, or just plain tonic water. Both preferred fish, egg, or light chicken dishes to red meat.

Another matter concerned availability of bathrooms. It was a firm rule that the Princess had to have a separate loo provided for her visit.

Fortunately, the Green Room, a capacious VIP area that included a small bar and several conference rooms, had already been installed in the new banquet wing of the Chicago Fitzgerald. It possessed several elegant pink marble bathrooms, and another was being created from the smallest conference room. The Green Room was also being redecorated for the Royal visit with the Laura Ashley floral prints that Diana loved.

But there were other matters more pertinent than wallpaper. Charles would carry on some of his talks in the Green Room; what would he need? Who did he wish included? Were there celebrities the Royals wanted to meet beforehand? What security measures? Of course, they had been told that members of Diana's security staff would personally come to Chicago the week before the gala, to check out every conceivable security angle before the Royals themselves arrived.

The steady roar of the plane was making Alexandra sleepy, and she finally dismissed the party from her thoughts. She had put on dozens of galas and fund-raisers, and in the end, despite the presence of the Royals, this was only one slightly more important party . . .

She dozed off.

— ◄► —

They were met at Heathrow Airport by Sir John Riddell, who took them to the helicopter pad, where they boarded a red Queen's Flight helicopter to take them to Highgrove, 100 miles west of London, near Bath.

Highgrove, from the air, was a beautiful, 200-year-old Georgian mansion situated on an extensive green sward. As they landed, Alexandra caught her breath at the sight of the old house. Its stones, Riddell explained, had been doused with buckets of tea to encourage their aged look. Part of the lawn was manicured green, but beginning near the house was a field of tall, waist-high grass in which white and yellow daisies and orange poppies grew in close-packed, lush profusion.

Diana, wearing blue-striped slacks and a Henley shirt, came running out to greet them. "Alexandra! Oh, it's so splendid to see you! Did the chopper shake you up too much? Charles and I love them, but they're not for everyone. The Queen hates helicopters with a passion. Hello, darlings," the Princess added, bending down to kiss each of the young ones in turn. "This is the first time I've met you in person."

Household staff arrived to take charge of their luggage. The two women stood back to look at each other. Diana's English-rose beauty was now at its zenith, her color fresh. Even at home her makeup was perfect, her eyes underlined with teal blue.

"You're blonder," Alexandra blurted, then bit her tongue.

"So are you," Diana retorted, unfazed.

"I confess to a few blonde streaks, myself," Alexandra confided, and they both laughed as Diana spontaneously threw her arms around her again.

"I'm *so* glad you're here. Otherwise I would be watching polo, and you can't imagine how dull that can be. Charles will join us for Ascot, maybe." Diana shrugged, her expression eloquent.

They entered the house. The long foyer was coral pink and ran from the front door through to the back, where French windows opened on vistas of garden.

"William and Harry are dying to show Trip and Andy their ponies. Would you like to see the boys' ponies?" Diana asked the Cox youngsters.

"Oh, yes, yes!" squealed both boys, with Stephanie chiming in.

"And pet rabbits? And a pond filled with carp?"

"What's a carp?" Stephanie demanded.

"It's a big, overgrown goldfish. We have dozens, and you can feed them if you wish. They come to the top of the water and go *poof*! and *bubble*! and *swish*! with their tails."

The children, with Brownie, were whisked away by the Waleses' nanny. The three Cox youngsters were agog with enthusiasm to see William and Harry and all the promised wonders, which included a playhouse, dovecote, stables, and several ponds.

"Come on, Alexandra. I want you to see the house. It's lovely." There were four reception rooms downstairs. Diana's sitting room was stunning with its pale yellow color scheme and Laura Ashley florals. There was another large, formal drawing room, furnished in antiques, and a study for Prince Charles.

Staff quarters and a large kitchen area were off the lower hallway, and a network of back staircases gave access to the nursery suite on the top floor.

The women strolled in what Diana called the garden, a vast, green area, its informal plantings lovingly designed by Charles to look like a wild meadow. There was an avenue of apple trees, now in tender, new leaf. Long grasses, undulating in the English breeze, were cut with narrow, mown paths that led to a walled garden, a few hundred yards away from the main house. Here grew more flowers, fruits, and vegetables.

"The garden is Charles's joy," explained Diana. "He's happiest when he's just kneeling and weeding and dreaming. He wants to add some lovely sounds, like running water and tinkling cowbells." She giggled. "But the cows were afraid of the bells, and running water makes me want to go to the loo."

Lunch was on a table on the lawn, a light buffet of quiche, green salad, and a delicately fluted pear flan. Cheese and biscuits were offered as well, arranged on bone china with the Waleses' crest. The children were eating upstairs, in the nursery.

"Who are you using in New York? For a designer, I mean?" Diana wanted to know.

"I do wear a lot of Bob Mackie . . . and Scaasi, and of course De la Renta." Alexandra shrugged. "One or two buying trips a year, and I've filled most of my needs. There's a shop on Park Avenue, Martha, where they know me, and I find that very convenient. I can arrive in New York, and they'll have things put aside for me. I don't devote half my life to fashion, like some women do. My time is limited, and I'd rather spend it on my music."

"I know," Diana said. "Fashion becomes one's obligation."

Diana talked of some of her frustrations, her long days of public engagements, her increasing efforts to redesign her gowns to wear more than once. Finally she sighed. "It seems so easy to talk to you, Alexandra . . . I'm a princess now. No one treats me like a human being anymore."

"But your friends . . . ?"

"I'm Royalty. Even they can't relax with me. Oh, it's awful!" Her eyes filled. "You don't have photographers spying on you all the time, just dying to get a picture with your legs apart or the sun shining through your dress. You can conduct your marriage in privacy." She sighed. "What a luxury. Everything *we* do happens in a fishbowl."

"I know," Alexandra said sympathetically. "But, Di, you deal with it all so well; you behave with such grace . . . really," she added, as the Princess shook her head.

"I don't. I don't stand up to it sometimes. And Charles is gone so much, Alexandra. Even today, he is at Cowdrey. The press says I'm living the life of a single parent. They count the days or weeks he's away from me, as if I couldn't count them myself."

Her voice trailed off.

"Haven't you discussed it with Charles?"

"Of course. But we're so very different, you see. He's been reared to live this kind of life, and he has so many obligations. The Queen and Prince Philip are often apart for months at a time. They don't seem to mind. But they're old . . ."

The Princess's face became expressionless, and Alexandra knew she was fighting emotions that she did not wish to reveal.

Alexandra waited until the staff had finished clearing the table, then said, "Di, I really think love is like an ember that never quite goes out. Sometimes it glows softly, and at other times it springs into flame and burns for many years. All we need to do is guard that glow. Keep it safe, so one day it *can* flame."

Diana looked at her. "I'm afraid," she whispered. "Embers sometimes die."

"They won't," Alexandra told her friend with more conviction than she felt. "They can't. Real love *never* burns away, Di."

——— ◄► ———

That night, Trip crept into the pale blue bedroom Alexandra had been given, and crawled under the blanket with his mother. His hair smelled of fragrant English shampoo.

"Why isn't Daddy with us?" Alexandra's son whispered into her ear. "Why did Brownie go into London tonight?"

"Daddy has business in Chicago, so he couldn't come," Alexandra explained. "And I promised Brownie she could visit her mother. She hasn't visited her in a long, long time."

"Are you going to see the Queen?" her son went on with his litany of questions. "Does Wills get to ride his pony every day? Will he be King sometime? Why won't I be King?"

Alexandra laughed, hugging her irrepressible eldest. "We're American, and we don't have kings, darling. But you could be President when you grow up, if you work very hard."

Trip thought. "President is boring," he said at last. "I want to have a pony, just like Wills and Harry."

———— ►◄ ————

The following morning, in meetings with Riddell and several other of the Waleses' staffers, Alexandra was astonished to learn that the Waleses would be bringing nineteen people with them to Chicago.

"Nineteen!" She stared at Anne Beckwith-Smith, whose hair, though darker than Diana's, was done in a hairstyle nearly identical to the princess's, and whose accent was every bit as upper-crust British.

"The Royals always bring staff," the lady-in-waiting explained. "There are security personnel for the Prince and Princess, the Royal physician, a baggage handler, several secretaries, their butler, Harold Brown, and the Princess's dresser. And of course, the week before a trip, security staff always visits the site to check every detail. A Royal trip is no casual event," Anne Beckwith-Smith added, smiling. "We can leave nothing to chance."

Alexandra took a brief nap after the meetings, lying on her bed and listening to the warble of birds in the garden, until she fell asleep. She dreamed that she was running down a long corridor searching for Richard. First she opened one door, then another, but he was in none of the rooms.

Finally she reached an open gallery where Richard stood talking with a group of chefs from his hotels around the world. She called his name and attempted to run toward him. Instead she found herself on an escalator running in the opposite direction. The harder she tried to stop, the farther away she found herself.

Then somehow Trip was with her. Blood was on his face. She tried to comfort her son and found him being torn away from her, screaming in terror.

She woke sweating and shaking.

"My God," she breathed, brushing her hair away from her face. She could still hear her son's beseeching cries. Nerves and jet lag did strange things to the mind. Better to get up and get on with the day.

Hanging in a small dressing room was the outfit she had chosen to wear for tea with the Queen that day, a pale blue silk Ferré cocktail suit with a yellow silk blouse that brought out the gleaming blonde highlights of her hair. Pinned to her suit was a pavé diamond brooch in the shape of a grand piano, a gift from Richard.

Choosing not to ring for a maid, she went into the bathroom to shower. As warm water sluiced down her body, she began to forget the dream. Definitely nerves, she decided.

Half an hour later, while Alexandra was still dressing, Diana popped in to invite her to her suite while she selected a hat and jewelry to complement her outfit.

"Great!" Alexandra said, her mood lifting.

Diana's suite was exquisite, in soft pastel hues and country chintz. The Princess was wearing a polka-dot suit in deep mauve and black with a fitted waist and deliciously flared long peplum. The famous Di look.

"The Emanuels," Diana said, twirling. "What do you think? It seems slightly 'forties,' don't you think, Alexandra?"

Diana's hat, a fetching black straw, was big-brimmed and looped with a ribbon in the same fabric as the suit. Alexandra was amused to discover that Diana owned ten black hats in varying shapes, some embellished with colored bows that could be detached for a new look.

They rummaged among the selection of jewelry that Diana's maid had brought them. There was a charm bracelet Charles had given Diana, one of the charms a tiny gold wombat, in honor of William's nickname. Although the most valuable pieces were in a safe, there were many expensive trinkets. There were also glittering *faux* pieces made of glass, paste, or plastic. Rhinestone teddy-bear heads and a fizzing-champagne-glass brooch caught Alexandra's eye.

"Which?" Diana asked playfully. "You choose for me, Alexandra."

Alexandra laughed with pleasure and sorted among the real gems until she found a pair of black-sapphire–and–diamond earrings shaped like crescents.

"These," she pronounced, holding up the sparkling pieces.

"Oh! The Sultan of Oman gave me these as a wedding gift."

"They're so lovely, they almost drip romance. Oh, Diana— I almost envy you all this."

"So much of my life is duty, though," Diana said, her

mood turning serious. "Even these," she said, pointing to the large, drawered jewel case. "These are all working jewels, except for a very few."

——— ▶◀ ———

At three-thirty, another helicopter arrived to take Alexandra and Diana to Sandringham, in the Norfolk countryside, 110 miles from London. They had to land away from the huge estate, in order not to offend the Queen with the noise, which Elizabeth loathed. From there a car took them to Sandringham.

Sandringham was a huge, Jacobean edifice of 270 rooms, with endless gabled roofs, onion-dome towers, and large, brick chimneys like mini-smokestacks on the roofs. It dominated grounds studded with huge-trunked oaks, and a garden of azaleas and rhododendrons created by King George VI. The estate housed part of the Queen's Stud, where breeding horses were kept, as well as the Royal Pigeon Lofts and kennels for the black Labradors bred by the Royals since 1911 as working dogs to accompany Royal hunters.

"Oh, heavens," exclaimed Alexandra. Surrounded by this living history, she was barely able to hide her awe.

"It's not glamorous here," Diana whispered as they approached in a black Daimler. "Just very horsey, don't you know? Lots of nice, saggy, squashy chairs. Oh, and don't stumble on the dog dishes. The Queen feeds her corgis herself, on chopped liver and dog biscuits."

Inside the front door was a large pair of scales, looking rather like matched buckets. Diana pointed them out with a giggle. "Those were used by Edward VII. He used to weigh people when they came here, and again when they left."

"Whatever for?"

"Why, to see if they'd eaten sufficiently well. They usually had."

They passed a salon where the Queen often sat. Here a large jigsaw puzzle had been laid out on a table.

"She hides the lid to make it harder. The puzzle is for anyone to do, but guests usually hold back a bit," Diana explained. "Imagine how awkward if you put in the last piece and the Queen was displeased."

Tea, at five o'clock promptly, was served in a white room filled with the Queen's Fabergé collection, case upon case of jeweled Fabergé eggs and other treasures studded with jewels.

Meeting the Queen, Alexandra panicked, lunging into a curtsy from which she miraculously did not fall.

"It is so pleasant to meet you," Elizabeth said, extending a gloved hand graciously. As she turned to speak to the Queen Mother, Alexandra managed to regain her composure. The Royals surrounded her. Prince Philip, handsome and attentive. Fergie, in forest green silk, throwing back her freckled face in laughter. Princess Margaret, in pale blue, the Queen Mother in mint green. Several other aristocratic couples whose names, in the excitement, had slipped by Alexandra.

The Queen's corgis, Susan, Whiskey, and Crackers, snoozed in a corner near their mistress.

"Are you quite in a panic?" Diana inquired quietly, giggling.

"A little," Alexandra admitted.

"Well, don't be. You're not the first. The Queen is used to people going into orbit when they meet her. That's why she always asks questions you can't say yes or no to."

Alexandra gazed around her with a growing sense of unreality. Tea. Dominated by the warm, brisk personality of Elizabeth herself, dressed for the occasion in peacock blue silk dotted with small, paisley shapes. A conservative, slightly frumpy choice, but on Elizabeth it seemed cozy and pleasant. The Queen wore a double-strand pearl necklace and small pearl earrings, her hair in her usual style.

The food itself was very British. Thinly cut brown bread, accompanied by butter in earthenware pots, and Cooper's jam. Various pâtés and fish pastes, to be spread on bread. Sandwiches made of thinly sliced white bread with the crusts cut off, filled with diced cheese and tomato, or cucumber. There was a jam-and-cream sponge cake, a chocolate cake, and little filled pastry boats with icing piped down the center. Brandysnaps and chocolate finger biscuits. Tiny, warm scones kept hot in a linen napkin, with thick, clotted cream and fresh strawberry preserves.

To Alexandra's amusement, she saw that there was a chrome double toaster on the Queen's left, into which Elizabeth herself, with housewifely aplomb, popped English muffins from a pile on a plate handed to her by a page.

Alexandra was seated at the Queen's left.

"Is the country in Chicago much good for riding? Where do you ride?" inquired the Queen in her warm, brisk voice as she poured the tea.

"It's mostly very urban, Ma'am," Alexandra responded. "I

do ride occasionally, but I confess I'm not a born equestrian."

Her mind rushed over all the admonitions and cautions she had been given before arriving here. You called the Queen "Your Majesty" the first time, and then "Ma'am." No one ever sat in the Queen's presence without being invited to do so. And once seated, no one left the table before she did—not even for calls of nature.

"And dogs? What sort of dogs do you have?"

"Actually, we don't have a dog," Alexandra explained, feeling very American and out of place.

"But you do have wonderful Lake Michigan, isn't that the proper lake?" The Queen said it to put her at ease. "I imagine you must do sailing there. I was told that your husband has sailed in the America's Cup and that you crewed for him."

As Alexandra began to relax, telling the Queen about her crewing experiences aboard *Lexy Lady*, the tea ceremony continued. Elizabeth spooned loose Darjeeling tea into the teapot with a silver spoon and added boiling water from the silver kettle. On the Queen's right waited six cups. She served only the top end of the table while her lady-in-waiting, today Ruth, Lady Fermoy, Diana's grandmother, went through the same ritual at the other end of the long table. Men got large breakfast cups, while women received smaller ones.

Ceremony, tradition, and duty—the bulwark of the Royals, their refuge as well as their job. Alexandra did not know if she would ever want to live this way, but it was fascinating to be a part of it for a few days.

If only Richard could be here.

4

Alexandra

1979

Alexandra made her debut the summer she returned from the West Heath School.

"Alex ... Alex ... " Roger Hunnewell Howe IV murmured in her ear, humming along with Bo Winniker's society orchestra as they executed a flawless fox-trot. "Do you know what you do to me? Do you know what you are *doing* to me?"

She knew, all right. The erection pressed against her thigh was solid steel, the only thing about Rog's white-tie-and-tails costume that was not absolutely proper. It was the fourth such pressure she had felt in the last hour. Could it be her stunning white Adolfo crepe gown, with its discreet décolletage that even her brother, Derek, said was "so virginal it has the opposite effect"?

They broke, and Rog twirled her with the expertise of one who had attended the obligatory dancing school at age fourteen. From the sidelines she sensed the eagle-eyed glance of her Aunt Sarah Biddle, who, with Felicia Revson, her father's friend, had culled the guest list and overseen every detail from the engraved invitations to staff gratuities.

She said only, "Please don't call me Alex. You know I hate nicknames. My name is Alexandra."

"OK, Alexandra." He pressed his body against hers. He had blond hair and the clean-cut look of a Ryan O'Neal. Down from Harvard for her Cotillion debut, he belonged to the select group of friends she'd known since preschool days, young heirs destined to be heads of large law firms, presidents of the Massachusetts Medical Society, or members of the Diplomatic Corps.

"Alexandra," he persisted. "You're so . . . "

Alexandra smiled dreamily and tuned out his chatter, wanting only to enjoy the ambiance of the night. The moonlight entering the ballroom windows was the color of the Cristal Roederer champagne now being served by the white-jacketed, white-gloved waiters. Sweet-smelling flowers were everywhere, all of them white in honor of the occasion. Roses, tulips, lilies, and plumeria.

The setting was The Country Club in Brookline, the first country club in the United States and so exclusive that its official name was only The Country Club, as if there were no other.

Among the hundreds of swaying couples were names that read like a roll call of Boston Brahmin families: Hunnewell, Biddle, Ward, Howe, Prescott, Shattuck, Forbes. Great-grandsons of industrialists who had made their fortunes in the War of 1812 danced with the great-granddaughters of tycoons who had opened up the country to railroads. Henry Kissinger was there, and two Supreme Court justices—John Paul Stevens and William O. Douglas, just retired—as well as Senator Edward Kennedy.

Alexandra was above all grateful to feel special, honored, and safe. Nightmares of that horrible, final *thump* in London still disturbed her sleep. In the six weeks since she'd come home, Alexandra had read the newspapers from front to back daily and had found only one small blurb in the *Times*.

British Peer's Son Killed in Hit-Run.

Shaking, she had read the one-paragraph story, which said little more than that Simon Heath-Cote had been killed in an accident after leaving a party, and no charges were being filed. Still, Simon's death had shocked her, and she could not let go of the idea that somehow, someday she could be held responsible.

The song ended, and Bo Winniker's orchestra swept into its version of "I Can Dream, Can't I." Rog escorted her back to the sidelines. Quickly, before someone else could ask her to dance, she escaped to the powder room.

The powder room was full of girls and women in long satin and tulle gowns. Some were this season's debs; others were in their second or third season. A few were mothers or older relatives. They applied lipstick taken from elegant little beaded or diamanté evening purses, resprayed hair mussed from too-exuberant partners, or waited while the uniformed attendant mended small rips or loose threads in the ballgowns. Becky Saltonstall was dabbing Halston from a small bottle into her cleavage.

"Alexandra! Alexandra! Have you seen Derek?" It was Pims, Pamela Lodge, Alexandra's best friend since kindergarten. Along with Muffy Copley and Alison Reid, she was sharing the coming-out ball with Alexandra.

Pims wasn't anyone's idea of a beauty. She had honey-colored hair pulled back into a braided chignon. Her face was sprinkled with freckles, and the pale lashes that fringed her warm gray eyes had been touched with mascara. Her body was sturdy and large-framed, which even yards of the obligatory white tulle and Schiffli embroidery did little to soften.

"Derek? He was dancing with someone," Alexandra said.

"Oh, balls," Pims said. She had a crush on Alexandra's older brother, who at thirty was finishing up his third term in the U.S. Congress. The five years had been flamboyant, and as a result he was thinking of running for the Senate.

"If you see them, would you steer him my way?" Pims added. "Tell him I want to raise funds for his campaign or something. I can't help it, Alexandra. I think Derek is dreamy!"

"Dreamy? His nose is too big, and his eyes are too little," Alexandra teased.

"You just think that because you're his sister. *I* think he looks just like Jack Kennedy. Check to see if I have big, sweaty handprints all over my back, will you?" Pims asked, turning her solid back to Alexandra.

"Are you interested in Rog at all?" Pims went on. "*He's* cute, don't you think? A little short but adorable."

Alexandra sighed. "Who cares about 'cute,' Pims? I don't want a cute man; I want something more."

"More, as in mature? Distinguished? Sexy?"

"Yeah, and very compelling and charismatic. But rich, powerful, and successful at the same time." Alexandra thought of her father, Jay Winthrop, who was all of these things.

Pims giggled. "You're not asking for much."

— ◄► —

At about eleven o'clock, the orchestra played a flourish. The dancing stopped, and the guests formed a semicircle around the edges of the ballroom. It was time for the debutantes to be presented.

Alexandra stood nervously with her father, Derek, and Rog Howe, waiting for her turn. She held a white nosegay of tiny roses and gardenias. She had not given much thought to this traditional moment—until now. Generations of white-clad young women had stood just as she was, trembling a little and yet proud, waiting for their adult life to begin.

"Don't be nervous, sweetheart," Jay Winthrop said, squeezing his daughter's arm. He was fifty-six, patrician in appearance, with his steel-gray hair, ruddy complexion, and trimmed mustache. At 6'3" he towered over most men of his generation, and his twenty pounds of extra bulk only enhanced his authority. She could not remember a time when she had not looked up to him. "You'll always be my baby girl, and now you're the prettiest woman in this room. I'm so proud to be your father."

"Oh, Daddy—"

"You're as beautiful as your mother, darling," he added, his eyes moistening.

Alexandra blinked back tears. The mention of her mother stabbed her heart. Cassandra Winthrop had not only been beautiful, but her many kindnesses and devotion to charity were legendary.

For an instant, Alexandra felt the gentleness of her mother's presence. A sad aura it was, too, as if Cassandra sensed the turmoil within her and knew its cause.

I'll make it up, Alexandra silently promised her mother. *I promise, I swear it. I'll live a good life, and I'll never hurt anyone. I'll do my music. I'll write songs for the world.*

Pims, the first of the debs, was being introduced. On Alexandra's right, Derek looked amused by the procedure, as befitted a handsome and supremely eligible bachelor who had attended hundreds of such affairs. For ten years Boston mothers had plotted to snare him for their daughters, but Derek, smiling, had eluded their grasp.

"She's about as exciting as New England boiled dinner," he suddenly murmured under his breath, referring to Pims, now clutching her bouquet and blushing furiously.

"Oh, Derek! Will you *hush*," Alexandra urged, stifling a giggle. "Muffy's going now. She looks so pretty. Just perfect."

Then it was her turn. Alexandra drew a deep breath, all levity gone. Taking her father's arm, she glided forward, a radiant smile parting her lips. Her aunt had rehearsed this glide with her, and the subsequent curtsy. Alexandra now moved with flawless grace, a tall, lissom young woman with instinctive presence, her white gown the perfect foil for her blonde beauty.

The crowd was a blur of faces, silk, and satin. There was a collective "ah."

"They think you're gorgeous," Derek said as he and Rog escorted her to her place in the line of debutantes and their attendants. "You'll have men telephoning you tomorrow until the phone rings off the hook. But to me you're still my Sissy, so don't forget it. I can still tweak your hair if I feel like it."

In her brother's arms, Alexandra gave herself up to the slow waltz rhythms. She shivered. This night . . . the dimmed lights, the admiring guests, the moonlight glowing outside the country club walls . . . What was going to happen now? What was it all for?

—— ►◄ ——

Aunt Sarah was extremely pleased with the evening.

"I think we can say you are the season's beauty, Alexandra," she said, seated regally at a side table from which she could review the shifting crowd.

Alexandra flushed, not knowing what to say.

"You'll have plenty of bouquets tomorrow morning, I can guarantee it. More than any other girl here tonight."

"Oh, Aunt Sarah . . . "

At one o'clock breakfast was served, and the debutantes and their friends feasted on scrambled eggs, sausage, toast, several kinds of marmalade, fresh-squeezed orange juice, and coffee. A chef prepared omelettes to order. There were three or four kinds of potatoes, from hash browns to cottage fries, all crusty with butter and dotted with fresh-ground pepper.

Derek, dragging himself away from a flirtation with Becky Saltonstall, who had been last year's beauty, filled Alexandra's plate. They selected a table near a window that looked out on a floodlit garden where couples strolled.

"Well, dear brother? Rumor has it that our father is urging you to find someone and settle down, and the sooner the better." Alexandra poked at her mushroom omelette, grinning at her brother, blue eyes sparkling. "Will it be Becky Saltonstall? Hmmmm?"

"Her? She's too fluffy for me."

"Too fluffy?"

"I want a Jackie Bouvier. Only Episcopalian. Heavy-duty glamour, class, and intelligence. *You* know."

Alexandra frowned. "I suppose any number of these girls could be a Jackie Onassis if the situation were right."

"By the way, Sissy, speaking of intelligent, you're not bad yourself. Any chance you might assist me a little in my next campaign? Maybe scout around and dig up some contributors? Don't want to count on Dad more than I have to."

Alexandra agreed, and they were talking politics when Derek glanced away, a grin spreading across his face. "Well, if it isn't Giancarlo. He's finally arrived."

"Giancarlo?"

Alexandra looked up as a man sauntered toward them across the room, his movements liquid. His evening wear was correct but more flamboyant than what the rest of the men wore. He was no more than twenty years old, slim, with lean, dark good looks. A spill of blue-black curls touched his collar, and his nose was as aristocratic as that of a Roman statue.

Alexandra realized she was not the only one eyeing him with surprise. From her vantage point, Aunt Sarah had begun to ruffle like an angry turkey.

"Glad to see you finally made it." Derek rose to greet the man, who, Alexandra was positive, was not on the guest list.

Derek casually introduced him. "Giancarlo Ferrari, of the Italian racing family. I met him at LeMans last year. He's terrific, Alexandra; he's going to be another Mario Andretti."

"It's nice to meet you." Alexandra extended her hand graciously. Giancarlo took her hand and then kissed it lightly in the European manner, holding it perhaps just one second too long.

"I invited him to stop by," Derek explained. "Met up with him at Locke-Ober's last night. Good party, eh?" Derek added, nudging the race-car driver. "My sister was the belle of the ball tonight. Too bad you missed seeing her bow."

The young Italian gazed at Alexandra with dark, liquid eyes in which gleamed a spark of aggressiveness. "You are very beautiful, *Signorina* Winthrop."

"Thank you."

"Would you care to stroll in the garden?"

"Why, yes," she told Giancarlo. "I'd love to walk with you. But first won't you join us for some breakfast?"

"Are you interested in cars?" the young racer asked as he sat down. "I will tell you about myself and my racing, and you will like to hear all of it, eh? I come from Torino, you know. I am going to be a world-class driver within a year at most. I will be famous everywhere."

Giancarlo left briefly to fill his plate, then returned to their table. He was amazingly handsome, though he talked endlessly about himself, telling her all about the race at Monaco, where he had driven a Ferrari 312B to take a first by sixteen seconds.

Alexandra listened, taken with the single-minded enthusiasm Giancarlo displayed. With vigorous gestures, Giancarlo took her around the track at Monaco. He zoomed them up the straight toward the Hôtel de Paris, around a fast bend near the Casino, through a hair-raising turn at the Mirabeau Corner, and along the famous Station hairpin.

"You are interested?" Giancarlo broke his monologue to ask her. "You want to hear more about me?"

"Of course," Alexandra said. And she meant it.

"Well, I am cousin to the Ferrari family who make the race cars. I have racing behind me for many, many years. My father has a home in Torino and a villa at Capri, another villa in Monaco."

"Of course." Boldly Alexandra allowed her glance to lock with his.

— ◄► —

Outdoors, a full, sterling-silver moon seemed to hang directly over the rambling country-club building and the beautifully kept grounds. Filmy clouds, like shawls of gauze, trailed behind it, sometimes partially hiding it from view. The air smelled deliciously of flowering trees, the last lilacs, and the scent of newly clipped grass.

Alexandra and Giancarlo joined the couples who were strolling the grounds. A breeze toyed with Alexandra's gown molding it to her body as she walked. She drew in a deep breath of summer air, feeling more alive than she had all night.

"Do you mind? My feet hurt," she said, stopping to grab hold of his arm while she slipped out of her dancing shoes with their three-inch heels.

They left the bricked walk and crossed the grass.

"Tell me how it feels to be at the edge of things, Giancarlo. To risk your life."

The racer laughed. "I'm not in danger, Alexandra." His accent delightfully fractured her name. "I have strong skills and the desire and the luck—I know what I want, and I go after it. If one does not do that, he should be washing dishes, not driving a car!"

They were going down a slight incline, and Alexandra stumbled slightly.

"Be careful," Giancarlo warned, grasping her arm. "The grass is slippery from the dew. We do not want you to fall down, eh? Or you may drag me with you."

His laugh was low in his throat, sensuous and suggestive. He's *so* sexy, Alexandra thought wildly, her body trembling from the nearness of this man she had just met.

She wanted Giancarlo to kiss her.

It would cap off the magic of the night and fix it forever in her mind, making it an evening she could never forget. She had been kissed before, of course, by Rog Howe and one or two others. But not by anyone like Giancarlo.

Deliberately she paused in the middle of a block of shadow, turning herself so that she faced him. In the moonlight he looked at her, his face carved by shadow into that of a young Pan.

"You are too beautiful for me to toy with, *bella*," he whispered. "I cannot take advantage."

"I want you to," she said.

"Here?"

"Yes, kiss me here; please kiss me."

"All right," he muttered.

But he hesitated a moment, gazing at her, his face serious. Then deliberately he pulled her to him, putting his arms around her hips and fitting her close to his body.

It was like being touched by an electrical shock.

Even as Alexandra gasped, Giancarlo moved his pelvis in such a way that his erection, even through cloth, seemed to find her crevices. Instantly she was aflame, her nerve ends seared.

Only then, when he had virtually anchored her to him, holding her buttocks with his left hand, did he move his right hand up to her face and pull her mouth toward his.

His lips were soft, supple, seeking out the tenderness of her mouth, his breath tasting of wine. Alexandra's inexperienced lips were still tight together. But Giancarlo gently thrust his tongue between them and softly showed her how to work her mouth and tongue with his. Her knees suddenly grew weak, and she had to grip his shoulders or fall down into the grass.

Delicious.

Heaven.

It was an entire body kiss, for Giancarlo's left hand kept her pinned to his groin, and as he devoured her mouth with his darting, sweet-tasting tongue, he also ground his pelvis into hers. He ran his hand up and down her buttocks, exploring the sweetness of her curves. Up and down, up and down, his experienced left hand smoothed itself into her crease. Each movement drew out of her a trembling response.

Inside Alexandra's body, something strange was uncurling, a bud of hot, exquisite sensation.

"Alexandra," he muttered once, leaving her mouth to trail damp kisses across her cheek to her ear, where he thrust his tongue inside with delicate skill. Alexandra almost screamed with pleasure. Her knees were shaking wildly, but he would not let her fall down. He continued to explore her as if she were nude, his agile fingers reaching into her soft, secret places.

This was not the kiss she had innocently asked for. Giancarlo was consuming her!

From somewhere nearby, she heard a giggle. A vestige of common sense returned to Alexandra. Another couple was walking the same path they had, and any minute now they would be seen.

"Giancarlo . . ." She tried to pull away.

Giancarlo didn't seem to hear, but dragged his slow, deep kiss downhill from her ear to the tender, vulnerable pulse area just under the tip of her jawbone.

"Please . . . someone is on the path . . . oh, Giancarlo . . ."

"I am sorry, Alexandra," Giancarlo said in a low voice, recovering himself. "It is just that—you are so *bella*, so *bella*. I could not help myself. You see how beautiful you are? You see what you do?"

Alexandra stooped to search for her shoes where she had dropped them in the grass when Giancarlo had kissed her. She slipped her feet into them, feeling the dampness of the dew that had condensed inside them. She and Giancarlo walked back to the clubhouse.

"I will call you tomorrow," Giancarlo told her. "I will take you out to a track that I know, where I am going to practice."

She nodded, unable to trust herself to speak. They were back at the veranda.

"Let's go around to the other side," she whispered to Giancarlo, feeling a stab of guilt. "I know another door, by the kitchen. I can slip in and get my purse and my evening wrap.

I need to put on some more lipstick."

"You need nothing," he told her gallantly. "You are *bellissima* wearing just moonlight."

—— ⋈ ——

Inside the clubhouse Alexandra slipped past the kitchen, feeling elated though still confused. She had only wanted a kiss, a bit of adventure to fix this evening forever in her mind. She had not bargained on—on Giancarlo.

She rounded a bend in the hallway, coming face to face with Felicia Revson, her father's friend.

"Alexandra, I was looking for you," Felicia said urgently, opening a door and pulling Alexandra inside a small room.

Firmly Felicia closed the door behind them. "All right," she said. "Now tell me where it is you've been—quickly, so that I can help you get out of this without your father going into orbit."

Alexandra found it difficult to meet the eyes of her father's attractive companion. "I . . . I was walking outside," she confessed.

"With that man Derek invited? Ah, I see," Felicia said, nodding. "Hurry—put on more lipstick. And here's your stole. You have love marks on your neck, so wrap it around you like this."

Grateful for the help, Alexandra repaired her face and combed her hair, restoring its glossy smoothness.

When she had finished, Felicia touched her arm, gazing into Alexandra's eyes with a look so warm that Alexandra knew why her father loved this woman. "Alexandra, I *have* been worried about you. Ever since you've returned from England, you have been so pale. Distracted. Is something worrying you?"

The urge to unburden herself was so strong that Alexandra had to bite down on her lower lip. She'd had nightmares almost every night since she got back from London. She did need someone to talk to!

But she couldn't possibly allow herself that luxury. Besides herself, there were Jette and Mary Lee, and the oath she had sworn to them.

"Nothing is wrong," she mumbled.

"Are you sure?" Felicia's eyes searched hers. "Alexandra, you know I care about you. You're a wonderful young woman, and at eighteen, you have the world in front of you. But just lately I sense that there is something very, very wrong. Are you sure you don't want to talk to me about it?"

"No," Alexandra whispered.

"Very well, then. But I have to tell you, darling . . . don't allow yourself to become involved with that young man. He is very attractive, but you've grown up in another world. Common backgrounds, ideals, beliefs, and interests are very important, especially when a man and woman form a permanent bond. I know, because I once married out of the group. Having things in common creates a deeper connection than mere love. It—"

"I'm not in love with him," Alexandra protested.

"Of course you're not. Tomorrow and the days to come are going to be very exciting for you, Alexandra. This is going to be the best summer of your life."

Alexandra forced herself to smile, guiltily remembering that Giancarlo had said he would call.

"We'd better go and find your father and aunt," the older woman said, as she gave Alexandra a hug that smelled of the subtle scent of Jean Patou's Joy. "And, please, darling, do try to relax a little. We all love you. Truly we do. You shone tonight, dear; you made tears come to the eyes of many people who were in that ballroom."

— ►◄ —

At home, Alexandra entered the music room that held the beautiful Steinway piano where she had spent so many happy moments seated next to her mother. She switched on the lights, sat down at the bench, and allowed her fingers to ripple over the keys. She felt tired, yet incredibly revved up.

Such a night. More than just a debut, it was . . . she didn't even know what it was. So many feelings seemed to war within her, fighting for expression.

She closed her eyes and allowed her fingers to find their way on the keyboard, letting the mellow notes pour forth. She liked the sound of one of the chords and repeated it, then again in a higher key. Suddenly she wanted very much to write a song . . . something that would express the confusion she felt now about Giancarlo. The pent-up, sexually charged emotions.

— ►◄ —

"Daddy? Daddy, would you do me a favor and listen to something? I have a song I want to play for you."

"Of course," Jay Winthrop said. They walked into the music room, and Jay settled himself on a couch that faced Cassandra's rose garden, now coming into glorious bloom.

Alexandra felt nervous as she sat down at the keyboard. She'd slaved over the song for days. Played it and played it, tinkering with the melody and chorus, with the lyrics that at first had been so difficult. Jay would be the first person to hear "Easy Woman."

"Well, baby, go ahead," Jay urged.

Alexandra played the opening notes, then began to sing in a voice that was faintly husky and smoky but strong enough to fill the room. The lyrics were full of sadness, fervor, and smoldering emotion.

She finished the last chorus and sat rigid and expectant while the last notes died away in the air. She finally turned to see her father staring at her.

"Baby, your song . . . It's so risqué."

"Daddy—!"

"Really, sweetheart, I wouldn't lie to you. It's a torch song."

"Daddy!" she cried again.

Jay winced. He rose and came to stand beside her, rubbing her shoulders with his strong hands. "You have such talent, Alexandra. But don't waste it on ditties like this. Enroll as a music major at Vassar, I know that's what you really want to do. But at the same time take a second major. That would be perfect. Language, maybe. Or communications. So that you could get a real job when you graduate. You could even work on Derek's staff. He'd love you to do that."

After her father left, Alexandra slumped on the piano bench, gazing blindly at the sheet music she'd so carefully written. Then she played the song again, and then another time, her voice filling the music room with defiant energy. When she had finished, she still thought it was good, finding nothing she would write differently.

"That was magnificent," Felicia said behind her.

Alexandra jumped.

"Sorry to startle you." Felicia walked into the room. She wore tennis whites and carried a racket. "I was on my way to practice my serve when I heard your wonderful song, Alexandra." Felicia was smiling.

"And?" Alexandra breathed. "What did you think?"

"Girl, you have a winner. I can't believe the emotions you packed into those lyrics."

"Daddy didn't like my title," Alexandra said resentfully.

Felicia laughed. "You might have made your debut, darling, but to him you're still sweet sixteen. Be a little forgiving, dear. What are you going to do with this song?"

"Do?"

"I have a friend at Arista Records, Alexandra—that's in Los Angeles. Perhaps I could give him a call."

Alexandra hesitated. She didn't want to be successful because of her family connections. She wanted to be famous because she was good.

"I don't think so right now, Felicia," she said. "I want to do this on my own."

———— ◄► ————

A week passed. Giancarlo had not called. Trying to put him out of her mind, Alexandra became engrossed with the idea of bringing "Easy Woman" to the attention of a record company. She began poring over issues of *Rolling Stone* and *Billboard*, searching for clues, finding no simple answers.

She decided that she needed to make a demo tape of the song and enlisted the help of Pims, who owned a tape recorder with several microphones.

"Oh, Alexandra, I just love 'Easy Woman,'" Pims raved after she had heard the song. "It's so . . . I don't know . . . sad and sexy, too. It makes shivers go all up and down me."

They spent an entire Saturday playing the song, until they finally had a tape that Alexandra and Pims agreed was acceptable.

"This is so exciting," breathed Pims. "You sound so great, Alexandra. I just know they're going to love it."

"My voice isn't so great, though," Alexandra said. "I just don't have the full, deep quality, the range. It's the song I want them to listen to."

"Oh, they'll listen OK. How could they help it? What do you think your father is going to say when they're playing your music on all the radio stations?"

"I hope he'll be proud of me," Alexandra said softly.

———— ◄► ————

It was a Tuesday morning in mid-June, the air fresh-washed after a late-night shower. Boston's summer humidity had not yet set in, and the day felt full of possibility.

"Miss Alexandra? Which dress will you be wearing for dinner at the Howes' tonight?" Colleen, her maid, had laid out several choices, including an elegant cream dinner suit and a deep blue Ralph Lauren silk dress. A bag filled with matching accessories had been neatly filed with each outfit and awaited her choice.

"Oh . . . the blue," Alexandra sighed.

"And which dress for the Hunnewell debut tomorrow night? There is still the peach silk you haven't worn. Although I believe, Miss Winthrop, that you should try it on again. You look as if you might have lost a few pounds. We don't want it to hang on you."

"All right, I'll try it on when I get back from tennis. I—"

The ringing of Alexandra's private phone line interrupted her. She dashed for it, her heart speeding up as it had been doing all week at the constant ringing. But each time she had been disappointed.

"Hello?" Her voice was breathless.

"Alexandra? It is you?" It was Giancarlo, his voice a caress.

"Yes . . . " Instantly she recovered her equilibrium. It would not do for a man like Giancarlo to sense her nervous excitement, her vulnerability to his charms. Besides, part of her was angry at him for making her wait.

"I take you to the track today, yes? In one hour I will be there to get you. You will be ready, wearing trousers and a scarf for the wind. My car, it has no top, and we fly, eh? I go past the speed limit; I carry one of those, how you say, CB radios?"

"I've made arrangements to play tennis in an hour, Giancarlo. And I have plans for dinner. Couldn't we do it tomorrow?"

"Tomorrow I will be in Daytona looking at the track," he told her with dignity. "Today I am with you. I will see you in an hour, eh, *bella*? You will be ready."

Alexandra hung up, a thrill running through her.

Now she would have to phone Pims and beg off. Luckily, Pims had a younger sister who loved tennis and would probably be happy to substitute. What would she do about John Copley IV, her date for tonight? She'd have to phone him, too.

"Colleen!" she called, dashing to the door of her dressing closet, where the maid was getting out a ball gown, taking it from the lengths of tissue in which it was stored to prevent crushing.

"Yes, Miss Alexandra?"

"I need something casual! Something gorgeous and casual and sexy! What have we got?"

—— ▶◀ ——

The car was a black Ferrari, so low-slung that it felt as if she were riding only an inch above the pavement. Its interior was like the bucket seat of a spacecraft. Alexandra was shocked by the car's responsiveness. Every time Giancarlo speeded up to pass another car, it felt as if they were going into lift-off.

To Alexandra's surprise, they drove to Logan International Airport, where he used a credit card to pay for two commuter tickets to Dover, Delaware.

"What?" she exclaimed, laughing. "We're flying?"

He nodded. "Dover Downs, yes? It's a short flight, eh? I hold your hand, we look out the window, count the clouds. I test several prototype cars there, they pay me."

At the gate refreshment stand, they purchased cream sodas and bags of chips. They stood by the window, munching.

"How did you become involved in racing, Giancarlo?"

"It was easier for me than for some," he shrugged. "I buy a car, I show them at Ferrari what I could do. They sponsor me and put me on a team! Then—"

Alexandra had to laugh. "Well, you don't lack for confidence, Giancarlo."

"I *cannot* lack confidence, *bella*. If I do—" He frowned. "Let us not talk of that. I am superstitious. I do not like to talk of what will never happen. I must trust in my body and my reflexes."

"And your car?"

He chuckled. "There, *carissima*, is where I never trust. There is always something waiting to happen. Suspension failure. Brake fade. Cracking of the discs. Or the brakes may lock— but I do not wish to talk of such things."

On the plane, Giancarlo regaled her with various tips and pointers on driving. "You feel the car," he insisted. "You feel it with your body, that tells you what to do. Then you must allow your instinct to direct you. No time to think; your body does thinking for you."

They arrived at eleven o'clock, the sun already hot, the sky a pale, cloudless blue. She had expected the sounds of motors, but there was only the roar of one huge engine being revved by mechanics in the pit.

To Alexandra the great speedway seemed oddly cavernous and deserted, with only a relatively few people rattling around in its pit area, most of them Ford Motor Company mechanics and engineers, along with a few wives who had gone along to watch.

Jackie Stewart wandered over to say hello. He too was involved in the testing program. In his white racing coveralls, he looked like the pictures she had seen in *Newsweek*.

The sun made its slow passage over the track, blazing hot, and it was seven o'clock before Giancarlo finally pulled the red car into the pit for the last time. He sprang out effortlessly and sauntered over to Alexandra, pulling off his helmet to reveal damp black curls.

"I must change and shower," he told her. "Then I must stop at my hotel room to make some phone calls before I take you back for the enormous lobster dinner, eh? The five-pound lobsters for each of us! At Locke-Ober, maybe? Or do you want Colonel Sander's chicken?"

"Lobster," she said, smiling.

She waited thirty long minutes while he showered, but finally he reappeared, looking fresh and relaxed, smelling of soap and a generous application of after-shave. He had changed into a blue silk shirt cut to emphasize the narrow lines of his waist.

He drove her through Dover to a large motel at the edge of town. Alexandra sighed. Today certainly hadn't been what she expected. All that time just sitting in the sun watching cars go around the track. Boring! He was so arrogant that she couldn't take him seriously, and he hadn't offered one single explanation as to why he had not called her in two weeks.

Giancarlo unlocked the door, and Alexandra looked around his room. Although it obviously had been cleaned up by the maid, even she could not make much headway through the bags of cookies, pretzels, Fritos, and barbeque- and onion-flavored potato chips that littered the top of the Formica dresser.

There were also six-packs of beer in a cooler, as well as many flavors of soft drinks, including orange, grape, and chocolate cream.

"Do you really eat and drink all this?" she asked, laughing.

"The racing, it makes me thirsty, and when I get thirsty, I want something to drink, and then I want the crackers and chips and dip . . . " Giancarlo had the grace to laugh at himself. He sat down on the bed and began making phone calls, to an airline, to a hotel in Daytona Beach, to Milan and Florence. Several of the Italian calls involved a dispute about a contract, Alexandra gathered from the few words of Italian she knew. But mostly it was fast talking, hand waving, and volubility.

While she waited, she glanced idly through the racing magazines that someone—the maid?—had stacked on the room's only table. Giancarlo hung up the phone and went into the bathroom. She sighed. She'd already waited forty more minutes. How long was all of this going to take?

"*Bella?*" he said softly, a moment later.

She glanced up and gasped. He had emerged from the bathroom totally nude.

Giancarlo's compact body was without an ounce of flab. A silky thatch of black curls decorated his chest, narrowed to form a thin line down his belly, and then widened again to cover his groin. Rising out of this glory of black silk was Giancarlo's phallus, so large and thick, so fascinatingly decorated with blue veins, that it commanded Alexandra's awed attention.

She sat frozen.

"*Bella,*" he whispered again, huskily.

"Giancarlo," she stammered. "We must go back to Boston now. My father and Felicia are giving a dinner party tonight, and they expect—"

With a natural gesture, he grabbed her hand and brought it to rest on his erection. Alexandra's words died in her throat. His skin felt smooth, dry, and hot. And . . . amazingly hard.

"Giancarlo . . . "

He pulled her up to him and smothered her protests with a kiss. His tongue instantly took up where he had left off two weeks previously, as it explored the depths of her mouth with sweet urgency. Her body responded with excruciating sensations of pleasure.

"No," she moaned with the last remnant of her sanity and resistance as she tried to twist away from him. "No, really, please, I can't. I mustn't. Really."

This was not the kind of love Alexandra had read about in romance novels. This was hot, hard, and quick. Giancarlo did not take time to savor her or to tease her. He simply stripped her, so that within seconds she was lying naked, exposed before him, trembling.

He lowered himself on top of her, wrapping his legs around her, his arms, too. Greedily his lips sucked her tongue, as he rocked into her with each thrust, pushing against her tight entrance.

"You are a virgin?" he exclaimed in horror.

She cried out, clinging to him, shaking under the violence of his efforts to penetrate.

"*Vergine . . .*"

He thrust deeper, wrapping her legs around his shoulders, exposing her to his passion. Again he thrust, groaning aloud. Through the pain, Alexandra felt a wild, crunching excitement, a build-up of . . .

Abruptly Giancarlo pushed violently forward, his whole body rigid as his lustful voice cried out in her ear.

Afterward they lay side by side on the Howard Johnson bed, Giancarlo snoring lightly beside her, his chest rising and falling with satisfaction.

Alexandra stared at the ceiling, tears welling in her eyes. She had lost her virginity. Thrown it away, really. She never should have come here with him. And she had taken absolutely no precautions, she realized with dread. She had been an absolute fool.

She sighed, sitting up and trying to glance at her watch again. But it was hard to see. It was now dusk, the motel room blanketed in deep shadow.

As suddenly as he had fallen asleep, Giancarlo stirred awake. He turned over lazily and smiled at her. "You are beautiful when you are naked, do you know that?"

He leaned forward and began to tongue her nipples, creating a ripple of sensation that quickly distended them to rich peaks. A new bud of desire began to flower between Alexandra's legs. Incredible. She attempted to ignore it.

"I really do have to go home," she said firmly. "My father will be worried. I told no one I would be gone this long."

"I will take you home very quickly. Is not a long flight." Giancarlo laughed, throwing himself on her again as impetuously as before. "But for now . . . I think it is time you came, too, eh? I will show you. I will make you happy. Happier than ever before."

━━ ►◄ ━━

Summer. In past years, for Alexandra it had meant outdoor concerts, tennis, horseback riding, and long weeks near Hyannis at a ten-room house the family affectionately called the cottage, overlooking Nantucket Sound.

This year summer meant Giancarlo and music. Long afternoons spent in motel rooms, and equally long afternoons at the piano. The more she saw of Giancarlo, the better she could write.

Several weeks went by, and the tapes of "Easy Woman" that Alexandra mailed out seemed to drop off the ends of the earth. A second batch of demo tapes fared no better than the first. Most came back with a notation stamped in bold, black letters: "Unsolicited Tapes Not Accepted."

It shook her faith in herself. After all, how many thousands just like her dreamed of having a hit song?

Alexandra listened to the tape once again, losing herself in the lyrics. Yes . . . it was exciting and fresh, and it created a mood. She would just have to keep believing in it.

Jay Winthrop made it clear he did not like Giancarlo and would prefer that she stop seeing him.

"Please, Daddy," Alexandra pleaded one day. "It's just a friendship."

"I think it's time we had a little talk about business, honey."

"Business? Daddy . . . "

"You have a very nice trust fund, sweetheart. You have 150,000 shares of Wintex Industrials . . . "

"He's not after my money," Alexandra said defiantly.

"Isn't he? You're not just an ordinary girl, Alexandra. There are fortune hunters in this world who are looking for an easy meal ticket."

"I know that. I don't love him, but I enjoy his company. Daddy," she added, sliding her arms around Jay's neck. "This is my debut summer. It's supposed to be *fun*. Anyway, Giancarlo's not the only one I date. There's Ben Maxwell, Bob Lowell, Walter Kutchins. I'm not going to marry any of them! I don't want to marry anyone."

"You mean not now," Jay said, somewhat mollified. "You'll marry eventually."

"Not unless I find the right one."

"You mean I'm going to have an old maid on my hands?" the financier teased.

She grinned. "If I want to be one. Don't you read the

papers, Daddy? Haven't you heard of women's liberation? Women have choices, and not all choices include men."

"Well, I know I can't stop you from doing what you want to," he said, touching her under the chin. "But no falling in love with that man, all right? I don't want my grandchildren racing Ferraris."

"Daddy—"

"Well? You *are* my daughter, Alexandra. Please be careful."

Giancarlo taught her to take a car to its limits, exhorting, lecturing, scolding, and praising her until she mastered the trick of feeling her car and using the gears masterfully to orchestrate its speed. She learned the proper way to turn and how to coax the most from her brakes, as well as what to do in a spin or a skid. She felt sure that if she were on the racing circuit, he would be just as harsh with her. But she still enjoyed the praise. She had never driven past 65 miles per hour until she met Giancarlo, and now she had clocked 105 on a deserted road. She loved it.

One July afternoon, she and Giancarlo spent an entire day making love at a motel in Framingham. Then, the room's airconditioning unit running against the July heat, they both drifted off to sleep.

Alexandra fell instantly into one of the troubled sleeps that had been bothering her since she returned from England. She dreamed she was driving a black race car that swooped around the track, screaming like a wild animal. Then she realized that the scream came from Jette. Jette was screaming at her to stop, stop before it was too late.

Tires squealed as brakes tried to grab pavement. She struggled and twisted, trying to wake up, but her body would not cooperate. She heard a horrible crunching sound, and then Simon Heath-Cote's body exploded onto the hood of the race car. His head was turned around 180 degrees on his neck, his glazed eyes red with blood.

She woke so suddenly it was like falling off a building. Her heart was pounding violently, and she felt sick to her stomach.

"Alexandra?" Giancarlo had wakened, too, and was holding her. "You are all right? You are safe now," he soothed. "You are fine; you are with Giancarlo."

"I had this terrible, terrible dream," she managed to say.

"Do you want to talk to Giancarlo? Do you want to tell?"

"Oh, no, I—I can't remember it all," she lied.

"Are you sure, *bella?*"

"Oh, I'm sure," she said, shuddering. She lifted her limp arm, which felt as if she had been swimming endless miles in Cape Cod Bay, and glanced at her watch. "Oh, God, Giancarlo, it's six already. I have to go. My father and Felicia are giving a party for Sammy Fain, and they expect me to be there."

—— ▸◀ ——

Sammy Fain was in town to attend one of the ASCAP meetings that were usually held in New York but occasionally in cities like L.A., Washington, or Boston. He had brought his dear friend of many years, Minnie Phillips, who was as spritely and charming as he was. Alexandra adored Sammy, who could sing and play anything, his voice sounding more like that of a man of forty than one in his late seventies.

Derek was present, partnered with Alexandra. The other guests were men with whom Jay wanted to keep strong political contacts, along with their wives.

After dinner, the group settled in the music room, and Sammy favored them with a medley of some of his dozens of songs, which had appeared in movies such as *Marjorie Morningstar, Tender Is the Night,* and *Alice in Wonderland.* He then played several songs he had just written and improvised one, which he called "Waltz for Alexandra."

When he had finished, they all clapped noisily, and Sammy rose from the piano and gave Alexandra a courtly kiss.

"I'd like to play and sing something for you, Sammy," she announced impulsively. "It's a song I wrote myself." She saw her father raise an eyebrow, but Sammy was nodding encouragingly. "I call it 'Easy Woman.' "

She sat down at the piano bench.

When she was finished, there was dead silence. She felt her heart sink. Then she heard wild clapping, and turned to see Derek, Sammy, and Minnie applauding, along with Felicia, the other guests, and, at last, Jay himself.

"Wonderful!" Sammy exclaimed. *"Brava! Brava!"* His face was alight with genuine pleasure.

Tears of happiness sprang to Alexandra's eyes. "Sammy," she managed to say, "I wonder if I could visit you at the Copley Plaza tomorrow, just for a while. I have so many questions . . . so many things to ask you. I've made a tape of 'Easy Woman' . . . "

"Bring it," the composer told her. "We'll play it, and we'll talk."

— ▶◀ —

"In the first place," Sammy Fain told Alexandra the next day, "if you want to get this tape listened to at all, you're going to have to go to a studio, where they can emphasize your sound with different electronic variations. The music business is one of the toughest businesses in the world. I'm sure you know that amateurs are a dime a dozen. Everybody thinks they can write a hit song. You've got to stand out. And then, after you get yourself a decent tape, your job is only beginning. It'll then be time to use pull—everyone in the record business that you know or your friends know. Pull out all the stops."

"Oh," she replied, remembering how she had brushed off Felicia.

"I'll tell you what. You make a demo tape that is absolutely fabulous, send me ten copies, and I'll promise to get them into the right hands. And you make another forty or fifty to give to everyone else you can find. Then we'll see what happens."

— ▶◀ —

At NBC Studios in New York on Fifth Avenue and Fiftieth, Alexandra watched, feeling intimidated, as jeans-clad technicians wandered back and forth, making adjustments to what looked like enough equipment for a rock concert. She had rented the studio, along with the services of an engineer and producer, for the day, and had been playing and replaying "Easy Woman" for hours.

Her voice was getting scratchy. She sat sipping lemon tea with honey, clearing her throat, and trembling. It was the hardest thing she'd ever done. The technicians were obviously good, but demanding.

"Success is never a one-shot deal, sweetheart," said the producer, walking over to her. "Here, freshen up that tea. It's a twenty-shot deal, or thirty, or three hundred. Whatever it takes, Alexandra. That's how many tries you've got to give. We'll get it right."

Back in Boston, Alexandra played the master tape for Felicia, delighting in the expression that crossed the older woman's face as she listened.

"Well, whatever the pros did for you, whatever their secret is," Felicia said, hugging her, "the results are fantastic."

The summer crawled along as Alexandra waited tensely for some response to the new demo tape. Two of Sammy's friends wrote personal letters of rejection. The rest she hadn't heard from yet.

Alexandra refused to give up. She hassled Jay, Felicia, even Pims's father, for more contacts in the record business, and when she received a new list of names, she copied more tapes, sent more letters, and began to make follow-up phone calls. Mostly she talked to secretaries. Apparently everyone who wanted to make it in the record business had the same idea as she did.

In mid-August, Jette phoned. There was music and laughter in the background, and Jette said she was calling from her dance class.

"Alexandra, I played your cassette, and it sounds great! You're going to be famous! What else is happening? Who are you dating? Anybody interesting?"

She told Jette about Giancarlo.

"Wow. A race-car driver? Really?" Jette said it with respect. "Is he sexy?"

"Oh, very. More than very."

"Good, because I have to tell you something, Alexandra."

"Yes?"

"I've started sleeping with men, too. I've done it six times now, can you believe it?"

"Six?"

"I've done it twice with Bryan Sellers, he's in a new movie with Clint Eastwood; he plays a bad guy. Then I met this other guy, Johnny Hertel. He has a part on 'Beverly Hills,' that new soap opera. I guess bad guys turn me on."

Alexandra was silent for a moment.

"Well?" her friend demanded. "Say *something*, kiddo. Tell me I'm a slut, a cunt, or even an idiot, but say something!"

"Jette . . . "

"Hey, there's been a sexual revolution, right? *Everybody* is thinking about sex, kid, especially out here in L.A. All that warm sunshine makes us horny."

"But . . . " Alexandra began, and then closed her mouth. She, too, had found a lover this summer, hadn't she?

Alexandra listened to more of Jette's chatter, mostly about her acting. Jette wanted to be seen as an actress in her own right, not as "Claudia Michaud's daughter."

"I'm going to make it, Alexandra. I am, I know I am! Michael Lembeck—he teaches my improv class—he says I have potential."

"That's wonderful, Jette. I'm so happy for you! Really!" Alexandra said.

"How's Mary Lee?" Jette asked.

"She's written me four postcards from Maui. She's been trying to make notes for a novel, but her mother found the notes and tore them up, saying there's only room for one novelist in their family. Can you imagine that? What a royal bitch."

"Yeah." Marietta Wilde had always made Mary Lee's life miserable, alternating between constant attention and total desertion. Mary Lee had never known what to expect or when the next unpleasant surprise would roll around.

"God, gotta go, the next class is starting. Call me! Or come and visit!" Jette ordered. "And say hi to Mary Lee for me. You lucky guys get to room together at Vassar for the next four years, while I'm out here slaving away and screwing my brains out."

"Jette!" Alexandra exclaimed, laughing.

"Sorry. I forgot you're kinda prim and proper," Jette added, her voice sounding suddenly melancholy. "Sometimes, Alexandra, I wish it hadn't happened."

She did not have to say what "it" was.

"I feel so dirty sometimes," Jette burst out. "So . . . I don't know. Some days I take about five showers, trying to wash myself clean enough. These other guys make me forget, Alexandra. They make me feel . . . " Her voice broke.

"Oh, Jette . . . " Alexandra sympathized.

"I . . . I'm sorry." But then Jette's voice changed again. "Oops, she's starting the class again; I've gotta go now, kid. Hang in there, and let me know more about this Giancarlo character. He sounds great."

— ▶◀ —

Giancarlo Ferrari, at that moment, was climbing the front steps to the Boston Public Library. He sauntered inside, the heels of his Italian shoes clicking on the marble floor.

Alexandra Winthrop was why he was there. The night he had met her, he knew she would be very good for him.

He needed some luck. The villas he told Alexandra his father owned in Capri and Monaco were figments of his imagination. In fact, he was not even a Ferrari—at least not legitimately.

He had been born Giancarlo Luigi Binaldi, his mother a semi-whore who had been briefly kept by a Ferrari, then dumped when she contracted tuberculosis. Even his mother did not know whether Giancarlo really carried the Ferrari blood in his veins.

That did not stop Giancarlo. From the day he had seen his first low-slung, impossibly curved, and gorgeous Ferrari 512, he had *become* a Ferrari and longed to drive one of the family's cars—to be on the racing circuit, worshipped by thousands. When his mother died, Giancarlo acted swiftly. He raided his mother's bank account and illegally sold her car.

With the money, he bought an old Ferrari, found two mechanics, and paid them with the last of his funds. He entered himself in the Targa Florio and won the race.

That was his start. Now he was on his way.

"I am looking for . . . " he asked the librarian. "How do you say it? A place where I might find newspaper clippings."

"For what paper?" she inquired crisply.

He hesitated. "I do not know; I am not sure."

"Well, we carry the *New York Times Index*, the *Boston Herald*, the *Boston Globe*, the—"

"No," he said. "London newspapers, 1978."

He waited while the woman dug some small boxes out of a filing cabinet. She led him to a room containing a number of microfilm machines, slid a small square of transparent film between two pieces of glass, explained how to use the machine, and left.

After hours of viewing columns on the screen, he found the clipping he sought. He read it five times, slowly because his knowledge of written English was rudimentary. Then he slid a dime in the machine and made a copy.

"The motorcycle!" she had screamed that day in the motel. *"Simon! Simon Heath-Cote! We killed him!"*

5
Alexandra
1989

Alexandra was tired after the long evening at Sandringham, the excitement of tea with the Queen, and the long chat she had with Diana, who seemed to have the energy of a seventeen-year-old.

Back at Highgrove, she excused herself to make a phone call. Dialing the number of Richard's office, she waited impatiently for one of his secretaries to pick up. What time was it in Chicago? 5:00 P.M.

"Good afternoon. Mr. Cox's office. May I help you?" a female voice chimed.

"This is Mrs. Cox. I'd like to speak to my husband—is he in?"

"He is still here but is just about ready to leave for a meeting, Mrs. Cox. I'll put you right through."

As she waited, Alexandra began to fidget with the telephone cord, listening to the soft recorded music on the hold line. Chicago seemed very far away.

"Alexandra? Punkie . . ." It was her husband's voice, sounding annoyingly fresh and enthusiastic.

"Hello, Richard," she said quietly.

"Hi, honey. How's it going? How was the trip over? Was the plane great? How's Diana?"

"Tea was unbelievable. It's me that's having a little trouble, Rich. I really need you here. Can't you fly over just for a day? One day? I want you to come to Ascot with me."

"Alexandra." All he had to say was one word. His voice sounded annoyed.

"Richard!"

"Alexandra, I can't. We've been involved in eighteen-hour-a-day meetings here, and things haven't been moving along. Their demands could bankrupt me. I can't back down."

Tears welled in her eyes. "I didn't ask you to back down! All I asked is a day or two of your company. Richard, I'm your *wife*. I'm lonely for you," she finished in a low voice.

"Lexy, Lexy. Jesus." There was a silence. "I wish I could. Try to understand," he began.

"What is there to understand? Richard, I'm not a fool," she said in anger and annoyance. "You've got four of Wall Street's top law firms working with you. Can't the lawyers handle the negotiations for a couple of days? Do you have to be there every single minute?"

"Punkie, it isn't a matter of just delegating—"

"And stop calling me punkie," she snapped. "You make me sound like some sort of a Las Vegas showgirl."

Richard's laugh was low and angry. "You're hardly a Vegas showgirl. What's got into you, Alexandra?"

"I'm just voicing a request."

"All right," he said impatiently. "I'll make the damned arrangements, then, if that's what you really want."

She took a deep breath, speaking loudly to be heard above the voice-static on the long-distance wire. "If that's the way you're going to be, forget it. Don't bother if you're going to come over here with that attitude."

"Jesus Christ! What do you want from me, Lexy? Look. If you really want me to come, I'll call up Twiston-Davies at the London Fitzgerald and ask him to rustle up the Ascot gear."

She softened her voice. "You'll look wonderful in it. Stop complaining."

"Hey, I'm not complaining; I'm just bitching a little." This time his laugh was genuine. "You drive a hard bargain, Alexandra."

"Let me know as soon as you have your flight schedule. We'll arrange for you to be helicoptered out here."

Alexandra hung up with a frown. In a way she'd won—she'd gotten her way, hadn't she? But in a way she'd lost, because his coming over here would be forced; it wasn't what he really wanted to do. She would have wanted the two days to be his idea.

Now she almost wished she hadn't pushed it.

— ▶◀ —

As it turned out, it was Charles who did not show up for
Ascot. The future King of England sent word from Balmoral
that he had gone there to fish and would not be back in time for
the horse races, Diana announced at breakfast. Coffee, pink
grapefruit, granola, and a boiled egg on toast were served by
Brown, the Waleses' butler. The Princess's hair was still damp
from her early-morning swim in the Highgrove pool.

"Oh, I'm so sorry," Alexandra said, struck by the wounded
look in Diana's eyes.

"It's quite all right. I'm accustomed to it, and I'm certain
we'll get along quite decently without him. It doesn't matter at
all," the Princess insisted. "Come upstairs with me, Alexandra,
do. You can show me what you're going to wear."

They ended up spending an hour in Diana's dressing room,
laughing and chatting. Diana showed her the deep rose silk
dress she planned to wear, designed by Catherine Walker. It was
embellished with navy trim and had a wide, plain navy blue
midriff. She would also wear a charming wide-brimmed hat
with navy on the underside. So very Diana, Alexandra thought.

The hem of the dress had been slightly weighted down
with lead, put in all of Diana's dresses ever since a brisk wind
had blown up the Royal skirt, the event captured in print by the
paparazzi. There were elegant two-tone Charles Jourdan pumps,
made to match. With the outfit, Diana would wear a pair of
diamond-and-sapphire earrings.

Diana modeled the ensemble in front of her long dressing-
room mirror, her smile radiant.

Then she took off the lavish hat. "Try this on, Alexandra.
I'm sure you'd look stunning in it. We're both blondes and tall.
Do you like hats?"

"I don't wear many," Alexandra admitted. She adjusted
the brim of the hat, which was slightly large for her, and gazed
at her reflection in pleasure. She imagined crowds . . . security
guards . . . photographers . . . Would she really enjoy such a life?

"You look so very 'me,' " Diana giggled.

Swept by a sudden wave of hilarity, they pulled out all the
hats and began playfully modeling them.

Maybe their laughter was a little too raucous. But they
needed it, and who was to say that the Princess of Wales and the

wife of America's most powerful hotelier could not laugh like schoolgirls?

A sky the color of freshwater pearls had promised rain all morning—a soft, misty precipitation that made leaves and manicured green grass seem even greener.

Royal Ascot was sheer English pomp and spectacle.

For guests of the Royals, it began at Windsor Castle, with pre-lunch drinks in the Green Drawing Room. Twenty-four Royals and aristocrats in full Ascot regalia mingled and chattered about which horses were favored. Some of the animals racing today had been bred by the Queen, who, relaxing her usual reserve, became enthusiastic about their prospects.

The Queen Mother. Diana's handsome brother, Viscount Althorp. The Duke and Duchess of Grafton. The Duke and Duchess of Wellington. The guest list read like a page from *Debrett's Peerage.*

Lunch was served in the State Dining Room. The ladies left their hats, the gentlemen their toppers, in a ground-floor cloakroom, and they sat at the long table. The china, bearing the crests of Queen Victoria and George V, changed patterns with every course. The table gleamed with sterling cutlery, sterling cruets, and crystal engraved EIIR, "Elizabeth II Regina."

After lunch, Prince Philip and the other male guests collected their umbrellas and top hats. The ladies gathered in their cloakroom, conversing while securing their hats with pins. The entire party then walked to the sovereign's entrance, where they climbed into a fleet of Rolls-Royces and Daimlers for the short drive to Windsor Great Park.

As they drove, Alexandra felt she was riding in the pages of history. At Windsor Great Park, they were handed into six open carriages. Emblazoned with the Royal armorial bearings, pulled by matched, gaily caparisoned horses, with postilions hanging on and footmen in the back, the carriages had been unchanged for centuries. In the first one, the Queen and Prince Philip already had their umbrellas up, and the Queen Mother was sheltering herself under a see-through plastic "brolly."

After a ten-minute ride to Ascot, the procession entered the racecourse, turning into the Royal Enclosure. Here the footmen jumped down to help the ladies dismount, and the Queen led the way through the covered entrance into the Royal box, which commanded a superb view of the track. It was decorated with bright red geraniums and other blooms brought from the Windsor hothouses. Immediately below this was the Royal Enclosure, a green, manicured lawn surrounded by railings, with two entrances, both guarded by bowler-hatted stewards who admitted only those who were wearing the proper badge.

The rain had turned to a fine mist again, and umbrellas were snapped shut. Alexandra gazed around her, smiling. It was like a photograph in *Majesty* magazine. Men strolled about, splendid in dark, tailed morning suits, wearing top hats on their heads and gold or zinnia-colored carnations in their left buttonholes. Most carried black umbrellas.

Women in summery garden dresses from Europe's major designers gathered in groups, their extravagant hats visible everywhere through the crowd. There were huge-brimmed floppy hats, saucer hats, tiny confections strewn with roses, white straws, and little creations with dotted veils. Clothes seemed to be the real order of the day, not the thoroughbreds.

Three of Diana's security men, also in Ascot gear, stuck close to her. Other security personnel were discreetly in evidence.

Until recent times, Diana told Alexandra, the right to wear a Royal Enclosure badge was strictly reserved for the upper classes. No person who was "in trade" or who had been divorced was ever admitted. In fact, in the old days, even divorcée Princess Margaret would have been excluded.

This ban would have included Richard, Alexandra thought with a twist of her heart. Queen Victoria, George V, and George VI would have snubbed her husband.

As Diana rushed up to greet Fergie, who was wearing a pale green watered-silk suit and floppy white hat, Alexandra felt a touch at her elbow. She turned, startled.

Richard stood before her, resplendent in his finery. He wore a dark gray morning suit with a pale gold carnation in his lapel. His waistcoat was lighter gray, and his tie was Ascot pink. His gray top hat was trimmed in a darker band of gray. In his left hand Richard carried the de rigueur umbrella. With his lean, compact body and dark good looks, wings of silver at his temples, he was stunning. No Lord here, no male Royal, could hold a candle to Richard Fitzgerald Cox, Jr.

"Rich . . . !" She breathed. Her heart gave a pounding leap of gladness and pride.

"Well, punkie?" he demanded. "Am I splendid, or am I splendid? Even if I haven't slept in thirty-six hours." His smile was tired, but he looked pleased with himself, laugh wrinkles crinkling from the corners of his eyes.

"Oh, darling—darling . . ." She threw herself into his arms, the Ascot crowd forgotten.

Diana appeared at Alexandra's elbow, with Fergie in tow. Despite the elegance of her designer dress, the Duchess of York was sunburned and radiant, her freckled face solidly English.

Diana introduced her to the Coxes. "Alexandra, Sarah has been dying to meet you. She loves 'Easy Woman.' "

"And 'Sensuous Woman,' " Fergie said, smiling. "Alexandra, where do you get your ideas? Do you compose sitting at the piano? Did Olivia Newton-John really commission you to write only for her?"

After a few moments of chatting, they began walking toward the Queen's viewing area, in the Royal Box. Tea would be served after the fourth race in a tea room over the entrance to the box. Later, the Queen and other members of the Royal Family would lead a procession through the densely packed crowd to inspect the horses in the paddock.

— ▶◀ —

The next day, as the *Fitz II* headed home, and while Brownie and the children slept in the smaller stateroom, Richard and Alexandra lay propped on pillows in their king-size bed.

They had just finished making long, delicious love, and Alexandra was satiated. Richard went over some papers while Alexandra leafed through *Jours de France*. Diana was featured on the cover, smiling and bare-shouldered in spectacular evening wear, a glittering sapphire-and-diamond necklace encircling her neck.

"Wasn't it wonderful?" Alexandra bubbled. "I can't believe all the fuss and bother."

"The Britons love their Queen," Richard said absently, turning a page in the thick report he was studying.

"They love Diana, too. She's done so much for England, really. She's made them fashionable again. She's set new trends; she's gotten everyone excited about British designers. She's starting to get serious about things. If only Charles had come."

"Mmmmm," Richard said.

Alexandra nudged him. "Are you paying attention? I said, it's too bad that Charles never showed up. Diana didn't say anything, but I could tell how hurt she was. I wonder why he didn't show up."

"Who knows about the Royals? I suppose he figures if he's making us an official visit, he needn't bother with something casual. Or maybe he had other obligations. You know he's a fishing nut. Or he was making a speech in some British slum. I wouldn't worry about it, Lexy. As long as he shows up at our party, what do we care?"

"But Di . . ."

He set down his report and looked at her. "Don't get too involved in her personal life, OK? She's a Royal now. They march to the beat of a different drummer—literally. Anyway, we have some problems of our own."

"Problems?" She was immediately alert. "Such as what?"

"Those stubborn union bastards. If it was just Robbie Fraser, I wouldn't worry. The man is tough, but he's reasonable, and he's got the brains to think ahead. But Emil Marchek— Marchek is another story."

"He's the one you said was being indicted?"

"Yeah, on eight charges. Defrauding the union pension plan. Marchek is one vicious son of a bitch, and he's got plenty of clout. Connections, too. He has people afraid of him; that's the bottom line."

"He had something to do with the videotape, didn't he, Richard? Don't shake your head," she added firmly. "When we get home, am I going to be able to stop worrying about this, or aren't I?"

After a brief hesitation, almost unnoticeable, Richard put aside the bound report and drew Alexandra into his arms. "Lexy, I promise you, there is nothing to concern yourself about. I swear it."

"Are you sure?"

He pulled back. "Yes, I'm sure."

——— ►◄ ———

At that moment, back at workaday Kensington Palace, in her bedroom suite, Diana was dismissing her dresser, Evelyn Dagley. They had just spent a session planning Diana's wardrobe for the following day, which would include three official appearances and an intimate dinner party Diana was giving for a group of close friends the press called the "Throne Rangers."

Diana didn't need Charles's presence to entertain her friends.

"Then it's the white-and-blue dress for the ground breaking?" the dresser persisted.

"Please. And the matching hat, the saucer hat with the bow. I'll look at the shoes in the morning if you could have a selection ready."

"Very good," the woman said, retiring after Diana had wished her goodnight.

Restlessly Diana walked across the large bedroom suite, which contained separate dressing rooms and baths for herself and Charles, as well as a uniform room for Charles and a "brushing" room, where minor repairs were made. She switched on her portable radio, searching until she found a pop station playing Duran Duran.

Music filled the room with a rhythmic rock. For an instant, Diana swayed to its beat. Then she flung herself on the king-size bed and sat with her left hand across her mouth, her eyes staring unfocused at the subtly patterned wall paper.

She was tired from the fun-filled schedule of the past weekend with Alexandra, the eager, jostling press of the heavy Ascot crowds, the photographers who had relentlessly snapped her every move and caught her off-guard making a face at something Alexandra had said. Even the good-byes to her friend were full of emotion.

No one had mentioned Charles's being gone, but the Queen had frowned. Diana knew his absence would not escape Royal censure. If the Queen scolded her son, it surely would not help *their* relationship.

She trembled slightly, remembering the picture of the Prince of Wales she had pinned to the wall in her room at the West Heath School. She'd had such a juvenile crush on him. He *was* virile, every inch of his body firm and sinewy. But . . . he was sometimes so middle-aged, so fussy and dogged about things, and there were little angers he took out on his staff. A very human king-to-be.

She still loved him.

Alexandra's Richard had made the effort to come to Ascot all the way from Chicago. How could a princess not have her prince? Where was he?

6

Alexandra
1978–1979

The medieval-looking campus at Vassar College was surrounded by brick walls and lined with gracious paths. The library, with its stained-glass windows and romantic turret crowned with Gothic crosses, resembled a castle. Ringed by magnificent old trees, a three-acre lake had been the haven for countless young women, including Edna St. Vincent Millay, Inez Millholland, author Mary McCarthy, and—more recently—Jane Fonda and Meryl Streep.

Alexandra and Mary Lee arrived at their dorm suite within hours of each other. It was their first reunion since London, and they greeted one another with squeals and hugs.

"Alexandra, you're so blonde! You look great! So sophisticated!" Mary Lee cried, whirling her around in a wild dance.

"And you're so tan," Alexandra marveled. "You're as brown as a Hawaiian. And *thin*."

Mary Lee flushed. "Thin? Me?"

"Heavens, yes. You've lost twenty pounds at least."

Mary Lee had definitely lost her baby fat and now boasted a size-eight body and beautifully sculpted cheekbones that made her slanting emerald eyes look huge. She had begun to smoke Benson & Hedges, blowing out plumes of blue smoke with the expertise of several months' practice. She looked tense.

"Tell me about Maui, Mary Lee . . . did your mother drive you crazy?"

"She's finishing another novel, and writing makes her bitchy," Mary Lee confided, tossing her thick, red-gold hair. "She and Tomas, her latest, were on the outs, and that didn't help either.

"It's an old habit," Mary Lee went on. "Anytime she's angry, she directs it toward me. You know, when Marietta saw that I'd lost weight, she cut up all my bikinis with a pair of scissors and made me wear a black one-piece with one of those ugly skirts."

"No way!"

"And then one night she threw a ripe mango at me—splatted it against the wall just by my head. When Tomas yelled at her, she threw another one at *him*. I had to clean everything up, and then she said it didn't look clean enough, so she threw another mango."

"God, Mary Lee, how can you put up with her?"

"She is my mother . . ."

"Were there any guys on Maui?"

"Not unless you wanted to date a beach bum or a waiter or a diving instructor." Mary Lee sighed. "Anyway, they weren't looking at me. I'm not exactly a beauty."

"Mary Lee, you are beautiful! You're so thin now, you could be a model."

"I still need to lose some more weight," Mary Lee said, stubbing out her cigarette in a sterling-silver ashtray she'd brought. "What do you say we finish unpacking? I've got a ton of stuff; how about you?"

Fall days at Vassar were crisp, the autumn foliage bursting with color. With her heavy class load, Alexandra spent most of her evenings in Thompson Library, in a piano practice room, or in a study room. She'd still received no word on "Easy Woman" and wondered how long it would be—if at all—before someone, anyone, got excited about her song.

Then one day the phone call came, as Alexandra was in the bathroom smoothing on body lotion after her shower. When Mary Lee told her that Arista Records was on the line, she let out a whoop, dropped the bottle of lotion, and raced for the phone.

For a wild moment she couldn't seem to find her voice. "Hello?" she gasped.

"This is Don Van Horn from the A & R Department of Arista Records," came the smooth voice. "I just want to tell you, young lady, that I've lived with your tape for weeks. I think we can do something with it. Clive really likes it. We'd need you to fly to Los Angeles and talk about signing a publishing contract with us."

She could barely take in all his words, hearing only that Clive Davis, president of Arista Record Company, had said he liked her song. "Oh! Oh, God! Oh, this is fantastic!"

"We think this song is just right to go on Olivia Newton-John's new album. Actually, why don't you have your agent or attorney call us to work out all the details?"

"Yes, yes, oh, wonderful," she interrupted Van Horn. "Thanksgiving break is next week . . . would that be all right?"

"Fine, we'll see you then. This is only the beginning, young lady. If you can keep it up, writing other songs as good as 'Easy Woman,' you'll be famous."

Still shaking with excitement, she then placed a phone call to Lee Phillips, one of the best music attorneys in Los Angeles—one of Minnie Phillips's sons. He agreed to look over the contract for her.

Hanging up, Alexandra felt a rush of pure rapture. Maybe she really was going to make it as a songwriter!

— ◄► —

After Thanksgiving, the weather turned bleak. In February several blizzards buried Poughkeepsie, immobilizing the town for days. Blanketed in snow, the campus was crisscrossed with deep paths made by students on their way to class. Cross-country skiers trekked the quadrangle, and the magnificent old trees became white-on-white lace sculptures.

One morning the phone rang. Alexandra had stayed up until 2:30 A.M. studying for an English literature test and had gone to bed bleary-eyed, her brain stuffed with obscure authors, poets, and dates. She was so groggy that when she reached for the phone receiver, she knocked it to the floor.

"Hello?" she mumbled.

"Alexandra? It is you?" The long-distance wire crackled with static.

"Giancarlo! It's—" She sat up and fumbled to see her watch. "It's 5:30 in the morning!"

He laughed. In the background she could hear voices. "Not here. It is 11:30 A.M., lunchtime."

She hadn't talked with Giancarlo since the summer, consigning him to her memories of a fabulous debut season, although there had been several nearly illegible postcards from Turin and Milan.

He told her he was calling from the Eifel Mountains of Germany, where he was qualifying for the Nurbürgring 1,000-kilometer race.

"When are you flying back to the United States?"

"Oh, soon," he said vaguely. "There is Daytona. You will fly down there and join me, yes? I will show you Giancarlo when he wins."

"But, Giancarlo, I'm in college. I have exams and two papers to write. I can't just fly down to Daytona Beach at the drop of a hat."

Mary Lee had sat up in bed and was now frantically motioning to her.

"Just a minute," Alexandra said, putting her hand over the mouthpiece.

"Daytona Beach," Mary Lee hissed. "Say yes! The weather here is the pits, and you know the Daytona 500 runs along that mile-long beach. They drive the cars along the water. We'll keep you company while he races."

"What?"

"Exams will be over in three days. We can go! You, me, and Jette. During the day we'll be together, and at night—well, then you can be with him."

Mary Lee was right. She wouldn't be bored if Jette and Mary Lee were there, and it would look better to her father if she traveled with friends.

"I'll come, Giancarlo! Give me the exact dates, and I'll get the tickets."

—— ►◄ ——

Alexandra, Jette, and Mary Lee booked a suite at the Daytona Fitz, through Jay Winthrop's connections with Richard Fitzgerald Cox, the owner. From their patio, they could look out on cars and four-wheel drive vehicles careening along miles of the hard-packed white sand for which Daytona Beach was famous, weaving in and out of the surf.

The three girls walked the beach, racing playfully in and out of the Atlantic waves, overjoyed at being together. Drivers swerved and did double takes at the sight of the trio—Alexandra golden blonde, slim in her French-cut bikini, Mary Lee tall and striking, Jette spilling out of a thong that left only three small triangles of chamois between her and total nudity.

"I mean, this is *so* great," Jette enthused, stooping to pick up a shell. "I miss you guys so much. I don't have any real friends in Hollywood. Some girls from acting class, but they're all so jealous. Everyone's afraid someone else will be prettier than she is, or sexier. God, I can't even imagine what it's going to be like when we start auditioning for parts."

"What's it like? Hollywood, I mean," inquired Alexandra.

Jette giggled. "What can I say? It's crazy land, La-La Land, Tinseltown . . . but I love it. Anything can happen to you there; that's the wonderful thing about Hollywood."

"Sex appeal," Mary Lee sighed as a couple of tanned, muscled surfers turned to gawk at Jette. "I wish *I* had half of what you've got, Jette."

"You *are* sexy, Mary Lee. But you have to feel it inside. You have to, you know, really dig men—want to feel a man deep inside of you, enjoy his body all over yours."

Alexandra and Mary Lee stared at their friend. "Do you really feel that way, Jette?" Mary Lee finally asked. "I mean, that's what the books all say. That it's supposed to be so wonderful."

"Well, it is," Jette said, suddenly scowling and poking the sand with her bare toe.

"But I really wonder—I mean . . . doesn't it hurt the first time?"

"Let's cool it for now on the specifics, huh, Mary Lee?" Jette said. "Later, maybe at the hotel, after we get some champagne, OK?" She ran into the surf, shrieking as a foam-capped wave buffeted her backward.

They had a wonderful dinner, feasting on fresh pompano, little ears of corn dripping with sweet butter, a Caesar salad, and slices of tart Key lime pie. Afterward, in their room, they had Jette, whose voice sounded the oldest, order champagne from room service.

They laughed, sharing the months they'd been apart, playing the demo cassette of "Easy Woman" over and over.

"You have it made, Alexandra," Jette exclaimed, hugging her friend.

"Maybe not. This isn't the cover song for Olivia's new album, it's just filler."

"It'll be a big, big hit, just wait," Jette predicted.

Mary Lee told them about interviewing John Cheever for Vassar's *Miscellany News*. The famous author had commented on her "glorious" hair. "He told me I had . . . I mean . . . he was so intense . . . Do you think he was coming on to me?"

"He probably was," Jette said, shrugging and pouring herself another water glass of champagne.

"But—I mean, he's famous . . ."

"Famous people are just as horny as the rest. I should know. I grew up with them." A note of bitterness entered Jette's voice. She quickly downed her champagne. "Anyway," she added, "let's just take a poll here. How many virgins have we still got among us? Just you, Mary Lee?"

Mary Lee flushed.

"Oh, well," Jette said, nodding her head wisely. "You'll be next. It's got to happen. If we don't give it away, it gets taken, right? Hey. This bottle's empty. Aren't we going to open the other one? Who wants to wrestle with the cork? I'm too drunk."

"Maybe we ought to save the other bottle for later," Alexandra suggested.

"No . . . let's have more now. Here, *I'll* do the cork if no one else wants to. Stand back. This one's going to explode through the ceiling."

Somewhere in the middle of the second bottle, Jette began to laugh hysterically. "You know . . . I haven't really been telling you guys the truth," Jette said, gulping back a sob. "It's not all that great . . . nine different guys, sometimes I've even tried cocaine, but nothing works, none of them could . . . you know . . . nothing happens. Not one little thrill, not even a tiny one!" She held up her glass. "Hit me with some more, Alexandra. I'm getting just a wee bit smashed, and I'd like to get more so. What is it with orgasms, huh? What's the big deal anyway?"

"Nine lovers?" Mary Lee squeaked. "You've had *nine*?"

"So what?" Defiantly Jette sipped champagne. "What difference does it make? People do fuck, you know. That's what makes the world go *'round*!"

"That doesn't sound . . ."

"Nice? It doesn't sound nice?"

"Well . . ."

"Hey, it isn't nice, but it's reality, kid. It's what a man and a woman do. One gets on top of the other, it really doesn't matter which, and they hump. Oh, don't look at me like that. My mother does it all the time, and so does yours. Even Alexandra's father. He's got a mistress, doesn't he? Felicia? The whole world sucks and fucks!"

Alexandra put her glass down. Why did Jette seem so angry?

They finished the second bottle. Jette's mood shifted again, and they laughed and engaged in endless girl talk, dissecting the men Jette knew in Hollywood and the ones Alexandra and Mary Lee had met at Vassar.

"Intellectuals!" Jette scoffed. "Half of 'em are wimps. Give me someone who's got lots of real sex appeal. Someone like Richard Gere or Mick Jagger."

She put her hand to her mouth, giving a little "oh" of dismay. They were silent.

"Oh, boy," Jette groaned finally. "London."

A cloud of gloom descended on them. "I can't forget it," Alexandra admitted. "I keep having these nightmares . . ."

"He was stoned out of his mind." Jette was adamant. "And that's why he crashed. Shit. If anything, he killed himself. The only reason we're in trouble is that we left the scene when we should have stayed."

"We were involved in his death," Alexandra repeated gloomily.

Jette said, "Yeah, well, the important thing is, did anybody talk? That's what's important." She looked from Mary Lee to Alexandra, her expression fierce. "We swore an oath, remember? A *blood* oath. We owe each other, right? Forever."

"Forever," Mary Lee said fervently, and after a second's hesitation, Alexandra chimed in, too. She had a vague memory of waking up in the motel room with Giancarlo, and she knew that she'd shouted something. But she knew she couldn't have said anything about London.

— ◄► —

Giancarlo arrived at the hotel early the next morning to take Alexandra to the speedway.

A woman hurried over to ask Giancarlo for his autograph as he entered the hotel lobby, and he signed her hotel napkin with a flourish, obviously enjoying his fame. Wearing expensive black Italian leather pants with a silk shirt, his skin tanned from hours spent on tracks, he looked spectacular.

Giancarlo loped over to Alexandra and scooped her up for a mammoth bear hug.

"Alexandra, you are here! You are the most beautiful woman I have seen in six months!"

"That's the last time you saw me," she giggled.

"That's right, *bella*. I have neglect you terribly, not seeing you sooner. I am afraid you might have forgotten me, eh? Not want to see Giancarlo again?"

"Oh, I wanted to see you a lot."

"You can show me later, eh?"

She laughed. Qualities that normally turned her off she found charming and provocative in Giancarlo.

◄ ►◄

The track at Daytona was already alive with spectators, and the arrival of Paul Newman, in wraparound sunglasses, his right arm in a foam air sling, caused a temporary frenzy.

Race-track groupies and beauty queens were everywhere, dressed in shorts and revealing T-shirts. One, a curvy blonde in a ponytail and tight Miami University T-shirt, hovered close to Giancarlo.

Giancarlo was strapped into his car now, lined up with other cars on the pitroad, the starting area. In the shiny, low-slung red Ferrari emblazoned with the number 12, he looked as much a part of the car as its engine.

Seeing Alexandra, he waved, and she waved back.

Alexandra found a rickety folding chair someone had left near the pit area, and sat down. The sun was already beating on her neck, and she was glad she'd remembered to bring a hat and her lotion.

As a pair of drivers walked past her, one gestured toward the track where Giancarlo was waiting, his engine revved and warming up.

"That crazy bastard Ferrari," the driver remarked.

"Yeah. Drives like it's a suicide run."

"Yeah . . ." The men moved on, and Alexandra frowned, feeling suddenly uneasy, realizing she'd feel a lot better when Giancarlo had safely completed his turns around the track.

Jette and Mary Lee arrived at the track just in time to watch Giancarlo run his laps.

"Oh," Mary Lee moaned. "I have a headache from all that champagne we drank last night."

"*I* don't," Jette said. "I feel great." She wore a bright yellow scarf over her mass of black hair and looked pretty and rested, as if she had gone to bed the previous night at 9:00, instead of 3:30 A.M.

The three of them stood as close to the fence as they could get. Giancarlo's car was no more than a red blur and a loud roar.

"I can't believe they're going nearly two hundred miles an hour," Jette marveled, putting her hands to her ears against the overwhelming noise.

"These guys are addicted to speed," pronounced Mary Lee seriously. "I learned about this in psych, people who are turned on by danger."

"Yeah! And I bet there's going to be some mighty dangerous guys at the party tonight." Jette nudged Alexandra. "We *are* invited to some of the race parties, aren't we?"

"Why, yes," Alexandra said, although Giancarlo had mentioned this only briefly. "I'm sure we're all going."

"But what to wear is the question," Jette began. "I have a sundress that—"

She broke off. On the track, a yellow car had edged close to Giancarlo, fighting for space at the curve.

Alexandra narrowed her eyes against the strong Florida sun. It looked as if Giancarlo was deliberately pushing his car into the other.

Within a split second, the yellow car spun sideways. It crashed over the boundary wall, landing on its side in an explosion of flames.

Giancarlo's red Ferrari sped on by, untouched.

All three girls screamed in horror. Photographers, fans, mechanics, and first-aid people ran toward the burning car. But they were held back by the flames and billowing black smoke.

"Oh!" Jette shouted in Alexandra's ear. "Oh, my God, he's burning . . . burning alive!"

Mary Lee was suddenly shoved aside by a man carrying a video camera. She stumbled and fell, letting out a sharp cry.

"I . . . I twisted my ankle!"

"Are you sure?"

"It hurts!" Little beads of sweat broke out on Mary Lee's forehead.

"We'll find you a doctor," Alexandra promised.

"Fat chance, when that poor man is burning up." Mary Lee began to cry.

Five minutes later they still had not been able to locate a doctor. Giancarlo came swinging up to them, helmet in hand, his hair and face drenched in sweat.

"I clocked 189.201," he told them.

Alexandra stared at him. He was grinning tensely.

"Giancarlo . . ."

"There are accidents," he said, shrugging. "They happen. But not to me."

Now all three girls were staring at the racer.

"Well? Why you look at me that way, *bella*? That German driver knew his risks, he took his chances, he didn't win. What else is there but to win?"

"I can't believe you!" Alexandra responded angrily. "You *caused* that accident, Giancarlo. I saw you. You pushed that driver, you pushed your car into his, you forced him to lose control."

Giancarlo squared his jaw defiantly. "I drove the best I could."

"The best you could! Look! They still haven't got the fire out yet. And you're talking about winning." Alexandra was in tears, her body trembling as nausea pushed up at the back of her throat.

"*You* don't know what you talk about," he snapped. "You are nothing but a pretty fool . . . a little rich girl who think she going to get some excitement, yes? That's all you wanted, Alexandra Winthrop. You just wanted a good fucking, no more."

"Go away!" Alexandra screamed. "I don't ever want to see you again. *Now!*" She turned to Mary Lee and sank down to hold her weeping friend's hand. "Don't cry, Mary Lee. We'll get you a doctor, I promise."

— ►◄ —

Mary Lee's broken ankle needed surgery to ensure it was set properly.

It took two hours for Dr. Richard Feldman to track down Marietta, who was enjoying a business lunch at the Four Seasons with her agent, Al Zuckerman. Angry at having been interrupted in the midst of an important negotiation, Marietta lambasted the doctor.

The girls could hear his end of the conversation. "Look, this is race week, and this hospital is packed with patients. If you want me to get a court order, I will. Fine. You, too. Good-bye!"

He hung up the phone with an angry click and turned to Mary Lee. "I'm sorry, but your mother refuses to come here and sign for your treatment, so I'll call a judge I know and get a court order. I think I can get it in a couple of hours . . . if we can find a judge at home. Things get crazy here in Daytona during race season."

"Oh." Mary Lee's eyes glittered with unshed tears. "This is just great. My mother won't OK my surgery. She didn't even ask to talk to me. She's got an auction. I'll have to go b-back to school with a cast . . . and maybe crutches . . ."

"I'll help you," Alexandra said. "I'll help you get to all your classes."

"I d-don't want classes, I-I want my mother. I still l-love her . . . " Mary Lee collapsed into heartbroken sobs.

"Marietta Wilde is such a bitch," Jette exclaimed when she and Alexandra were alone in the ladies' room. "Even *my* mother isn't *that* busy."

"Well, she *is* a famous—"

"So what? You're too damned sweet and forgiving, Alexandra. Famous shouldn't mean anything when it comes to your child. She jerks Mary Lee around like a pull-toy on a string. You know what?" Jette added bitterly. "I'll bet anything that she sends Mary Lee piles and piles of gifts when you guys get back to Vassar. Maybe even a car. Yeah. And then she won't call her for another six months."

Alexandra nodded, feeling sick at heart. This trip to Daytona had turned into a fiasco. She had never expected Giancarlo to be so ruthless. As soon as Mary Lee could travel, she was going to take her back to Vassar and try to make it up to her for what had happened.

As for men . . . Alexandra didn't care if she ever met another one again.

— ◄► —

It was the usual post-race party, swarming with drivers, women, and hangers-on. But even the pulsing rock music someone had turned on—Hall and Oates—didn't liven things up.

Giancarlo walked past several groups that became strangely quiet as he approached. They blamed him. He knew they considered him wild, crazy, suicidal.

He browsed the length of the buffet table. He never ate before racing, and he was ravenous now. When he was satiated,

he'd think about getting laid. Alexandra Winthrop was finished—for now. She had acted as if he were a murderer. He
wasn't. When they stepped into a car, drivers knew what they
were dealing with. They all knew it could happen to them.

In a fire, you only got one breath, drivers knew. You had
to shut your eyes tight and hold your breath, because if you
breathed once, the oxygen was burned out of your lungs, and
you would pass out.

Giancarlo felt a pair of hands slide around his waist from
behind, hugging him along his groin. There was a giggle in his
ear.

He turned. It was Ingrid Hillstrom, a track groupie he had
had sex with a couple of times, a curvy brunette who made a
living as a sometime singer in rock groups.

"Ingrid," he said.

"Long time no see. This is Bitsy. She's here with me; she
just got kicked out of Miami University for partying naked in
the fountain. Way to go, eh? Show those old professors how to
live."

A second girl stood next to Ingrid, and Giancarlo recognized the blonde ponytail he had seen earlier at the speedway.
Bitsy was wearing a boob tube made of Lurex that revealed the
outlines of very pretty, small, uptilted breasts. She had a button
nose and bright blue, wide-set, intelligent eyes that seemed to
be laughing at him.

"You want a drink?" he offered, speaking directly to Bitsy.
"There is plenty of beer and cocktails. Or there's grass, or some
other stuff . . ."

"I'll take all of it," Bitsy said calmly.

"All?"

"Whatever. I'm going to party tonight. Then tomorrow I
have to think what to do next. Maybe I'll go and live with
Ingrid; she's getting an apartment up near Washington, in
Georgetown."

He began to relax a little. *Two of them*, he thought. Why
not? Alexandra and her friends were gone, little rich bitches, off
to Vassar again, safe and secure in their family fortunes, while
he had to scratch.

"Come on, Bits," Ingrid said to her friend, as if reading his
mind. "Let's have a little shrimp, and then maybe we ought to
go for a walk on the beach with Johnny. Go skinny-dipping or
something. I love swimming naked, and I know you do."

"OK," Bitsy said.

It turned out that Bitsy had some coke, so they squeezed together in the ladies' room, snorting white lines with a rolled-up twenty-dollar bill from a little mirror Bitsy carried in her purse.

"*Fantabulous*," Ingrid said, sucking in an ecstatic breath.

Bitsy said nothing, her eyes locking with Giancarlo's. He felt a wild surge of sexual desire and power. Some woman was banging on the door, wanting to come in, and they all laughed uproariously. Finally, the coke coursing through their veins, they exited in a laughing conga line.

Thirty minutes later they were running along the water's edge, splashing about naked. Giancarlo pulled the two women to him, kissing their slippery, soft, and wet breasts in turn.

Ingrid felt his erection push against her legs under the water.

"Oh, wow. I feel something."

"Something big," Bitsy added, diving underwater to fasten her mouth around him for a few seconds of glorious warmth and swiftly moving, teasing tongue. Her mouth felt indescribable, and Giancarlo tensed.

"Not yet, baby," he murmured, hands reaching for her blonde hair.

Ingrid agreed. "Not here," she giggled. "Let's go back to our hotel room, OK? I don't want to get sand in my pussy."

"What do you want in your pussy?"

"Oh, something real nice . . . and Bitsy wants something nice, too."

With some difficulty, they located their clothes, which they had thrown in a heap at the water's edge, and rapidly dressed. The girls' hotel room was only a short walk down the beach, and they zigzagged up the sand. Finally reaching the hotel, they burst into the room, stripping clothes as they went.

"Ohhh," Bitsy cooed happily. "What are we waiting for? Let's ball!"

They did, mouths locked onto genitals, tongues busily licking and sucking, hands busy, too, and Giancarlo's cock pumping. To Giancarlo's delight, Bitsy was a screamer, and he made sure she had plenty of opportunity to make her ecstasy known. Giancarlo lost track of the times he had thrust forward into a pulsating, soft, tight, wetness, uttering his own screams of pleasure.

They snorted another line and popped a few 'Ludes that Giancarlo had bought earlier. Then back to the daisy chain again, until finally Ingrid passed out.

Then it was just he and Bitsy, but by now even Giancarlo was beginning to lose steam. He pulled out and rolled over on the mattress beside her. Within five seconds, he was asleep.

Giancarlo opened his bleary eyes and looked with horror around the hotel room. Morning light streamed in the window through a wide gap in the hotel drapes, which his companions had not bothered to close all the way.

Ingrid lay sprawled on her stomach across one queen-size mattress, her buttocks thrust into the air, while beside Giancarlo, Bitsy was curled into a ball, her blonde ponytail tangled.

Giancarlo dragged himself off the bed and stumbled for the bathroom. *Fungari!* He had to race today . . . He was going to have to hurry, or he'd miss his starting time.

He jumped in the shower and turned on the cold water full blast. Under the spray, he grabbed a razor from where it lay on the tub edge and ran it over his cheeks. The inside of his mouth tasted like an oil slick, and his eyes felt as red as a taillight. He scrambled back into his clothes and left the room at a run.

On the pitroad, strapped into his car and waiting his turn, Giancarlo drew deep breaths of air and tried to convince himself that he was feeling *fantastico*.

He was going to win. Nothing was going to stop him.

The Ferrari screamed around the track.

Inside, drops of sweat streamed down Giancarlo's forehead. Heat, sucked up from the 125-degree track surface, was pushed into the engine compartment by the rocketlike speed of the car.

The roar of motors around him was deafening, and he breathed the stench of exhaust fumes. His arms ached from gripping the wheel, and his eyes itched from looking directly toward the sun once every fifty seconds as it flared like a supernova off his sand-pitted windshield.

This was what he was born to do. He did it better than almost anyone on earth, and after today maybe he would be a step closer to being the best.

After several laps, he accelerated out of the fourth turn, flashing like a rocket. He was inside his own inner space, in complete union with the universe. As the starter unfurled the white flag, indicating one lap remaining, Giancarlo approached a yellow Ford, aggressively nudging its rear bumper, feeling the impact through his own car as the metals touched.

He swung the red Ferrari out around the Ford, a process called slingshotting that the other driver was powerless to stop, short of forcing both of them into the wall. Inside, Giancarlo was laughing.

But before he finished passing the Ford, there was a slight wobble in the tail of the Ferrari. In the flash of only one second, Giancarlo felt his car skid sideways.

The nose of the car smashed against the concrete wall, and the Ferrari bounced off, heading tail-first for the pitroad. Race fans jumped to their feet and began screaming; it was the sudden, ugly, spectacular violence many had come specifically to see.

But Giancarlo didn't know any of that.

The roar in his ears was the roar of despair. On impact, red-hot pain raced through his head, creating orange patterns like a thousand Chinese firecrackers.

J

Jette
1979–1980

"Mees Jette, you be back three o'clock?" Rosaria, her mother's maid, wanted to know.

"Yeah, or maybe four or five. Now, Rosaria, remember, if anyone calls, anyone at all, take down the message." Jette made scribbling motions with her hands for the benefit of the Mexican maid.

"Sí, sí."

"Don't mess it up, Rosaria. I'm expecting calls. Important calls. Maybe."

"Sí."

Jette was dressed for browsing on Rodeo Drive in a long denim skirt, layered T-shirts, a new Kenny Lane necklace, and Gucci boots. She sauntered out to the five-car garage and slid into her mother's BMW. Claudia was in Monterrey, Mexico, filming another Western comedy with Burt Reynolds. Before that, she had been in Acapulco with Burt, and before that, in Phoenix at Elizabeth Arden's, dieting and revitalizing her body at $5,000 per week. Occasionally she had stayed home to supervise her daughter's entrance into acting.

Which, thus far, had not been spectacular.

"You're a Michaud, so you can get into any acting class just based on that. You won't have to push and shove," Claudia had told Jette two months ago, picking her up at LAX.

— ◄► —

Claudia Michaud, a veteran of more than twenty-six pictures, was still a star despite the box office failure of the last two. She wore a skintight white jeans outfit studded with silver rivets, her platinum hair wrapped in a white scarf to conceal her identity from curious fans.

Of course, it didn't. Six people had approached Claudia for her autograph while they were walking from the gate to the baggage claim area in the international terminal.

Standing at the luggage carousel, Claudia outlined her plans for her daughter. Improv and dance classes with the best coaches in Hollywood. Appointments at the "in" dentist, Dr. Nelson Stanley, to begin the process of having her teeth capped, a necessity since the camera was cruel and pinpointed even tiny flaws.

"And you need a diet," Claudia added, scrutinizing her daughter. "Eight, ten pounds maybe. You're too voluptuous."

"A diet?" Jette squeaked.

"Most certainly. You are charming, of course, darling, with a very pretty figure, but the camera adds at least ten pounds. With that large bosom of yours, it will add even more weight."

Incredulous, Jette stared at her mother. She knew she had something—and it was something pretty spectacular.

"Now, don't be hurt, Brijette. This is only business; it's just what you have to go through, that's all. You're going to be very marketable when we finish with you."

Jette busied herself with the bags, turning away so that her mother wouldn't see the tears that sprang to her eyes. She couldn't believe this. She'd written her mother in advance, telling her she wanted to follow in her footsteps—and she'd thought her mother would be pleased and encouraging. Instead Claudia was treating her like a Barbie doll that needed a little strategic repair before it could look really right—before it could be *marketed*.

She set down a Gucci garment bag stuffed with school uniforms, and turned to face her mother. Her chin was high, and her dark eyes flashed. "In the first place, I want to be called Jette, not Brijette. I like Jette much better. In the second place, I like myself the way I am now, and I'm not going to change." Her voice quivered. "I'm not going on a diet. I'm not having my teeth done. And that's that."

"Surely you don't object to a few little caps? *Everyone* has those done."

"Mother—"

"Darling, be realistic. You are a Michaud, but there are hundreds of beautiful girls in Hollywood, and *they've* been smart enough to do the right things. They know how fierce the competition is."

"I know how fierce it is, too," Jette declared defiantly.

Claudia raised an eyebrow, carefully feathered with ombré pencil. "Of course. You grew up right here in Beverly Hills; you've seen it all. Still—" Seeing Jette's face, she stopped. "Anyway, we don't need to discuss it now, do we? I've got to go on location in a couple of weeks to some dreary hole in Mexico. But Rosaria will be home, and I know you'll love your room. I had it redone in lavender and celadon, and I've discovered the most marvelous little closet shop. They put shelves in simply every *inch* . . ."

— ⋈ —

Jette loved her acting class. The readings, the tension of trying to get the nuances of a role, the laughter when someone totally flubbed his or her lines. Nina Foch was an exacting instructor. And Jette discovered that Claudia was right about one thing.

The competition.

It *was* daunting.

"And don't think that because you're the child of a star, it's going to guarantee you a fast ticket," Foch stated, her eyes seeming to pick out Chris Lemmon, also in the class, and Jette. "Sure, stars' children get an edge. I'd be lying if I told you it wasn't true. But the road is paved with star babies who didn't make it."

Carefully Jette backed the BMW out of the garage, avoiding the left-hand post, where last week she had scraped a fender. She flicked the electronic opener to close the door, and reached for the second device to open the wrought-iron gate that guarded the property. The well-oiled gate slid smoothly open on its tracks.

As she nosed the BMW onto the street, a familiar tour bus paused in its circuit. Thirty-five faces swiveled to inspect Jette in the BMW, who smiled and gave them a finger-wiggling wave.

The bus lumbered off toward its next stop on the tour of one hundred stars' homes, and Jette headed left, toward Rodeo Drive. It was a perfect California afternoon, dazzling sunlight glowing on green fronds of palm trees and blazing poinsettia hedges and hibiscus.

Beverly Hills. Everything here was bluer, greener, bigger, and richer.

Most of the homes were architectural fantasies, a potpourri of styles from the 1920s and '30s. There were Frank Lloyd Wright homes and Dutch Colonials, side by side with half-timbered Tudors, even an Islamic-style home with exotic, pointed widows and an eight-sided chimney.

Every morning, gardeners hosed down the streets and sidewalks to keep them clean and sparkling.

Jette drove east on Sunset, past the renowned "pink palace," the Beverly Hills Hotel, on her left, toward Rodeo Drive, which was only a few blocks away. The streets snoozed in the golden California sun. Jette had grown up on these streets, had wandered in and out of Lucille Ball's kitchen, and had fallen off her skateboard in front of the driveway of Phyllis and Alan Factor, of Max Factor fame. She had petted Bill Cosby's wire-haired terrier and taken swim lessons with Dean Martin's children in the Martin pool.

She was glad she'd come back here instead of going to Vassar. She was a California girl, and she was going to have a house exactly like one of these someday. And to do that, she needed a job. A very good part, that's what she needed. Why hadn't it been forthcoming yet? She had already registered herself at Complete and Atmosphere, the two biggest extra-casting offices in town, and it wouldn't be too long before she could register for speaking parts.

Turning onto Santa Monica, Jette spotted a white Porsche coming from the opposite direction. Her mother's platinum-blonde head, wrapped in an Hermès scarf, was plainly visible behind the wheel. She jerked the BMW to a stop.

"Jette!" Claudia Michaud pulled up alongside her daughter, rolled down her window, and waved cheerily, as if she had not been away five weeks but a few hours. "Where are you headed?"

"Oh, just some shopping." Jette was overjoyed to see her mother. "But I won't go now; I'll turn around and go back home with you, Mother."

Claudia reached up to adjust the knot that tied the silk headscarf at the nape of her neck. Piles of Vuitton luggage were jammed on the passenger seat and in the little car's back ledge. "Well, darling," she said. "I suggest you drive straight to Giorgio's and pick out something low-cut and spectacular, because we're going to a party tonight, and I think this might help your career."

"What?" Jette blinked.

"Mrs. Bradley Goldfarb wants us to attend a dinner party at their house—you remember Bradley, don't you dear?"

"I guess," Jette said reluctantly. Bradley Goldfarb was in his seventies.

"Well, he owns the Rams, and he has that little football field on his property. For the players to practice their plays or whatever? She's having three tables of twelve," Claudia added. "People in the business, dear. People who have contacts. Did you know he's also the single largest individual stockholder at Warner Brothers?"

"Great!" Jette began to cheer up. She'd been begging her mother to help her, and now there'd be a whole house full of people who might be able to give her leads to a speaking part in a movie.

Claudia put the Porsche in first gear. "Buy yourself something sensational, Jette, and then stop and have something done to your hair. I'll phone Vidal as soon as I get home, and he'll work you in. For me, he'd better." Claudia glanced at her watch. "Let's say in about two hours? That should give you plenty of time."

—— ◄► ——

On the way to the Goldfarbs' house on Bellagio Drive in Bel Air, Claudia filled her daughter in on exactly what she should and should not do. "We're not here for fun," Claudia pointed out. "This is strictly business. We're here to make contacts for you, and to let people see you. The last time most of them saw you was at your Sweet Sixteen party."

"I don't look sixteen now, do I?" Jette inquired anxiously.

"Heavens, no," Claudia drawled. "Wherever did you find that cheetah dress?"

"There was a new little shop," Jette said. "Is it too much?"

"Not if you like fringe."

Dusk's muted purples darkened the large homes that perched on the hills and canyons of Bel Air. As Jette and Claudia wound upward, they caught occasional glimpses of the lights of Los Angeles, just beginning to sparkle below.

Jette relaxed on the passenger side of the BMW her mother

had chosen to drive that night, enjoying the way the animal-print dress, with its hundreds of delicate leather fringes, swayed deliciously when she moved. It was such an *adult* dress—exactly the kind that Claudia would have chosen for herself.

She'd had to battle Vidal a little—he'd wanted to give her something clipped and curved and extreme. She'd finally persuaded him to comb and curl her out in a rippling, tousled, *au sauvage* mane of hair. It looked wonderful. Not that good taste was an issue here. In Beverly Hills, getting noticed was the issue.

"Now, remember," her mother added. "Tell everyone you're taking classes with Nina Foch and that she says she hasn't seen anyone as good in ten years."

"Oh, Mother."

"It's the way people do things here, my dear. You can't be shy. There are thousands of girls who would kill for the opportunity you're getting here tonight."

"I know," Jette said, feeling a lilt of excitement and anticipation.

They pulled up to a gatehouse set in the midst of tropical greenery. The additional wooded acres made the estate one of the largest in Bel Air.

A gate attendant came out to check their names against a list, and then the electronically controlled gate slid open. Claudia aimed the BMW around a curved driveway that widened to a large, brick-cobbled parking area that could hold fifteen to twenty cars. Two parking valets, in white windbreakers and black pants, waited to park their car.

The mellow notes of a piano drifted out of the large, Spanish-style house, along with the sounds of laughter and voices.

Jette hesitated, suddenly panic-stricken. Did she look OK? Maybe she'd overdone the cheetah thing. The dress had seemed wonderful in the shop, so slinky and sexy.

"Brijette! Don't daydream!" Claudia poked her in the side. "Get out, hurry, the valet is waiting. And pull down your skirt, will you? No sense letting him see to Sunday."

The party began as a hundred other Hollywood parties did, but for Jette it was a debut. When she was younger, she had only strolled through, greeted a few people, been shown off, and then happily escaped to the TV set with a liberal plate of party refreshments and—sometimes—a stolen drink. This time it was different.

"Claudia!" A woman exclaimed.

"Jennifer—you look wonderful!"

Claudia embraced their hostess, who wore a yellow crepe gown with a neckline that swooped down to show a dangerous amount of her considerable, creamy bosom. She had white-blonde, pouffed hair and was immaculately groomed.

"Jennifer, you remember my daughter, Brijette, don't you? I wanted to show her off tonight; she's just back from London."

"Indeed." Jennifer Goldfarb eyed Jette, taking in the mane of dark curls and the voluptuous fringed gown that clung to her figure, revealing inches of firm young cleavage. "You were filming there?"

"Actually, I was in school." Jette had been nervous, but the assumption that she was already an actress caused her stage fright to evaporate. "I'm using the name Jette," she informed Jennifer, smiling confidently. "Don't you think that's a bit more interesting than Brijette? I mean, Brijette makes everyone think of Brigitte Bardot."

"There are worse things to think about, my dear," Jennifer said, amused. "Come in and say hi to Bradley. He's out by the pool. More hors d'oeuvres, Bill," she added, speaking to their houseman, who had appeared at her side.

Inside, the immense tiled floor was covered here and there with magnificent oriental carpets. Stuccoed walls contrasted with tropical plants creating oases of greenery.

"The Pecks are here tonight," Jennifer told them as they descended to a wide veranda bright with potted geraniums and fruit trees. "And Bob Conrad, and Larry Hagman from 'Dallas,' and Burt Bacharach, of course. He's here with Carole Bayer Sager, and Jack Nicholson just arrived."

They stepped outside, where guests were gathered at the edge of a large, kidney-shaped pool. People looked up, and there was a tiny, electric reaction to the dazzling new arrivals.

"Claudia! How was Mexico? Are you totally frazzled?" Claudia was immediately pulled away by Jacqueline Bisset, one of her close friends, and Jette, left to her own devices, stood holding a glass of champagne.

The pool was a glorious shade of turquoise, its surface shimmering under the glow of expertly placed spotlights. Banks of pink and salmon hybrid bougainvillea and floribunda roses added bright splashes of color. At poolside, Henry Mancini, Jimmy Stewart, and Ricardo Montalban shared a joke. Jimmy Connors was entertaining a group of people with stories about

Wimbledon. Jette recognized Shirley MacLaine, wearing a dress that seemed to consist mostly of silk flowers. Bradley Goldfarb himself stood talking to Myron Orlando, one of Hollywood's best agents.

Jette's newly acquired confidence wavered. Why would any of these people be interested in *her*? She wasn't famous yet.

She wandered on. Shirley MacLaine didn't recognize her at first and uttered whoops of delighted laughter when it registered that the glamorous young woman was the former tomboy Brijette. "Darling, I really can't believe it. That hair—it's sensational. Who did it?"

"Vidal Sassoon," Jette said.

"Oh? A little different, isn't it? For him? Well, it's a lot prettier look than Farrah Fawcett ever dreamed of . . . and if she's here, don't let her overhear me say it." The star leaned forward. "What are you doing these days?"

Jette seized the opportunity to explain about her acting classes.

"Oh, that's very nice . . ." Someone was waving to Shirley from across the pool. "Do excuse me, I have to mingle, darling."

"What wild animal do you represent?" asked a tall man with a good-looking face and blow-dried gray hair. "The cheetah?"

His eyes traveled up and down Jette's dress, lingering on the row of fringe that covered her breasts.

Jette stiffened.

"I'm an old friend of the family. Court Frank," he explained.

"Oh, yes," Jette smiled. Now she remembered. Courtney Frank was a developer-builder who had made millions on properties in Beverly Hills and Los Angeles. All of his condo developments had long waiting lists.

"Let me get you another drink. And then I'll take you under my wing, little kitten. Nobody should leave a pretty lioness just standing at the edge of the prairie with no one to talk to."

"Cheetah," Jette giggled. "And it's the plains. Cheetahs live on the plains."

"Plains, prairie, whatever. So you're jumping into the fucking rat race, yes? Of course, I have a few contacts myself. I know a few studio heads. And I'm in a new investment group. We're going to be financing a new TV series—an evening soap."

"Mmmm," Jette said, torn between her conviction that here was a Hollywood BS artist—a rich one—and her hope that he really might be a legitimate contact.

"We could have lunch," Frank suggested, his eyes roving. "Call my office tomorrow. Either Polo Lounge or Bistro Garden."

Before she could reply, his head swiveled. "Uh-oh. Guess who just walked out by the pool? And it isn't Shirley Temple Black. I wonder if they are actually guests."

Jette couldn't help turning her head to look. Two men had just descended the wide steps from the house, each accompanied by a beautiful starlet. One was an older man, definitely Italian, with a barrel-like body, iron-gray mustache, and impassive expression. It was the younger man on whom Jette's eyes fastened with a little visceral shock that rippled all the way through her stomach.

He was tall and had rugged, flat cheekbones, a strong, square jaw, and a beautiful Roman nose. On his temple was a silvery half-moon scar. He wore white linen pants that emphasized a flat stomach. A dark blue shirt open at the collar revealed a tangle of black chest hair. A navy blue cashmere jacket complemented the outfit.

He was staring at her, too—directly into her eyes. Jette shivered. No man had ever stared at her that way before.

"A regular Romeo, isn't he?" Frank remarked. "Best-looking Mafia man in the country, I'd say."

"Mafia?"

"Yup, Mafioso. The Provenzo family, from Chicago."

"I don't believe you."

"The old one is Sam Provenzo, the godfather. The young one is one of his sons—I don't know which one, he has eight. I can't imagine why Bradley invited them. Oh, I see," he added, as another man emerged from the house. "That explains it—that third guy is Jimmy Weingarten."

"Who?"

"From Caesar's Palace, kid, don't you ever go to Vegas? He's brought them to the party. Bradley is going to have a shit fit when he finds out he's got Mafioso at his party."

Frank rambled on, offering tidbits of gossip, but Jette didn't bother to listen. She watched as the men and their dates ambled around the poolside.

Once more, the younger man glanced over. Again their eyes locked across the shimmering surface of the pool.

Jette agreed to make a lunch date with Court, then excused herself and started around the pool.

The young man's date, a six-foot-tall redhead, had left for the powder room. Jette seized the moment and zeroed in on him.

"I'm Jette Michaud," she told him, deciding to be bold. "Claudia Michaud's daughter. And you're—?"

"Nico," he said, his eyes boring into her. "Nico Provenzo."

They stood looking at each other, Jette's stock of conversational ploys temporarily exhausted. She felt a deep tremor. Jesus—even looking at him made her panties moisten.

"Aren't you kinda young for this crowd?" he asked her.

"Me? Young?"

"Yeah, I'd say you don't fit."

She glanced around the terrace area, where guests milled and laughed and caterers were putting the finishing touches on three tables that had been spread with yellow linen cloths.

"What did you expect?"

"Not so many old ones," he told her. "I'm not going to get old."

"You're not?" He could only be a few years older than she was, Jette thought—not more than twenty-three, anyway. She laughed. "How do you know that? Give me your hand," she ordered. "I'll tell you if you have a long life line."

She took his hand in hers, feeling her heart jolt as she touched his skin. He felt very warm, even hot. She knew she'd only sought an excuse to touch him.

"Your hand is soft," he said. "Nice."

Jette giggled. "Hey, I'm the one doing the reading."

"I know soft when I feel it."

"Right. Hold out your hand and relax it," she began. "I have to look at your lines."

He grinned, revealing very white, even teeth. "OK."

Jette looked down at his hard, muscular hand. The palm was squarish and definite, fingers long and strong. Lover's fingers, she found herself thinking. Intelligent hands, rebellious hands. He wore a gold nugget ring carved with the family crest. He teased her by spreading out and flexing his fingers.

"Stop," she giggled. "I can't read you when you do that. There. Good. Now, this is your mount of Mercury, and this your mount of Venus." She pointed to padded areas underneath the fingers. "Here is your heart line, and this is your—"

She caught her breath. Nico's life line did not look like the one depicted in the book. It ended only halfway up his palm. Well, maybe she'd got the picture wrong. Anyway, she had to say something.

"This is your life line," she hurried on. "Very interesting, and you have a very nice heart line, which is tasseled at the end—these little lines that kind of fan out. It means you're going to have several love affairs."

"Oh?"

He winked at her and deliberately lifted up one of the fringes on the bodice of her dress, suggestively pulling her toward him with the little snippet of leather. But before they could continue, the older Provenzo, Nico's father, came striding toward them, ignoring Jette.

"Business," he said to his son curtly, motioning with his head over to the pool area, where several studio heads stood with Jimmy Weingarten.

Nico glared at his father.

"Nicolo," the older Provenzo said in a deep, gravelly voice.

"I'll come when I am ready," Nico replied.

"It's OK," Jette said nervously.

"When I am ready," he repeated.

—— ►◄ ——

Bistro Garden, on Canon Drive, was full of studio people dressed in Hollywood's standard casual garb. Some sat at small tables outdoors, soaking up sun while they gossiped and made deals. Others were gathered indoors, where hanging plants and vines provided more of a garden atmosphere.

Jette was ushered to one of the best tables, where she found the developer engaged in a phone conversation.

She sank into the chair the waiter pulled out for her. Two tables away, Barbra Streisand sat with Jon Peters, her hairdresser and current lover. Jette waved to Barbra, who had been one of the guests at her Sweet Sixteen party.

The waiter came to take her drink order, and Jette hesitated, knowing she was underage. Finally she said, "A Virgin Mary, please."

"*Are* you?" Frank inquired, grinning at her with his hand over the phone.

Jette didn't bother to answer. Near the door, Kate Jackson was entering with a couple of other women Jette didn't recognize. Jette politely let her eyes slide by the TV veteran. In Beverly Hills, only tourists openly gawked.

"Well, cutie," Frank said, finally hanging up and returning the phone to the waiter. "You look as sweet today as maple sugar candy. But I hope not as virgin as that terrible drink you ordered."

He opened the menu. "This place has wonderful veal piccata," he added patronizingly. "If you've never had it, you'll love it. Or the chicken Milanese. That's fantastic, too."

"I usually have the Chinese chicken salad," Jette said firmly.

Frank himself ordered salad, no dressing, only a lemon squeeze. Throughout the meal, he continued a long, gossipy monologue that encompassed everyone he recognized in the room.

Bored, Jette interrupted him. "I wanted to ask you about those people at Bradley Goldfarb's. Sam Provenzo and his son. You say they're from Chicago?"

"Interested, huh?"

She flushed and began fussing with her table knife. Interested? She'd only slept a few hours last night, her mind replaying every word she and Nico said to each other. "I'm just curious, that's all."

"Provenzos control gambling and drugs in Chicago, and they're getting into some picture deals here in L.A., I hear. They're connected with Mo Bernstein, down in Florida. He's a real heavy kingpin."

"Oh," she breathed.

"They aren't Seventh-Day Adventists, babe. You turn on to violent guys? Is that your thing? Does a guy like that really make you cream your panties?"

Jette was beet red, sorry she had ever brought up the topic.

"Well, you don't mess with those people, girlie. They'd eat you for breakfast and spit out the cherry pits."

She hated his vulgarity. "I'm *not* a child," she said.

"Hey, there's nothing wrong with being fresh and young, eh? Especially when you look like you. Great tits, and ass to boot. A little chocolate truffle. Yeah," he elaborated. "Dark chocolate hair, and nice, pink, minty, edible insides."

Jette stared at him incredulously. "I'm looking for a job as an actress, not as an after-dinner mint," she snapped.

Frank didn't even seem to notice he'd been put down. "Well, I can certainly connect you in the job department." He smiled. "I was just on the phone to Robert Ehrman, who's a big honcho with NBC. If you wanted to be just a little nice for me, that is."

Jette had really lost her appetite now. Oh, boy, this was as blatant a casting-couch ploy as she could imagine. What a total jerk.

But he had given her an excellent idea. Ehrman was one of her mother's old friends—the very one, in fact, whose advice she had sought in a rather messy divorce that made *National Enquirer* headlines for months. They were still close today.

Anyway, she didn't have to wait for Court Frank to call him, or her mother either. She could do it herself.

She took her napkin out of her lap and plunked it on the table, gathering up her purse.

"Sorry, *sweetie*," she said, imitating her mother's breezy star-brushoff. "I forgot to tell you, I have an appointment at two-thirty. A massage, don't you know? So relaxing. All those nice, scented oils."

She got up and left, smirking as she felt his frustrated eyes fasten on her departing, swaying backside.

——— ◄► ———

As soon as she mentioned Claudia's name over the phone, the secretary put her through. Robert Ehrman agreed to meet Jette for lunch in Burbank at the NBC executive dining room.

"But twenty minutes max," he specified. "That's all I can give you, and even then it's stretching it."

"I'll talk fast," she promised.

Ehrman was about forty-five, with a suntanned face and a head of dark hair, except for some premature silver on both temples. He was treated deferentially in the private dining room. At the next table was another notable with a silver head of hair. Johnny Carson was deep in conversation with two studio executives—something about Charo and censorship. He looked annoyed.

Jette told Ehrman about her class, trying not to exaggerate too much, and her interest in acting. "Actually, I have done some work," she informed him. "When I was four, I was in *Vixen Heart* with my mother. I played her when she was a little girl. I had six lines."

"I remember that picture. You do have a certain look," he conceded, assessing her with the swift, sure glance of a man who judges people every day. "Innocent and yet baby-doll sexy. If you photograph half as well as you come across in person, you could be dynamite."

"Really?"

"Of course," the production chief equivocated, "that means diddly without a screen test. Anyway, I've already got three girls testing for a certain part that's being cast right now. I suppose I could call over there and schedule you."

Jette was almost jumping up and down in her chair. He was going to screen-test her! She had a chance—and she knew that once they saw her, they were going to love her.

"Calm down, calm down," Ehrman said. "It's only a test. Tomorrow morning at six-thirty for makeup call, OK? Stage 9. Tell them I sent you for the part of Jenette."

"Jenette," Jette babbled, unable to stop herself. "It even almost sounds like my name . . ."

"The role is a baby-doll type in the evening soap we just launched, 'Canyon Drive.' The ratings are already starting to climb, and we need lots of new, hot, sexy blood to keep it going in the same direction. We want you to give Darryl Boyer a run for her money." Ehrman pushed back his chair and stood up. "Say hello to your mother for me, will you?"

— ◄► —

The next morning, Jette drove Claudia's BMW through the studio gates on Alameda in Burbank and stopped at the guard's box to give her name, which was checked off on a list. She drove on through.

The NBC studios were a huge, rambling collection of sound stages that looked like warehouses. At 6:30 A.M., Jette saw no stars—only production people intent on their tasks. Young women in tight jeans scurried back and forth, carrying clipboards. Workmen unloaded something from a truck backed up to one of the loading docks. An electrician hurried by with an armful of thick cables.

With some difficulty Jette found the parking area she had been told to use, then she wandered among the unmarked driveways another ten minutes until finally a young woman pushing a coffee cart told her where to go.

She followed the directions, managing to find Stage 9 without asking again.

Damn, but she was nervous.

Ten minutes later, she was seated in a small, cluttered makeup room, where Linda, a makeup girl, dabbed pancake on her with a brown sponge.

"I don't have to do too much to *you*," Linda told Jette, as she penciled eyeliner on her lids. "You've got a natural face and awfully good cheekbones. And your hair is great."

"Really?" Jette was thrilled with this compliment from a professional.

"Yeah, you look familiar, too. Haven't I seen you before?"

"My mother is Claudia Michaud."

"Yeah?" The pencil paused, then resumed. "I hear she's a real sweetheart, always signs autographs. Who's she dating now, Burt Reynolds?"

"I guess," Jette said. Claudia's affairs were erratic and often lasted no longer than the filming of the picture.

"Is Burt a good lover?"

Jette giggled. "My mother didn't tell me."

Linda continued to chatter, while Jette sat stiffly underneath the plastic clothing shield that had been wrapped around her shoulders.

She'd learned her script, but this would be real, not acting in a class. A *baby doll*. What, specifically, did you do to be a baby doll? Oh, this was going to be awful . . .

A face peered around the doorway of the makeup room, and Jette looked up, expecting to see the production assistant who had brought her here. Instead she saw the heart-shaped face of Darryl Boyer herself, the new female star of "Canyon Drive."

"You're testing for Jenette?" Darryl didn't seem to be addressing the comment anywhere specific.

"Are you talking to me?" Jette asked.

"Sure, who else? I'm not talking to the makeup girl."

"Well, excuse *me*," huffed Linda, snapping the eyebrow pencil back into her box.

Darryl Boyer stepped into the small room that reeked of face powder and pancake makeup. She was about 5'4", an exquisite woman with huge pansy eyes augmented for the TV screen with several rows of false lashes. Her hair was blonde, streaked, and tousled into a spiky look that was already catching on. Millions of American women wanted to look exactly like Darryl Boyer.

"They were only supposed to test three," she said to Jette as if it were her fault.

"Mr. Ehrman told me to come," Jette defended herself.

"Oh, that Robert," Darryl retorted, her tone scathing. She was already dressed for the day's shooting in a black crepe gown that clung to her perfectly wrought curves. "Let me have a look at you," the star ordered, stepping closer to Jette.

"Me?"

"Who else is testing for Jenette? Cleopatra? I just want to know what's going on. The person has to be exactly right, or it's going to royally fuck up my part. And I've told them that, too. Now, come on, stand up, honey. I want to have a look."

Jette sat where she was, her eyes filling with tears of humiliation.

"Come on," Darryl pressed. "I've got to get back, so hurry. Stand up and show me what you've got."

Jette drew a quick breath and stood up, flicking off the makeup shield and tossing it to the floor. Then, with another liquid shrug, she lifted the bottom hem of her sweatshirt.

She wore no bra. Her magnificent breasts were firm and white, each peaked by a ruby-pink nipple. They were breasts to kill for, and there wasn't a plastic surgeon in Hollywood who couldn't have made his fortune if he could have duplicated them.

"This is what I've got," Jette snapped. "Better than yours, too, I might add."

As the makeup girl burst into laughter, Darryl gasped and fled from the room.

Jette, lowering her sweatshirt, began to laugh, too.

"That was perfect," Linda giggled.

"What a bitch she is," Jette managed to reply.

"Did you see her face?"

"What a riot!"

Linda calmed down and retrieved her pencil. She started to make repairs. "Jesus, you can't laugh like that; it ruins your eyes. You are something else, kid. You are really something. But there's only one problem: if you get this part, that Darryl Boyer is going to be climbing up your ass."

"Do you really think I'll get it?"

"Honey, I don't see how you can avoid it."

—— ◄► ——

As it turned out, Linda was right. Jette got the part of Jenette, at $750 a week, a modest rate carefully negotiated for her by Myron Orlando, her mother's agent. He wrote escalators into the agreement, so that if she stayed for more than eight episodes, her pay would go up to $900 an episode.

"You can't ask for the big prices yet, baby," the agent told her from behind his imposing bleached-oak desk. "It all depends on how much the viewers like you and how much fan mail you get. Right now, everyone is gaga over Darryl Boyer, and any show she's on is sure to be a hit. Which is very good. Some of the luck will rub off on you."

"But . . . what if she doesn't like me?" Jette inquired guiltily.

"Who the hell cares if she likes you?"

"But—"

"You go on home, study the script they gave you, and make sure you've got the lines down cold. Always be *on time* for your call. You do those things, and look good in the clothes they give you, and nobody is going to complain."

Jette was so excited that when the elevator hit the lobby floor, she rushed to the phone booth and called Alexandra. "Guess what! Something great's happened; it's so incredible, you're never going to believe it!" She almost screamed with delight.

She and Alexandra talked for forty wonderful minutes, and Jette told her all about the show, which starred not only Darryl, but also Ann-Margret and Rob Cramer, who had recently been written up in *TV Guide* as "TV's Most Desirable Hunk."

Alexandra's laugh trilled across the telephone wires from Poughkeepsie. "Jette, you'll give a new name to flash and trash. I can hardly wait to watch you on the little screen."

— ▶◀ —

By the time Jette reported for her first day on the set of "Canyon Drive," she had passed through the gamut of emotions, from exhilaration to terror.

"Actors are human," Claudia had casually assured her. "They sweat, and they have to pee once in a while, and they forget things. Why do you think there is more than one take? But *always* memorize your lines," she added. "Never try to wing that."

Veteran of years of Hollywood back stabbing, Claudia had advice about Darryl, too.

"OK, you did antagonize her. But if you keep your mouth

shut and stay out of her way, she might just leave you alone. Remember, she doesn't really want people to know what you did—because she's afraid they might laugh at *her*."

The morning Jette was to report to the set was one of Los Angeles' famous smoggy days, when pollution had bleached the sky into a pallid, pastel blue. Still, to Jette, the air seemed to vibrate with possibilities.

A production assistant introduced Jette to the behind-the-scenes people—the director, assistant directors, associate producer, secretaries, script girls, grips, gaffers. Everyone eyed Jette with curiosity. After all, she was the daughter of a movie star, and even on the set of a TV show, movies were revered.

"We're a big family here," Pamela Randolph informed Jette. The older actress was quick to take Jette under her wing. "All you have to do is remember one thing. Lady Darryl is hell on people who blow their lines. Darryl the Peril is what some of us call her."

"Great," Jette said.

"Oh, don't worry. Right now she's all wrapped up in planning her wedding to Richard Cox. You know, that handsome Fitz Hotel guy, and she's too busy to give you more than a token bark."

They filmed the hospital scene where Jette was brought in as a young, beautiful amnesiac who could not remember her name. Dozens of extras played doctors, nurses, and visitors.

It was noon before Darryl appeared on the set. That afternoon they would shoot the scenes that included her. Even without makeup, she looked like a star. Her small body was clad in teal blue velour sweats.

"Well, if it isn't Little Miss Tits," Darryl drawled, approaching Jette, who sat in a folding chair, nervously studying her lines.

Jette had thought long and hard about what to do when they finally came face to face, but no good solutions had come to her, so she spoke impulsively.

"Look, Darryl, I guess I got carried away, but I was so nervous. I acted like an idiot. I hope you can forgive me. Thank God, the makeup girl hasn't said a word. I told her not to."

Darryl searched Jette's face for evidence of sarcasm, but she saw only sincerity. Grudgingly Darryl nodded. "Well, I guess anyone can make a mistake. One thing, though."

"Yes?"

"I want the close-up shots and the good angles, under-stand? Ben Martigliana, the chief cameraman, is a good friend of mine, and he knows how to give me good close-ups. Nothing personal, but I've paid my dues, and you haven't."

"OK," Jette said, shrugging.

The first AD—assistant director—called to Darryl, want-ing to discuss some blocking changes with her, and Jette kept on smiling until the blonde actress was safely out of sight. Then she expelled her breath in a long, relieved sigh.

That was over. Maybe now Darryl would leave her alone.

—— ◄► ——

"Cut and hold!" yelled the director. The red camera lights blinked off, and the three cameramen temporarily relaxed. It was the tenth take.

Jette, Darryl, and Rob were filming a scene where Darryl, as Rhea, discovered Jette in bed with her movie-star husband.

It was a seminude scene, as realistic as network censors would allow. The director had requested a closed set to make the actors more comfortable. Jette was in bed with Rob, wearing nothing but bikini bottoms and pasties to cover her nipples, these to preserve her modesty in front of the limited crew and a network executive who had dropped by to observe the day's filming.

"She's fluffed her lines again," Darryl complained loudly. She was referring to Jette. She stood in the doorway of the set, hands on her hips, wearing a beige suit with flared jacket and navy piping. "Can't she memorize her lines, for God's sake? What's so tough about saying, 'I'm sorry, Rhea, I'm really, really sorry'?"

Jette yanked the sheets up to cover her breasts and sat up, looking at the director imploringly. "I did memorize them! But it's a tongue twister, and it's a stupid line anyway. And besides, I'm sitting here half-naked with about ten people watching me."

"That should hardly bother *you,*" Darryl remarked.

"OK," smiled the director. "No problem. Let's get a writer out here; we'll change that dialogue. On the double!" he added, speaking to a production assistant, who immediately scurried off.

Jette pulled on a robe, and they waited for the writer to be located. Darryl asked for a telephone and spent the time laugh-ing and talking softly, her face relaxed. It was the first time Jette had seen her look soft and vulnerable.

"Who is she talking to?" Jette finally asked Pamela Randolph.

"Oh, it must be her fiancé, Richard Cox. She's madly in love with him; it's the only thing that keeps her human," Pam said, expertly threading a stubby needlepoint needle with yellow Persian wool.

"Who is he?" Jette wanted to know.

"Well." Pam stopped what she was doing. "He's just about one of the most eligible men in the country, that's all. Tall. Dark good looks, silver at the temples. And filthy rich. He owns the Fitzgerald Hotel chain, with about 150 hotels all over the world. They're getting married as soon as the show wraps for the season, and that's all she's living for. The way she figures it, once she's married to him, she won't have another financial worry for the rest of her life."

"But—she's a star," Jette said, accustomed to her mother's freewheeling independence.

"Honey," said the fifty-year-old character actress, "actresses are like butterflies. They have their season, no question. But wings fray. Skin ages. Suddenly you have cords in your neck and wrinkles on your upper lip. Need I say more?"

They were called back to the set, and Jette took off her robe and slid into the satin-sheeted bed.

— ►◄ —

Overnight, Jette began to receive fan mail. It arrived in huge, gray-grimy U.S. Postal Service bags. Most of the letter writers seemed to think Jette *was* the baby-doll character she played. They told her to shape up or excoriated her for her seductive behavior, asked for pictures, or (if male) told her in endless, steamy detail what they wanted to do to her.

One day on the set, Jette noticed the associate producer, Rusty Copa, talking with a man who, although his back was turned to her, looked familiar. When the man turned, she saw that it was Nico Provenzo.

Her heart gave a spinny, sparkly dip, and she ran toward him, waving and calling his name.

"Jette Michaud," he said, obviously pleased to see her. In daylight the intriguing half-moon scar on his temple gleamed silver.

"What are you doing here?" Jette asked in delight.

"Meeting with some people. And you?"

"I got a part! I'm an actress now—I'm in 'Canyon Drive.' Isn't it wonderful?"

He smiled, and his eyes caressed her body warmly. "Come with me and have a drink," he proposed.

"Now? I have a wardrobe fitting and one helluva long day, but could we make it at eight-thirty? I think I'll be through by then."

"The Ambassador," Nico specified.

—— ►◄ ——

At 8:45 P.M., fifteen minutes late, Jette sped into the parking lot of the Ambassador, a sprawling, 500-room, quasi-Spanish-style complex of main building, bungalows, and cottages that reeked of Hollywood history.

Jette was dressed for major allure. She had borrowed one of her costumes from Wardrobe, a black-and-white silk dress with gored skirt and beaded, off-the-shoulder straps that made her skin look creamy. She had also combed her hair from the underside up, until it tangled all around her in full, rippling, glossy waves of black.

In the bar, Jette and Nico sat drinking martinis.

Nico told her he was an undergraduate at Georgetown and had received his MBA from Harvard three years ago, the first member of his family to take a degree. His father had chosen Nico for this honor when he was only six, and he had been allowed no choice about attending.

He was the youngest of four brothers by his father's first wife, and the elder Provenzo had since remarried, fathering another four boys.

"Eight?" Jette inquired incredulously. "Your dad has eight children? All boys?"

He nodded. "He is extremely virile. In my family, sons are considered most desirable. We are a fiercely loyal family, Jette. All Sicilian families are. No matter what differences we may have with one another, or how angry we become, we would give our life for each other, do you understand that?"

"Close, huh?"

"Family comes first. That is how our children are brought up—to respect and to walk in the family footsteps. It's the old way and a good way—not like so many Americans these days, with no roots and no loyalty, people who are no more solid than snowflakes or raindrops."

She dared to ask about the scar. "A car accident," he told her shortly, his eyes flicking away. He was lying, she realized, but somehow that made him seem even more intriguing.

He took her to Spago for an intimate dinner, and by midnight they were at the Beverly Hills, where Nico was staying. Jette rode upstairs with him in the elevator, her heart pounding.

A bucket of iced champagne awaited them in Nico's room, two fluted crystal glasses nestled on sparkling ice.

"We'll drink from one glass," he told her softly, his eyes locking with hers. "Then from each other."

Jette found her reply clogging in her throat. Was he talking about . . . ? Holy Mother of God, he was. He was going to kiss her all over her body. Drink champagne from her breasts, lick it from her stomach, and . . .

Jette was on top of Nico, her slender yet rounded body impaled on his hard and lean one. Her hips undulated frantically up and down on his shaft, while, with his finger on her clitoris, he artfully stimulated her. Sweat poured from their bodies, as Jette felt afire with an urgency she had never felt before.

They had done everything. Nico had licked and teased her nipples into poignant erection. He had poured champagne onto her breasts and licked it up, his smooth, wet tongue driving her to incredible throes of distraction. His tongue probed greedily between her vaginal lips, penetrating the slick yet muscular, pink depths of her being. He poured champagne on her thighs and lapped it up with exquisite tongue strokes.

Several times Jette hovered on the brink of a strange, swelling feeling of near-explosion. Only nothing happened. After a few seconds, the feeling died.

Orgasm. That's what the feeling was, and as soon as Jette became aware of it, she began trying to pull the sensation closer and to control it.

Again it slipped away. She was almost sobbing from frustration. *Why couldn't she have one?* She'd reached "almost." Why hadn't she gone over the edge and exploded?

"Are you getting there?" His head was thrown back on the pillow, his teeth bared, nostrils flared.

"Yes, oh, yes," she lied, as they increased the friction of their movements.

She was almost there.

"Come to me," he murmured. "Come to me, Jette. Come to me . . . Come . . . Come . . ."

She tried. She squeezed her eyes shut tight, and she thought about the wonderful explosion that was going to be hers in just a few seconds. Yes—just a few more moves . . . she had to concentrate really hard . . .

"Come!" Nico grunted out in a louder voice. "Come! Come! Come!"

So Jette faked it. She drew a deep breath and undulated her hips, and she let out a cry of excitement that she hoped was genuine enough to fool him. The minute she cried out, Nico pushed his pelvis into hers and gripped her with strong fingers until she thought he was going to squeeze her to death.

His climax seemed to last forever, a frenzy of bucking and shuddering and groans. This was his fourth time.

Afterward, Nico sank back into the sheets, lying there very still, and Jette rolled off him. She cuddled up beside the bulk of his chest, sliding her arm around him. His curls of deliciously fragrant chest hair tickled her skin.

"You were wonderful," she breathed dutifully. "It was so . . . so wonderful."

He didn't respond. If anything, his body seemed to grow more tense. Jette tensed a little, too. Maybe she had been too effusive.

"You had no orgasm," he informed her curtly.

"What? I did, too. It was so nice," she murmured, wiggling even closer to him.

"You lie," he said, sitting up and pushing her aside. "What do you think I am, some ignorant *paesano* who can't recognize when a woman has pleasure?"

"Please . . . Nico . . ."

"It's an insult for a woman to fake with a man." Nico got out of bed and began to dress in quick, angry movements. "It tells him he is a failure to her. That he could not pleasure her."

"Not so," Jette said. "All it means is that she didn't get the feelings. So what? She still enjoyed it, didn't she? I mean, *I* still enjoyed it."

"Enough," he said savagely.

Oh, God. Jette was ready to sob from disappointment and hurt. She had wrecked it all with a careless word, insulted his manhood. She couldn't believe this. Not two minutes ago their naked bodies had been locked together, floating on a sea of passion. Now he was acting as if he hated her.

"Hey," she pleaded. "I'm sorry, I didn't mean any harm. I was only trying to please you. I've never had a climax before; I don't even know how to get one. I wanted you to be happy," she wept. "Please, don't be mad . . ."

"It cheapens both of us when you fake. Never do that to me again. Not ever."

He sounded so cold and harsh. She sat on the edge of the bed, too upset to reach for her clothes. "You told me to come," she said. "You kept demanding that I come. I wanted to. I tried."

Everything she said only made it worse.

"Get dressed. I'll call and have my chauffeur drive you back to the Ambassador for your car," he said, reaching for the telephone. "I dismissed him, but he can come back."

Sobbing, she reached for her clothes.

—— ► ——

It was weeks before Jette recovered from the humiliation of being rejected by Nico. At Spago, Nico had given her his elaborately embossed business card. Now she alternated between wanting to tear it into little white bits and wanting to dial the number listed there.

He didn't call.

She didn't call.

But she didn't tear up the card either.

Even the fifteen-hour days of work on the set didn't exhaust all of Jette's nervous energy. She drifted through several weeks, fighting her depression. Her fan mail increased, to Darryl Boyer's displeasure.

Nico wasn't the only man in the world, Jette assured herself. There were lots of other ones out there.

One day a stuntman who specialized in auto chases, an Israeli with a head of glossy black curls, came on to Jette. When he told her stories of fighting on the Gaza Strip and sleeping with his machine gun, Jette went with him to his room. She fucked him for seven hours.

She didn't come with him either.

—— ► ——

Spring on the Vassar campus was a glorious explosion of flowering trees. White dogwood glimmered in the woods near

Sunset Lake, and flowering crabapples created blazes of pink. Delicate apple, peach, and pear blossoms softened the stone and brick of the old, Gothic-style dormitories.

Alexandra was on her way to her French class, her mind worrying away at the French verbs she was still trying to memorize for the day's quiz.

Hundreds of students had been drawn outdoors by the balmy weather, and they lazed on blankets on the grass.

Starting across the lawn, she was suddenly stopped in her tracks by the voice of a woman singing on a portable radio. Olivia Newton-John was singing "Easy Woman."

As the lilting power of the song swept across the grass, she felt the blood rushing to her cheeks, a delicious quicksilver feeling in her veins.

Her song! On the airwaves for millions of people to hear.

Alexandra was late for the French class, but she was no more capable of moving than she was of levitating fifty feet. As she stood paralyzed, she experienced a moment of pure joy that was worth all the waiting, discouragement, and rejection.

"Easy Woman" was a real song now. It had been born and belonged to the world.

—— ▶◀ ——

Jette, in Los Angeles, heard the song the same day and rushed to the phone to call Alexandra. "It's going to be a hit," she gloated, as proud as if she had written it herself. "I just know it, Alexandra! You're going to be so famous. You'll have to get yourself an unlisted number. Or even better, another phone line to handle all your calls."

"Better yet," Alexandra said, laughing, "why don't you come out here to visit us for a couple of days and be my personal secretary?"

"I'll do it," Jette said.

—— ▶◀ ——

True to her word, Jette flew to Poughkeepsie, and two days later, the three friends were lounging on the grass in front of Main Building, enjoying the spring sunshine.

"Oh!" Jette exclaimed, stretching. "This is so wonderful. This campus is like a serene, safe world. You just can't imagine how much I needed this. Hollywood is so full of crap sometimes. You just don't know."

"It's that hard, being a TV star?" Alexandra inquired.

"Fifteen-hour days," Jette sighed. "And I think Rob Cramer is gay. And—" She stopped. "Oh, never mind."

"Well, this is one weekend you can relax," Alexandra promised. "We're taking you to dinner, and then we'll have some wine in the room and just talk."

Alexandra had brought several books to study, and Mary Lee lay on her stomach, scribbling something in a notebook. Her ankle was mended, she had lost even more weight, and she was wearing her titian hair in a thick, Valkyrie braid.

"What's in the notebook?" Jette asked her friend.

"Oh, nothing. Just some ideas I'm writing down for an article," Mary Lee said vaguely.

After half an hour, Mary Lee excused herself, saying that she had a language lab to go to and would return to meet them for dinner.

"Jette, is something bothering you?" Alexandra remarked, when the tall, striking figure of her roommate had disappeared down one of the campus's tree-arched walks.

Jette hesitated, then burst out, "Have you ever faked an orgasm?"

"Done what?"

"You know. Faked. Pretended." To her dismay, Jette burst into tears. "I . . . I did, and it t-turned out t-terrible."

Sympathetically Alexandra moved closer on the blanket and put her arm around Jette's shoulders.

"It was so humiliating . . . he . . . he just sent me home."

Alternately sniffling and blowing her nose on a tissue, Jette told the story of meeting Nico Provenzo. The only thing she left out was that his family was Mafia. She thought it would shock Alexandra too much.

"You mean, you faked it, and he got mad at you?" Alexandra said at last, shaking her head.

"Yeah. Silly, isn't it? I hate it. I mean, why *can't* I? Everyone else does. They must, or otherwise why would he have expected it? And," she concluded miserably, "if I have to fake, it would at least help if I knew what I was faking. I mean, I obviously did it all wrong."

Alexandra's laugh rippled into the blossom-scented air.

Jette couldn't help it; she giggled, too. "Well? Have you got any information?"

Alexandra whispered, "You have to . . . you know. Have a spasm inside you."

"What?"

"Well, when you come, it makes everything contract, and your body goes into these wonderful ripples. So, if you *were* going to fake, you would have to start rippling."

Jette nodded, bemused. "How?"

Alexandra giggled. "You have muscles down there, Jette. You can move them and contract them. Like when you pee."

"Good. OK. I can do that."

"And breathe fast, and kind of moan, too. You lose all control; you make any sounds that come into your head. Making noise makes it easier, Jette; it actually helps make the climax bigger. I think it frees your inhibitions."

"I see," Jette said, although she didn't.

"But the most important piece of advice I have," Alexandra added, "is, don't *think* about it so much. In fact, don't think about it at all."

Later, in the dormitory room, it was like old times—the three of them gossiping, laughing, teasing while they applied their makeup and debated what to wear to dinner.

"What's with Mary Lee?" Jette asked Alexandra when the other girl had disappeared into the bathroom to rebraid her hair. "She seems so depressed. And she's much too thin, God, you can see her ribs and hip bones."

"She *is* depressed. Ever since we came back from Daytona. Her mother sends her these awful letters where she bawls her out, calls her too fat, you name it. Then she telephones and says the same things. Mary Lee just sits there and takes it. She doesn't say a word, just 'Yes, Mommy,' and 'No, Mommy,' and 'I'm sorry, Mommy.' "

"That's terrible!"

"Mary Lee wants Marietta's love so much that she accepts all the verbal abuse," Alexandra added. "How awful to have a mother who wants to hurt you. Mary Lee keeps writing things in her notebook, and she puts it where I won't read it. And she makes a lot of phone calls at the booth in the lobby."

Jette shook her head. "Weird. Maybe tonight we can get her to talk about it, huh? If she can't talk to *us*, who can she talk to?"

But when they returned from dinner, several students drifted to their room. The party lasted until 3:30 A.M., with the young women telling wild stories and finishing several bottles of wine.

The next morning, Jette said good-bye to her friends in the lobby of the dormitory wing, as she waited for the limousine service to take her to the airport.

Mary Lee seemed tense and fidgety. She said to Jette, "If you hear any gossip about my mother, would you write me? Or if you read anything in the paper, no matter how small, send me the clippings. I can't afford a clipping service."

Jette looked at Mary Lee oddly. "Sure. I'll do that. Well, look for me on the tube, guys," she added as she hugged her two friends, then slid into the limousine. She rolled down the smoked-glass window so she could wave.

Alexandra and Mary Lee watched, their arms around each other's shoulders, as the limo picked up speed, taking Jette back to her world.

—— ▶◀ ——

Back in Beverly Hills, Jette plunged into her work, determined to forget Nico, missing orgasms, and the question of her femininity. Bags of mail continued to arrive for her, more each week. Several times she earned herself an approving nod from the director and once, to her delight, patters of applause from the crew for a particularly difficult scene.

Daily, huge bouquets of deep red roses arrived for Darryl on the set, sent by her fiancé, Richard Cox. The actress arranged them in rows on tables in her dressing room, keeping them until the velvety petals drifted off the stems. Theirs was a storybook romance. Rich, handsome man meets beautiful actress. Instant love.

The wedding was scheduled for five days after the season's shoot was completed and the show was in summer hiatus. In a flash of generosity, Darryl had invited everyone from "Canyon Drive"—from cast to gaffers and publicity girls—to attend the wedding, which would be held in the garden of the Bel Air Hotel.

—— ▶◀ ——

The last episode of the series, a crash in a private plane, was being kept under wraps. Not even the cast knew which characters would survive the disaster and reappear next season.

Endlessly the cast speculated about who would be written out of the series. The soap's three main writers became tight-lipped and reserved, scurrying back and forth for story conferences.

"I think *my* character is going to go," Pamela fretted one afternoon while she and Jette were waiting for Wardrobe. "I'm over fifty, the viewers want a younger woman, my fan mail hasn't been nearly as big as Darryl's. They aren't exactly standing in line to cast a woman with crow's-feet and neck wrinkles."

"Balls," said Jette. "They love you, and you know it. And you don't have crow's-feet."

Pam's smile was sad. "Honey, I've not only got crow's-feet, I've got a crow's-beak—well, almost. But to look on the bright side of it, they can't exactly kill off the matriarch of the whole family, so maybe I'm safe for a while."

One morning as Jette was in a stall in the women's room near the sound stage, two women entered the room and began smoking a joint. As they talked, Jette recognized the voices of Linda, the makeup girl who had witnessed her first confrontation with Darryl, and Tillie Milgrom, the makeup girl frequently used on her own show.

"Crazy," Linda was saying to Tillie. "That Darryl Boyer really takes the cake. I heard she's sleeping with Rusty Copa and Ben. *And* her fiancé."

Jette froze, fascinated by the gossip about Rusty Copa, associate producer of "Canyon Drive," and Ben Martigliana, the chief cameraman.

"Yeah, she'd sleep with a snake if it could get her a part," Tillie said lazily.

"She's *got* the part; now she's trying to protect it. I heard her talking with Copa today. She must give damn good head, because he was really listening to her," Linda went on.

"Yeah?"

"Yeah, and from what I heard, I can tell you one thing for sure—the first person to crash and burn is going to be Jette Michaud. She's a nice kid. But, hey, she's going to be snake food for Darryl the Peril."

Finally, the two exited, leaving behind a cloud of smoke thick enough to get high on.

Jette emerged from the stall, overwhelmed with disappointment and hurt. She was going to be written out. Her eyes filled with tears. She'd only been on the show for seven episodes— she'd barely had a chance to begin. How could she be cut now?

She frowned, thinking it through. If Darryl could influence

the producer, then she had to do it, too—only better. How could she get to Rusty Copa?

Then the answer came to her. Nico.

——— ►◄ ———

It was one of Chicago's famous windy days. The Yellow Cab Jette had hired pulled up in front of the Provenzo Plaza Building, an eight-story condo complex located just off Lake Shore Drive.

"Little Sicily, huh?" said the talkative Greek cab driver who had been coming on to Jette for the entire ride.

She fished in her purse for the money.

"Look, you want I should wait? Or I can come back. Whatever you want. Here's my card. Peter Spiro. Call me anytime. *Anytime.*"

"I don't know exactly how long I'll be," she said, adding the business card to the growing collection she was effortlessly building in her wallet.

"Be careful," he called to her as she got out of the cab.

Jette slammed the door and, holding down the hem of her clingy red silk dress, made her way through the wind toward the building entrance.

She pushed her way inside the soaring marble lobby, bringing a gust of air with her.

"Who are you here to see?" asked an armed security man sitting at a marble-topped desk equipped with telephone, computer screen, and closed-circuit TV.

"Nico Provenzo," she told the guard, showing him Nico's business card. "What apartment is he in?"

He inspected it closely. "You expected?"

"Yes," she lied, "it's . . . a business matter."

Maybe he believed her, maybe he didn't. "Name?"

"Ms. Michaud."

"You'll have to wait while I call up."

Jette paced the lobby, her high heels clicking on the polished marble. She felt pleased with herself for getting this far, glad she'd decided not to call before coming. Nico would not turn her away now. If nothing else, he would be curious.

She got out her compact and gave her face a quick inspection, adding just a touch more lip gloss to her full, plummy lips. This wasn't going to be any worse than her screen test, she decided. She'd survived that. She would manage this, too. She'd just talk fast.

———— ►◄ ————

Upstairs, on the sixth floor, seven men were having a meeting, a radio playing in order to foil any federal local law enforcement listening devices homed in on the building.

The Provenzo Group, Inc., was the name on their ivory vellum letterhead. Sam was the chairman of the board. Giovanni "Van" D'Stefano, President of the Italio-American Savings and Loan Co., which the Provenzos controlled, was president.

Patriarch Sam Provenzo looked down the polished oak table. What he saw made him both proud and uneasy.

To his right was Richard Fransworth, né Ricco Fronditti, vice president of the same bank. A graduate of the Wharton School of Business, he was in charge of the family's considerable banking interests. Like D'Stefano, Fronditti was a Provenzo cousin and blood loyal.

Next to Fransworth, Sam's oldest son, Marco, forty-six, leaned back in his chair, tapping the table with his fingers. Marco was in charge of gambling, bookmaking, illegal off-track betting, and floating roulette, craps, and blackjack tables.

Next to him, Joe, forty-four, surreptitiously smoothed back his black, glossy hair. Dapper Joey, the lady-killer of the family, wore tight pants, silk turtleneck, and suede blazer. Joey's area was drugs . . . marijuana and heroin, of course, and also cocaine.

At the end of the table sat Leonardo, at forty almost totally bald, his skin bluish from the heavy beard he had to shave twice daily. Lenny was the best businessman of the bunch and was in charge of the legal enterprises from construction to meat packing to laundries.

And next to Lenny was Nico, the youngest of the grown sons.

Nicolo. At twenty-seven years old, he was the baby of the family and Sam's not-so-secret favorite. They shared the same birthday and the same genes. Nico had been placed in charge of matters relating to motor vehicles—thefts and chop shops. Also his were the money-laundering projects in Los Angeles, Dallas, San Francisco, and Seattle, which needed a subtle business savvy. Nico had wanted more, but Sam hadn't wanted to give him anything too fast, telling him to work and struggle. No son of his was going to have anything just handed to him. Sam didn't want pussies for sons. He wanted men.

As D'Stefano finished summarizing a rosy profit report, he looked around the table. "Any remarks?"

"Just a little matter of cleaning up some more of this money," Lenny began. "We've got to be thinking of better ways—bigger ways. It's difficult to—"

"You get paid to do difficult," Sam growled. He turned to D'Stefano. "Well? Let's get on with it. I ain't got all day to sit here with my finger up my ass. What's next?"

"The 'pross' ring," D'Stefano said, referring to prostitution. "We thought, Nico's been doing good so far, and he's got contacts in L.A. anyway. We want to set up another call-girl operation. Similar to Vegas. Starlets, small-time actresses, former showgirls—$1,000-a-night pussy, the best. Give it to the kid. Let him see what he can do."

Heads all turned to where Nico sat scowling.

"Oh, yippee," he said sarcastically. "Just what I want, the pussy detail. I want into drugs. That's where the real action is."

"You'll take what you get," the banker snapped.

"I get *shit*, that's what I get!" Nico snapped back. "I graduated from fucking Harvard with an MBA; I did everything you asked. Now I want in."

The others shifted uneasily. Nico was too young and inexperienced, even with degrees. But to Sam, family loyalty was absolute. Either you had it, or you were no longer family. You were history. Toast!

D'Stefano looked at Sam, then cleared his throat. "So OK," he summarized. "Nico, you'll start on the call girls. High-grade cooze, remember. Next. This Gordon Seyburn guy, he's thirty days late with his note."

"Well," Lenny began authoritatively. "It's simple enough what to do. We just work out a bump in the interest rate with half the principal due in the next ninety days. We—"

"Bullshit!" Nico banged on the table with his fist. "What are we, a bunch of pussies? Fucking nuns with a fucking calculator? We'll go in there with a hammer and teach the guy some respect. The guy likes Vegas, right? He'll have to play craps from a wheelchair."

"*Bastardo!*" Sam said under his breath. "Stupid kid," he began. "Who do you think you are anyway? Al Capone? We're a business now, not a bunch of thugs."

"We are Mafioso," Nico said softly. "*Siciliano.*"

Everyone at the table stirred. Sam rubbed his right hand across his heavy, gray mustache. His heart hurt for the stubborn reaction of this son. "You listen to too many stories, kid."

"We're pussies!" Nico snapped again.

"Now, hey, wait a minute!" Lenny yelled, jumping to his feet.

"*Bocchinoro!*" Nico screamed, and sprang toward Lenny. Before Lenny could even bring up his hands to protect himself, Nico was on him. Lenny staggered backward, blood spurting from his nose.

The other two brothers pulled Nico off.

"Jesus fucking Christ!" Sam exploded. "What is this, we can't have a meeting without you tearing each other's throats out? Angelo!" Sam's head bodyguard, Angelo, stuck his head cautiously around the edge of the door. "Go the fuck to the kitchen and get some ice, will you?"

Sam turned to the conference table, now in disarray. Lenny was hunched over, cursing and wiping his bloody nose. Nico was being held back by his other two brothers, his body rigid, his eyes blue lasers.

"Let him go."

They all looked at Sam.

"Did you hear what the fuck I said? Let him go." Sam spat on the floor. "Sit down, all of you. We'll go on with this."

Cautiously Joey and Marco released their grip on Nico. He shook them away, his eyes hard, and he stalked out of the room.

After Nico had gone, there was a silence.

"He's crazy," Lenny said, shaking his head angrily. "A temper like a fucking hair trigger. He'll get us all killed one of these days."

Sam growled, "*Basta.*"

"He can't be trusted," Lenny insisted.

"*Basta.* Enough."

———— ►◄ ————

When Nico stepped off the elevator, he looked as if he wanted to kill someone. Jette started up from the couch, her composure disappearing at the sight of him.

"Nico?"

He stopped where he was. He did not smile. "Jette."

"Hi."

His eyes held hers. "What are you doing here?"

"I came to see you. I . . . I just have to talk to you. Just for a minute, sixty little seconds."

"You're not pregnant, are you?"

"No," she flashed. "And if I was, I'd never tell you."

They regarded each other, the fire between them suddenly revived.

"Boy, have I blown it," she forced herself to say lightly. "I've flown all the way to Chicago, and you still hate me."

"I don't hate you."

"Oh? Well, why don't you take me out to lunch? Because there's something I have to talk to you about, and believe me, it's *not* a baby."

He hesitated. Then something in his eyes stilled, like waves calming. He even smiled. "All right," he agreed.

He took her to a restaurant called Spiaggia, on North Michigan Avenue, and insisted on ordering for her—risotto with eggplant, tomato, and mozzarella, and grilled sirloin fragrant with rosemary, pepper, olive oil, and lemon. Dessert was a plate of strawberries surrounded by warm, broiler-browned zabaglione.

During the meal, they talked lightly of Los Angeles restaurants that Nico knew and Alexandra's song "Easy Woman," now in the number 2 spot and pushing for number 1. "I love music," Nico said. "It's pure; there's no contamination. You can get away from yourself and into something better. I listen to Gregorian chants when I really get tight."

Jette was just about to mention Rusty Copa when the waiter brought the check and Nico put a large bill in the plastic tray. He pushed back his chair.

"Come. We'll go for a ride," he said. "I've got a Lamborghini I keep in the garage under the condo building—it's fantastic."

"A ride? But Nico, I just was going to tell you—"

"Later," he promised.

He took her on a wild ride along Chicago's freeways, north toward Morton Grove.

Eighty miles per hour.

Then ninety.

Then ninety-five.

Jette gasped, frightened and exhilarated, as Nico darted around cars and trucks. He was an arrogant driver, tailgating cars that blocked him, forcing them out of the lane. He drove as if he were in a trance, a half-smile on his lips, utterly relaxed.

A traffic jam lay ahead, and Nico cursed and put his foot on the brake. They slowed just in time to avoid rear-ending a Mercury Cougar.

Jette seized the opportunity.

"The reason I came here . . . I have a problem with 'Canyon Drive,' " she began. "They're having a plane crash in the last episode and are going to use it to cut two or three characters. I'm going to be one of them. Darryl Boyer wants me out because she's jealous, and Rusty Copa will do anything she wants."

He glanced at her. "Copa?"

"You know him, don't you? I saw you talking to him. Please," Jette said, touching Nico's arm. "He's . . . it isn't fair. He'll do anything she says because he's sleeping with her."

He turned and looked at her. "And who are you sleeping with?"

"No one! I—I really love this part. Can you do anything for me? Just one phone call," she suggested hopefully.

"And you think Rusty Copa would listen to me."

"I *know* he would. You're powerful, aren't you?"

He smiled.

"People listen to you, don't they? They respect you," she went on, responding to the way he was nodding at each flattering thing she said. "If you could just make sure I stay on the show, I'd never forget it, Nico. I swear."

His blue eyes burned. "OK. A favor. Yeah, I can do it."

"Will you? Oh, God! Thank you!" She clapped her hands together in delight.

"For you I'll do two favors," he added softly.

When Jette stepped inside Nico's eighth-floor condominium, she couldn't help gasping. She'd been expecting something like the downstairs lobby, all pillars and mirrors.

Instead, Nico had decorated his apartment in stark blacks and whites. The carpet, white. The walls, black. A huge coffee table made of black onyx. A big, curved couch of white, soft leather.

And along one wall, in several floor-to-ceiling ebony cases, was Nico's collection of guns. A regular arsenal, Jette thought.

She stood fidgeting while Nico turned on a stereo. The room filled with the liquid trumpet of Wynton Marsalis.

Nico stood in front of her and slid his arms around her, his touch surprisingly gentle. Then, his hands clasping her waist, he picked her up and set her down on an ebony buffet. He unbuttoned her dress and slid it up over her head. It dropped to the floor, a vivid scrap of red. Her bikini panties followed. She wore no bra.

Then Nico separated her legs and moved closer, standing between her thighs to embrace her.

His tongue probed her mouth with slick, moist urgency, darting in and out, hinting at other possibilities. Jette clung to him as her flesh came exquisitely alive.

When she was weak with kisses, Nico finally pulled back. "You must give up your body to me," he said.

"What?"

"Completely. Not just partly. And no lying this time." Lightly he ran his hands down her sides to her hips, then slid them inward along her crease to the soft, springy fluff of her pubic mound. "I will teach you, little girl . . . if you really want to learn. Do you?"

"Oh, yes," she sighed.

He lifted her down from the buffet. "First let's go in the hot tub," he said. "You are still too tense; I can feel by touching you. The warm water will make you feel very relaxed, very sexual. Go now," he added, patting her rump. "Down the hall and to your right. I'll fix us drinks and bring them in."

She started to obey.

"And, Jette?"

"Yes?"

"When you are in the warm water . . . touch yourself. Enjoy your own body. It is very beautiful, you know."

Nico walked into the condo's large kitchen. Although well equipped, the room was seldom used for cooking anything more elaborate than the occasional pasta dish that Nico prepared for himself.

Jette Michaud, so beautiful, so bright and alive. She could be addictive—if he let her.

He poured vermouth and Bombay gin into glasses, over cubes of ice, then added a dash of bitters. Doubles. He'd accept Jette as a challenge. He'd make her come, all right—give her much more than she bargained for. He would make her beg for mercy.

Lifting up one of the martini glasses to take a swallow before he carried them into the bathroom, Nico was struck by a familiar unease. It was partly a physical sensation, partly mental, consisting of ripples of colored light that seemed to fade in and out, flickering across his eyes.

He fought it back with fierce intensity, digging his fingers into his temples until it went away. He trembled with the effort.

—— ►◄ ——

He had first experienced the aura twelve years ago, alone in the back room of the party store where, at fifteen, he'd been working as a numbers runner. He'd woken up to find himself lying on the floor, cases of soda and beer all around him. He had cut his temple on the corner of a wooden beer case, a semicircular cut full of blood. He couldn't even move for at least ten minutes, but just lay on the floor, shocked, disoriented, helpless.

One afternoon about three months later, he saw the intense colored ripples and then woke up to discover himself sprawled on the floor of the upstairs hall in his father's Oak Park mansion. Elena, the Armenian cleaning woman, was bent over him, slapping his cheeks and calling out his name.

Nico was flooded with such panic and revulsion that he had to turn aside his head to vomit. If his brothers ever learned of this . . . the prospect was unthinkable. In the Provenzo family, there was nothing more offensive than weakness.

"Mist' Neek!" The maid shook him hard. "You OK? You want me to call docta? Call your fatha?"

She could not have said a worse thing.

Groggily, Nico staggered to his feet. He grabbed her arm, pulling the woman downstairs with him and out to her old car. Shoving her inside, he pinned her against the seat back, his hands locked around her throat.

"If you ever come back to work for my father again, I'll kill you," he hissed.

"Please— Please—" The woman struggled weakly.

"I'll slit your throat. Do you hear? Leave now, and never come back. Never. You hear?"

She must have read correctly the ferocity in his face, because she never showed up for work again, so Nico did not have to kill her. He did kill Rosy Bennuchi, one of his father's *capos*, five years later, when Bennuchi witnessed one of Nico's blackouts. When the body was found, the killing was blamed on a rival family.

After that incident, Nico swallowed his pride and found

himself a doctor. This doctor told him that what he had was a form of epilepsy, controllable by doses of Dilantin.

Epilepsy. To the Provenzos it meant shame and dishonor.

Nico filled the prescription. The seizures went away . . . almost.

"I don't want you driving until we get this regulated," the doctor told him. "You might not be able to have a driver's license until we can control your seizures. Come in next week, and we'll see."

No driver's license? How would he explain that?

Nico did not go in the following week. Instead, he fire-bombed the doctor's office, destroying all his records. He upped his dosage to two pills a day, and when the Dilantin ran out, he broke into a pharmacy and stole more, enough to last him three or four years. Medicating himself, he had kept the seizures mostly under control since then, but always he was watchful.

Damn, he thought now. He would have to add one more pill each day. He remembered Jette, waiting for him in the hot tub. She was lucky she hadn't seen him seize.

He never allowed any woman to see that shameful part of him. Not *anyone*.

— ◄► —

Jette leaned back. Water bubbled all around her, making her feel intensely sexy and relaxed. One of the jets was directly behind her, a bubbling, erotic force. She wiggled close to it, enjoying the roiling, concentrated current.

She let her fingers slide between her legs. But she didn't want to touch herself. She wanted him to.

There was a sound in the doorway. Jette looked up to see Nico enter the bathroom, two martini glasses balanced on a small tray.

"I've been waiting *soooo* long," she cooed.

"Phone call," he said brusquely.

He wore only black string-bikini briefs. As he slipped off his black briefs, his penis, embellished with blue veins, hardened and distended. Jette eyed him in greedy pleasure. As he stepped forward, she reached for him with both hands.

"Make me happy," he said, sitting down on the edge of the tub. Swimming up in front of him, she took him in her mouth.

"Yes," sighed Nico, relaxing and giving himself up to her tongue. "Yes. Oh. Yes."

An hour later, Jette lay sprawled on her back on the carpet, her legs arched wide apart so that Nico could drink of her hot, sweet flesh. She was so close. Ecstasy was within one tiny millimeter of her grasp.

Moaning, she writhed her hips up and down, fighting to hold on to the sensation.

"Let go," Nico whispered, lifting his head. "Just let it happen."

"I . . . I'm trying . . ."

"Don't try. Push into me. Push your hips up and down. Fuck my face. Yes . . . yes . . . I want more of that sweet little tight cunt."

Both of their bodies were bathed in sweat, sweet-smelling and wonderfully sexy. Finally, all the fibers of Jette's body began to convulse, then explode. She gasped, her hands clawing the floor, caught in something uncontrollable.

Nico reached for a vial, snapped it in two, and thrust it under her nose.

The effect was instantaneous. Jette's orgasm leaped into another dimension, explosive, powerful. She became a rocket shot into space, flaring tongues of fire a galaxy long.

Her heart hammered frighteningly fast. She heard a high sound and realized it was her own scream of ecstasy.

As the magnificent orgasm went on and on, so did her scream. Her voice filled the bathroom. Nico said something. She didn't hear.

She flamed beyond his reach, incandescent.

8
Mary Lee
1980–1982

Maui, in early summer, was spectacular. Its colors, from Pacific blue to palm green and all the hot pinks and salmons of the bougainvillea that rioted everywhere, were intense. In front of Marietta's beach house grew small yellow bananas, along with avocados, hibiscus, passion fruit, and jackfruit. A papaya tree always held at least three fat orange-yellow fruits, ready to pick.

But Mary Lee was bored. Totally, colossally, unmitigatedly bored.

The village of Hana was exactly that—a village. Situated at the eastern end of the island, its population was less than two thousand. Mature movie stars and wealthy Japanese had homes here. Not much action for young people.

She filled the time with walks on the beach and frequently snorkeled at a small, hidden cove perfect for viewing the brilliant colors of fish amid volcanic rocks and coral. She read every book in Marietta's extensive library of bestsellers and begged permission to type on Marietta's new Digital computer—a state-of-the-art machine.

"I'm so bored. I want to try writing a magazine article," Mary Lee pleaded.

Marietta Wilde, at forty-six, was sinewy and fiery. Born Mariquita Guajardo into poverty in Mexico City, she fought her way out of the barrio and entered the United States as an illegal alien. At age twenty-seven she enrolled at UCLA and changed her name. She spent the next year searching for someone to marry her so she could get her green card. An unplanned pregnancy—Mary Lee—temporarily stopped her search.

Three weeks after the baby's birth, Marietta visited a butcher shop to purchase some hamburger. The forty-five-year-old owner took one look at her, and a month later they were married. Once she had her citizenship papers, Marietta filed for divorce and tried to get the meat cutter to assume legal custody of Mary Lee. He refused.

Since that time, Marietta had written six bestsellers and had become a regular on the network talk shows. Her flamboyant quarrels and lawsuits had been exhaustively covered by the tabloids. She was recognized and given best tables by the maître d' of every important restaurant in the country. And, as she was the first to point out, that made her a *real* celebrity.

"You? Write a real article?" Marietta now scoffed.

"Why not? I can write. I'm on the Vassar paper."

"Oh, that. A *college* paper. That's not real writing."

"It isn't?"

"In the first place, no good writing ever gets done by a person under twenty-five. Nobody in your generation can even spell their way out of a paper bag. As for my word processor, I can't possibly risk you damaging it. I have to get parts for repairs all the way from Honolulu."

"But I won't damage anything. I know how to type, Marietta."

"By the way, aren't you putting on weight?" said Marietta sharply, changing the subject.

"Putting on weight?" Mary Lee gulped.

"You jiggle, dear. Your hips. And your inner thighs, you seem to have very little muscle tone at all. Don't you ever exercise?"

Mary Lee hung her head, demoralized as always by her mother's pronouncements.

"Oh, and one more thing," her mother added. "I forgot to tell you, Tomas and I are taking one of those puddle jumpers over to Honolulu to soak up some nightlife. You'll be all right, won't you? I'd bring you along, but you would be a fifth wheel, Muggy. You do understand."

"Sure," she said.

"We'll be gone a couple of nights. Maybe three or four. Tomas is such a wonderful dancer. Maybe it's all that sparring and footwork he does." Marietta purred. "We're leaving at two," she added.

"Two? Today at two?" Mary Lee blinked. It was already one-thirty.

As soon as Marietta and Tomas roared off in his white Bugatti, Mary Lee went back into the big beach house, which her mother had bought with her royalties from *Love Pirates*.

Restlessly Mary Lee wandered about. The famous novelist's bedroom, lit by blasts of Maui sunlight, looked like an explosion in a boutique. Clothes hung from chairs or reposed in circles on the floor where they had been flung. Used tissues littered the floor around the wastebasket, and there were two packages of condoms and a half-used tube of K-Y lubricant lying on a dresser top.

Also on the dresser was a pink coral bracelet purchased on the island, and Mary Lee picked it up and tried it on. Too pink, she decided. There were matching earrings, too small and dainty to look good on her larger-boned frame. She tested them anyway.

She put down the earrings, and that was when she saw the small gold key. It lay right on the bureau top, as if her mother had forgotten to put it away.

Mary Lee picked up the key, suddenly intensely curious.

She continued to prowl the room, but now she had a purpose. In only five minutes, she found the filing cabinet that had been installed at the very back of her mother's walk-in closet. Mary Lee pushed aside the folds of satin, spandex, and chiffon. She inserted the key in the lock, and the top drawer glided open.

The drawer was stuffed with sacks of manila envelopes, labeled in her mother's handwriting. Some were many years old, judging from their faded, dog-eared condition. Mary Lee picked up the nearest one and read the label.

Darius K.

Darius Kenneally, author of the bestselling *Darius Diet* series, had, ten years earlier, been Marietta's fiancé. The relationship had ended badly when Marietta successfully sued him.

Mary Lee opened the envelope, seeing to her surprise that it contained legal papers, letters from attorneys, and a number of other letters, closely written in a man's handwriting. Some professed love; others were rife with four-letter words and accusations.

She shuffled through the other envelopes. Some were thin; others were so stuffed with papers they had to be secured with rubber bands. The names on them belonged to Marietta's discarded friends, former lovers, hated sister, divorce attorney (with whom she had had a brief affair), and various lovers, as well as from other writers and even Marietta's editor and agent. A relatively fresh envelope had been started for Tomas Puentes.

Her mother's whole life was contained in this file cabinet. Feverishly Mary Lee pulled open the bottom drawer and discovered piles of notebooks and loose snapshots, some apparently taken in the barrio. There were a few polaroids showing Marietta posing nude. No wonder her mother had hidden the file cabinet behind her clothes!

It's fate, Mary Lee thought wildly. She backed out of the closet, moving almost in a drunken stupor, and had to lie down on the big, satin-covered bed until the dizziness ebbed.

Suddenly memories began to gush through her brain, like a faucet turned on full blast.

The morning when she was eight and had gotten her new dress soaking wet in the rain. Marietta made her crawl inside the clothes dryer, threatening to turn it on and tumble Mary Lee dry.

The party Marietta took her to, one summer when she was ten. An Arab prince kept admiring Mary Lee's coppery-gold hair. Marietta, who had been drinking wine all afternoon, laughed loudly and offered to sell her daughter to the Arab for $50,000.

Mary Lee put both hands over her eyes and writhed on the bed, fighting the panic. She could write well enough to do the job—but did she have the guts? She would have to.

Mary Lee went back into the closet and knelt down in front of the file cabinet, taking out the envelopes one at a time and piling them in a neat stack.

Three or four days would be plenty of time to make copies of everything.

— ◄► —

Rushing into the dormitory, Alexandra stopped to get her mail, noting that there was a letter from Jette. She tore it open as she walked.

Finally had the big "O," Jette wrote. *God, I thought I was in the middle of an explosion of the galaxy. I'll explain sometime. I think I have sold my soul to the devil . . . and I love it, love it. He got me back my part on "Canyon Drive," too.... Some kind of magic, huh? Oh, yes, his name is Nico Provenzo. I adore him! He's so ...*

Jette went on for several more paragraphs, describing the wonders of her latest lover, who, Alexandra realized, was the same man who had dumped Jette when she couldn't produce an orgasm on demand. She put the letter inside her purse, troubled. Why would Jette put up with a man like that?

Alexandra sat down on her bed. The past months, since "Easy Woman" had earned a gold record, had been frantic. Success was great, but the people at Arista Records hadn't been as happy with her second, third, and fourth efforts, their verdict being "good but not great."

Could she measure up again, she wondered, or had she only gotten lucky? It seemed the harder she tried, the more her goal eluded her.

Mary Lee was another worry. Always studying, or hunched over her typewriter, pounding out something she would not let Alexandra read.

Suddenly Alexandra heard a retching noise from the bathroom. She got up and tapped on the door. "Everything OK?" she called.

"Just lovely," came the sound of Mary Lee's muffled voice.

"You sure?"

"I'm OK, I tell you!"

A few minutes later, Mary Lee emerged from the bathroom, white and shaking. Clad only in a bra and French-cut panties, she was shockingly bony. "It's probably a bug of some kind; it's going around." Mary Lee's eyes did not meet Alexandra's. "I think I'll just lie down on the bed."

"Mary Lee," Alexandra said, alarmed, "I don't think it's the flu. You were making yourself heave, weren't you?"

"I wasn't."

"You were; I know you were. Oh, God, Mary Lee, how can you do that to yourself?"

"I'm too fat."

Alexandra stared. "Mary Lee, have you looked at yourself in a mirror lately? All your ribs show. Your hipbones, too."

"I still weigh about ten pounds too much," Mary Lee insisted. "Look at my stomach. It sticks out."

"What stomach? Mary Lee ... God ... Where did you get the idea you were too fat?" Then Alexandra stopped, sucking in her breath. Of course, she thought. The Royal Bitch strikes again. "Mary Lee, listen to me. You're very attractive. Very striking." She started toward the phone. "I think you have anorexia. I'm going to call a doctor."

"No!" Mary Lee's eyes were wide with desperation. "Please. I'll eat, I promise. I just don't want to go to a doctor. *He'll call her.*"

Alexandra sank into a chair, frustrated. "I'm your friend, Mary Lee. You can talk to me, whatever it is."

"I'm writing a book," Mary Lee blurted.

"You mean a novel like the ones your mother writes?"

"Not a novel. A biography. An unauthorized biography."

"Of who?"

Mary Lee paused, her eyes showing fear and determination. "My mother," she said.

"Your mother!"

"I've been working on it for months now. I'm interviewing a lot of people—she's got tons of old enemies. And I have some other fantastic material, too. I'm calling the book *Cobra Lady.*"

Alexandra gaped at her roommate. "But, why?" She shook her head. "Oh, God, please, Mary Lee, don't do it. It's crazy. It's your revenge, but you'll only get in terrible trouble."

"I don't care!" Mary Lee cried. "And it isn't revenge. It's . . . I can't explain it. Anyway, people want to know everything about her. I know her better than anyone else."

"But as her daughter, not as her biographer. Mary Lee, you're playing with fire," Alexandra insisted. "You *know* how she'll react—she'll pulverize you!"

"She already has, Alexandra. I'm going to put everything down in print, and don't you dare try to stop me. This is more important to me than anything—I'll even drop out of Vassar if I have to."

"Don't do that."

"I will. I'll do anything. Just let me write, and don't ask me any more questions."

An hour later, as soon as Alexandra left for a class, Mary Lee unlocked the top drawer of her desk and took out the manuscript of *Cobra Lady.* She hefted the stack of paper, amazed at how heavy it felt already. There were seven hundred typed pages, and she still had four chapters to go.

She sat down at her typewriter, rolled in a sheet of fresh paper, and stared at it for only a few seconds before she began to type.

In 1972 Marietta's relationship with Darius Kenneally took an ugly turn, when . . .

— ►◄ —

That summer was hot, humid, and endless. Mary Lee stayed in Poughkeepsie working as a fill-in reporter on the *Poughkeepsie Journal*. For almost no pay, she wrote everything from birth announcements to obituaries. Her big story of the summer was a piece about a climbing accident in the nearby Catskills in which a local teenager had died. Mary Lee wrote it so vividly that the copy editor, a hard-boiled journalist who crabbed at her mercilessly about her spelling, actually complimented her.

"Not too shabby," he remarked. "In fact, we could enter it in the Press Association contest, except you've got to be working here to be eligible, and you're going back to snotty Vassar, so you won't be."

Mary Lee only smiled. Little did he know that by this time next year she would be a bestselling author. No one knew anything about that except for Alexandra and the literary agent to whom she had sent the manuscript.

She had racked her brain trying to decide which agent to use. Finally she remembered a man her mother had criticized several times, calling him a publishing rogue who thought he could break all the rules and get away with it. Her words sounded like a good recommendation to Mary Lee, so she sent a letter to Robert "Bobby" Leonard, who had immediately asked to see the manuscript.

That had been several weeks ago. She hadn't heard from him. Had her book gotten lost in the mail? She fantasized a hundred terrible things happening to her precious 850-page manuscript, including an explosion on the plane that airfreighted it. She didn't have a good copy, just her first draft covered with scribblings. If the Fates would only get her pages to New York, she'd never again be so dumb as not to make a copy.

That Monday, returning to the apartment she had taken in Poughkeepsie, Mary Lee found a typed postcard in her mailbox. It said, "This is to acknowledge receipt of your manuscript. It will be read in as timely a manner as possible. Thank you." The card was signed Robert Leonard.

As she stood in the hallway by the row of metal mailboxes, she felt relief, then the realization that Leonard's postcard was the standard acknowledgment. That must mean her manuscript was going to be treated routinely, exactly as everyone else's was treated. Didn't he realize what fantastic material she'd included? She used excerpts from the letters, and from Marietta's diary.

Climbing the stairs to her little apartment, she heard the telephone ring. She fumbled with the key, trying to open the door and get in before the ringing stopped.

She rushed inside just in time to catch the phone on the seventh ring. "Hello?"

"Am I speaking to Mary Lee Wilde?" asked an unfamiliar voice.

She nearly fainted. "Yes? Yes . . ."

"This is Bobby Leonard. I stayed up all night reading your manuscript, and I must say I'm very excited. In fact, I've already made a phone call to Annie Wilkins at Crown, and she's extremely interested."

This wasn't real. This was a joke. Someone had paid him to call her and say this.

"She is?"

"That is, she's interested if you're really Marietta Wilde's daughter and if you're willing to do some publicity for the book. Are you willing to do publicity? A tour? Radio, TV, all that?"

Mary Lee hung onto the phone, suddenly galvanized by terror. All along, she'd known this would happen. Now it was a reality.

"Well?" the agent demanded.

"I . . . I can do publicity. Yes," Mary Lee whispered. "And I *am* Marietta's daughter. Didn't you see the pictures I sent with the manuscript?"

"Can you come to New York next Thursday? I'll set aside the entire day to talk to you, and we'll discuss the manuscript page by page. Then we'll sign you up . . ."

—— ◄► ——

The skyline of Manhattan loomed in front of her, cement canyons, towers, and spires rising out of an East River mist. To Mary Lee, it looked positively frightening.

She was in the backseat of a New York taxi, being jounced

from side to side as a surly driver swerved through the heavy morning traffic.

My God, the book wasn't a fantasy anymore.

When the cab pulled up at the agent's office on lower Fifth Avenue, she thrust a bill into the driver's hand and fled into the building.

In the tiny lobby, Mary Lee stood gasping for breath, her heart slamming in the throes of a panic attack. She should never have written the book! Alexandra was right; this would be disastrous. Her mother would annihilate her. This was all a terrible, terrible mistake.

She could feel the grapefruit half she had eaten for breakfast begin to splash up into her esophagus. Maybe she should just leave, just skip her appointment with Leonard and forget the whole thing.

"Honey, are you all right?" asked a heavy-set woman who had joined her at the elevator. The woman had a dignified bearing and skin the color of strong coffee, and she carried a small paper bag.

Mary Lee jumped. But the woman's eyes were kind. She blurted, "I . . . I . . . I'm going to see Mr. Leonard."

"Now, you don't have to be terrified," the woman assured her. "Just picture him wearing nothing but a pair of suspender socks. Socks with holes in them. Big holes, with the toes poking out."

Mary Lee couldn't help giggling.

"Always imagine 'em naked. Works wonders," the woman added. "I'm Rachel, Mr. Leonard's receptionist. I was on my break. Come on upstairs, honey, and I'll get you a cup of coffee. Some of this cheese Danish wouldn't hurt either. You are the *skinniest* thing."

Ten minutes later, half a Danish and a cup of coffee had helped alleviate Mary Lee's panic attack. By the time she was ushered into the agent's office, she felt only nervous.

"Well, hello there, Miss New York Times Bestseller," drawled the "rogue" literary agent, looking up from a desk piled so high with letters, manuscripts, contracts, and papers of all kinds that its surface was totally lost to view.

"Hello," she managed.

He eyed her sharply. "Come in and find a seat, will you? This place only looks disorganized. Actually I'm a stickler for detail, and I know where every single thing is. And if you believe that, you might want to make a little purchase of the Brooklyn Bridge. Only fifty dollars; for you I'll sell it cheap."

Mary Lee felt the tension evaporate out of her body. Bobby Leonard wasn't how she imagined a literary agent at all. He looked more like a sportscaster or football coach. He was in his middle fifties and tall, his dark hair was liberally sprinkled with gray, and he had the rangy build of a former athlete. His gestures and voice were those of the happy, expansive extrovert. He wore jeans and a tweedy sports jacket.

"Sit down," he instructed again. "Oops, all the chairs are covered. Here, I'll move something."

The piles he moved appeared to be book manuscripts labeled with the names of Robert Ludlum, John D. MacDonald, and others just as well known. Mary Lee caught her breath, shocked at her proximity to top authors.

She sat down, gazing around the agent's office, which wasn't what she had anticipated, either. Although luxuriously carpeted and furnished with a goodly collection of celebrity photos and other memorabilia, it was far smaller than she had expected.

"So," Leonard began. "You are the author of that wonderful and wicked book, *Cobra Lady*."

"Yes . . ."

"You did write it yourself?"

"Oh, yes!"

"No help from anyone?"

"None." Mary Lee sucked in her lower lip, then responded, "I know I'm young; I know it's not that believable I could have written a book like that, but I did. I've been writing for the Vassar *Miscellany News* for two years, and right now I'm employed at the *Poughkeepsie Journal*. I can write. I've always been able to. It's my one talent, and I promise you, if you help me get my book published, I'll write lots of books—dozens."

"Dozens? Well, good, that's what I like to hear. I love prolific writers." Leonard's smile was warm. "OK, Mary Lee. I'm going to tell you your strengths and your weaknesses. You have a way with words that's almost like Leon Uris. You make things come alive. And there's a . . . a sharpness to your work, a delicate touch that really goes for the gut. Dynamite, kiddo, in the right hands, which are mine."

"Oh . . ." She was stunned by his words.

"Of course, there are a few weaknesses in the book, too,"

the agent went on. "That's why I wanted you to come to New York. Organization, Mary Lee. The manuscript's a little weak in that area. You jump around too much; you jerk the reader around, pulling her from place to place, year to year. It gets confusing. Your first chapter is much too long; it drags, and a few of the other chapters need to be cut, too. In fact, the book needs cutting by at least twenty thousand words."

"Twenty thousand words?"

"Minimum. Get rid of the deadwood and flab," the agent said. "But it won't be as bad as it sounds. We'll do some word-by-word cutting, some sentences and paragraphs, and in one case, a whole chapter. Don't look so horrified," he added. "Every author has to do revisions. Didn't you know that? When we get done, this book is going to be lean and mean."

She stared at him, appalled. How could he tell her he liked it and then tear it apart like that, saying her book had deadwood and flab? She'd worked so hard on every word, every sentence. And to cut twenty thousand words was impossible. It would rip out the very heart of her book.

Almost in tears, she rose. She had to get out of here. She'd hail a cab—back to La Guardia—

Apparently Leonard had not noticed her panic or her preparations to flee. "Damn," he said, rooting around the clutter on his desktop. "Where's a blue pencil when you need it?"

Mary Lee hesitated.

"Come on," he said impatiently. "I'll show you what I'm talking about."

"But—I thought an editor did things like that—"

"Lady, the most beautiful diamond in the world can't shine if it's never been cut and polished. And in this case, if it doesn't shine, it isn't going to sell."

She had no choice—she couldn't run away. Leonard would not let her. He was a brilliant editor, explaining everything he did so clearly that after an hour or so she forgot her hurt and became fascinated. She began to see how she had padded many anecdotes with useless beginnings and used weak modifiers that served no purpose.

"Cut! Cut! Cut!" Leonard exclaimed happily, crossing out a whole page with one stroke of the pencil. "This is fantastic; we're making marvelous progress here. Clean. Streamlined. Taut. Tight. The critics are gonna love *you*, little lady, because your diamonds are going to glitter."

By six-thirty they were both exhausted, and Leonard took her next door to a small bar, ordering her a double Bloody Mary without asking what she wanted.

"Now, don't go home and get in a tizzy about this," the agent said. "Just go through one page at a time, and make all the changes I told you, then send it back to me in four weeks. I want to have a book auction for you. I think we could do very well. Crown wants to make a floor bid . . . they're just waiting to see the finished manuscript so they can decide how much to offer."

She sipped the large, spicy drink. She hadn't eaten much lunch, and now her muscles felt very loose, and her head was spinning.

As Leonard explained the procedure for the literary auction, Mary Lee noticed a man who kept eyeing her. Seated at an adjacent table, he was nearly thirty, stocky and blond, with wire-rimmed glasses and a rumpled, intense look she found very appealing. He looked like a programmer, maybe. Their eyes met, and to her shock, the man winked.

She blushed bright red, clutched her drink, and looked down at the table.

"—so an auction can get very tense," Leonard was saying. "But if we have a lot of bidders, as you can see, the price can easily go up into six figures. In fact, I did one last week that went into seven."

She began paying attention again. "You mean . . . a million dollars?"

Leonard shrugged. "For this book, it'll be a lot less. I can't make *any* promises. But I'll tell you this. I'm a tiger when it comes to money, and that's probably why half the editors in the Big Apple hate my guts."

In a few minutes the agent excused himself, saying he had to go back up to his office to make "California phone calls." Mary Lee lingered in the bar with another Bloody Mary, too excited to leave.

A wave of euphoria engulfed her. She had a month until school started again. She'd quit her job at the *Journal* and work full-time on the revisions of *Cobra Lady*.

"I love that braid of yours," a voice murmured at her elbow. "So unusual."

She jumped and turned to see the blond man, his eyes glowing with unmistakable, lustful interest.

A bar pickup. She and her friends agreed that such ploys were very tacky. Ordinarily she would have stammered out some reply, then fled to the ladies' room to avoid him.

But today she felt too potent.

"Why, thank you," she responded, playing the role of a sophisticated woman. She smiled at him, remembering that Marietta smiled a great deal when she was being very charming.

"Can I join you? Are you a model?" He sank into the chair vacated by Leonard and leaned his elbows on the table, looking into Mary Lee's eyes. "You have that model look. I can always tell."

After twenty minutes and another Bloody Mary, she knew. Oh, yes, he wanted to go to bed with her. The first man who ever had. She should sell a book every day, it made her feel so sexy. Boldly she held his gaze, moistening her lips with her tongue.

She realized he had taken her hand. His palm was warm, his fingers very strong.

"Where do you live?" he asked urgently.

"I don't live in New York; I'm staying overnight at a hotel, the—"

"We'll go there," he said, pulling her to her feet and dropping a bill on the table to pay for her drink.

In the cab, wedged close to the blond man (he never did tell her his name), Mary Lee felt a momentary flash of panic. But he began kissing her hungrily, his tongue darting into her mouth, tasting of the beer he had been drinking. And of himself. She had never tasted a man's mouth before. It was absolutely incredible.

They stopped kissing briefly, grinning at each other. She was beyond thinking.

While the cab driver impassively drove, she allowed herself to be wrapped in a pounding, pulsating embrace that was more like a battle than a hug. Between kisses, they nuzzled and stroked, patted and inserted hands into each other's clothing, grinding their pelvises together. They groaned aloud with their need.

Then they were out of the cab, running into the hotel lobby, holding onto each other, laughing. Several people stared at them as they skidded past, hurrying straight to the elevator bank. On the way up to her room on the thirty-sixth floor, he pushed her against the wall of the elevator and, shoving up her skirt, pulled her panties down.

"I want to fuck your hot pussy now," he groaned. "Oh, God, spread your legs."

She clung to him, panting, feeling as if she had stepped on a roller coaster and could not get off.

"Bend," he panted. "Bend your knees. Yeah."

She did as she was told, tipping her pelvis to give him better access. She didn't know what the hell she was doing but was beyond caring. She just kept thrusting at him.

Before long Mary Lee felt a sudden movement, heard his fevered groan, and felt a hot, thick liquid spurt all over her naked thighs. Dimly Mary Lee knew she was very, very smashed. She realized that she didn't even know this man's name, that she'd never see him again. They could be caught in this elevator, and she would hate herself tomorrow.

It didn't seem to matter. Tomorrow was too far away to be important.

He was kneeling, his tongue licking at her pussy, so greedy for her that he took her entire labia in his mouth, sucking her into his warmth. She moaned, the sound shuddering into a soft scream. He took her by the hips and pulled her down to the elevator floor, pushing her knees apart.

With the last of her strength and sanity, she reached out to push the stop button, bringing the elevator to a halt between floors.

When he entered her for the second time, she screamed again. It was good, so good. She didn't care if they even got caught; this was the most incredibly exciting and dangerous thing she had ever done. Even better than selling a book.

—— ►◄ ——

Five weeks later, Mary Lee sold her book to Crown for a $280,000 advance against royalties. Bobby Leonard said the price was fantastic for a first book.

The day she received the check for her first payment—one-third of the advance—Mary Lee went into Poughkeepsie and opened a money-market account. Then she went to a used-car lot and bought herself a 1980 Camaro, a sporty, low-slung car with only ten thousand miles on its odometer.

On the day she picked up the car, she went into downtown Poughkeepsie and found a bar near the *Journal*, the hangout of reporters and a few ad men. She ordered her favorite, a Bloody Mary.

"Hey, there, little stranger." It was Howard Boykin, her former copy editor at the *Journal*. He slid into her booth.

Boykin, at thirty-two, was already hard-bitten and world-weary. He was short, mustached, and balding, and he could be cruelly acerbic when criticizing reporters' writing.

"What's doing?" he asked her casually. "Anything happening with that book you were working on?"

"Yes . . ."

"Really? Don't tell me you sold the sucker. That'd be too much."

"I did, actually." She found herself telling Boykin about the book and how excited her publisher was with the manuscript.

Boykin clapped his hand to his head, laughing aloud. "I can't believe it—! You really did sell it. Jesus Christ, and I got you started. What are you going to do now? Finish up at Vassar? Get a job? With the book sold, I bet you could go to New York and get a real job. In fact, I know a woman at the *New York Daily News*. Give her a call. Tell her I sent you. Give her clips from the *Journal*, especially that mountain-climbing story, and copy a couple chapters from your book. She'll be interested, all right. Shit," he said plaintively. "They're getting younger and younger, aren't they?"

Mary Lee was so startled at Boykin's suggestion that she nearly choked on her drink. Boykin was already on his fifth beer, and as they talked, he kept leaning closer to her, his hand brushing against her arm.

With a shock, Mary Lee realized that he was coming on to her. Nervously, she began edging away from him. She remembered that wild night in New York—but she wasn't that kind of person, not really, and this was Howard Boykin, someone she knew.

"Excuse me," she sputtered, getting to her feet.

"Hey! Where you going?"

But she was already on her way to the parking lot.

She drove aimlessly, savoring the feel of the Camaro. A Holiday Inn loomed to her right, and something made her pull the Camaro into its parking lot. It was now dusk, and she hadn't had any dinner. She felt pangs of hunger and dizziness. A salad, that's what she'd have. And maybe another Bloody Mary.

In the bar, several solitary business travelers hunched over their drinks.

"Hi," one of them said to her. "You stuck here in the armpit of the Western world, too? Oops, you don't live here, do you?"

"No, I don't live here." Mary Lee sipped her drink, suddenly feeling very, very relaxed. The familiar, heady cloud of delirium had begun to overtake her again. She'd received a check last week that was more than this guy would see in five or six years.

As with the other man, this excited her, making her feel powerful. He couldn't possibly turn her down.

"You're very pretty," he told her, smiling back. "Your hair . . . I bet you look gorgeous when you comb out that braid. I bet you look *real* gorgeous. I'll bet it streams all the way down your back."

Yes. It was going to happen.

— ►◄ —

Mary Lee never realized how quickly time could pass or how irrevocably her life could change. Encouraged by her conversation with Howard Boykin, she returned to New York and called up Leona Hardy, the arts-entertainment editor on the *New York Daily News*.

Hardy agreed to see her and to look at her clips and the copies of the first two chapters of *Cobra Lady*.

"Very impressive," the editor said when she had finished reading these. "In fact, *very* unusual. We could definitely use you. The only trouble is, what happens when *Cobra Lady* comes out? What about your job?"

"I'll take a leave of absence without pay," Mary Lee promised. "The publicity tour will only be about four weeks, they told me. After that, I could work steadily. I won't take any vacation for that year. I really don't need any vacation anyway."

"Mmmmm. And Vassar? I assume you are planning to drop out."

"I'll transfer to NYU, finish my degree there," Mary Lee improvised. "At night."

"All right. As long as it doesn't interfere with the job. We'll give you a chance . . . but mind you, your pay is going to be dirt bottom, and it'll be mostly scut work for a while."

"OK," Mary Lee crowed joyfully.

Leona Hardy smiled. "Don't be too happy, honey, because we are going to work your crackers off."

She had a job. On the *New York Daily News*, a newspaper read by over 1.5 million people each day.

When Mary Lee emerged from the newspaper building on East Forty-Second Street, she was trembling with excitement. It did not take her long to find herself in another of the bars that had now assumed such forbidden importance in her life.

A big triumph. A big fuck. The two were now linked.

This was another newspaper bar, jammed with weary-looking types in shirtsleeves, tipping back doubles with half an eye on two big-screen TV sets that were permanently tuned to sporting events. Mary Lee took a seat at the bar, as far away from the TV screens as she could get.

Four seats away, a man glanced her way, and then glanced again as Mary Lee gave him a sly smile. He picked up his drink and slid it down the bar to where she was, taking the seat next to her.

"Are you a model?" he asked her.

—— ►◄ ——

Marietta Wilde came storming through Mary Lee's small apartment on West Twenty-Sixth Street, brandishing a copy of *Cobra Lady*. Its jacket suggested golden snakeskin, on which a photo of Marietta had been superimposed.

"I couldn't believe it!" Marietta screeched. "I just could not believe it when Al Zuckerman sent me a copy of this book. I could not *believe* it!"

Marietta wore a plum-colored Donna Karan suit and dark red Hermès silk scarf, their colors matching the fury of her complexion.

Mary Lee had been expecting this for months. Dreading it. Lying awake nights in a frenzy of sweating fear. But now that the moment was actually here, she felt oddly exhilarated.

"I wrote it, Mother," she said.

"I know you wrote it, you imbecile! You blithering, libeling imbecile!" Marietta's hand lashed out, and two vases crashed to the floor, broken glass and flowers flying.

Mary Lee stepped back.

"And I'm glad I wrote it," she said.

"You're *glad*?" Marietta hissed. "Don't you realize what

you've *done*? You got into my file cabinet, didn't you? You read all my letters. You read my diary, for God's sake."

"Yes."

Marietta's face went white. "Is that all you can say is 'yes'? I can't believe you. You went into my private papers and copied what you found there. Do you know something, honey pie? That's very illegal."

"But I've talked to—"

"You are going to get *sued*. I'm going to sue the ass off you and that publisher of yours for everything you make on the book. They're not going to realize a penny, and neither will you. I'll tie you up in the courts for years."

"You can't sue if the material is true," Mary Lee retorted. "And, since you've worked so hard at being an international playgirl and celebrity, you've given up your right to privacy. At least that's what the publisher's lawyers told me."

"What?"

"And it's all true, isn't it, *dear mother*? Every fact I put in that book, every word. But I'll tell you a small secret. I didn't put *everything* in. I kept a few things out . . . like the fact that you made me crawl into the dryer when I was eight years old and made me stay there for three hours. With the door shut. I could have smothered."

"You little . . ."

"That's called child abuse. Think about it, *Mommy*. If you dare to file any kind of a lawsuit against me, I'll countersue for abuse, and I'll win, too. Lots and lots of money. Plus the wonderful publicity for you. Just the kind you like, isn't it?"

Marietta made a muffled choking noise.

Mary Lee went on, "Remember the Mexican maid we had then? Remember Maria Torres? She saw it. She knows everything, doesn't she? She'll testify for me."

"You little bitch!" Marietta grated. "You ugly little pig. Yes, pig . . . I even took you to a plastic surgeon once to see what could be done about that snouty little nose of yours, but he said it was impossible to fix."

Mary Lee gazed at her mother with detached triumph. In a way, this was the real purpose of her book, come to fruition. They were even, and she was free. Free forever from the horrible woman who, by some fluke, Fate had assigned to be her mother.

Her mother continued to rave, maligning everything from Mary Lee's appearance to her quietness, to her sneakiness, to the fact she had wet her bed until she was seven. "And you think you told everything; you think you published all the dirt, right?"

"I did my best, Mother."

"Well, your best wasn't good enough, *tootsie,* because there are a few facts you did not have access to, and these concern your own father."

"You don't know who my father is," Mary Lee said calmly. "He was one of the professors at UCLA, only you don't even know which one."

"You think that, don't you? You really think that." Marietta's blue eyes glittered. "Well, I lied; what do you think about that? His name was Walter Jurgen, and he was a professor of philosophy. And do you know what he died of? He died of Huntington's disease."

"So?"

"Think about it, dearie. Huntington's disease. Which is totally crippling and totally *inherited.* So there's a very good chance you might be carrying it around in your genes right now, right this very minute. How do you like that?"

Marietta's smile was wide—triumphant and gloating. "And that's why I never loved you, never wanted to love you. Because I knew all the time that you were going to get a horrible disease and die, probably in your early thirties. And that's—what?— only ten years away."

Huntington's disease. Mary Lee waited, stunned, while Marietta contemptuously dropped the copy of *Cobra Lady* into the center of her living room floor and marched out of the apartment, slamming the door behind her.

As soon as Marietta was gone, Mary Lee's bravado collapsed. She fell on the couch, sobbing wildly. She was in such pain that she thought she would choke. She could have borne anything but hearing her mother admit that she didn't love her and never did.

What a mistake she had made in writing *Cobra Lady,* what a devastating mistake. She hadn't freed herself from her mother, she'd only made things worse. Marietta was a genius at knowing exactly where and how to wound, and nothing was going to hold her back now.

Her mother didn't love her.

Never had and never would.

And she might have a terrible disease that could kill her in only ten years.

She got up to go to the bathroom, and she was so weak she

staggered against the door frame and nearly fell. She sank to her
knees and began to cry again, her sobs softer this time, the cries
of an abandoned little girl.

Mary Lee opened her eyes and looked around. Dusk had
fallen, and the apartment was lit by one small lamp. In the
middle of the floor lay the wreckage from the vases her mother
had smashed, along with the copy of *Cobra Lady.*

Mary Lee crawled to the book and picked it up, smoothing
a small rip in the shiny jacket. Marietta's face looked up at her,
small, beautiful, vixenish.

She began leafing through the book, stopping to read a
sentence here, a paragraph there. The first two chapters concerned Marietta's early life, and Mary Lee turned the pages
slowly, rereading them. She hadn't included the names of the
professors with whom Marietta had had her early affairs, because she didn't want to disrupt their personal lives over something that happened so long ago. But in her notes she still had
their names.

Mary Lee got to her feet and walked to her old file cabinet,
in which she'd preserved all her notes for the book. Feverishly
she rummaged through them until she came up with what she
needed: the names of the three professors at UCLA with whom
the long-ago Marietta, then known as Mariquita Guajardo, had
been sexually intimate.

She reached for the telephone and dialed information.

⸻ ◄► ⸻

Michael Jackson belted out something funky and sexy from
his newest album.

It was another smoky bar, one where singles from the
nearby financial district mingled. Hundreds of bodies were
crammed into a small space, and the noise was deafening.

Mary Lee shouldered her way up to the bar to order herself
a drink. She had concealed her crying jag, soaking her swollen
eyelids under a cold cloth liberally doused with witch hazel.
She'd put her hair in two braids tonight, winding them elegantly
around her head. She wore a new emerald green jumpsuit she'd
just bought at Bloomingdale's, with a matching jacket that
made her look like a *Vogue* cover girl.

She felt drained and sad, but also relieved and triumphant.
Her telephone call to California had revealed unexpected infor-

mation. Walter Jurgen hadn't died of Huntington's disease. He wasn't even dead. In fact, he had just retired from the university the previous year and was now devoting his time to a book on the history of creationism. Her father—maybe. But it was more likely he was not; otherwise, surely there would have been a hint before this.

Marietta had lied. And, although Huntington's disease no longer worried Mary Lee, she was still saddened by her mother's hatred. Maybe Marietta just lacked the maternal instinct—a birth defect, so to speak, in mothering capacity.

Mary Lee didn't feel exactly comforted by that thought, but at least some of her hatred for her mother had been lanced. From now on, she would try to treat Marietta as a *force majeure* . . . like a tornado or hurricane, a phenomenon you guarded against but didn't take personally. A storm was a storm.

A man appeared at her elbow. "I hate these meat-market places, don't you? The only reason I'm here is that I have to hand over some papers to a friend of mine, and he said to meet him here at the bar. Unfortunately he hasn't shown up."

She looked at him, immediately interested. A shock of dark-blond hair kept falling across his forehead, he had the wide, muscular body of a man who works out regularly, and his three-piece suit was very well cut.

"Of course," she teased. "The bar, a perfect place to exchange papers. Especially with all these attractive women mingling about."

He grinned back. "I admit I'm enjoying the scenery. Especially the scenery very close at hand."

They bantered for a few minutes, while Mary Lee felt the familiar lift of bar-pickup excitement. He looked as if he might earn more than she, a prospect that dimmed her desire a little bit. Still, he was more than attractive. There was a dimple in his left cheek that flashed charmingly when he smiled. She found herself longing to touch it.

"I'm Jake Scott," he told her. "The whole name is John Ellison Scott, Jr. Don't like the junior part of it very much. I'm in the trenches at J. Walter Thompson—right around the corner," he added, referring to the big advertising firm. "And you? You look so familiar, I could swear I've seen your face before. Pretty recently, too."

She flushed. Usually her encounters were more anonymous than this. "Oh, I don't think you've seen me."

"Oh, but I'm sure I have." He studied her. "You look like

a model, but somehow I don't think you've ever done any modeling. You don't have that narcissistic look. So it must be something else, but what? Funny, I never forget a face . . . TV!" he exclaimed, snapping his fingers. "That's where I saw you. On television."

"No."

"Oh, yes, it was 'Good Morning America,' I'm sure of it. You're Mary Lee Wilde, aren't you? You wrote that book about your mother."

Her rapturous mood had vanished. She pushed away her drink and turned, murmuring, "Excuse me." But a group of people blocked her way, and she had to wait for them to pass.

"Shy, are you?" Jake was still beside her. "Look, if you want to get out of here, just stay behind me and let me lead. It's the least I can do. And then if you don't want to talk to me, you don't have to."

"Please, I—"

He started pushing his way through the heavy crowd, and Mary Lee, after hesitating, decided to follow him. Within a few minutes, they were standing on the sidewalk.

"Damn," Mary Lee said. "I hate rain in New York. Especially in March."

"Where are you headed?" Jake wanted to know.

"Look—thanks for getting me out of there. I'll just catch a cab and go home."

"Not in this rain, you won't. I'll go and make a phone call; I'll get us a limousine."

"A limousine?"

He grinned. "Why not, for a beautiful lady author? Look, Mary Lee," he added seriously, "I know we met in a singles bar and you think I hang out in places like that. But that's not the case at all. And I know a class act when I see one. I would like to see you again. I'd like to see you a lot."

"I . . . I can't . . . please . . ."

She hadn't brought an umbrella, and even as they talked, the rain had intensified, sweeping down in icy, gray, rippling sheets.

"Do you have someone else?" he persisted. "Are you engaged or married?"

"No—really—"

"I swear, I look lots better when my hair is combed. I'm housebroken, like children and animals, even cats, and I don't eat crackers in bed. Not very often, anyway. I even clean up dirty dishes the same night."

He *was* cute. But with every word, he was making himself less anonymous. And the more real he became, the more panicky she got.

"Oh, go away," she snapped. "I don't care if you do eat crackers in bed once in a while. You won't eat them in my bed."

He threw back his head and laughed, ignoring her rebuke. "OK, I promise. Not even a Ritz, which is my all-time favorite."

"Please—"

"But let's not get ahead of ourselves, OK? I'm not trying to get naked with you. I know a woman like yourself must get a lot of offers, but I promise, I'm legitimate. I'm the kind of guy your mother always urged you to meet."

She glared at him.

"Well, maybe not *your* mother."

"Please—" Still, her insides started to soften. He really was adorable.

He went on, "Mary Lee, let me call a limousine service and take you out to dinner someplace, and then home. If you don't want dinner, I'll settle for just taking you home. Trust me," he told her convincingly.

She allowed him to hire a limousine and drop her off at her apartment. She gave him a cup of coffee.

The following night, she grudgingly allowed him to pick her up and take her to dinner at Lutece. The night after that, it was dinner in Chinatown, at a hole-in-the-wall restaurant with barbecued ducks hanging behind the counter, a menu entirely in Chinese, and the most fabulous dim sum she had ever tasted. Then they strolled on the street, window-shopped Chinese bazaars and antique stores, and bought Chinese ice-cream cones, flavored with ginger.

Jake made no physical advances, except to hold her hand. He treated her with warm, casual deference and called her his "braided lady." He sent her flowers five times, helped her pick out a word processor, and taught her how to play racquetball at the United Nations Tennis and Racquet Club.

It was four weeks before they went to bed. Jake Scott wasn't a one-night stand at all.

— ◂ —

"Oh, I can't believe you're really Alexandra Winthrop, buying a tape right here in my store just like everyone else," gushed the owner of the Poughkeepsie record store, who had recognized Alexandra's name from her check. "I loved 'Easy Woman.'"

Alexandra smiled shyly. Being recognized always made her feel pleased but nervous.

"Are you working on another song?" the woman went on. "I can't wait to hear your next one."

Flushing, Alexandra finished paying and hurried outside, blinking back tears. Only yesterday on the phone, it had been Derek who asked the same question. "You're not *really* thinking of trying to make it in the music biz?" her brother had remarked. "I mean, 'Easy Woman' was just a case of being in the right place at the right time. After you graduate, why don't you get on board my staff, help me with my campaign? I promise you some exciting work, something with a real future, not just daydreams."

"But I want to write songs. It's what I want to do. It's—"

"Honey, one record does not a career make. You told me yourself you haven't been able to come up with another one that Olivia liked. Whereas if you work with me, there'll be all kinds of excitement and interesting people to meet, too."

"I'll think about it," she'd snapped.

Now, walking toward the Vassar campus, she felt a wave of depression sweep over her. They were right—she might have had a wild success with "Easy Woman," but that's where it had all ended. Somehow, she hadn't been able to come up with another winner.

God, was she all dried up, already finished with her career before it even got started?

She walked back to the music building, to her favorite practice room. She sighed as she prepared herself for yet another session at the piano.

She played for twenty minutes or so, working on a song she wanted to call "Sensuous Woman." All she had was a title right now, though. The real meat of the song seemed to elude her.

After the tenth effort to polish a particular phrase, she finally let the notes die away. It just wasn't working.

That night, Alexandra phoned Jette in Los Angeles, hoping that her friend's zest and enthusiasm would pull her out of her own blues. Mary Lee's publisher was throwing a big party for her in New York, at the Fitzgerald Hotel, and they both planned to attend. The Cobra Lady herself was, of course, boycotting the whole affair. She had issued a statement to the press: "My daughter deliberately set out to hurt me, and she has succeeded. I will not sue her, although I have legal grounds to do so."

"What an incredible bitch," Jette marveled. "No wonder Mary Lee hates her so much. Anyway, how's the music going, Alexandra? Are you still writing?"

Alexandra was close to tears. "It's going absolutely no-where," she burst out. "I mean, what am I doing wrong, Jette? I spend hours and hours at the piano, I've got thousands of notes and rough starts, and it all goes absolutely nowhere. I can't believe I could only have one good song in me . . . but the harder I try, the worse it gets."

"Sorta like having an orgasm?" Jette inquired.

"What?"

"Well, the harder you think, the more it gets away from you. So you try even harder. You start watching yourself . . . 'how am I doing?' . . . only now you're numb and getting desperate."

Alexandra blinked. She clung to the phone, not knowing whether to laugh or cry. God, she couldn't believe it, but it was true.

"Remember the advice you gave me?" Jette giggled. "You said I had to stop thinking about it so much and stop trying to force it. And then another time you told me that coming is like sneezing; it builds and builds, and you can't stop it, and then it explodes."

"All right," Alexandra said, laughing. "Oh, Jette. You are something else. You really are. I don't know what I'd ever do without you."

Later that night Alexandra went to the piano in the sitting area of her dormitory floor, instead of the one in the practice room. She sat down to play, but this time, instead of concentrating on what she wanted to accomplish, she just let the notes roll out—any notes, whatever her fingers chose to play.

A girl walking down the hall wearing an oversized Yale T-shirt and big bunny slippers paused to listen. Encouraged, Alexandra stepped up the tempo a little. Thoughts of Giancarlo came to her—not as he'd been at the end, but the way she remembered him best, in bed, rolling on top of her in wild, abandoned sex.

She forgot about her audience and continued to play, engrossed in her memories. Finally, she looked up to see a circle of students standing around the piano, swaying to the rhythm. Encouraged, she kept on playing, adding a swingy, suggestive chorus, repeating it in several keys.

"Sensuous Woman" she'd call it. She *felt* sensuous.

9

Alexandra and Richard
1982

Mary Lee's publishing party was being held at the revolving restaurant atop the eighty-story New York Fitzgerald Hotel. The guest of honor wore a sea green Ungaro silk suit, cut daringly low. She had on her four-inch "come fuck me" heels. Her hair, plaited into two double braids, wound around her head like a gleaming, Nordic crown.

Mary Lee was beautiful, in a fine-honed, sculptured way. Her complexion was flawless cream and peach, her hair a rare shade. Francesco Scavullo had photographed her for a *Vogue* article about celebrity fashion.

Alexandra, gazing proudly at her friend, was not sure exactly when or how this transformation had come about. Surely the publication of *Cobra Lady* had something to do with it. Or maybe it was just the conflict with her mother coming to a head at last. Or the fact that Mary Lee had gained ten much-needed pounds.

Jette had flown in from California, and the three of them had had a brief reunion in Alexandra's suite before the party, accompanied by shrieks, kisses, and hugs. They had not forgotten to place a call to their friend Diana, in London and now married to Charles. Diana had sent Mary Lee a huge bouquet of flowers.

"Oh, God!" Jette cried. "I can't believe we're all together

again. Mary Lee, you look drop-dead smashing. And, Alexandra, you look more and more like Grace Kelly every time I see you!"

Photographers surged around them, snapping their flash-bulbs at Jette, who, as a star on "Canyon Drive," was endlessly written up in magazines and the gossip columns. She was more glamorous than ever, her teeth beautifully white, her makeup nearly as heavy as it was on TV. Women all over the country were now doing their eye makeup the way Jette did, in rich sables and cinnamons, and teenage girls begged their hair-dressers for a "Jette cut."

After a few minutes of posing, Jette good-naturedly shooed the photographers off, then began telling the two girls about her sometime boyfriend, Nico Provenzo.

"We're jet-set lovers," she giggled. "He flies out to L.A., or I fly to Chicago. But I'm so damned busy . . . even Estee Lauder wants me to sign a contract to have a fragrance named after me. They want to call it Jette. I've had two or three meetings with them. They want me to do a publicity tour—can you believe it? Plus all the work on 'Canyon Drive.' I never get any sleep with all I have to do."

Jette skittered from one point to the next, buzzing with anxious enthusiasm.

"Hey, calm down, this is me, this is us," Alexandra said. "You're talking like a little windup doll, Jette. Are you sure that everything is all right with you? That Nico Provenzo—he's the one who treated you so badly, isn't he? I can't believe you're still seeing him."

"He's wonderful," Jette said after a tiny hesitation.

"Why? What's wonderful about him? The sex?"

"Yes, the sex, Alexandra." Jette's full, red lips pouted pret-tily. "You don't understand . . . I tried it with other guys. Lots of them. But they don't do it for me; they can't make me come. Nico gets me off nearly every time. He's a genius at it." Jette giggled. "You don't want me to go through life never getting my bell rung, do you?"

Alexandra stepped back. "Good Lord, Jette, how can you talk like that? There's more to a relationship than just . . . that." She reached out to hug her friend. "What is this Nico like as a *person*? Is he kind and loving? Does it make you feel happy just to be with him? Does he share his feelings with you?"

Jette pulled away, frowning. "Alexandra, it's not like that with us. I don't want to marry him. He doesn't want to marry

me. That's the way we like it. Maybe someday we'll live together, but who knows?"

"But, Jette—"

"Hey, what is this, lecture time? I flew all the way to New
York to have fun, not to attend sex education class."

Alexandra knew when it was time to change the subject.
"Let's go to the bar and see if we can get another drink. And
have you seen Darryl Boyer? She's supposed to be coming here
tonight, too—along with her husband."

"Oh, Darryl," Jette said, shrugging.

"Is she still a real pain on the set?"

"Does George Burns smoke cigars? Everyone thought she'd
be different after she got married, but no such luck."

They wove their way through the crowd that was gathered
around an elegant Chinese buffet.

Editors in chief, publishers, literary agents, and authors
chatted, balancing drinks and small plates. Bobby Leonard, with
his recently acquired tan from a quick business trip to Australia's Gold Coast, was the focus of attention.

The publishing world was a very small one, Alexandra
realized. She nodded to several people she knew, mostly guests
who had been invited to add glamour to the party.

Halfway to the bar, as Jette was sidetracked by another
photographer, Alexandra noticed a man and woman enter the
room. More photographers scrambled to get close to the couple.
She recognized Darryl Boyer. The man with her had to be
Richard Cox.

"Go away, go away!" Darryl was telling the photographers
angrily. "Go bother someone else! This is a private party, not a
photo session."

"Please, Miss Boyer, just one picture—turn this way—give
us a big smile—"

"I said, go away," snapped the star.

The eager paparazzi ignored the rebuff, circling even
closer. Richard Cox was about to remonstrate with them, but
Darryl cried out, "I said, buzz off, dickheads!"

Cox reddened, pressing his lips together.

Alexandra looked away, embarrassed for him. Hadn't he
known she was like that before he married her?

The Coxes were absorbed into the party, and Alexandra
drifted toward the bar, where she talked with Jette, Senator Carl
Levin, and Mary Lee. Peter Ginopolis, a Greek movie star who
had written a Crown book on bodybuilding, joined them.

After a while, Alexandra excused herself to visit the powder room. On her way, she saw the Coxes again in the corridor, locked in disagreement.

Alexandra froze.

"Why were you talking to that female Dr. Spock for so long?" Darryl was inquiring in sarcastic tones. "She was such a frump. Do you think I'm going to read her stupid book?"

"I didn't ask you to read her book."

"Not yet you haven't. Richard, I do *not* want to quit everything and go to Chicago and raise babies!" Darryl snapped. "Really, I don't know how you can push me to do it."

"I haven't been pushing you to do anything, Darryl."

"Well, I'm *not* some kind of a baby-making machine—"

Blushing, Alexandra hurried past the quarreling couple, relieved when the rest room's door closed behind her.

— ▶◀ —

Later, a large cake was wheeled out, decorated with a replica of the book cover, with sugar-icing typewriters and flowers around the edges. Mary Lee and her editor, Annie Wilkins, stood together to cut it, while the guests crowded around them, oohing at its artistry. Photographers snapped more pictures for *Publisher's Weekly,* the *New York Daily News,* and the *New York Times.*

Alexandra found herself standing next to Richard Cox.

"This'll be the first time I ever got to eat a book," he suddenly remarked to her.

"You mean the cake? I think Mary Lee is going to take part of it home with her and put it in the freezer. As a memento, you know, sort of like a wedding cake."

He turned to face her. God, he was attractive, with dark hair, feathers of silver at each temple, and penetrating blue eyes. His square-jawed face wasn't Robert Redford handsome, but rather nicely craggy and strong. He had a cleft in his chin, she noticed. But his looks weren't the entire attraction. There was an energy about him, a personal magnetism she really liked.

"I'm Richard Cox. You're Alexandra Winthrop, aren't you?"

"Yes, how did you know?"

For the first time, he smiled. He had straight, white teeth, and his smile was a charmer, with deep lines carved on either side of his mouth.

"I raced your father three or four years ago in the Mack-inac races," Cox explained. "Afterward, he talked about you, his beautiful daughter who's attending Vassar and writes popular songs." He paused. "Besides that, I asked someone."

Richard gazed at her in a warmly appreciative way that made Alexandra's skin feel hot.

"I understand your wife is Darryl Boyer," she managed to say.

"Yes."

"She is very beautiful."

"Do you really think so?" He frowned ever so briefly, then added, "Yes, but the truest beauty includes an inner radiance—such as yours, if I may say so."

She fought the tendrils of physical attraction that already were twining between them like vines. She didn't need this—he was a married man.

She started to walk away.

He strode after her. "Hey, I didn't mean to scare you."

Oh, he was *so* attractive. Alexandra forced her lips into a smile. "I know, Mr. Cox, but I promised to rejoin my friends."

— ►◀ —

Alexandra's graduation from Vassar marked the end of three years of hard work. The ceremony was steeped in tradition. Undergraduate women in white gowns formed an honor guard celebrating graduation by carrying on their shoulders a long chain woven of fresh-picked daisies.

Afterward, on the lawn in her cap and gown, Alexandra embraced her father, Felicia, and Derek, who had flown down from Boston in Jay Winthrop's new private jetcopter.

"Baby, I was so proud. I can't tell you how proud." Her father hugged her, tears in his eyes. "I only wish your mother could have been here. She would have loved seeing you in your cap and gown, marching through the daisies; she would have been so happy."

Alexandra clung to her father, her eyes also misty. "Maybe she was here, Daddy. We can't know."

They strolled about the campus, while Alexandra pointed out various landmarks and introduced her family to her professors and friends. Later, in the lobby of Main Building, Jay Winthrop drew his daughter aside.

"Alexandra, Vassar seems to have been such a special

world for you. Do you wish you'd stayed the full four years, instead of graduating in three?"

"Oh, no, Daddy, I really want to work on my music."

"And maybe work on your brother's campaign staff," her father prompted. "Your music is wonderful, and I admit I was wrong in thinking you shouldn't get involved with it. But it wouldn't hurt to spend a few months getting your feet wet in politics. You might find you like that, too."

Alexandra looked at her father. He enjoyed playing the behind-the-scenes role of a "kingmaker." She knew he was ambitious for Derek, too. Would it hurt to get involved for a few months?

"And you could meet someone interesting," Jay added.

A memory of her encounter with Richard Cox flashed through Alexandra's mind. As she so often had, she pushed the picture away with a sigh and a twinge of guilt.

Her pensiveness inspired her father to continue. "What you need is a decent social life. As soon as we get home, I'll have Felicia throw you a couple of small parties, get you in the swing of things again. And naturally we'll find something for you on Derek's staff."

"Oh, Daddy—"

"Now, just promise me you'll give one summer to pleasing your old dad. After that, you can do whatever you want."

"One summer then."

———— ►◄ ————

That summer in Boston, Alexandra felt certain that she was poised on the brink of some intense, life-changing experience.

Could it be her music? She was working on several more songs and had decided to continue the "woman" theme of her first two successes.

She thought of Richard Cox from time to time and allowed herself the guilty pleasure of investigating him in the library. Before his present marriage, she learned, Cox had been married to a glamorous and respected socialite who had died of a head injury sustained in an auto accident. He had no children. And he was more than twenty years older than she.

She also fulfilled her promise to get involved in Derek's political campaign. But she didn't want to be just a precinct canvasser. She wanted to do something more meaningful.

"Derek, maybe I could be your campaign manager?" she inquired during dinner at home one night.

Her brother cleared his throat and looked embarrassed. "Um, Sissy, I know you're a wonderful organizer, but what would I do with Bo Donohue? He's been working with me for six years now. I can't exactly toss him away like a used Kleenex because my little sister wants to help."

At thirty-three, Derek was a handsome, hearty-looking man with a mane of tawny hair, his looks a definite political asset. An article in *People* billed him as "The U.S. House's Most Eligible (and Elusive) Bachelor."

"Please, Derek, I don't want to be just another body at the phone banks. I studied some political science and have organized several fund-raisers for you, remember? One of them made more than $50,000."

Derek nodded. "OK, I had a woman quit last week—you can be my scheduler. But it's awfully hard work . . ."

"Wonderful! I can take it, at least until Election Day." She saw her father's smile of approval. "Try me."

"All right," he agreed. "But, Sissy, this is serious. We're not talking some college project here; we're talking about my election, and I don't intend to lose."

Annoyed, Alexandra made a face at him. "I'll work as hard as you do, so don't worry. Oh, and there's one more thing."

"What?"

"My name is *Alexandra*."

Derek waved off the maid's offering of cheese and fruit along with after-dinner sherry. "No thanks, none for me. I've got a meeting with the State Democratic Committee, and I'm late already." He turned to his sister. "Show up at my office tomorrow morning at nine, and someone will show you the ropes."

Before Alexandra could do more than nod, he had hurried out of the dining room.

Jay Winthrop frowned. "If he's going to a political meeting, I'll eat my hat."

"Now, Jay," Felicia said in her warm contralto.

"Well, where *is* he going tonight? One of his women? Damn it," Jay fretted. "I wish he'd pick one and settle down. Three or four months with each one, and he's on to the next."

"He just doesn't want to make a mistake. He's not ready to commit himself yet."

"He's thirty-three years old," muttered Jay. "He'd better

settle down if he ever wants to make it to the Vice Presidency. Last I heard, they don't ask tomcats to run."

"Jay!"

"Daddy!"

Jay Winthrop had the grace to look embarrassed. "Well, baby," he said to his daughter, "it's a good thing he's going to have you working with him. You'll keep him on an even keel."

———— ◄► ————

At work, Derek was a far different person from the laid-back, often irreverent brother she knew at home. He arrived at his headquarters before 6:00 A.M., frequently not leaving until after midnight.

His stamina was legendary, and his staff members told stories of campaign trips where he stayed up for thirty-six hours, barnstorming, pressing the flesh, and phoning important money men, ward leaders, and support groups.

He had a staff of nineteen, all of whom were extraordinarily loyal. Ken Corey, the speech writer, explained some of the reasons: "Derek might seem offhand sometimes, but he's got charisma, and he can project it in the media. Mark my words, he'll make it soon, maybe by 1994. His people stick by him because they smell success. They all want to be on board the P-train. And I mean P for President."

The humid summer inched along. The Republican candidate had begun to fight dirty on the issues of abortion and crime. Derek drove himself, working eighteen-hour days, whistle-stopping through every town in Massachusetts.

And Alexandra made sure everything ran smoothly. It was a balancing act, but one day Corey told her casually, "We haven't had any major fuckups in the past month, or many minor ones either."

The tough compliment pleased her far more than any she had received from her professors at Vassar.

———— ◄► ————

One day in late June, when she was at the Fitzgerald Hotel to make final arrangements for a speech that Derek was to give to the Boston Bar Association in the ballroom the following day, she ran into Richard Cox.

"Hello, there, beautiful music writer," he said.

"Richard Cox!" She could not hide the excitement that coursed through her. He was wearing a Savile Row navy blue pinstriped suit and a pale blue shirt that emphasized the deep aquamarine of his eyes. He looked even more attractive than when she had seen him at Mary Lee's party.

"What are you doing here?" she blurted, then blushed, remembering that he owned the hotel.

He smiled. "I make periodic trips to visit my hotels. We're in the process of hiring a new head chef here. Would you like to join me for a meal? I always ask candidates to prepare me a sample of their art, and I was just on my way to the private dining room. Please join me. I don't like to eat alone."

"Why, I . . ." She felt flustered. What was it about the man? Just being in his presence made her heart leap inside her chest.

"All right," she assented, "although I haven't much time. I'm campaign scheduler for my brother, Derek. He's running for the U.S. Senate in Massachusetts."

"Yes, I know. I promise you, your time will be well spent. This man has trained in Paris at the Cordon Bleu and then worked three years as sous-chef at La Tour d'Argent. I understand he's excellent."

They boarded an express elevator. Several other people entered with them, forcing Alexandra and Richard to stand closer together. She could smell his scent, a combination of after-shave and a light, lemony European soap. As she felt herself responding to him, she became intensely aware of her own body. Beneath the silk blouse she wore, she was conscious of her nipples thrusting at the lace of her bra.

When they transferred to the penthouse elevator, she was left alone with him. Although they had this elevator to themselves, he stood as close as before. Trembling, she stepped backward to make the distance more comfortable.

"The chef's name is Jean-Yves Lauriat," Richard was saying. "He is very French and very eccentric, I'm told—but then, often the great chefs are. And surprisingly, he isn't fat. He told me that he runs twenty-five miles a week through the Bois de Boulogne."

The elevator opened onto a wide reception area lit by banks of windows overlooking the city skyline and Boston Harbor.

"Mr. Cox, a telephone call, from a Robert Giambelli," said a bellboy, approaching them.

He took it on a red house phone, gesticulating as if the other speaker were actually in the room. He returned, shaking his head. "A kitchen employee at my New York hotel was fired for repeatedly being late to work. Now the union has filed a grievance against us. Jesus, unions. One hundred and fifty hotels, one hundred and fifty headaches each day. They just can't seem to grasp that the hotel's prosperity is their prosperity."

They walked into the small executive dining room, where a table had been set with a dark-blue cloth and gleamed with silver, crystal, and bone china with the Fitzgerald crest. A centerpiece of irises was arranged in a silver salver.

A waiter showed them to the table, and Richard ordered wine. "But enough talk of unions," he said to Alexandra, smiling. "Let's talk about you."

"What about me?"

"I'm interested in your music, how you got started, what it means to you."

Alexandra was pleased at his interest and found herself talking freely, telling him things she had not told even Jette.

The meal was elegant, each course intricately garnished, a feast for the eyes as well as the palate. There was a light asparagus bisque. An endive-and-walnut salad, the Belgian endive julienned and garnished with chopped walnuts and dewy green watercress. Next came lobster stew *sous croute,* a savory blend of lobster, leek, Jerusalem artichoke, onion, carrot, and mushroom, flavored with garlic, tarragon, and a pinch of cayenne. The dessert was an elegant creation made from a light filo dough, encased in solid Dutch chocolate. Within the case was a feathery raspberry soufflé. The entire presentation was shaped into an *F* for Fitzgerald and garnished with plump, perfect raspberries.

The phone rang twice more while the soufflé was being served, but Richard told the waiter he would return the calls later. The dessert was too stunning to miss.

"Oh," sighed Alexandra, surfeited. "I love my father's cook, but she never dreamed of such creations. Superb, Richard. He's too good to pass up. I hope you hire him."

"I've already decided to." His eyes met hers. "I have a talent for knowing exactly what I want."

At his remark, Alexandra felt her heartbeat speed up. Hastily, she reined in her thoughts.

As if he could read her mind, Richard said, "You know, I

was divorced last month." Alexandra's head began to spin as he continued. "I'm not ashamed to say that I've made mistakes and I'll probably make more." He paused. "But one mistake I *didn't* make was running into you here today."

"What?"

He grinned. "I knew you were going to be at the hotel today."

"What?" She couldn't help laughing. "You mean, you were lying in wait for me?"

"I confess." His eyes were intense.

She had dated Harvard and Yale men, as well as associates in prestigious Boston law firms, finding them interesting but not compelling. This man was far, far different. Compared to those relatively callow young men, Richard was a shark. A very, very sexy shark.

"Well," Alexandra said, taking a deep breath and glancing at her watch. "I've already overstayed; I have an appointment at three o'clock and six dozen phone calls to make."

He ignored her excuses for what they were. "Alexandra, I want to see you again."

"I—I can't."

"Why not?"

"Because—I really must leave," she stammered, pushing back her chair.

Instantly he rose, too. He was only a few inches taller than she, and their eyes were nearly level, his capturing hers.

She turned and began to stride out of the small dining room, nearly colliding with the chef.

Richard caught up to her. "You're afraid of me, aren't you?"

The chef tactfully disappeared into the dining room.

"I'm *not* afraid."

"Then why are you running from me? Alexandra, I'm flying down to Connecticut tomorrow. I have to deliver some legal documents. I'm planning to have dinner at a nice old inn near Westport where the food is wonderful and I know the chef personally. Please, come with me."

"I can't," she repeated, shaking her head.

"I'll pick you up at nine tomorrow morning. Wear casual clothes, and bring something to change into for dinner."

She hesitated.

"You'll love flying," Richard persisted. "With me."

The double meaning did not escape her. She drew in a

long, slow breath and expelled it, knowing already what she was going to say.

"Well, all right."

———— ►◄ ————

"So you're seeing Richard Cox?" Jay Winthrop was in tennis whites, on his way to play at the club. His doctor had forbidden him singles, but he was permitted doubles, and he usually played daily.

"I'm not *seeing* him, I only agreed to fly to Connecticut with him. Apparently he has some business there, and he asked me to join him for the day."

"I see."

"Daddy, you wanted me to get out and socialize."

"But with a man twenty-five years older than you are? If you were to marry him, it'd be his third marriage. Of course, he's very wealthy," Winthrop added thoughtfully. "I hear he's adding more hotels to that chain of his every day. I sailed against him several times at Mackinac; he's a good competitor. Really quite a guy."

"It's only twenty-*three* years, Daddy. And just one date," she said, flushing.

"That's good," Jay Winthrop said. "Because, baby, from what I've heard—Cox works hard, and he plays hard. And he's dated more gorgeous women than the Aga Khan."

"Why shouldn't he?" She heard herself defending Richard. "He's extremely attractive."

Jay frowned. "If you were thirty and he were fifty, I wouldn't be as concerned. But you're barely twenty-one; that's just so damned young. It's practically cradle robbing."

"Daddy!"

"Sorry. But that's how it seems to me. Be careful, Alexandra, that's all I ask. And think very, very carefully before you get involved with Richard Cox. He's on the rebound from a divorce. Odds are he isn't looking for another wife, only a playmate."

———— ►◄ ————

Alexandra was up at dawn. Outside her window, the sky was awash with pale salmon clouds, lit from behind by the sun. A perfect day.

She went for an early-morning jog under the trees that

bordered the eighty-acre Winthrop estate, drinking in the fresh, clear morning air, feeling more alive than she had in months, every muscle taut and finely tuned.

Returning, she showered and then went down to the kitchen, where she assembled a breakfast of fresh-squeezed orange juice, a croissant, and coffee. She was too excited to finish her croissant.

Back upstairs, Alexandra put on a pale blue Calvin Klein tank top, which skimmed delectably over her breasts. She added white denim jeans and a navy blazer that brought out the Wedgwood blue of her eyes. She rolled up the sleeves for a more casual, raffish look, then wrapped several lengths of a rope-chain belt around her waist, showing off its slimness.

His eyes were going to go straight to the tank top, she realized, but she didn't want to change. She wanted him to admire her.

Her father was right; he *was* older. But so virile, she decided as she sat down at the dressing table and began applying eye makeup. A man in his midforties was in the prime of his life— at the peak of his powers, with the experience to know how to please a woman in every way imaginable . . .

She shook the thought from her head. She would see him this one time, and then it would be over.

— ▸◂ —

She had flown many times before, of course, but never in so small a plane. It vibrated and shook as it suspended them in air so clear that she could see every tree on the ground, every glittering pond, brook, and stream, every green patch of woods.

"Beautiful!" she called to him over the roar of the motors. "Just beautiful."

His sunglasses gave him a dashing look. "For you . . . my gift. You can have it all if you want it."

What did he mean? That he would buy her everything, even things that were not for sale? She managed to comment, "Such a gorgeous day!"

"You're even more gorgeous. I thought we'd fly over Providence, and then down along Long Island Sound. I have a small house on the Sound near Westport, and I keep a car there. And a selection of bathing suits, in case you forgot to bring one."

"You forgot to tell me we were going swimming."

"So I did."

She smiled. A beach house along the Sound. She felt sure he had it all planned. First, a romantic walk along the beach. Then lunch in some out-of-the-way seafood place. A swim in the Sound with her wearing some nothing of a bikini he provided. Then . . . his mouth, hers, their bodies wrapped together, moving in a dance of love . . .

By the time they reached Westport, Alexandra had had plenty of time to ponder Richard Cox. First, she was no match for him. He was older than she, far more experienced, and far more determined. She sensed that what he wanted, he usually got. But then, he was vulnerable to the wiles of the many women who looked for rich and powerful men, using beauty to get security. Did he accept the implicit bargain and simply take what was offered, knowing his wealth was part of the attraction?

As they taxied up to the small terminal, Alexandra decided she would not be like all the movie stars, models, and socialites Richard had been involved with. She would not give in to having sex with him, no matter how persuasive he was.

"Well, we're here," Richard said, pushing his sunglasses up over his forehead. "I've got a car I keep at the airport. Let's go claim it and deliver the contracts I told you about—that should take us only about half an hour. After that, I'll show you the beach."

His eyes glittered, and she sensed his desire, delicate but persistent, like the spicy after-shave he wore. She felt her body respond to it.

A sapphire sky arched overhead, and small waves lapped on the shoreline where skittery curlews ran. A couple of fishing-net floats had washed ashore, their paint scoured by years of sea immersion.

Alexandra and Richard walked side by side, barefoot, their trousers rolled up past their knees. She had left her jacket on the sand in front of the redwood-and-glass beach house that was not small at all, as Richard had suggested, but big enough to sleep ten.

Richard strode ahead of her to examine one of the floats, and she could not help noticing that he had very sexy legs.

She averted her eyes. Everything about him turned her on, from the shiny fullness of his black hair, only slightly receding from his temples, to the surprising thick strength of his hands. Jette had once told her that the size of a man's hands was a good indicator of the size of his "three-piece set," as the California girl colorfully put it.

Richard seemed almost to read her mind. "Please, don't be afraid of me." He stopped in the sand and turned to her, putting his hands on her shoulders. She shivered.

He said, "You *are* afraid, aren't you? You keep pulling away from me."

She looked into his eyes. "I'm not like all the other women you date."

"I'm very aware of that."

He was about to kiss her, she could sense it.

"Let's go have lunch," she suggested quickly. "I'm just starving—aren't you?"

His eyes speared her, and for a wild instant she feared he was going to kiss her anyway, stealing what she would not give. Then he dropped his hands. However, his expression told her he wasn't finished with her yet.

"How about that wonderful seafood place I told you about?" he said. "It's right on the water, and the clams casino are superb."

——— ▸◂ ———

Richard Cox pursued Alexandra with gifts, flowers, and glittering afternoons on his sloop, *Stormy Lady*. His instinct for the perfect gift was uncanny. She loved pink roses, with their delicate petals and heady fragrance. Richard sent her huge, lush bouquets every day, until her room, then the rest of the house, was filled with roses, an extravagance of pale pink.

One morning, just as she was leaving for Derek's headquarters, a package arrived by messenger. It was larger than a laundry basket and was swathed in lengths of pastel ribbon, with an enormous bow in which pink rosebuds had been fastened.

"Another token from your admirer?" Jay Winthrop inquired on his way to breakfast.

"It seems so," Alexandra said, blushing.

"If I'm not mistaken, those are air holes," Jay observed. "You'd better open this package right away."

She did. Inside was a pair of large, pink-and-white, lop-eared rabbits. They were the size of small dogs, their noses wriggling, their fur incredibly soft. They nestled inside a brass cage that contained everything for their needs, from a supply of green pellets to water containers. And each wore a pink bow around its neck.

"Oh! I can't *believe* it!" Alexandra knelt down and picked up one of the rabbits, burying her nose in its white, glossy fur. For an instant she was an eight-year-old again.

"I've *always* wanted a rabbit! And these are Lops! How could he have known?"

"This is a man obviously out to win your heart," Jay Winthrop said, one eyebrow raised. "I think this is a serious pursuit, my dear girl. What are you going to do about it?"

"Do?" But Alexandra knew exactly what he meant. "Why, I'm going to enjoy the summer, Daddy. That's all."

"At least he wants to please you," Jay said, heading into the breakfast room. "Your job is to figure out whether you want to be pleased."

Did she want to be pleased? By Richard Fitzgerald Cox, a man whose financial power was growing by the week, if she were to believe the recent *Fortune* cover story that called him the tenth richest man in the United States?

While they had not been sexually intimate, they shared kisses that racked both of them with desire. At those moments, it was only a shred of determination that kept Alexandra from giving herself to him.

But as she got to know him better, she became troubled by his preoccupation with his business. The phone frequently intruded on their time together, and even that time, she often felt, had been carefully scheduled to fit around his work. Also, Alexandra was dismayed by Richard's reticence in expressing his feelings. She knew he wanted her physically, but how did he *feel* about her?

She wanted a man with whom she could share everything—thoughts, dreams, feelings. She wanted a husband who was also her best friend.

——— ▸◂ ———

In the polls, Derek was ahead 58 percent to 42 percent. Alexandra arrived at headquarters at seven in the morning and stayed until after midnight—an exhausting regimen that was beginning to take its toll. She was fighting off a cold, maybe because it had been weeks since she had slept eight straight hours. Nighttime fantasies about Richard Cox and the sheer labor of politics were a lethal combination.

"You OK, kid? You look kinda white." One morning Derek breezed into the big office area where they all sat at open desks. He looked suntanned and vigorous. Long hours seemed to invigorate him. He was a political party's dream.

"Sure, I'm fine. I just have a small cold; it'll be better by tomorrow," she said, her voice a little hollow.

"All those late hours with that new boyfriend of yours, eh?" Derek chuckled. "You can't burn the candle at both ends, Sissy, not when you work with me."

Alexandra said nothing. She *was* very tired.

"I'll tell you what," Derek went on jovially. "I hate droopy, draggy staff people, so I want you to take four or five days off. Get away from Boston; go out west someplace where the air is clear."

"Four or five days? But, Derek, you need me."

"Sure, I need you, but not that much. You gotta have bounce and enthusiasm if you want to work with me. You need new sparks and an oil change."

In spite of herself, she cheered up a little. "Where should I go?"

Derek grinned, striding over to a U.S. map thumbtacked to the wall. "Simple enough to find a place . . . what would you like? Mountains? Rivers? Trees? Canyons? Mesas? Desert?"

She laughed. During campaign time, Derek seemed fueled by ten times as much energy as the average person. "I don't know."

"I'll help you, then." Derek picked up a piece of yellow chalk, closed his eyes, and turned around several times, as if he were playing Pin the Tail on the Donkey. He lunged forward and made a mark on the map. "Montana! There's a good state for you, nicely wild and woolly." He leaned forward, peering at the marked spot. "Billings. Bozeman. Helena. And the Rockies, Sissy. Half the state is mountains. And look, here's Glacier National Park. Should be plenty of clear air there."

"Derek." She laughed again. "I can't go to Glacier National Park just because you pinpointed it on a map."

"Why can't you? You need a vacation from politics, and that's about as far away from politics as you can get. Get your famous friend, Richard Cox, to take you. See him out in the wild—that'll tell you whether he's really a man or not."

"I know he's a man."

"*Do* you?" Derek leered.

"Oh, stop," she said impatiently. "We're not . . . I mean . . . oh, never mind!"

The phone rang for Derek, and he went into his office to answer it, leaving Alexandra to ponder his suggestion. She *did* need some time away. And . . . yes . . . maybe she would have a chance to see more of the real Richard.

She reached for the phone.

—— ◄► ——

Three days later, when Richard had cleared his schedule and Alexandra had recuperated from her cold, they flew in Richard's Lear jet to Kalispell, Montana.

Luckily, both possessed broken-in boots, but Alexandra needed gear for the cool mountain slopes, and they outfitted themselves for hiking at a store called Fran Johnson's.

"Where did you get all this hiking knowledge?" Alexandra asked Richard curiously as they emerged from the shop. "I thought—"

"You thought I was a citified greenhorn? Hey, I've been tramping mountains since I was ten years old. My father used to take me. I've hiked the Adirondacks, Smokies, Rockies, and Cascades. I head for the peaks whenever the world seems to be closing in. It's the best therapy in the world."

She looked at Richard with new interest.

They had booked two rooms at the Many Glacier Hotel, which hugged the edge of Swiftcurrent Lake in the majestic shadow of Mount Gould, with a stupendous view of white-capped peaks, mirrored in the clear water that was literally within feet of their rooms.

As she emerged from the car they had rented in Kalispell, Alexandra looked around with awe. All around her were jagged peaks cut with gorges and escarpments, ridges and cliffs, heavily forested up to the tree line. Although it was early August, the upper areas were dusted with snow.

This world was so rugged, pristine, and intimidating that Alexandra felt her heartbeat quicken. She'd be sharing all this with Richard.

"Excited?" He was smiling at her. He looked younger than she had ever seen him, his face completely relaxed.

"Oh, yes! It's like stepping back fifty thousand years, like seeing the world when it was still new. I love it, I just love it!"

"I love you," he said.

"What?" Holding one of the shopping bags, she turned, startled.

"Your enthusiasm, Alexandra. Your warmth. You are the warmest person I have ever known." Richard cupped her chin with his hands and pulled her to him for a kiss.

It began innocently enough, a butterfly kiss that brushed their lips together. But quickly it escalated, as he scooped her to him and the bag fell out of her fingers to the ground. His arms wrapped around her, and she melted into him. His mouth sought hers, opening her lips to probe her sweetness with his tongue.

Alexandra's heart began pounding wildly.

A group of hikers returning to the hotel noisily trekked past them, giggling.

"Never mind them," Richard said, as they pulled reluctantly apart. He looked flushed, too. "Guess I'd better register and get this stuff into the rooms."

They sat down on an outcropping of granite, putting their day packs on the ground. All around them were the magnificent spruces, firs, and lodgepole pines, the rugged snowcapped mountains. A little blue cirque lake seemed to cup the sky. Somewhere a bird sang, and the air was clear and sharp.

"Look," Richard said quietly. "There, to your right, just past that stand of pines."

Alexandra followed his direction. Four white-tailed deer, delicate and nervous, had materialized out of the trees, picking their way cautiously.

She and Richard watched for several minutes, until something spooked the deer and they bounded away, their tails raised like white flags.

"Such beauty," Richard said. "It's here, in a place like this, that I really believe there is a God."

"He does seem close, doesn't He? As if we somehow wandered into the beginning of creation."

"You and I, Adam and Eve?"

"A pretty modern Adam and Eve," she pointed out, laughing. "Me in my Gore-Tex jacket, and you with your goggles and their ultraviolet protection."

He laughed, too. Then he grew serious. "Do you know something, Alexandra? I feel more relaxed with you than with any other woman I've ever known. More content. Less hassled and pressured." He sighed, leaning back on the rock and giving his face up to the sun. "I guess I've needed this break—more than I realized."

"It must be very stressful," she remarked. "Your lifestyle. You're always striving after goals."

"And failing sometimes. My marriage to Darryl was certainly a failure. I guess I just wanted to prove to the world that Richard Cox could have any woman he wished."

"We all make mistakes," she said, liking him very much for that admission.

"I did love my first wife, though. Glenda was a very sweet woman and would have been a wonderful mother if we'd been able to have children. A hysterectomy ended that. She begged me to adopt, but I refused."

"Oh, Richard."

"I knew I was hurting her," Richard said bitterly. "Damn, I knew it, and I couldn't seem to give in. I wanted *my* child, *my* heir."

"But an adopted child would have been yours, too."

"I realize that now," he said quietly. "But by the time I had figured it out, she was dead. And damn it, now I hunger for children, Alexandra. I'm forty-four years old, and I haven't got forever."

They sat for long moments; the only sound came from the nearby rushing creek.

"Well, let's walk some more," Richard finally said, his voice husky.

They put on their day packs and began walking again, feeling closer.

But Alexandra felt a pang. In her memory, she saw Simon Heath-Cote lying crumpled on the road, his neck twisted, his glazed eyes staring horribly at nothing. Jette was raped. What would Richard possibly think? He had shared his most intimate secrets, but she could never share this one with him. She had sworn a solemn vow.

"You're quiet," he said, taking her hand to help her over a rocky rise in the trail.

"Am I?"

"Yes, dear Lexy, you are."

"Lexy?" She gazed at him, startled out of her mood.

"Yes, Lexy. It suits you. Shorter than Alexandra, and sparkier. Sexier, too."

He stopped. They could hear falling pebbles on the trail

ahead of them, coupled with a snuffling noise. "Bears," Richard said, reaching for the bear bell, which neither of them had remembered to use.

Alexandra caught her breath, stepping backward. Her heart leaped into her throat as three brown shapes lumbered out of the brush, snuffling and grunting.

"Richard . . ." Alexandra said nervously.

He rang the bell again, the sounds echoing against the granite walls of the escarpment.

"Come, Lexy, love, let's stroll away from here. I don't think they want to mess with us, and I *know* we don't want to mess with them."

That night they had a simple dinner at the hotel. Then they went for a leisurely walk along the lake, where Richard photographed the stunning view—the mountains reflected in the inky water, the clear image broken only by the occasional jump of a fish—and took many shots of Alexandra.

In the evening shadow, the temperature had dropped at least twenty degrees. Alexandra could feel winter, the snows to come in only a few weeks.

They walked casually, talking, teasing, and bantering. "You know, I think we could use an after-dinner brandy, Lexy. Care to join me?" smiled Richard, taking her hand.

Back in Richard's room, the bottle of Courvoisier stood on the dresser along with two glasses. But instead of offering her some brandy, Richard closed the door, then reached out and pulled her into his arms.

For a long time, they just stood together quietly. "Alexandra," Richard finally whispered. "You don't know how I've longed for you. I wanted to be doing this." Richard gently lifted the cashmere sweater over her head. As Alexandra obediently raised her arms, fire consumed every nerve ending of her skin.

My God, she thought with a rush of panic. Was this really happening? Now it seemed hard to believe she had expected to resist intimacy with Richard.

Then she couldn't think about it at all, for Richard was pulling the sweater away from her, along with the matching silk turtleneck and the half-moon wisps of ecru lace that cupped her breasts.

"Beautiful," he murmured huskily as he bent to kiss her full breasts. "I knew you'd be just beautiful. So perfect. I love every part of you. Oh, Alexandra."

His tongue teased such a sensation from her that she uttered a low, throaty moan.

Richard was a persistent and adoring lover. He unfolded all of Alexandra's treasures with slow, loving, worshipful attention.

"Your skin is like satin," he whispered. "So soft, so very soft. I love your softness."

His kisses burned a trail from her breasts to the taut ripples of her rib cage, then downward to her stomach. His hands and mouth explored her adoringly, leaving no part of her unkissed or unexplored. His caresses were at first gentle and soft, then more urgent, until he was moving with fierce passion.

As their legs entwined and their mouths locked, Alexandra's senses drank him in. His sharp, musky scent. The faint, sensuous scratch of his whiskers against her skin. The sweet enfolding of their legs, hers long, smooth, and soft, his firm and hard-muscled.

His tumescence pressed into her stomach, and she reached down and took him in her hand, feeling the live strength of him, the pulsating male power. They changed positions, and she bent to kiss him there, burying her nose in the crisp, silky hair. He strained his hips up to meet her mouth.

"Oh, God— Jesus—"

He uttered sharp moans as Alexandra encircled him with her mouth, taking in as much as she could of the full, throbbing length. She tongued him greedily, until his cock strained and pulsed and his body seemed to vibrate.

"Stop!" he cried out hoarsely, almost unrecognizably. "Not . . . not yet . . . I want this to last."

He pulled her toward him and then turned her around so that she crouched over him, with her slim, rounded buttocks near his face. For an instant she felt shy, but it dissolved in pleasure as his tongue made regular, fiery strokes that laved her in glorious, vibrating ecstasy. Alexandra gasped and moaned.

He knew exactly when to tongue her hard and when to stroke her enlarged clitoris in short, delicate circles. He knew when to thrust his tongue into her opening, probing the soft, slick skin until she moaned and sobbed and cried out with abandon.

He also knew the exact point that placed her on the edge of the precipice, so that she trembled violently, only a hairbreadth away from cataclysmic release. He stopped, just at that point.

"Quickly," he breathed, again turning her. "Quickly now."

He lowered himself on her. He inserted the tip of his cock into the slippery opening of her vagina—but only enough to tease her, to run its blunt, velvet head up and down her slickness, enflaming her.

"Please," she begged raggedly. "Please, please . . ."

"I will. Oh, I will."

But not yet. She had never had a lover like this. . . . Finally, when the sweet torment became unbearable, he thrust himself deep within her.

His thrusts began slowly, and he methodically rotated himself as he pushed in, so that every inch of her was touched by him, filled and pleasured.

Then he quickened his rhythm until they rocked and bucked together, thrust and pounded, sobbed and gripped each other's shoulders, frantic fingernails drawing warm blood.

Their sweat lubricated them, a sweet, salty, natural sexual oil. Alexandra felt a deeper joy than she had ever known, flowers of delight blooming. Then suddenly her body rippled from tiny, sharp explosions, an exquisite rending apart of the psyche that at the same time was a joining.

Alexandra screamed out her pleasure, hearing Richard's hoarse cries of fulfillment.

She and Richard had, for a seemingly endless moment, blended their bodies and souls in perfect harmony. Something that human beings live and strive for. Willing to bear anything—every hurt and sacrifice of life—to achieve.

10

Alexandra
1989

The voice of Olivia Newton-John singing "Ever-Loving Woman" filled the air with a rhythmic energy. Alexandra's private aerobics instructor, Christine Bane, was using it for their cool-down after the hour of vigorous twists, jumps, reaches, and kicks.

"Whew," said Dolly Rutledge, leaning against the wall of the Cox exercise room and wiping streams of perspiration off her face and chest. "I thought I'd die with some of those movements."

"I always think I'm going to die," Alexandra said, pulling the sweatband from her forehead and waving good-bye to the young instructor. "But it's only temporary."

"It feels damn' permanent to me," Dolly puffed, peering at her leotard-clad reflection in the mirrored wall. "I'm not twenty-eight, that's my trouble." Well preserved, with a trim figure and sun-streaked hair, Dolly was an attractive forty-eight-year-old.

"Take it easy," Alexandra said. "Do some more walking to cool down."

"Christ, look at me, will you? Puffing. Panting. Sweating. And I'm starting to get love handles, too. I hate them with a passion."

Alexandra laughed as she walked over to switch the stereo to a more mellow Lionel Richie. "Hey, you look great. And as for me, I could use a good soak in the Jacuzzi. I didn't get much exercise when we were in England, and my muscles feel stiff today."

Adjacent to the mirrored exercise room was a large area for bathing and changing. The Coxes had installed a steam room, sauna, and whirlpool, along with a refrigerator stocked with fresh fruit, juices, and Alexandra's favorite brand of diet cola.

The two women stripped off their leotards and tights, took turns stepping briefly under the shower, then lowered themselves into the hot, steamy, bubbly water.

"Ah, God, but this is good," Alexandra sighed.

The women relaxed in companionable silence for several minutes. Alexandra leaned her head back on the edge of the pool, letting her thoughts drift back over the trip to England, to Diana, and then to the party again, as Dolly filled her in on their progress. Chefs from five international Fitzgerald hotels had been contacted, with Georges Taxier, from the Paris Fitzgerald, selected as head chef. He was submitting menu suggestions, and chefs and sommeliers from the Hong Kong, Chicago, and London hotels would be in charge of hors d'oeuvres, wines, and desserts, respectively.

Spectacular, they had ordered. The purpose was to stun the guests.

Dolly had ordered laundry-basket-sized, hand-woven West Virginia baskets to be placed in the hotel rooms, filled with gourmet delicacies and wines to represent the offerings of the entire hotel chain. Orders had been placed with Ralph Lauren for satin bathrobes, gray for men and pink for women, each to be monogrammed with the initials of the guest.

Contracts had been signed with six limousine services to provide VIP airport pickups and transportation services for the entire three days of the event. Now they were working on arrangements for a helicopter tour and harbor cruise; a shopping tour at Tiffany's, Cartier, and the other stores on Chicago's Magnificent Mile; and a view of the Mackinac-Chicago yachting race, which would be run that week. Calls had been placed to several set designers.

But Alexandra wasn't entirely satisfied.

"Theme," she said aloud, frowning. "Dolly, we need something that's going to create magic—something they'll talk about for years."

Dolly laughed. "But we're having the future King and Queen of England. Isn't that enough to talk about?"

"Of course. Still . . ." Alexandra lowered herself further into the steaming water. "I want something more."

"The Garden of Versailles?"

"Possibly. But not so ornate."

"Well, I'm sure you don't want the Garden of Eden," Dolly said, her voice just a hint sharp.

Alexandra fretted. "I want magic. Glamour. Maybe a little stardust."

"Moondust?" Dolly said tentatively.

"Garden of the Moon Princess," Alexandra announced softly.

Dolly stared at her in surprise. "Garden of the . . . what—?"

"Dolly trust me—it's going to be fabulous. The theme, Moon Princess, is just perfect; since Diana's going to be there, it can honor her. Our colors will be silver and blue. Pale, pale silver and blue. And, Dolly! We'll hire a set designer, of course, but we are also going to hire the Twyla Tharp Dance Company."

Dolly looked even more startled. "What?"

Alexandra was so excited that she sprang up out of the hot tub and strode over to the bench where a stack of thick bath towels awaited. She dried herself with such vigor that her skin tingled.

"Dolly, picture it. Flowers everywhere, white on white. Ivory, cream, and stark white. Glittering Italian lights, maybe interspersed with silver net and Austrian crystals to sparkle like dew. Fountains that we'll build, with a water display that keeps changing and lights trained on the water, changing in shades from blue to lavender to silver, so that it looks fabulous and fantastic and not quite real. Yards and yards of extrawide white silk moiré—maybe looped and swagged, I don't know."

"Good Lord."

"But the most stunning thing of all will be the two small stages we'll construct."

"*Stages?*"

"Yes, your mention of set designers gave me the idea. Each will be constructed to look like a beautiful, silvery half-moon, on its side, raised to the balcony level so that people will have to look up," Alexandra went on. "And on each of those silver half-moons will be a beautiful tableau of dancers—sometimes two, sometimes three—depicting the Moon Princess and her consort, or her ladies-in-waiting."

Dolly stood up in the water. "Dancers? But, Alexandra—"

"Yes! They'll form a beautiful, moving tableau. Living decor. And by using the entire dance company, we can have the dancers performing all evening long. It'll be just a knockout. And best of all, Diana *loves* dance. She wanted to be a ballet dancer, and she still adores everything about dancing."

"It is a wonderful idea," Dolly said. "It gives me shivers just to think about it. But Alexandra, the cost. My God, the set designer and construction alone . . . and a whole dance company! You're talking about several million dollars!"

"Richard didn't seem concerned about the cost, so I'm not going to be either," Alexandra explained.

"If you say so," smiled Dolly.

An hour later, Alexandra was in her office, finishing her telephone call to the famous choreographer, while Dolly, on another line, was attempting to reach James Combes, the Hollywood set designer.

". . . Yes. That's Mrs. Richard Cox. Of the Fitzgerald Hotel Coxes. Yes. Absolutely. Please have him call me as soon as he comes in." Finally Dolly hung up, looking frustrated. "He's about to leave for Majorca, but maybe it's only a short trip. Oh, Alexandra . . . you know we have only two months."

Alexandra, excited because Tharp had agreed to her plan, did not wish to hear about obstacles. "We can do it. We will. But I need your vote of confidence on this, Dolly. I have to have your enthusiasm."

"I know—"

"Dolly, *I need you to be with me.* If you're not able to handle it, now is the time to back out. I promise I'll never blame you."

Dolly flushed. "Alexandra, your ideas are fantastic, and this party will make my reputation. Of course I want this party."

Alexandra smiled. "I guess I'm a bit edgy. This party will make *my* reputation as a hostess! We'll do it."

Later that day, Alexandra slipped from the house, telling her driver to take her to the Chicago Fitzgerald, where she had arranged to meet Richard for a drink. She hadn't seen much of him since they had returned from England, but Alexandra knew something was wrong. The exhaustion etched on Richard's face was unmistakable.

As she rode through the Loop, Alexandra gazed impatiently

out of the smoked-glass limousine window, which seemed to put distance between herself and the city, darkening the June sunlight.

Money. Could Richard possibly be worried about money? The idea was so unusual that it startled her a little. But quickly Alexandra pushed it away. It was ridiculous to pair Richard and money worries in the same thought. He had so much money that even the interest on the interest was a fortune.

The limousine pulled up in front of the towering Fitzgerald Hotel, and the doorman rushed up to open the door for her. She walked inside the huge main lobby, drawing a deep, pleased breath, as she always did. She loved this place, from the four glittering Waterford crystal chandeliers to the pink marble fountain, which she had commissioned. She had worked with the artist herself, and as a result, it reflected her own personality. She really felt very much at home here.

In the bar, Richard was seated at one of the tables near the wall, a drink in front of him. She was struck by the expression on her husband's face as he waited, unaware that he was being observed. Creases of anxiety furrowed his brow and scored a line between his nose and mouth.

"Rich—" she began, going toward him.

"Hello, stranger," he said, rising so she could slide into the banquette. He smiled, the furrows of worry vanishing. As always, he looked fabulous. He was so at ease in his body, in the clothes he wore. Today he had on a dove gray pinstriped suit, with a light gray shirt and a maroon-and-gray-striped necktie. Richard didn't like to fuss over his clothes. He made several trips to London each year, efficiently buying four or five suits at a time from his tailor on Savile Row.

She sat down, smiling back. "I guess I *am* a stranger, at that. It's getting pretty bad when we have to make a date to see each other. How're the meetings going?"

"As expected." He shrugged. "But let's not ruin a perfectly good cocktail hour over that. What are you drinking?"

"How about something festive and cool? Maybe a frozen strawberry margarita?"

Richard grinned. "That's festive, all right. Olé."

He summoned the barmaid and ordered the drink and a platter of crudités with caviar dip.

"So how are the kids?" he began. "What are their names anyway?" Again that wonderful grin crinkled his face. "Tr . . ."

"Oh, you," she said, laughingly.

Her drink came, the vegetables soon after, and they sat talking companionably about how nice the hotel looked and about some repairs Richard wanted to make on *Lexy Lady*, their sailboat.

Finally Alexandra said, "But the most exciting news is, Rich, I have a theme for the party! And it's going to be wonderful; I'm so excited."

"Dancers?" Richard said dubiously, after she described the theme. "A whole dance company?"

"Yes! In fact, I had Dolly call 'Lifestyles of the Rich and Famous,' and Robin Leach wants to do a feature on the party. That would be worth millions in publicity for us, darling. For the hotels. It'll pay for the cost of the party three times over."

Richard smiled and raised his glass. "To the city's number one hostess. Alexandra, you are something else."

11

Alexandra
1982

Giancarlo Ferrari nosed his battered Plymouth Duster down P Street, looking for a parking spot as Georgetown simmered in a late-August heat wave.

Merdo. He was tired and sweaty, but he'd just scored some excellent coke, and he was in a big hurry to get to Ingrid's apartment, so they could party.

Life had been hell since the racetrack accident at Daytona. He'd broken almost every bone in his body. He spent two months in the hospital and another year in physical therapy and would never again be totally free of pain.

At the end of a year, Giancarlo could walk normally, although his joints were still painful. His reflexes were shot, they said, and the bones in his neck were held together by "spit and tar paper."

"One false move, and you've had it," his doctor warned. "I mean it. Don't even slip and fall on the ice!"

Now he eked out a living as a manufacturer's rep selling stick-on racing stripes and decals to auto-parts stores, but it was Ingrid who really supported them. Bosomy Ingrid, her brown hair now spiked and bleached platinum blonde, sang at a torrid Alexandria nightclub called Cheeks. Giancarlo had married her in order to get his green card and stay in the United States.

In addition to the $900 a week she earned singing, Ingrid made a little money on the side. There were men who came to

Cheeks with more in mind than just music, and Giancarlo and Ingrid used the extra income to buy coke, hash, and Quaaludes.

Circling the block for the third time, he finally spotted an old Toyota pulling out. Triumphantly he braked with a screech, tooled backward, and swerved into the spot.

Climbing the narrow, steep front stairs of the house, Giancarlo puffed with the exertion. The frequent cocaine he ingested kept him slim, but he was out of shape.

"Where the *hell* have you been?" Ingrid greeted him sourly. Although it was two-thirty in the afternoon, she had just gotten up. She looked surly and sleepy, her eyes puffed, her white-blonde hair sticking out in unruly, tight frizzes. She wore nothing but a pair of bikini panties.

"I was scoring, what else? And I was meeting with those people from Racing Stripes. They want to put out a new line; they wanted my advice." Three years of living with Ingrid had improved Giancarlo's English.

"Yeah, right."

"They might even want me to do an endorsement for them . . . my picture in the magazines, eh, *bella*?"

Ingrid nodded. She'd heard all this before. Few of Giancarlo's schemes ever materialized. "Well, is it good stuff? How much did you get?"

"Four grams," he told her.

Ingrid pouted. "You couldn't get any more than that?"

"Not with the money you gave me, and we're going to have to find a new contact. Ty got busted." Giancarlo pulled the folded plastic sandwich bag out of his pocket and went over to a small side table. Here, in a lower drawer, Ingrid kept the paraphernalia: a small mirror, straws, razor blade, and a silver coke spoon, plus rubber tubing and syringes.

He felt his stomach churn with anticipation.

"Come on, come on," Ingrid urged impatiently. "Get going, will you? My head feels like I'm on the inside of a set of cymbals. Let's do some shit."

Giancarlo carefully spooned a portion of the white powder onto the surface of the mirror and with a razor blade formed it into two thin lines.

"Party time, here I come," Ingrid said, placing a straw up her right nostril and pressing her other nostril shut. She tilted back her head ecstatically. "God . . . I feel like the dog's dinner today, but not for much longer . . ."

"Hey, leave some for me."

"Don't be greedy. *I'm* the one who paid for this shit, in case you didn't notice."

Giancarlo took the mirror away from her and repeated the procedure, drawing in the powder with a quick, deep sniff. He was a coke-head now, and he knew it. Without Ingrid, he'd be on the street doing robberies to support his habit.

Thank God for Ingrid. He went to the couch and knelt down in front of her. "Lean back, *bella* . . ." Parting her legs, he buried his face between her firm, creamy thighs. She lay perfectly still, not seeming to notice his ministrations until she suddenly let out a wild squeal, her whole body shuddering with release.

Afterward, they put on a reggae tape and danced to UB40 and Bob Marley. Giancarlo was really flying. He felt powerful, almost as good as he used to feel at Daytona or Monaco, screaming around the track at nearly two hundred miles per hour.

His nostrils hurt, though. Thinking Ingrid might have some cream, he headed for the bathroom and rummaged around underneath the sink, where they kept a cardboard box stuffed with various medications.

As he was reaching for the box, he spotted a plastic bag at the back of the cabinet. Inside were what looked like a pair of his old racing gloves and a folded-up white racing suit.

The racing suit still had track dust on it. Looking at it, he could almost feel the hot sun and hear the screaming crowds. Shit. He didn't need these old memories. Why'd the bitch save the stuff?

His mood spoiled, Giancarlo stuffed the racing suit back into the sack. But as he did, a sheet of paper fell out—a photocopy of a newspaper article.

Then the day came back to him, his one and only foray into a library, three years ago. And before that, Alexandra Winthrop, sprawled naked beside him in bed, caught in the throes of some nightmare.

"*The motorcycle! . . . Simon! Simon Heath-Cote! We killed him!*"

— ▸◂ —

Derek's campaign was more intense than ever. He needed to win big if he wanted to fulfill his political plans. At campaign headquarters, Alexandra was on the phone with a woman who wanted Derek to speak to her chapter of Parents Without Partners.

Alexandra made the arrangements and hung up feeling tired but satisfied. She'd already put in a nine-hour day, and it looked as if she'd be here another hour or so. But the work didn't bother her. Nothing bothered her. She was still floating on a cloud of euphoria from her trip with Richard.

The phone rang again, interrupting her reverie.

"Alexandra Winthrop?"

"Yes, may I help you?"

"I bet you do not remember me," said a deep voice.

"I'm sorry, who is this?"

"You're sure you don't recognize me, *bella?*"

"*Giancarlo?*"

"That's right." His voice sounded different, the accent less pronounced.

She didn't know what to say. "I—I heard you were in a terrible accident. I'm so sorry, Giancarlo."

She could almost hear him shrugging. "I took chances, I lost. I'm not calling for pity, Alexandra. I'm calling about your brother. I need to talk to you about him."

"I'm sorry," she explained, puzzled, "but Derek is so busy right now, with the election coming up. Almost every minute of his time is booked."

"I didn't say I wanted to see *him*. I want to see you."

She drew in her breath, dismayed. Did Giancarlo want to start up their affair again? Oh, God, that was the last thing she needed.

"I'm sorry," she said stiffly. "But I have a meeting tomorrow, an all-day meeting. You've caught me in the middle of the busiest time, and it's only going to get worse through November."

"Tomorrow afternoon at Anthony's Pier 4. Meet me in the bar at twelve-thirty. I have something to show you, and I think you are going to be very interested."

"Giancarlo, I've just told you, I can't."

"Anthony's," he repeated. "And if you don't come, Alexandra—I'll go to your father."

"What? Really, I—"

He clicked off the phone.

Something to show her? What did he mean?

Instinct told Alexandra she should look intimidating for this meeting with Giancarlo.

She spent an hour combing her closets, finally selecting a yellow Adolfo suit, its jacket and skirt trimmed with black piping. A black V-necked blouse and yellow-and-black shoes completed the outfit.

She pulled her hair straight back into a golden knot at the nape of her neck, emphasizing her bone structure, making her look strikingly chic.

She spent another hour on her makeup, dusting her face with translucent powder until her skin was perfect, not a pore or a line showing. On her lips, she brushed a deeper red than she usually used, and she used a subtle blush. She shadowed her eyes with iridescent seal brown, then touched her lashes with several coats of mascara. The final touch was a citrine necklace and earrings by Paloma Picasso.

She studied her reflection in the mirror, amused. She didn't look like herself at all. She looked like a model on the cover of *Vogue*, more mannequin than human. Very, very unapproachable. Good, she thought. She hoped Giancarlo squirmed.

Arriving at Anthony's, she hesitated in the reception area, unable to see in the dimness of the bar. A waiter approached her.

"Miss? Are you meeting Mr. Ferrari?"

"Yes, I am."

"This way, please."

She followed him through the bar, aware of heads turning as she passed.

"Alexandra?" Giancarlo was sitting in the last booth. He half-rose as she approached, his expression startled. The three hours she'd spent getting dressed had definitely been worth it.

"You look beautiful," he muttered. *"Bellissima."*

"How are you, Giancarlo?" Confident now, she slid into the booth and ordered a wine spritzer from the hovering waiter. Giancarlo already had a large manhattan in front of him. A Filene's shopping bag rested on the seat beside him.

"In the accident, I broke every bone," he told her. "I can't race anymore. One wrong move, and poof."

Examining her former lover, Alexandra thought that he barely looked like the same person. He was still handsome, but he looked worn somehow. His pallid skin seemed to hang too loosely over his bones, and there were dark circles underneath his eyes. He looked more like a man of thirty-five than the twenty-three she knew he was.

Had the accident aged him that much?

The waiter arrived with her drink and gave them menus, but Giancarlo waved him away. "I can't stay for lunch; I just wanted to give you this," he told Alexandra. He reached for the Filene's bag, handing it across the table to her.

"For me?"

"Yeah, *bella*, just for you. A few little . . . mementos."

His black eyes were focused on her with intent, predatory interest, and Alexandra realized there must be more in the bag than just "mementos." She didn't want to take it.

"I really must leave," she began.

Giancarlo rose, pressing the sack into her hand. "But first, you will need to open this, Alexandra."

"No."

"Then I will take this to your brother's office," he said quietly.

Defeated, she sank back down, reaching for the bag. Inside there was a medium-sized box with a Gucci label. She pulled off the box lid to find two packages tightly wrapped in wrinkled tissue paper.

"Go on," he urged. "Unwrap them."

She reached for the smaller bundle and gingerly pulled away its wrapper. Inside was a small toy motorcycle, partly smashed.

"I . . . I think I'd better go now."

"Not yet," he insisted. "Open the other one."

She unwound the tissue with trembling hands. Inside was a Ken doll, stripped naked, its plastic skin smooth and pink. The doll's head had been twisted around so that it stared across the doll's shoulders.

A broken neck.

Oh, God! Giancarlo knew. She felt waves of sickness begin in her stomach. There were two more items in the box. Numbly she lifted them out. One was a Xerox copy of a newspaper clipping, an article about the hit-and-run killing of British aristocrat Simon Heath-Cote.

And the other . . . Her heart froze.

The other was a photograph of Alexandra and Derek.

Blackmail.

She realized she was swaying sickly, and she braced herself on the Formica tabletop.

"I see you get my meaning."

"How much?" Alexandra whispered.

His eyes fell to her right hand, on which she wore a sapphire surrounded by small diamonds, a gift from her father.

"I don't carry much money," she told him coldly. "I'll see that $2,500 in cash is delivered to you tomorrow. Where are you staying?"

Giancarlo named a small motel in nearby Quincy.

"You'll have it by 10:00 A.M.," she told him. She rose and walked out of the bar with smooth, angry grace.

In the car, Alexandra's hands shook so badly she could barely fit the key in the ignition. She had to get out of the parking lot before Giancarlo followed and saw how shaken she really was.

She backed her car out and turned into the traffic. *She was being blackmailed*! And he would keep coming back for more.

She couldn't go to the police. Even if she didn't care about her own life, she could hardly release facts that would affect Jette and Mary Lee.

She took a deep breath and tried to think calmly. She would have to go to the bank tomorrow and withdraw the necessary cash.

How quickly her life had changed.

—— ◄► ——

Giancarlo ruined the rest of that fall for Alexandra.

Somehow, probably during one of her nightmares, she'd revealed the secret to Giancarlo. They had all sworn an oath, and she had let her friends down, endangering their futures and their happiness. And Derek's, too.

A week later, Giancarlo phoned again. He wanted another $2,500. He suggested that this time Alexandra simply mail the cash in an envelope.

Adding to her misery, Richard seemed to have changed since the trip to Montana. He had become completely reabsorbed in the pressures of his life. Negotiations for the purchase of hotels in Montreal and Vancouver meant endless trips back and forth to Canada.

Richard canceled several dates, saying that meetings or business trips had come up unexpectedly.

"I had to rearrange *my* schedule, too," she told him the

third time it happened. She had stopped by his office at the Boston Fitz to meet him for lunch. "But *I* managed to set aside the time."

"Oh, Lexy, Lexy," he apologized. "It's just business. God, I hate being this busy, having to plan every minute of every hour. Anyway, you know I've made Boston my home base for the fall because of you. I usually work out of Chicago. That has to count for something, doesn't it? At least a few brownie points."

"Of course it does," she said, weakening as he smiled at her.

He came around his desk and took her in his arms, pulling her close. "Mmmmm," he murmured. "You smell wonderful. What are you wearing?"

"I have on Opium today," she said. "But I think it's a little too musky for me, don't you? I like a lighter scent."

Richard nuzzled her, his breath warm on her neck. "If you say so. All I know is that you make my nose happy . . . and a few other parts of me, too."

Just then his secretary buzzed a call through.

"Oh, *no*," Alexandra moaned.

"Sorry, Lexy. I'll cut this one short."

The voice that came over the intercom was female. "Richard? Darling? I've been trying and *trying* to reach you. That secretary of yours always tells me you're in a meeting."

"Katrina. How was Jerusalem?" The warmth in Richard's voice chilled Alexandra's soul.

"Hot, dry, and full of gorgeous Israeli men. None as gorgeous as you, though, and the shoot was miserable. I sprained my ankle when they made me stand on this stupid wall and I fell off."

"Seriously hurt?"

"Oh, just an Ace bandage. When am I going to see you? It's been weeks . . . weeks!"

Alexandra, a captive audience to this conversation, realized that Katrina must be the twenty-year-old model who was a current *Cosmo* and *Vogue* cover girl and who had also caused a sensation by posing for the *Sports Illustrated* swimsuit issue. Katrina was six feet tall, as golden-skinned and exotic as a harem princess.

"I've been busy," Richard excused himself, with a pained look at Alexandra.

"Oh, Richie," Katrina cooed. "You *always* plead business, you bad, bad boy! I'm in New York. Why don't you fly out for a long weekend? We'll make love in the hot tub again, like we did last time, hmmmmm?"

Richard had the grace to flush beet red, and Alexandra rose quickly. "Sorry . . . I'll let this conversation be private," she told him, not bothering to lower her voice.

The woman on the intercom heard her. "Richie? Have you got someone with you? Is that your secretary?"

"No, hon, it's a friend. Look, Katrina—"

Alexandra didn't wait to hear him sweet-talk some other woman. She stepped outside Richard's office, closing the door behind her with more force than was required. She stood for a minute, drawing a deep, angry breath.

Oh, God! Katrina and Richard had seen each other only weeks ago! The shock of betrayal was chilling.

She strode past his secretary's desk, her high heels digging into the deep-piled carpet. She told herself that Richard had a right to do anything he wished. She didn't have any claims on him.

She'd better face hard, cold reality. Their time in Montana was only an interlude. Now it was back to business as usual for him—beautiful, ego-building women.

She hurried to the bank of elevators, painfully aware that Richard hadn't followed her out of his office. An elevator was just arriving, and Alexandra practically ran inside, stabbing the lobby button.

The doors seemed to take forever to whisper shut. When they finally did so, Alexandra slumped against the wall of the elevator, feeling her body shake all over.

As the elevator came to a stop at the ground level, Alexandra fumbled for her handkerchief and wiped her eyes, setting her jaw grimly.

— ◄► —

"Miss Alexandra?" Bridget, Alexandra's maid, had her hand over the telephone mouthpiece, her eyes questioning. "It's Mr. Cox again."

"I told you, Bridget, I don't want to take his calls."

"He sounds so upset."

"I don't care if he sounds upset. I *don't* want to talk to him," Alexandra snapped. She took the receiver away from her maid and laid it in the phone cradle with a firm click.

Bridget looked hurt.

"Oh, Bridget," Alexandra said in exasperation. "I'm sorry. I really am. I haven't been in a very good mood lately."

"He's sent all those flowers," the maid pointed out. "I don't know how many bouquets of roses. Pink, your favorite."

"Take them to a nursing home or something. And take one or two of the bouquets for yourself. I *don't* want any more reminders of him, and that's final."

Five days had passed since the call from Katrina. Alexandra had tried to bury herself in work. However, even eighteen-hour days were not much of a panacea, not when thoughts of Richard intruded on her mind constantly. His smile, the way he had held her, the way they had made love. How was she ever going to forget him?

Alexandra planned to attend another $1,000-a-plate fund-raiser that night, a ball sponsored by the Democrats for Derek Winthrop. Disconsolately she rummaged in her closet, poking through the racks of dresses.

There was a Mary McFadden evening gown she had just purchased. Strapless and pale aqua, its skirt was McFadden's characteristic crinkled column of pleats, the bodice exquisitely embroidered with beadwork. The robin's-egg shade would accent her blondness and the creamy beauty of her shoulders.

She pulled out the dress on its hanger and laid it across her bed. Since the dress was elaborate, the jewelry should be simple. The pearl necklace, interspersed with diamond rondelles, that had belonged to her mother . . .

She sighed, sitting down on the bed. Who really cared? This was just another party . . . another ball full of men who would come on to her because she was a Winthrop. Oh, what was the use?

She allowed the tears to flow, sobbing until the huge block of pain centered in her chest began to melt a little. She was just feeling sorry for herself, she decided. And she'd always hated people who wallowed in self-pity.

Finally she stood up and reentered her closet, searching for her pale aqua evening pumps. There was a benefit to attend tonight, and she'd attend it smiling. Derek needed her to be at her most charming, and she would not let him down.

The main ballroom at the Boston Fitz was thronged with seven hundred couples, the men in black tie, the women in glorious evening gowns. Against a backdrop of tiny white lights, diamonds glittered on wrists, throats, and ears, a light-catching display meant to show off a man's status as well as a woman's beauty.

Sprinklings of celebrities added to the luster of the evening—Ted Kennedy; Michael Dukakis with his wife, Kitty, glamorous in blue silk chiffon; the mayor of Boston; Derek, circulating with the ease of a professional politician.

Alexandra circulated, too. Suddenly a voice behind her said, "Why won't you return my calls, Alexandra?"

Alexandra whirled. "Richard!"

He didn't look apologetic. "I wangled a ticket at the last minute. I wanted to see you."

Despite a stab of longing and sorrow, she replied, "I *don't* want to talk to you." Her heart seemed to have leaped up into the center of her throat.

"Obviously not."

"I mean it!" she insisted, her voice rising in near-panic at the seductive nearness of him.

"Of course, you mean it. Look, could we just step into a corner for a minute or two? I promise, I won't make things tough on you. I just want to explain about Katrina."

"There's nothing to explain," she responded stiffly.

"I think there is; otherwise why would you have stormed out of my office like that and then refused to return my calls? Alexandra, Katrina is—was—just a date. Someone to fill time with. Nothing more than that. She means nothing to me whatsoever. In fact, I've told her I won't be seeing her again."

"That's very noble of you." Blindly Alexandra turned and fled across the ballroom, weaving her way among the well-dressed couples chatting in small groups.

"Stop running," he ordered, setting a brisk pace beside her. "Why are you so bent out of shape?"

"OK," she said, turning to face him. "I'll tell you what the problem is. I'm not able to deal with life as you choose to live it. You're far too sophisticated for me. As I told you when we first met, I'm traditional. I don't want a man who's got a beautiful model hanging from each arm and a hundred more waiting in the wings."

"Give me a chance," he pleaded.

"I did give you a chance. We saw each other half the summer and half the fall. We went away on a trip together. And all the time you were seeing me, you were also seeing her. And maybe more women, too; I don't even know. Do they all have to be beautiful?" she asked him cuttingly. "I mean, did you ever consider finding someone who was more than just a cover-girl face and body?"

"Yes," he said.

She shook her head angrily. "I don't believe you . . . and I'm not going to be one of your conquests. Go away, Richard. I really mean it. We belong to two different worlds."

———— ▸◂ ————

When she returned from the ball, she found Jay waiting up for her. "Have a good time, sugar?"

"Oh, Daddy—" For a second she almost broke down, but she reined in her emotions. She didn't need Jay fussing over her. "A pretty good time. But boring. All those people."

Jay raised his eyebrows. "Make up your mind, kiddo. 'A pretty good time' or 'boring'? It has to be one or the other."

"I suppose it does."

"Anything wrong, dear? You seem kind of down lately. Not your usual self."

"Oh, I'm fine, Daddy. Just, well, maybe a little blue."

"I see," Jay said, nodding. Affairs of the heart he could understand. "Now, don't you give up, sweetie. There aren't too many beauties like you around. You could get any man that you want."

She looked at her father—gray-haired, distinguished, born and bred in another generation.

"Daddy, I wish it were that simple," she whispered, running upstairs.

In her bedroom, she dismissed Bridget and got undressed, hanging her gown back on its padded hanger, tissue paper arranged to protect it from dust. Still in her strapless bra and silk panties, she replaced the shoes in their box and then began absentmindedly straightening her closet.

It was nearly 4:00 A.M. when she heard the telephone ring. She sighed and picked up the receiver. "Hello?"

"Dancing until dawn, eh? I tried calling all night, but you did not answer."

"Giancarlo?"

"I tried calling all night, but you did not answer," he repeated, as if this were something she had deliberately done to thwart him.

At the familiar accent, Alexandra sank down on the bed, clutching the phone. "I can't give you any more money, Giancarlo. My account at the bank is supervised by the trust officer and my father's accountant. They're bound to notice all my withdrawals and ask questions. I really can't—"

"Twenty-five hundred is peanuts. I'm going to need a lot more this time, at least ten thousand."

"Ten thousand!"

"You heard me, *bella*. I watch TV, you know; I know all about that brother of yours, Congressman Derek Winthrop. The polls say he's going to win the election and be your next Senator. Unless something happens, eh?"

Alexandra sagged against the headboard, her head reeling. Her worst fears were being realized. She would have to talk to Derek now. He had to know what was happening.

"Alexandra? Are you there, *bellissima*? Are you still on the line?" Giancarlo's voice brought her back to ugly reality.

"Yes, I'm here. Look, Giancarlo. I—I need to raise the money. I'll have it for you in—in a few days."

"Tomorrow," he specified sulkily. "In the mail, like before. Ten thousand in cash."

"It will take me a day or two to get the money. It's the weekend, Giancarlo. I can't go to the bank until Monday morning."

She forced herself out of bed at six-thirty, knowing Derek was leaving for a speech in Holyoke.

She went downstairs, where she found her brother finishing his breakfast of a bran muffin, orange juice, vitamin pills, and coffee. Derek watched his weight at home, since he had to eat out so much.

"Derek? Could we talk? Just for a few minutes?"

"I don't have a few minutes, Sissy," he told her, pushing back his chair. "I have to leave to pick up Bo. He's going to drive down with me."

"Please," she begged. "Fifteen minutes."

"Sorry, babe, I'd love to, but I just can't. Tell you what, though. We'll have lunch tomorrow at Anthony's. Just you and me."

She swallowed dryly, remembering the last time she'd been there. "It can't wait until tomorrow," she replied hesitantly. "I'll ride with you while you go to pick Bo up. Then I'll take a cab home. I *have* to talk to you, Derek."

It was one of Boston's misty, pearl gray autumn mornings when water droplets clung to every dead leaf and branch, shimmering on telephone wires like Cartier diamonds. Only a few cars were on the road, families going to church.

Alexandra told Derek her story.

"I can't believe this," he shouted, his voice filling the car. "I fucking can't *believe* this, Alexandra! Three eighteen-year-old kids, and you get messed up in heavy-duty trouble like that? Jesus, a guy dead. Oh, Christ. And election day is only ten days off. Holy shit!"

"I'm sorry," she whispered.

"Sorry!" Derek's face was congested with fury. "Sorry is not even in the ballpark, lady. Sorry doesn't even come close to hacking it. Jesus fucking Christ, and we have to pick up Bo in ten minutes. You just don't care, do you?" he lashed out at her. "You really just don't give a flying fuck, do you, about what happens to me or to anyone else in your family? Word of this could kill Dad. I suppose you never thought of that, did you?"

She sat rigidly, fighting the waves of nausea that threatened to overwhelm her. "W-what are we going to do?" she managed to ask. Derek was driving too fast for the wet roads.

"*We* aren't going to do anything. I am. I'm going to call the best criminal lawyer I know, and I'm going to lay it all out to him. The whole nine yards. He'll figure out what to do to smooth things out."

By now Alexandra had started to cry, and her body began heaving with sobs. "I . . . I'm sorry," she choked.

"Fuck, I'll fix it. I'll get Dave on it, and we'll work it out. If necessary, we'll just feed the guy a payment or two until the election is over, and then we'll worry later about what to do after that."

They drove into Norwood in silence. Derek let Alexandra off at a restaurant, where she planned to call a cab to take her back to Brookline. As she got out of the car, she felt her legs tremble.

"OK, now, Sissy," Derek told her, rolling his window down. His anger had evaporated, but his mouth looked grim. "I don't want you to say one word about this to anyone else. *Not to anyone*, do you understand me? I don't want one single soul to know I'm connected in any way to Giancarlo Ferrari. OK? Will you agree to that?"

"Of course," she said, relieved the matter was now in her brother's hands and those of his lawyers.

"Do you have cash for the cab?"

"I think so." She began to fumble in her purse.

"Here, take this." Derek handed her several bills. "And, Sis
. . . don't worry. Just go into headquarters today and do your
regular work. And if that shit Ferrari calls you again, tell him
you've put the money in the mail."

Derek continued into the town of Norwood to pick up his
campaign manager, forcing himself to drive within the speed
limit.

Fuck. What he'd learned today from Alexandra was political dynamite. His future was on the line. It didn't have to be
major dirt to topple him—just enough to make him lose *this*
senatorial election. He had no intention of allowing even a
whisper of scandal to come between him and his future quest
for the Presidency.

He pulled up at a gas station where there was an outside
phone booth. Hunched in the phone booth, Derek dialed Rudy
Schmidt, a detective in a Washington agency he had used
several times on congressional business. He offered Schmidt
$1,000 if he could get information on Giancarlo Ferrari and
have it for him by that night, when he got home.

"That quick? Congressman Winthrop, I got sources, but it's
Sunday, and people—"

"Tonight, Rudy. I need it tonight or not at all."

"OK, OK."

The talk in Holyoke was one of Derek's best. His rich, full,
well-enunciated Boston voice excited the imaginations of his
listeners. He knew how to move an audience, how to hold them
breathless in expectation. He *loved* politics.

He and Bo drove home, discussing last-minute strategy and
some of Derek's plans once he became elected. But Derek's
mind was only half on his conversation with his campaign
manager. The rest of his mind was on Giancarlo Ferrari and
what the detective would have to say when he called.

"He's a coke-head," said Rudy Schmidt. "I mean, heavy-
duty. He's even getting perforated nostrils from all the nose
candy. Plays around at working, but he probably only makes
about 15K, if that. He's basically a gigolo. Married a nightclub
singer named Ingrid Hillstrom so he could get his green card.
Now they're both living in a third-floor apartment in Georgetown. She's the big earner in the family. Pulls down about
$1,000 a week at Cheeks, this nightclub she works in, and the
rest of it from hooking."

"Oh, Christ," Derek groaned.

"They buy a lot of coke, and every once in a while Ingrid sells some of it. They give *beaucoup* parties in their apartment. Sometimes she sells the coke there, to her friends. Just your average, red-blooded American couple."

"Parties?" Derek fastened on the one word. "They give a lot of parties?"

"Three, four times a week, the neighbor said. Real late parties, since Ingrid's last set isn't over until 2:00 A.M. Any more information you want?"

"Not now," Derek said. "I'll get in touch if I need anything more. Cash is being messengered to you; you should get it Monday. I don't want to send a check. And, Rudy—"

"Yeah?"

"Not a word about this, not one fucking word, or your ass is grass in Washington, do you read me? Do you get my drift? I do not want one other person knowing I even asked about a scumbag like Ferrari, and if anyone ever does find out, I'll know who the source is, and I'll nail you."

"Sure, Congressman."

"That's not a threat, it's a promise."

After he hung up, Derek paced his bedroom for several minutes. He never folded under pressure, and this was the worst pressure he had ever been under. Two coke-heads. What if Ferrari were to die of an overdose?

Derek started to sweat. Hot, salty beads of moisture began to collect along his shoulders and back. He could smell the fear on himself, and he didn't like it.

He was a Congressman, a member of the House Ways and Means Committee. As recently as last night, certain people had hinted about bigger things for him once he got into the Senate. There was no way in hell, no possible way, that he was going to allow that to be wrecked.

Derek paced. Two coke-heads who gave frequent parties. If Giancarlo were to die, the police would surely connect it to drug-related activities.

The police. They made regular drug busts on places like Ingrid's, and they were known to royally fuck up half of their raids in some way or another. What if . . . ?

Derek returned to the telephone and dialed. His call was to a certain Bubba McCafferty, a forty-nine-year-old police lieutenant on the Washington, D.C., police force. He knew him to be heavily on the take and the man's price. He was also willing to pay it. A job on his security staff, one paying $50,000 a year until retirement. Then great bennies.

All for just one little drug bust. A *special* one.

— ⋈ —

Music pounded into the room, Talking Heads singing "Burning Down the House."

"What do you think, Bitsy? Some party, eh?" Giancarlo, stoned on coke, was playing the role of host.

"Oh, it's a great one," Bitsy Lancombe told him. She was between men and between jobs and had decided to stay with Ingrid for a while, maybe take some classes at Georgetown University.

"Aren't you going to try any stuff? We got good blow, the best. In your honor," Giancarlo said, his laugh loose in a way that Bitsy found offensive. He wandered away before she could answer.

She was just starting toward the dining el, where the bar was, when a sudden crash exploded through the living room.

"*Raid!*" screamed a male voice. "Police raid! Everybody freeze, right where you are."

Ten uniformed men, wearing flak jackets and brandishing guns, burst in. Like commandos they covered the room, gun barrels constantly moving. "*Freeze, assholes!*"

Women screamed.

"Eh," Giancarlo began in a conciliatory tone. Under stress, his Italian accent was much thicker. He took a step forward from the group around the coffee table, using both hands to gesture in protest. "Eh, *paesano*, you got the—"

Blasts of gunfire filled the air, bullets ricocheting wildly around the room, the party goers screaming to the floor. Blood spurted out of Giancarlo's forehead, some of it hitting Bitsy. Then something else hit her face, knocking her backward.

As she fell, the screams, shouts, and explosions faded into the background. Her face was consumed by pain.

One of her eyes stopped seeing, but the other one saw Giancarlo's body sprawled on the floor, covered with splashes of red.

— ⋈ —

Two days later, seated at her desk, a huge stack of pink

phone message slips in front of her, Alexandra sipped coffee, her stomach unaccountably queasy. In front of her lay the *Boston Globe.*

Her eyes scanned the paper, searching for any word of Derek. *Feminist Groups Come Out for Winthrop,* said the headline. She read the article carefully, then clipped it for their file, which was thick with similar pieces from every newspaper in Massachusetts, from the *Lowell Sun* to the *Worcester Telegram.* The media were now regarding Derek's Senatorial bid as a sure thing.

Absorbed in her thoughts, she turned the page. That was when she saw another headline, as vividly as if it were in red neon: *Former Race Driver Killed in Narcotics Raid.*

With shaking hands, Alexandra pulled the page closer to her, staring at the small print, which seemed to waver in front of her eyes.

WASHINGTON—(UPI)—Former race-car driver Giancarlo Ferrari, 23, was killed last night in a police drug raid on the Georgetown apartment of his wife, Ingrid Hillstrom, a nightclub singer. Police say the shooting resulted when Ferrari made a move toward a concealed gun.

Four others were injured, one seriously. Elizabeth Lancombe, 26, has been hospitalized with a bullet wound in the face. Her condition remains serious . . .

Alexandra read the article again, with mounting horror. Giancarlo dead! Nausea flooded through her, and she rushed to the ladies' room, arriving just in time to lose her breakfast into the commode.

Giancarlo . . .

She kept seeing his face. She wiped her mouth and stood in the stall, weeping. Then slowly, insidiously, another feeling crept in. Relief.

— ▶◀ —

Derek won the election with a 16 percent margin over his Republican opponent.

Richard Cox sent a congratulatory telegram to Derek and one to Alexandra as well. It ended with SO PROUD OF YOU, MUCH LOVE, RICHARD. She stared at it for a long time before sliding it into her desk drawer.

The morning after the victory celebration, Alexandra had an appointment to visit her gynecologist for her annual Pap smear. After having spent most of the night watching the election returns with Derek, her father, Felicia, and members of Derek's staff, she felt exhausted.

Dr. Janice Lord entered the small enclosure and, after the usual pleasantries, proceeded with the examination.

"Have you had a pregnancy test, Alexandra?" she asked.

"What?!" Alexandra nearly jumped off the table.

"I'm sorry. I thought that was why you were here. You seem to be pregnant, and you gave the date of your last menstrual period as mid-August."

Alexandra lay very still, feeling hot rushes of blood fill her face, then surge away again. Those nights at the Many Glacier Hotel with Richard. She had noticed the missed periods, but that had happened before.

The gynecologist was smiling, although her eyes searched Alexandra's face. "I hope there's no problem."

"No," Alexandra said dazedly. "No, of course, there's no problem."

Alexandra drove aimlessly, her heart hammering in her ears.

What should she do? Much as she loved Richard Cox— and she did love him—she felt as if she had been maneuvered into an untenable position. Once he learned about the baby, he would probably want to marry her. But did she want to marry a playboy? Would he ever give up his models and actresses, the Katrinas and Darryl Boyers?

Still, Richard was her baby's father. Alexandra could not help feeling he had a right to know.

That afternoon, Alexandra placed a call to the Boston Fitz, where Richard had been keeping his office. A secretary told her that Richard had returned to Chicago and could be reached there.

— ◄► —

Chicago was blessed with an Indian summer, the windows of the highrises along Lake Shore Drive bathed in sunlight. Lake Michigan was dotted with whitecaps.

Alexandra registered at the Drake Hotel, then took a cab to the marina, where Richard's assistant said he could be found on his boat, *Stormy Lady*.

She paid the driver and got out, hugging her light jacket closer against the crisp breeze that blew off the lake. Waves spanked against the pilings, and gulls wheeled overhead, crying out sharply. Most of the boats had been pulled out of the water for the season, and the slips were empty.

A wave of sadness overtook Alexandra.

He was standing on the pier as she walked up.

"Richard—"

He turned, and she saw surprise and pleasure spread across his face. "Why, Alexandra."

"I have to talk to you."

"All right, sure. Just let me finish, and then we'll get some coffee."

He took her to a little cafe that overlooked the marina.

"How about some chowder?" he suggested. "They make the best—stuffed with clams, and the flavor is out of this world."

"No, thank you. I couldn't eat."

"Just coffee, then," he said, ordering from a middle-aged waitress. "It's great to see you," he added, taking both of Alexandra's hands in his. "Just great. I missed you so much. Are you through being mad at me?"

His hands were warm and muscular, and his eyes were so blue—she'd forgotten how penetrating they could be.

"It's not a question of being mad at you, not anymore." She looked down at her hands. "I'm pregnant, Richard."

"What?" Comprehension spread slowly across his face. "Oh, Lexy, oh, Alexandra," he said huskily. He squeezed her hands so hard she thought he would crush her fingers. "Oh, my God." He laughed. "This is wonderful. I can't believe it, it's just great! A baby. Our baby. We'll get married. Jesus . . . I can't believe you're going to make me a father."

He got to his feet, putting down a $20 bill and pulling Alexandra after him. "Come on, Lexy . . . we're got so much to do . . ."

He had her out of the door and halfway to his car before she could interrupt him, half-laughing. "Richard—you didn't even let me finish what I was going to say."

Obediently he stopped and turned to her. "OK, punkie. What is it you were going to say? You don't want to be married to me? Is that it? Lexy, you've *got* to marry me! You're not going to try to have this baby alone, are you? You haven't got some other man, have you? Or—God, no—you wouldn't be considering . . . You wouldn't do that to your baby, would you, Alexandra?"

"No, I wouldn't." To her horror, she started to cry. She wiped at her eyes, sniffling. "I *didn't* do this to rope you in, to get you to marry me! I didn't want to be pregnant now . . . and I don't want a marriage based solely on the fact that I'm going to have a baby!"

"Oh, Lexy. Oh, my darling." He pulled her into his arms, holding her close. "Is that it? Do you think I'm marrying you just because the stork got a little ahead of itself?"

She pulled away from him a little, crying again. "D-don't refer to it in those awful, coy terms. 'The stork.' Ye gods."

"Parturition, then. Do you like that better?" Tenderly he wiped away the trail of tears from her eyes. Then he hugged her tightly again. "God . . . baby, I love you."

"And Katrina? Do you love her, too?"

"I knew you were going to say that. I tried calling you to explain—"

"Explain what?"

"I never slept with Katrina after I started seeing you. I swear it. Those times she was referring to . . . it was all before you. I'll confess, I haven't been a monk. Alexandra . . . I'm not perfect, but don't crucify me for it. I love you. I want to be your husband—I've wanted to for a long time."

What could she say? She wanted her baby to have a good life. And she did love him.

"Yes," she said as they finished walking to Richard's car. "We'll be married. As soon as possible—maybe the first week in December. But, Richard, I want you to promise me there will never be other women. I can't exist in a marriage where there is any of that. There has to be trust."

"I promise, darling," he said. "But how could you think it could be any different?"

She searched his eyes. "This isn't just a whim. I know I'm old-fashioned, but it's the way I feel."

"I love you that way." Richard took her hand and brought it to his lips. "I don't want any other woman but you. Not now. Not ever!"

— ◄► —

December 7, 1982. A date she'd always remember.

In a small room in Trinity Church, in Copley Square,

Alexandra waited for the ceremony to begin, surrounded by her bridesmaids, Jette, Mary Lee, and Pims.

Wearing her flowing Scaasi gown embroidered with bugle beads, with petal-like V-neck and puffed sleeves of silk taffeta, Alexandra floated on a cloud of excitement. The gown was exquisite, designed for her alone. It featured a cathedral train with a hem trimmed with traceries of lace roses. Her headpiece was a simple circlet of woven pearls. She would carry a bouquet of pink-tinged Princess Di roses and white cymbidium orchids.

"Pinch me, and see if I say ouch. I can't believe this is really happening," she said to her friends, who were stunning in gowns of deep, almost black, garnet velvet and silk moiré. Wearing gloves of black, dotted mesh, each would carry a stem of rubrum lilies boasting six elegant, deep-pink-centered blossoms, wrapped in tulle.

"Alexandra! You are perfect," breathed Jette and Mary Lee almost in unison. The women hugged each other, all of them going a little misty with tears.

Jette's escort to the wedding was the star of a new NBC police drama—a man she saw only when Nico was unavailable, which was 80 percent of the time.

Mary Lee's Jake had flown in from New York with her, but the couple was at an impasse about marriage. He wanted it; she didn't.

"I don't think I'm the wedding-bells type," Mary Lee had explained. "Poor Jake; sometimes I think he feels I love my job more than I love him. Did I tell you NBC called? They're looking for a journalist to cohost a Sunday-night news show, and they're actually considering me."

Felicia, elegant in deep mauve, entered the room to hug Alexandra and to loan her a pair of pearl-and-diamond earrings for her "something borrowed." Alexandra was also wearing a pearl bracelet that had been worn by her mother, and by her grandmother before her, at their weddings. Underneath the long gown was a beautiful antique lace garter, threaded through with pale blue silk ribbon, her "something blue."

"Oh, Alexandra," Felicia exclaimed, when she had helped Alexandra put the earrings in her ears. "I can't believe how beautiful you look. I just want to say . . ." Alexandra realized that her father's friend was close to tears. "I never had a daughter, but if I did, she'd be you, dear. I love you."

"Oh . . . I love you, too, Felicia. I think I'm going to cry." Touched, Alexandra reached out to hug the older woman.

Felicia smiled tearily. "Oh, God forbid you should cry now. Your makeup! Anyway, I think I hear the quartet playing the Verdi piece now; that means it's almost time, honey. I have to go and be seated. And the wedding planner wants to start lining everyone up."

In the church vestibule, Jay Winthrop was smiling at Alexandra, his face pale and clearly showing his deep emotion. He was handsome and distinguished in his white tie and tails.

Alexandra felt a surge of affection. "Daddy!"

"Baby. I've never seen anyone more beautiful. Honey, you glow."

"Oh, Daddy . . ."

"I guess now that there's a new guy in your life, Daddy's going to become old hat . . ."

"Oh, Daddy, never." Her gown rustling elegantly, Alexandra flung her arms around her father.

"Well, sweetheart, at least you are getting a fine man. I've known Richard's family for forty-five years. He's a little driven, but I know he'll take care of you. But, honey, I do want you to know something. I'm so proud of you, and I'll always love you as a daughter, but more than that, I'm your friend, too. I hope you'll always come to me if—"

She buried her face in her father's starched front. "Daddy, I love you, too. I'm so happy. I could never find this kind of happiness anywhere, I just know it."

The wedding planner began to position them and give last-minute advice, making sure that the small flower girl and ring bearer, a grand-niece and -nephew of Jay's, were ready.

Jette took an excited breath. "It's time, Alexandra . . . Are you scared? Oh, you're going to knock Richard over; you look like the cover of *Bride's* magazine."

Alexandra clung to her maid of honor. "God," she said, fighting sudden panic. "My last minute as a single woman."

Jette giggled. "You're not going to change your mind, are you?"

"Now?"

"Yeah, well, I guess it is a little late, isn't it? Now, come on. I think somebody is waiting for you."

The strains of Verdi filled the church as Alexandra stood, poised, with her father. Derek was head usher, and Richard's best man was his cousin, Benny, Thomas Benton Cox IV, from Philadelphia.

The church was breathtaking. On either side of the center

aisle, every two or three pews, swags of Swiss organdy had been looped, fastened with big bows with long streamers pooling onto the floor. Lavish bouquets also were affixed to the pews—rubrum lilies and lush, pale pink roses. More flowers were massed at the alter, along with tall cathedral candles made especially for this day.

Alexandra caught her breath as she heard the first notes of Purcell's elegant Trumpet Voluntary.

"This is it, honey," Jay said, his voice hoarse.

Alexandra gripped her bouquet, her smile soft and tremulous. Slowly, gracefully, the bridesmaids began the long walk down the aisle.

Later, she would remember that paced walk down the aisle on her father's arm as a beautiful blur of candlelight, roses, and the turned faces of the guests, many of whom had flown in from New York, Chicago, and Los Angeles.

Then it was only Richard she saw. Standing at the altar waiting for her, his face was alight with anticipation and love.

Alexandra's eyes moistened again, and her heart soared. The guests, the flowers blurred, and all she could see were Richard's eyes locked with hers.

Then, slowly, to the regal notes of the Trumpet Voluntary, she walked the remaining few steps to meet him.

She had chosen the words of the ceremony carefully, to reflect the love and caring she wanted to carry through to the rest of her life; now the beautiful words seemed to fill the church with significance.

She gazed at Richard, her hand steady as he slipped a diamond wedding band next to the magnificent engagement diamond he had given her.

Sliding a gold ring on Richard's finger, she smiled into his eyes, which met hers with such love that she felt her heart pound. She loved him so very much. They were going to be happy. She felt it with every fiber of her being.

Then it was over, and they were walking back down the aisle together, into a new life as Mr. and Mrs. Richard Cox, Jr.

—— ▶◀ ——

With its crimson-and-cream mansard-towered palaces, Biarritz was playground to the superstars and the superrich. The

Grande Plage stretched its white crescent of sand through the center of the city and was washed all day by huge, white-capped breakers.

A Biarritz Fitzgerald was undergoing renovations, so they were staying at the Hôtel du Palais, built in 1854 as a love gift from Napoleon III to his wife, the Empress Eugénie. Its decor was Belle Epoque, and its exquisite, landscaped gardens famous for blue hydrangeas.

Their room was the real center of their life. They made long, slow, delicious love all afternoon, bodies entwining as sunlight silted through the windows to bathe their bodies in its glow. Then there were the sweet morning times, when they stirred lazily, turning to each other still half asleep.

"Why are you crying, babe?" Richard asked quietly one early morning. He had pulled her so close there was not a millimeter of space between his nakedness and hers.

"I . . . I don't know . . . I'm so happy."

"So am I, Lexy."

"I hope it lasts. I want it to last. Richard," she said, clutching him. "We've got to work at it! We can't let it slide down the drain the way so many couples do. Promise me, you'll always put us first."

"Baby, baby," he said, holding her. "I swear it. Don't worry so much."

Finally, when they were wonderfully weary and satiated from their lovemaking, they would leave their suite, famished. Biarritz was a gastronome's delight. La Rotonde, the Hôtel du Palais's formal, Napoleonic dining room, had a spectacular view of the city, and its specialties were duck with raspberries and lobster with steamed peppers. There were cold, cracked crab, pink boiled langoustines, wild-boar pâté, and roast pigeon with wild-mushroom ravioli.

After the enormous lunches, they went for drives in the countryside, visiting colorful, sun-washed Basque villages surrounded by mountains. They drove the Basque Corniche, a twisting road where every dip and curve revealed swooping vistas of sea and mountain, the Atlantic Ocean frothing and roaring at the foot of steep chalk cliffs.

In the hamlet of Louhossoa, the designer Iris Mansard had her studio in a charming, 300-year-old, whitewashed house with blue trim. Its balconies spilled over with geraniums and were hung with huge, shaggy swags of wool that resembled white

Spanish moss. Here Mansard herself spun, dyed, and wove the wool from the Pyrénées sheep to create fashionable jackets and coats.

Richard bought Alexandra two jackets and then, apologetically, asked if they could stop at the Biarritz Fitzgerald. He wanted to check on the status of the remodeling.

"On our honeymoon?" Alexandra began, then cut off the protest when she saw the expression on her husband's face. "Of course, darling," she said. "Whatever you want."

"It's only for an hour," Richard assured her. "Why don't you take a walk in the town and maybe do some shopping? I've kept you too busy to browse, and now's your chance."

Alexandra enjoyed her window-shopping expedition past the many surfing shops (Biarritz was Europe's reigning surfing capital), lovely French-style perfumeries, and Cartier and Hermès boutiques.

At a shop featuring handmade infant clothing, Alexandra paused to glance longingly into its windows at the lacy, hand-embroidered christening outfits.

She touched her stomach lightly. In April she would have her own baby to care for. She believed it would be a boy, and she and Richard already had their son's name picked out: Richard Fitzgerald Cox III. Jokingly, they had already begun referring to him as Trip or Tripper.

"So there you are," Richard said forty minutes later, catching her as she emerged from the shop, carrying a package that contained not only a christening outfit, but also several hand-knit crib blankets. "I see you found the baby shop."

"Oh, I did! Rich, aren't these beautiful?" Impulsively, she lifted her purchases out of the sack, too happy to wait until they got to their room to display them.

"Beautiful," he agreed, fingering the spills of lace and embroidered linen. But he seemed preoccupied.

—— ►◄ ——

Back in New York, a Christmas snow dotted the city, transforming it into a living holiday greeting card. Inside Kenneth Jay Lane's boutique in Trump Tower, knots of shoppers leaned over display cases, examining the glittering costume jewelry. Lane's client list read like a star gallery of New York. Elizabeth Taylor and Jackie Onassis sometimes picked up baubles here, and today Michael Douglas was browsing among the display cases.

Inside a private office area in the back, a stereo played soothing Christmas music, and the bustle of Christmas was muted.

"Are you sure you want a rose motif?" Kenny Lane said. The jeweler was seated at a desk, sketching rapidly on a piece of paper.

"Yes, but not one rose." Richard Cox leaned forward intently.

"More than one? But in good taste, of course. Not gaudy," the jeweler attempted to guide his client.

"Let yourself go on this one, Kenny. I want it to be a stunning, legendary piece."

Lane began to look excited. "I am picturing at least fifty five-carat South African diamonds, *blanc exceptionnel,* that's blue-white, the best. With numbers of smaller stones, set pavé. We'll mix them with pink diamonds, for the color."

His pencil moved swiftly, and what he drew was a necklace of diamonds that had five petaled roses, three blossoms strung in the first row, two more in the second.

"Wonderful," breathed Richard, gazing over the jeweler's shoulder. "This is it, Kenny. This is what I want. I'm giving it to her when our child is born, our son."

Lane looked up. "When is the baby due?"

"Late April, the doctor said."

"That's four months away!" Lane looked horrified. "My God, do you realize what has to be done? I've got to contact the best diamond men in Europe so they can be searching for matched stones. Do you realize how many we'll need? I've got to draw up the design in detail and then arrange for the mounting. Paris, probably. Couldn't you give her the necklace next Christmas, maybe?"

"April," Richard said stubbornly.

"But this is far too little—"

"I don't care what you have to do. Get twenty diamond brokers on it if you have to. Pay bonuses, have people working overtime. I want to bring this necklace to my wife on the day she delivers my son."

Along with the real necklace, Richard also arranged to have a duplicate made as a security measure. The fake would be of cubic zirconia and pink Austrian crystals, identically cut to match the diamonds.

12

Alexandra and Richard
1983–1984

"Hold on to my hand, Richard . . . Tighter, Rich . . . Oh, God! This is . . . oh . . ."

He was sweating as much as she was. "I'm holding on, babe. Just breathe like they taught you."

"Oh, Jesus . . ."

Alexandra lay in a bed in a private delivery room at Massachusetts General, sweat-soaked blonde hair spread out on a hospital pillow. Even perspiring and in pain, his wife was beautiful to him.

As she cried out again, Richard swallowed. "I don't think it will be long now," he told her gently. "Dr. Lord said you were dilated five centimeters. You're doing great."

His wife suddenly stiffened, her eyes staring into space as if she were listening to something Richard could not hear. She moaned, a deep sound that seemed to issue from the very center of her. "Richard . . . God . . . I think the baby's coming . . . pretty fast. I think you'd better go get Dr. Lord . . ."

She arched her back and groaned again, the sound urgent.

Fifteen minutes later, Richard was capped and gowned, standing in the delivery room that smelled of disinfectant. His hands clenched into white-knuckled fists, he watched the wailing, squalling delivery of his son, Trip—the unexpected blood and the child's surprisingly angry cry.

A nurse placed the infant on Alexandra's stomach. She

lifted her head, a beautiful smile on her pale, exhausted face.

"He's so pretty," she whispered in a cracked voice. "Richard . . . our son . . ."

He moved closer. A son. A pounding joy made him delirious. "You did wonderful, Lexy. Oh, babe. He's perfect."

The infant boy had stopped squalling. He had his eyes open, and his hands, curled into fists, were impossibly tiny and pink. He had a full set of everything, including a beautifully shaped and surprisingly large penis. The sight of the baby's genitals attacked Richard like a spear to the heart.

This child would be a part of his own life until he died, and after that he would carry on the bloodline, adding Richard's genes and Alexandra's to the long line of humanity.

"Mr. Cox? I really must escort you out of the delivery room now. You can see your wife in a few minutes."

He shook the nurse away. His eyes glazed as he stared at his wife and child. Then the tears spilled. He stood there shamelessly crying, heedless of the others in the delivery room. He was so full of love and hope and miracle that he could only weep.

That night, Richard came to Alexandra's room. He found her in a pink satin robe, standing to gaze through a glass wall at the mini-nursery connected to her room. The room was already filled with bouquets of roses and pots of spring tulips.

Richard felt less vulnerable now. He had had a chance to get something to eat, to recuperate, and to pull on the mask he usually wore to face the world.

He greeted Alexandra with a kiss, and they held each other. She looked remarkably fresh, her eyes glowing. They turned to gaze through the glass.

They stood watching the baby, making the comments all new parents make, finding resemblances to both of them, and to Jay Winthrop, who had given the child his well-shaped ears and high forehead.

After a minute, though, Alexandra's strength gave out. Richard helped her into bed again and pulled the coverlet up.

"I've brought you something," he said, unable to wait any longer. He handed her an antique mother-of-pearl box, which glimmered softly.

"Oh, what a wonderful box," Alexandra said, delighted. She turned it over in her hands.

"It's pretty, but it's not the real gift," he said.

"You mean there's something inside? Oh, Richard . . ." She

found the small, gold clasp and released it, lifting the cover of the box. Then she gasped in astonishment. Lying on white velvet was the necklace designed by Kenneth Jay Lane. Pink and glowing, it sparkled under the light like the spill of a maharani's treasure. A rope of blazing diamonds supported five beautifully shaped roses formed of deepest pink diamonds, with more white diamonds set pavé.

"My God," Alexandra breathed.

"Take it out of the box."

"I—I can't. My hands are shaking too much."

As he helped her, the necklace spilled from their fingers, light refracting and concentrating in prisms. At any party, no matter how expensive or glittering the jewels of other women, this would be the focus of all eyes. Only the simplest of gowns would be suitable for its magnificence.

"It's beautiful," she breathed. "Oh, God, this is a work of art. It's a masterpiece. This is—I just love it. It's so . . . Richard, I love you."

"Put it on. Here, I'll do it for you."

He had planned what he would say to her, and now the words came to him, made husky by the emotions he felt.

"There are fifty large diamonds, dear Alexandra, and each diamond stands for a year I want us to be together. And there are 108 smaller stones. Each one represents a reason why I love you, but there can never be enough, because I love you for so many, many more reasons than that."

Alexandra was crying as she reached out her arms and pulled him into them. They clung to one another. Then Richard began kissing her neck where the five beautiful roses rested. He planted a kiss on every diamond, warming them with his breath. "You're my heart, darling, the very meaning of my life."

—— ►◄ ——

It was another sunny morning in Los Angeles. Birds twittered in the tropical shrubbery outside the Spanish-style bungalow that Darryl Boyer was renting in Beverly Hills for $10,000 a month. She had forgotten to pull the drapes the previous night, and light spilled in with venomous brightness.

On her bedside table was an empty Absolut bottle, along with a carafe that had held fresh-squeezed orange juice. Her head was pounding. Usually she didn't drink so much, but last night she'd needed it desperately.

She'd been fired from "Canyon Drive." The reason given was that she was "too difficult on the set," according to Bernie Adler, her attorney/agent.

She had met him for lunch at Musso & Frank Grill on Hollywood Boulevard.

"Baby, baby, you really blew it," Adler said, shaking his head.

Darryl pushed away her salad, unable to take another bite. She was a star—bigger than Linda Gray or Joan Collins or any of them.

"They're buying out the rest of your contract, honey, because they said they can't deal with your shtick any more. I fought for you, Darryl. I yelled and screamed, and I even invoked the gods. But it wasn't enough."

"Wasn't *enough*?" She stared at him, incredulous.

"Babe, they say you've been drinking on the set and yelling at the crew. They've had to do as many as twenty takes on one of your scenes. You're late nearly every day, and once you never bothered to show up. They gave me a whole fucking list, Darryl, in writing. Do you want to see it?"

She waved a hand. "I was sick that day; I was on the rag."

"So? Take some Midol. You've also been feuding with the other actresses—Jette Michaud in particular."

"She's a bitch," Darryl muttered.

"Is she? Who the fuck cares? Do you realize what's happened, girl? You have made yourself persona non grata to the entire TV industry. You've just fucked up a five-million-dollar contract—but good. Right now you couldn't even get a job turning over game show letters."

She glared at Bernie, aware that a table of tourists was staring at her.

"And one more thing," Adler said, looking uncomfortable.

"What's that?"

"They said you're starting to age—on camera, I mean."

"What?" Darryl's hand flew to her neck, where she fingered her throat with frantic, squeezing motions.

"The camera doesn't lie, sweetie. Not that it matters now, anyway. Why don't you start looking around for a nice job in public relations, Darryl? You're still a celebrity. You could be a spokeswoman for one of the big cosmetics companies. I'll put in a word for you."

That had been yesterday. She'd tried to drink herself into oblivion, but even the vodka hadn't cooperated.

Curley Hingham, the gossip columnist, called her at 9:00 A.M., wanting to get "her side of it." "Everyone's going to want to know, hon, and you want them to get the real story, don't you? You know I always try to research my facts."

"Research your own butt," Darryl said rudely, slamming the phone down in Hingham's ear.

She rummaged in the kitchen and found another vodka bottle and some Diet Coke. She mixed the two together in a blue crystal goblet, daintily adding a slice of lime to the edge of the glass. Finally she started to think of a plan, and the plan was simple and effective.

What did a woman do when she was in trouble? She turned to a man. And what man did Darryl have in her background who was megarich, world-class powerful, and who once had been crazy after her body?

Richard Cox could make a few phone calls, she'd bet.

Better than that, she thought feverishly, she could get him back. His current wife was all legs, blonde hair, and that old-fashioned kind of 1950s-pretty starlet face. A sweet woman, Darryl thought contemptuously, soft and mild and afraid to stand up for herself.

Calming down a little, Darryl sipped on her drink. There was no real reason she should fail. She was smart, clever, and determined. Best of all, she was absolutely desperate.

"Dickey, baby, I saw a picture of you in the paper last week. You looked soooo sexy I had to rip it out and hang it in my bedroom." Darryl's smoky voice purred across the telephone wire.

Richard immediately took warning. "What is it you want, Darryl?"

"Oh . . . I'm going to be in Chicago tomorrow; I'm getting in around eleven. I thought we could have lunch. Or something."

"Darryl, it's good to hear from you, really, but I'm tied up all day tomorrow in meetings. And I have to fly out tomorrow night for Vancouver."

"Just one little lunchie," she pleaded. "A quick one? A quickie?"

"What are you trying to say?"

"I just need to see you. It's been two long years," she said, her voice dissolving in easy tears. "You don't know . . . oh, Dickey-bird . . . you don't know what they've done to me!

They've hurt me so bad . . . they've killed me."

He prayed one of his secretaries was not listening in on the line. "Come on. What do you mean, they've 'killed' you?"

"I mean they've dropped me from the show! Dumped me off 'Canyon Drive'! I'm not bullshitting you, Richard. I'm just desperate; I don't know what to do or where to turn. I just feel so helpless. Please? Please see me? I promise I won't come on to you." She started to cry.

Despite serious reservations, Richard agreed to see her. Carefully he set it up to thwart any possible advances from his ex-wife. The place he chose for them to meet was a little Chinese restaurant, the Mandarin Inn, family-owned and -run, a plain place full of wooden booths and waiters fresh off the boat. Nothing glamorous or sexy.

Darryl arrived wearing a black Donna Karan dress with a front wrap that barely concealed her firm, silicone-augmented breasts. She wore enough Opium to fill the entire restaurant, and her hair was streaked and tousled.

"Jesus, Darryl. I hate to say it, but couldn't you have dressed a little more appropriately? That dress is coming apart in front."

"Do you like it?" Her huge, moist blue eyes were brimming with seduction. "I remember all the things you like, Richard. All the sexy things. Remember that time when we—"

"That's in the past," he cut her off hastily. "Tell me about your problems with 'Canyon Drive.' "

For the next forty minutes she listed her complaints and vendettas, giving him details on what she had heard from her agent and director, as well as everyone else involved in the TV show.

"But the bottom line is, you're out," Richard summed it up at last.

Her eyes filled with tears. "I don't want to be out. Please, do something. Just get me back on the show again."

"Darryl, I'll try to help. I'll make a few phone calls. But I don't have that kind of influence—"

"You know everybody, for God's sake!"

"I'll do my best, Darryl."

"You don't mean it. You're just saying that to get rid of me, aren't you? You're afraid you might be attracted to me again. You're afraid we might go to bed together and be really, really good, the way we were before. And we would be, too. Dickey, I do know how to please you. I learned your body like a book. I learned *everything* you like . . .''

Richard talked with Rusty Copa, Robert Ehrman, and Bernie Adler, but all three said Darryl was not worth the trouble.

"She's over the hill," Copa added bluntly.

"Keep her on at least until the end of the season," Richard suggested.

"No way, José. We've already written her out, and we are *not* going to resurrect the bitch, not for anything."

Hesitant to put his assistant at Darryl's mercy, Richard phoned Darryl and broke the news, repeating as much of the conversations as he dared.

"Oh, God," Darryl breathed into the receiver when he had stopped talking.

"Darryl, you're not finished. There are other parts, other roles. Your agent will find you something."

She screeched, "Didn't you talk to him? He'll find me something, all right—as a mouthpiece for some stupid company that makes douche bags and panty liners!"

"I'm sorry," he said.

"Sorry! You're not sorry! You're a man, and men only get better as they get older; women get worse!" Her voice sounded slurred and whiskey-coarse. "I look old, that's the trouble! They told me. I'm getting lines. I'm going to have to get a face-lift. I should have got one two years ago, and then I wouldn't be having this problem!"

"Darryl, you don't look old yet," he found himself saying.

"Ohhhh," she sobbed into the phone. "I don't know what I would do without you, Dickey-bird. I can turn to you anytime, can't I? Anytime, day or night . . ."

Holding on to the phone, he froze in dismay. "Darryl, I have a wife now, and a baby son. I won't jeopardize my family."

"*I'm* your family, too," she sobbed.

"Darryl, you're my ex-wife. That hardly qualifies as family."

"You owe me," she wept. "You owe me."

— ◀▶ —

A November rain rattled against the windows, spitting hard, cold raindrops against the glass.

Bitsy Lancombe stood in the downstairs hallway of Ingrid's

apartment building on P Street, fumbling with her key to the tiny mailbox. Her hand shook violently, and she had to aim the key four or five times before it finally entered the lock. She had just returned from one of the computer classes she was taking at Georgetown University, and she was exhausted.

She was only twenty-seven, but for all practical purposes her life was over. How could she find a good job when she was too tired to go to class? Who would want to hire her with her face looking as it did?

The ricocheting bullet had struck Bitsy's right eye, shattering it and causing the surrounding skin to droop grotesquely. She had undergone five corrective operations, and although the ophthalmologist and plastic surgeon seemed pleased with their work, Bitsy was not. The glassy artificial eye she saw when she looked in the mirror made her skin crawl.

She reached inside the mailbox and pulled out three letters. Two were bills for Ingrid, and the other was a letter from Hooper, Schwartz, Canfield, and van Wooten, the law firm she'd engaged for her suit against the Washington, D.C., police.

Her hopeless lawsuit. Giancarlo *had* appeared to be reaching for a gun, several witnesses had stated in depositions. End of story.

She thrust the letter into her purse and rushed up the three flights of stairs, unlocking the apartment door and hurrying inside.

"Did you stop at the Safeway?" Ingrid wanted to know as Bitsy entered. Her roommate was wearing a fuchsia pink teddy and a pair of thongs and had just washed her hair.

"What . . . oh, no, I forgot."

"Jesus, you never remember anything anymore, do you? I need some tampons, and we need beer. And by the way, you haven't paid your rent yet this month. I hope you're not going to be late again."

Bitsy's trust fund paid $2,500 a month, just barely enough to pay her tuition and the lawyers.

"Sorry," she mumbled, throwing herself onto the couch.

"Jesus, what's the matter with you *now*?" Ingrid demanded.

"Nothing . . ."

"I thought you had a computer class today."

"I did, but I left it. I . . . they were staring at me."

Ingrid expelled a sigh. "They were not, Bits. You look fine. When are you going to accept it? You look as good as you ever did before, if not better. After all, they did fix your nose, too.

The one that French guy broke."

Tears filled Bitsy's eyes. "I look like shit," she whimpered. "I'm disfigured."

"Oh, crap," Ingrid said. "I hate it when you're so negative."

Ingrid went into the bathroom, picked up her hair dryer, and began blow-drying her hair. "Will you just try to lighten up a little?" she fumed. "How can I have people here when you put everyone in such a down mood?"

"Why did they shoot him?" Bitsy asked.

"Oh, no," Ingrid groaned. "Not your theory again. You sound like a fucking broken record. Because he was a jerk," she added flippantly. "Who knows why they shot him? If he'd just stayed where he was and not moved, none of it would have happened. Just forget it, would you? Giancarlo was just a cokehead. At least you pay some rent."

"I still think something was fishy," Bitsy muttered.

"I still think you're full of shit. And I'll tell you something else," Ingrid went on. "I want to give a party here tomorrow night. If you're going to act like this, you can just go someplace else."

"Please, Ingrid. Where would I go?"

"I don't know. Go out to the movies. Go to a bar."

"A bar?" Bitsy shuddered all over. "How could I go there? People would look at me . . . men . . ."

"Oh, fuck!" Ingrid burst out. "You look perfectly OK. Your hair looks a little limp, that's all, but if you'd go and get yourself a perm and a little blonde streaking, you'd look great."

That night, after Ingrid left for work, Bitsy searched the apartment inch by inch, from the untidy litter under Ingrid's bed to the bathroom cabinets full of bottles. She even took off the couch cushions and probed among the lint and stray pennies.

All she found was a plastic bag under the bathroom vanity. Opening it, she found an old racing suit and a pair of fireproof racing gloves. The suit was dirty and dusty and reminded her of a garbage man's coverall.

She sat staring at them for a long time. Unconsciously she rubbed at her right eye socket, which often ached. There was a secret here—and she was determined to find out what it was.

— ⋈ —

Alexandra was pregnant again, and she and Richard were ecstatic. Another child! Richard plunged into his hectic life with even more zest. Now it was even more important for him to continue to build his hotel empire.

One December night, Richard had returned, via company jet, to his Chicago office, following a roast he had attended for Milton Berle at the New York Friars Club. He and David Kwan had begun putting together a deal, and he was in a hurry to dictate a file memorandum on what they had said. He always documented any discussions he had with possible financial backers.

As the private elevator whispered to a stop at the forty-fourth level, he emerged, loosening his formal bow tie.

His office door was ajar, and he pushed it open, annoyed with his assistant, who apparently had forgotten to lock up when she left. He switched on the light.

"Hello, Dickey-bird." Darryl sauntered across the king-size office, totally nude except for her spike-heeled shoes, her body silhouetted against the breathtaking, sparkling view of Chicago at night. She was smiling, her blonde hair bed-tousled, her only other adornment a diamond pendant on a chain so long that the stone rested between her round, pink-tipped breasts.

"Darryl—Jesus."

"Well? How do you like me? Do I look wonderful, or do I look wonderful?" She pirouetted before him. The long, curved line of her buttocks and legs was still magnificent. Her skin had an oily glisten. "I went and had a few things lifted, a few more things tightened. What do you think?"

Richard shed his evening jacket and held it out to her. "Put this on, Darryl, for Christ's sake! How did you get in here?"

She refused it, preferring to display herself for him, then flung herself on one of the long Italian leather couches. Stretching out, she began fondling herself, running her fingers through her fine, blonde pubic hair.

He strode over to her and tossed the jacket on top of her. With three more steps, he was at his telephone.

"Security, get somebody up here—now! To my office!" he snarled into the receiver. "We have an intruder. And call Slattery."

"Please, honey, please." Darryl was sobbing now. "Richard, I *had* to come. I need you. I need your friendship . . ."

"You need a psychiatrist, Darryl!"

"Please, oh, Richard, please," she wept.

"Boss? Oh shit." Richard turned to see Blackjack Slattery, his chief of security, and two uniformed guards.

"Get her out of here," Richard snapped. "Find her some clothes, and ship her out in a cab. And tomorrow we're going to talk about how she got in."

It took both guards to subdue her, her oiled body squirming in their hands as she screamed and kicked. But at last they had her straitjacketed in the sleeves of Richard's evening coat. They found her black mink coat and her street clothes stuffed in a large Gucci tote that she had hidden behind the couch.

"Don't call the police," Darryl begged, her makeup streaked with tears. "Please don't! I can't stand the publicity!"

Calling the police was the last thing Richard intended.

"Get dressed then."

Sobbing, she turned her back and pulled on her skintight black sweater and leather skirt. "I hate you," she wept. "I just hate you so much."

By the time Richard arrived at their penthouse, it was after 2:30 A.M. Alexandra lay asleep in bed with the light on, an opened book on her stomach. He stood staring down at her, thinking how beautiful she was. She stirred, murmuring sleepily, as he slipped into the big bed beside her.

"I had a problem tonight," he began.

"I had problem, too . . . no husband . . . nobody warm to hold," she mumbled. She reached out for him, and he felt the full, warm, feline length of her nakedness against him.

"Lexy, Lexy," he whispered.

"Make love," she begged.

He lost himself in the silken flesh of his wife, hearing her soft moaning cries as she climaxed again and again.

In the next three weeks, Darryl phoned Richard's office sixty-two times. Richard beefed up the hotel security and swore his assistant to secrecy.

Gloria had been with him for fifteen years and was a streetwise divorcée supporting several children. "Just get her another part, Mr. Cox, maybe in a movie this time. That should shut her up."

"But she's blacklisted in Hollywood."

"So? They make movies in a lot of other countries, don't they?"

It gave Richard an idea. He telephoned David Kwan.

"I'm thinking of bankrolling a couple of movies, and I

know you've been looking for blonde American actresses. Well, I think I know how we can help each other out."

"You have someone?"

"With star quality," Richard promised. "All I ask is that you film in Hong Kong."

⸻ ◄► ⸻

The year of Trip's birth, Richard became infused with an even stronger desire to build a dynasty.

As his empire grew in complexity, so did the problems. One morning in December, when Trip was eight months old, Richard met in his office with Robbie Fraser, the president of the American Service Workers Union.

"So you're going to go big, really big," the union man began, in his gravelly voice with its faint Scottish burr.

"I'm going to be the biggest," Richard said. "Within three years. Four at the max."

"Takes a lot of other people's money to do that," Fraser responded.

"I'm willing to take the risks. It will happen," Richard said confidently.

"But not on the backs of my union members. Cox, there are a lot of issues we haven't really addressed yet."

"Such as?"

Fraser took twenty minutes to enumerate them, ending with a veiled threat of a strike. It was a threat that Richard did not miss.

"Look, I understand the union's priorities, but I hate anything that smacks of blackmail. I won't tolerate it, and I won't buckle under it—that's something about me you've yet to learn, Fraser."

"And you've got something to learn, too, Cox," Fraser said. "Times are changing, and the union is, too. There are new people coming up, tough, mean sons of bitches. They're old-fashioned brawlers and grapplers. I hate it, but I can't get around it."

"You're referring to Tank Marchek."

"And people like him." Fraser sighed. "I'm warning you; maybe not this year, maybe not next, but it's coming. They want what they want, and they'll get it, too."

"Not while I'm at the helm."

"Then maybe you won't be at the helm," Fraser said quietly.

"What's that supposed to mean?"

"Take it to mean anything you want, Cox. I just want you to heed the warning. We're floating now, we're not asking anything you can't give, but in the next few years, that is going to change. You're going to have to give us what we want, or there will be a massive strike. It could cripple whatever chain we target. And the Fitz just might be our target."

After Fraser left, Richard forced himself to lean back in his chair. Maybe he should slow down a little. Every hotel cost hundreds of millions, even the small but elegantly luxurious Park Royal Fitzgerald he had just acquired on Central Park West. What if the economy took another perilous dip, upsetting the balance of cards he had built?

He'd protected himself against that by working with Drexel Burnham Lambert, the junk-bond specialist. Maybe he should consider a $500 million bond issue with a slightly higher interest rate. That would take the pressure off him for at least two years. He had the momentum going, and he knew he was not going to stop.

⸺ ►◄ ⸺

Alexandra glanced at the big clock on the wall of the labor room. The minute hand had crawled only five minutes further. She tried to stretch out more comfortably, arching her spine to ease the backache that had plagued her for the last six hours. Dr. Lord had told her the infant was in a breech presentation, and she would have to have a cesarean section. They were waiting now for an operating room.

Where was Richard? She had left a message with Gloria to try to reach him, and his assistant had felt sure she could track him down within the next twenty minutes.

Alexandra twisted uncomfortably, hoping she'd be able to see her husband before they took her to surgery. She didn't want to go under anesthetic without him.

"Mrs. Cox? How are we feeling? Is there anything you need?" The nurse came back to put the blood-pressure cuff on her arm. "No liquids, of course. But maybe another blanket, or an extra pillow?"

"No, thank you. Just my husband. Has he called yet?"

"Not only has he called, but he left a message that he'll be here in about ten minutes," the woman reassured her.

Alexandra leaned back with a sigh of relief. He was going to be with her, just as he had promised.

Richard rushed over to her as they were transferring her to the gurney to take her to the operating room.

"Babe? Lexy?" Even through her pain, Alexandra could sense his anxiety.

"Rich . . ."

"Baby, baby, I dropped everything and came as soon as Gloria called. Dr. Lord told me they're doing a cesarean. I've called for the chief of staff to assist her, and we're getting the best anesthesiologist in the state. I've also got a group of neonatologists standing by. And all the latest equipment."

He looked so tense that Alexandra summoned up a smile and reached to squeeze his hand. "It's going to be all right," she said softly. "Rich, Dr. Lord said his heartbeat is very strong."

"His?" Richard questioned.

"It's a boy," she told him, breaking the news at last. "They did an ultrasound, and little Andrew Winthrop Cox is waiting for us."

"Mrs. Cox? Mrs. Cox? Are we awake now? Wake up."

"Mmmmm . . ."

"You've got a beautiful boy. Seven pounds, six ounces."

"Oh," Alexandra breathed, unsure whether she spoke aloud. "Is he all right?"

"Just perfect. He's got blond hair. A few wisps of it, anyway. A very nice boy."

Andy. Alexandra felt a surge of satisfaction. Another healthy son. Richard would be so happy . . . and she was, too. She still wanted a little girl, but maybe in a few years.

"I want to see my husband," she whispered. "When can I see Richard?"

Later, when they had wheeled her back up to her private room, now filled with masses of pale peach roses, her husband leaned over her bed, taking her in his arms. "Lexy," he said in a choked voice. "You don't know what this means to me. Two boys. You've given me so much . . . and I have something for you. As a token. I had Kenny make this up for you."

He pulled away and took out another box, similar to the mother-of-pearl box her diamond necklace had come in, but smaller.

Alexandra opened it to discover a pair of pierced earrings that matched the necklace. Rose-pink diamonds dripped in a cascade of glitter.

"They're glorious," she breathed, touching one of them. Light caught it in roseate pinpoints.

"Do you want to put them on?"

She sank back on the pillow, exhausted. "I do, but . . . ."

"I'll put them in your ears, darling." Tenderly Richard pushed back the blonde hair from Alexandra's temples and fastened the posts of the earrings in her ears. His touch was so gentle that a warm peace and contentment enveloped her.

Her bedside phone rang.

"Damn," she said. "I wonder who that is. Not your office?"

"I'll get it." Richard picked up the receiver and said hello, but after he listened for a couple of seconds, she saw his expression change.

The voice on the other end of the line had a Hispanic accent.

"Mr. Richard Cox?"

"I'm Cox."

"I'm Lieutenant Gomez of the Los Angeles Police Department. Your secretary told us how to reach you. Mr. Cox, I'm calling about Darryl Boyer. She is your ex-wife, isn't she?"

"Yes."

"Well, your ex-wife's housekeeper found Miss Boyer after she took an overdose of drugs and alcohol."

Richard uttered a low groan. Alexandra was staring at him, her eyes wide and alarmed.

"Who is it?" she questioned.

He covered the phone. "Just a minute, Lexy . . . What's her condition? Is she alive?"

He saw Alexandra's eyes widen further.

"They've pumped out her stomach, and she's still comatose, but the chances are good she'll survive," Gomez answered.

"Why are you calling me?" he demanded, both sorry and angry at Darryl for being such a damned fool.

"The maid said she didn't have any other relatives."

"Well, I'm not a relative," he snapped. "What hospital is she in?"

Gomez named a Los Angeles hospital.

"When I get back to my office, I'll call her doctor and make sure she has everything she needs." He hung up.

"Richard . . . who was that? Who's in the hospital?" The

diamond earrings glittered in Alexandra's ears as she tried to sit up.

"It's—Darryl," he told her reluctantly.

"Darryl!"

"Baby, she took an overdose of sleeping pills in L.A."

Alexandra looked shocked. "But I don't understand. Richard, why would they call you here?"

"I don't know, Lexy, but don't worry about it. It was just one of those mix-ups. The maid didn't know who else to name."

"So she named you? Why would you be called unless . . . Oh, God, Richard! Have you been seeing her?"

He flushed, remembering the night Darryl had surprised him in his office.

He went to the bed and took his wife's hands in his, trying with the pressure of his hands to convey all he felt. "I told you, I don't know why they notified me. I haven't seen Darryl in years, Lexy. I don't want to see her. She doesn't mean anything to me. *You* mean everything to me, Alexandra. You mean the world."

She gazed at him, her eyes ringed with exhaustion. "God, I want to believe you. You promised, Richard, when we got married that there would be no other women."

"And there aren't! Damn it, Lexy! She's an unbalanced woman, and I'm not responsible for some Los Angeles police lieutenant calling me here. There is no way I could have predicted that would happen. Believe me when I tell you that. I adore you, Lexy. I always have, and I always will."

Alexandra finally nodded, reaching out for him. They held each other, Richard caressing Alexandra's back until she relaxed slightly. "I love you, too," she whispered.

As he stroked his wife's back, Richard struggled to hide his dismay and anger at Darryl. Damn it, he never should have had any contact with her at all. He never should have sent her to Hong Kong, to David Kwan.

13

Jette
1984

Flashbulbs popped, and people were screaming. Groupies, fans, and tourists pushed against the ropes in an attempt to get closer to the celebrities who were arriving to attend the premiere of the new Richard Gere picture.

Jette and Nico sat in the backseat of a white stretch limo in the lineup waiting to disgorge passengers in front of Mann's Chinese Theater on Hollywood Boulevard.

Ahead of them, Elizabeth Taylor was getting out of her limo, fighting a mob of reporters with microphones.

"Oh," sighed Jette happily. She clutched at Nico's hand. "Look! We're next in line."

She smoothed the flounces of the white Nina Ricci evening gown she wore. It was midthigh, triple-flounced, strapless, and sensational. She wore huge, dangling white earrings and carried a white feather boa.

"All these stars showing off," Nico growled, affecting a bored expression.

Jette leaned forward to look out her shaded window, and as she did so, the dress rode up her thighs. Nico reached out and tugged it down, his touch surprisingly gentle.

"Watch it," he told her. "They've got TV cameras out there. And pull up your top, too; it's slipping."

"Pull here, pull there," Jette griped. "So what? Dolly Parton shows hers off; why can't I?"

"You're much classier," he said. "You have to remember that."

The driver came around to open the door, and Jette stepped out onto a red length of carpet.

Before she could take even a step, people came running toward her, sticking microphones in her face and yelling out questions. "Jette! Jette! Is it true you've actually dated Richard Gere?"

"Him? Oh, no, it was just publicity stuff," Jette began.

"But weren't you his lover? Weren't you—"

"Come on," Nico said, grasping her arm. "No more questions. Leave her alone," he snarled.

He escorted Jette into the theater, where a crush of people mingled, drinks in hand. Stars, studio executives, PR people, agents, directors, and rich groupies who had managed to wangle invitations. The men were in black tie, the women in designer gowns.

"I'm sorry," Jette murmured to Nico as they made their way to one of the four bars. "All those questions. Richard Gere. I really haven't . . . I mean, he *is* something else, but you're the only man I want."

"I'd better be."

"Oh, you are."

Over the past three years, Jette had come to know Nico better than any woman ever had. But he still puzzled her sometimes. He could be extremely tender with her, soft and loving. In public, though, he often acted very distant. She supposed it was because he was *Siciliano*, as he so often reminded her. They didn't want the world to see any weakness, and to them, loving a woman was weakness.

At the same time, Nico was fiercely possessive. Once, after they had made love for four straight hours and were both dripping with perspiration, he had said to her, "You love me too much, Jette."

"What?"

"You don't know me. You love me and know nothing about me; you only know me as a lover. I am much more than that, little Jette. And I will be more for you one day, when things evolve in my family. I only demand one thing of you."

"What's that?" she asked.

"I won't go where any man has gone before."

"And what's that supposed to mean?" Although she already knew.

He put his hand on her warm, wet pubic mound. "This. It's mine. It's going to stay mine."

More flashbulbs were popping in the theater lobby as Nico excused himself and went to the men's room. Shirley Eder, a popular syndicated columnist, came rushing up to Jette, trying to get an item for her column.

"I am definitely interested in moving over to the big screen," Jette told her. "But I'm too smart to give up my part on 'Canyon Drive.' The road is paved with stars who gave up roles on popular series and were never heard from again."

Shirley was scribbling on a small steno pad. "And who is your escort tonight, Jette? He's such a hunk. Is he an actor?"

"Oh, he's a Chicago businessman."

"What business is he in?"

"Various enterprises," Jette said vaguely. "He makes deals."

After Shirley left, Jette was looking around for Nico, when a tall, handsome man happened to glance at her at the very moment she was looking at him. She drew a blank for an instant, then remembered him as Derek Winthrop, Alexandra's brother. She'd met him at the wedding. She remembered flirting with him then; actually she'd been outrageous. She couldn't help smiling.

"You're the most gorgeous woman here," he said, coming up to her. His smile lit up his face and sparkled in his blue eyes.

"Not when Elizabeth Taylor is present," she told him coyly.

"Say, you've got her beat hands down."

"Oh?"

"I'm a man who speaks my mind. I think you're beautiful," he told her bluntly. "I can be reached at the Senate Office Building; you can ring straight through to my assistant."

Jette was flattered. She had known celebrities all her life, but few in the political arena. Derek Winthrop wasn't as handsome as Nico, but she sensed power in him. Interesting. Definitely interesting.

She eyed him flirtatiously. "I might call . . ."

"I hope you do."

Just then Nico came walking back and led her into the theater. "Even the bathrooms have faucets like dragons," Nico remarked. "Who was that guy?"

"Oh, you know. Just somebody trying to make small talk."

He took her arm and pressed it to him more tightly than was necessary. "Don't play dumb. He wasn't making small talk.

He was coming on to you."

"So what if he was?" Jette cried. "Men come on to me all the time, Nico. It's part of the business. People don't think anything of it."

A mistake.

His voice was icy cold. "Part of what business?"

"Why—the film business. Nico, people flirt with other people; it's just a way of complimenting them. It doesn't *mean* anything." She was getting angry now. "Anyway, what do you care?" she cried recklessly. "You're not planning to marry me, are you? I mean, the only woman who's ever going to be good enough for you is some Italian virgin."

His eyes met hers, their blue light as chilly as diamonds. "I happen to value virginity."

"What? Oh, you value virginity! Oh, that's just wonderful! That really makes me laugh," she hissed. "You, who use amyl nitrate as a regular part of sex, and who own a whole supply of cock rings and vibrators and body oils. Cock rings. I didn't even know what one was until I met you."

"Jette—" he began warningly.

"Oh, yes, you love to fuck me, but that's all I am to you. Just a good piece of ass."

"Shut up," he told her. "This is a public place."

"I won't shut up. Nico, I'm not just a . . . a good lay! I've been good to you. I've—"

"Be quiet, or I'll get up and leave," he snapped.

Five minutes later, he did.

Jette sat alone in the darkened theater with her eyes fixed on the screen, but she saw little of the picture. She was too hurt. Afterward, she allowed the limo driver to drop her off at Spago, where Cybill Shepherd was having an "afterglow" party.

The party was jammed with people, an eclectic mix of studio types and stars. The stereo was pumped up loud, Linda Ronstadt singing a new Alexandra Winthrop ballad. It was just another Hollywood party as far as Jette was concerned. She'd come a long way since that party three years ago at Bradley Goldfarb's. Now she belonged.

"Well, we meet again," Derek Winthrop said, emerging from a crowd clustered around the bar.

"Did you wangle an invitation to this party, too?"

He grinned. "Guilty as charged. It helps to have friends in high places. Listen. What do you say we cut out, go and get a drink, maybe talk a little."

Jette hesitated. If Nico found out, he'd be furious.

"Hey, I'm not going to attack you. Just a drink."

"I've only been at the party five minutes. I guess I could . . . I'm in the mood for a really sweet drink. Something tropical, with fresh pineapple in it and about a thousand calories."

"I know just the place," Derek promised.

— ◄ —

Two months later, Jette had gotten to know Derek Winthrop *very* well. He intrigued her with his witty and charismatic exterior, his utter assurance that others would respond to him. And respond they did. It amused her to go to dinner with him in Boston and find crowds of people flocking to the table to meet not her, but him.

It was a bicoastal affair. Every Friday, he had his secretary send her flowers, and twice a month, he'd send tickets for weekend flights to Boston.

She found him a mediocre lover. At foreplay, she would rate him a 7, and at staying power, about a 5. Just as he was beginning to climax, he would ask her to talk dirty and sometimes even to hurt him a little by squeezing his balls.

It was harmless enough. He probably couldn't come without it, she figured. Jette didn't expect and didn't get orgasms with Derek. Nico Provenzo was probably the only man in her life with whom she would ever share that experience.

A U.S. Senator and a Chicago Mafia man. Incredible.

Now that she was juggling two love affairs, life took on a sharp focus, a razor-edge excitement. Neither Derek nor Nico knew about the other. Both men came occasionally to L.A., Nico for mysterious "family business" and Derek to attend conferences on Latin American trade.

Jette used her answering machine to separate the two phases of her love life. If she was entertaining one of her lovers, she switched off the ringer and turned down the volume on the machine so that her messages couldn't be overheard.

One June weekend, however, when Nico was in L.A., she forgot to switch on her machine.

She and Nico were lying in bed reading the Sunday *Los Angeles Times.* Her bedroom, swathed in yards of lavender chintz, was a musky haven of untidy bedcovers, sexual odors, and spicy smells from a huge pizza lying in a cardboard box between them.

When her white, gilt-embossed telephone trilled for attention, Jette instantly cursed her carelessness. Nico always asked who her calls were from, and if she didn't pick up the receiver, he would wonder why.

Jette reached for the bedside phone. "H'lo?"

"Baby," Derek Winthrop's voice said in her ear.

"Sorry, wrong number," she responded, hanging up.

The phone immediately rang again, and again Jette jumped for it.

"Wrong number!" she snapped into the receiver. This time she surreptitiously flicked off the ring button. Later, she'd tell Derek that a fan had been bothering her, or something.

She returned to the bed and plumped down on the king-size mattress. "Cripes!" she exclaimed. "Honestly, Nico, I think I'm going to have to change my number again. I keep getting these weird calls."

"What weird calls?" Nico looked up from the article he was reading, looking as if he'd stepped from the pages of a *Playgirl* calendar, his muscular chest matted with black, silky hair.

Jette giggled nervously. "You know, crazy calls. I get them a lot. And letters, from sickos. Guys who write me in care of the network, talking about marriage, or why did I get the abortion on TV, or why did I wear a fur coat that killed seventy-nine animals. Or God told them to get in touch with me so we can mate together, combine our genes, and save the world." She giggled. "That really happened. Cybill got a letter like that."

Nico's laser eyes searched hers. "Yeah?" he said softly.

"Yeah." She cuddled up to him, grabbed the paper away from him, and added in her most cajoling voice, "Hey, come on, sweet guy, do you have to read that boring old stock market stuff? I mean, it's always the same, isn't it? Buying, selling, everyone getting filthy rich."

Nico stared at her, and for a second Jette felt a stab of uneasiness.

He finally told her, "People are pyramiding their investments, buying on margin, acting like fools. In fact, I see signs of a stock market crash, maybe in the next year or two. If you've got any stocks, I suggest you think seriously about unloading them."

"My business manager does all that."

"Well, maybe you need to talk to him. Or I'll do it for you."

He put down the paper and reached for her, smothering her face and neck with kisses that became licks of his sensuous, darting tongue. Jette relaxed, sighing with pleasure. She had to be more careful with the answering machine. She didn't want to lose Nico.

——— ◄ ———

That year, Alexandra had her third platinum record with a ballad, "Forgiving Woman," written for Kenny Rogers and Barbara Mandrell. "Forgiving Woman" had crossed over from the country category, had a bullet, and was already number ten on the *Cashbox* hit list.

All of Alexandra's songs now had the word *woman* somewhere in their title. It was her trademark.

"So what's new in the music world?" Jette asked Alexandra one rainy Saturday afternoon in July. She had arrived to spend a long weekend with the Coxes.

Alexandra was glowing. "I have so much I want to write. I'm just having this amazing creative surge. I've been talking with the A & R people at Arista Records, and they want to put out an album with just my songs, sung by different artists."

"Sounds wonderful."

Alexandra went to the white Steinway grand piano that dominated the Cox living room. "Do you want to hear my latest?"

"I do, but can you play 'Easy Woman' first? I never get tired of hearing that song. It reminds me of the way I feel about Nico."

Jette threw herself onto one of the long, chintz-covered couches, put up her feet, and closed her eyes.

Alexandra's mellow voice poured into the room. *I've never been an easy woman,* she sang. *Until I met you . . .*

Jette listened, entranced. The song reached into the center of her, drawing out a poignant sadness.

"Wow," she said when the last husky tones of Alexandra's voice faded into the air. "All I can say is, wow! How can you think up such sad things?"

"Did you think that song was sad, Jette?"

At that moment, Trip toddled into the room; the nanny, behind him, carried three-month-old Andrew in her arms.

"Mommy, Mommy!" Trip ran up to Alexandra.

The children were beautiful, with round faces and blond

hair, pretty enough to model, Jette thought. But Trip was especially striking. Even now you could sense the man he would someday grow up to be.

"Trip heard the piano and wanted you to sing him something," Brownie said.

"He did, did he? Well, it so happens I've written him a little song. I just finished it last night."

"Song," Trip begged, looking expectant.

Alexandra poised her hands over the piano keys. "This is a song about a squirrel," she began, her voice warm. "A very special squirrel." She played an introductory chord.

"Kw . . . kwirl?" Trip was learning to talk, his vocabulary far larger than that of most fifteen-month-old boys.

"Squirrel," Alexandra repeated. "A happy, jumping, laughing squirrel named Herbie who loves to dance."

The song was light and bouncy, and even Jette couldn't help tapping her feet. Trip, hanging onto the piano bench, banged out the rhythm with one chubby fist. Jette laughed, enchanted. Somehow, Alexandra had ended up with it all. A wonderful, handsome husband who just happened to have billions of dollars. Two beautiful baby boys. And her creativity—music seemed to pour out of her effortlessly.

Alexandra hadn't become just a rich man's wife, Jette thought. All along, she had maintained her identity.

The song was finished. "More kwirl! More!"

Laughing, Alexandra scooped up her small son and placed him on the piano bench beside her. Jette held baby Andy in her arms and felt some of the warmth of this happy family take hold of her.

Not that her own life wasn't good—it was. She had what millions of women dreamed of. Why, then, did she envy her friend so deeply? Why did she feel as if *she* were the one who had been cheated?

Later, after the children were in bed, Jette and Alexandra stayed up late, drinking wine. They phoned Mary Lee long distance, and each got on a different phone. The three chattered away nonstop for two hours.

"I'm still waffling about marriage," Mary Lee confided after telling them about her new talk show, her recent interview with Henry Kissinger. "I mean, should I or shouldn't I? Jake's given me an ultimatum. I have six months to pick out a ring.

After that, if I haven't committed myself, we split."

They hashed over the pros and cons. Alexandra thought Mary Lee should take a chance, since Jake happened to love her so deeply. Jette believed Mary Lee's uncertainty might mean that Jake wasn't really the man for her.

"I was counting on you two to help me," Mary Lee said an hour later. "But I guess the jury's hung, isn't it? Anyway, have you heard? My mother's in the hospital. They're doing tests to find out why she's losing her memory."

"Losing her memory?" Jette asked.

"Yeah." Mary Lee sounded troubled. "The great Marietta Wilde, author of God knows how many novels, and now she's having trouble remembering where she keeps her car keys. I don't know if you've noticed, but she hasn't had a new book in three years. Her editor turned the China one down. Said it wasn't publishable."

"But I don't understand," Alexandra said.

"I do," Mary Lee said. "The doctors are looking for a vitamin deficiency, or a drug side effect, or some imbalance in her brain chemistry. But *I* know what it is, all right, and it isn't anything they can fix with a vitamin pill."

"What?" Jette asked. "What is it?"

Mary Lee's voice was tinged with bitterness. "Alzheimer's disease. It's so ironic, don't you think? She lied to me and told me I had a horrible disease, and now it turns out she's got one. Eventually I'm going to have to take care of her. So I guess in a perverse way, she still gets her revenge."

Later, Jette and Alexandra sat in Alexandra's bedroom, sipping more wine, laughing and gossiping. Jette began telling her friend what she hadn't mentioned on the phone—the wild sex with Nico, the amyl nitrate orgasms, the complexities of trying to manage two lovers.

The only thing Jette didn't reveal was the identity of the second man. She didn't think Alexandra would be pleased to learn she was having an affair with her brother.

At 1:30 A.M., the phone rang.

"It's probably Richard." Alexandra was pouring more wine. "He's in Phoenix again. Third trip there this month. Pick it up, will you? I've got my hands full here."

Jette reached for the phone. She was beginning to feel high from the wine.

"H'lo?" she said.

"*Jette*? Is that you?" Derek sounded astonished and none too pleased.

"What are you doing calling *here*?" she hissed.

"What do you mean, why am I calling? Alexandra's my sister."

Jette handed the phone to Alexandra, who stood with the wine carafe still in her hand, looking puzzled. When she realized that the caller was Derek, the look of puzzlement on her face increased.

She finished the brief call from her brother, something about a fund-raiser. "Jette . . . " Alexandra said after she hung up. "Why did you ask Derek why he was calling here? I mean, why wouldn't he call?"

Jette shrugged uncomfortably and looked away.

Alexandra frowned. "Jette? Derek isn't—that is, *Derek* wouldn't be one of the men you date in California, would he? I know he's been flying to the Coast a lot lately, and I've wondered."

Jette picked up her wine glass and sipped, uncertain what to say. Alexandra was persistent. "Come on, Jette, talk to me. Reassure me that my brother isn't one of the men you're dating in California. Not that you're not a wonderful person, because you are, and I love you, but my brother has to watch himself politically."

Jette set down her glass. "What's that supposed to mean?"

They had both drunk too much. Alexandra's honey blonde hair looked slightly disheveled, and her cheeks were flushed, her eyes unusually bright. "You don't talk much about what your friend Nico does for a living, but I heard some of the people at Arista talking about him."

Jette looked away. "I'm tired," she said. "I think I'll fold my tent and just steal into the night."

Alexandra followed her down the hall. "Jette? I wish I weren't so tipsy; maybe this would make more sense. Are you telling me . . . you're dating a Mafia man and my *brother*?"

"I haven't done anything but have a lot of very nice screws," Jette burst out, going into the beautifully furnished guest room with a view of the Chicago skyline.

"Oh, Jette," Alexandra said in dismay.

It was noon before Jette finally crawled out of bed and made her way to the breakfast room of the Cox home. She had dressed in tight jeans, a designer fringe vest, and ropes of silver-and-turquoise Indian necklaces, belts, and bracelets. Her jet-black hair streamed down her back in its usual riotous curls, and she wore no makeup.

"You certainly look like Pocahontas this morning," Alexandra remarked. She was sitting at the large table with a cup of black coffee.

Jette stopped, offended. "Sorry, I forgot this was Chicago. Out in L.A., we consider Chicago the provinces."

There was a silence while they gazed at each other. Then Jette slumped down at the table and scowled at the pitcher of fresh-squeezed orange juice and plate of warm croissants a maid quietly served. "Sorry. Anyway, I'm not hungry."

"I'm not either. I'm thinking about Derek's political career. You want to chew it up and spit it out like apple seeds."

"Wow," Jette said, her eyes filling with sudden tears. "You really hate me, don't you? I guess I'd better catch a cab."

"Oh, shit," Alexandra said. She wore jeans, too, with a much-washed T-shirt from an Olivia Newton-John concert. "Quit feeling sorry for yourself. You know I love you, Jette. I just don't want you to louse up a great guy's career by a thoughtless act."

"You're angry at me because I dated your precious brother. I'm not really good enough for him, that's what this is all about."

"That's not true at all!"

"Isn't it? Come on, face it."

Another silence. This one stretched out for minutes, during which a young maid came through the louvered swinging door from the kitchen and set darkly bronzed, hot bran muffins on the table, along with a fresh pot of coffee.

"Thank you, Yolanda," Alexandra said. "Just leave us now; we'd like to talk."

The maid left them alone, and Jette sullenly reached for a muffin, breaking it in half and taking a large bite.

"I hate us quarreling," Alexandra finally said.

"Well, I hate it, too."

"I mean, we don't see each other very much, and now look what we're doing. But Derek is my brother, and I can't allow him to wreck his political credibility. You don't know how my father has dreamed of having a President in the family."

Jette looked up from her plate. She allowed her eyes to meet Alexandra's. "Hey, he has free choice. He's single. I'm single. What's the problem?"

Alexandra shook her head. "You don't know? The *problem* is that you haven't told him that your other boyfriend is Mafiosa. Is that really fair, Jette?"

"OK, OK," Jette said, ashamed.

"You have to break it off with him. Today if you can. If you don't . . ." Alexandra's eyes filled with tears. "If you don't, well, our friendship won't be over, Jette, but it will never be the same."

Before she left, Jette hugged Alexandra and promised to call Derek as soon as she got to L.A. "I swear I'll never see him again—scout's honor! And I'll send back all the things he gave me. Even the piñata."

"The piñata?" Alexandra laughed in spite of herself.

"Well, we were in Mexico one time around Christmas, and he bought me this chicken piñata. It was so pretty, all yellow and pink paper feathers . . ."

Alexandra felt a stab of guilt. She never could stay mad at Jette very long. "Oh, Jette. You don't have to send it back. Oh, God. I love you, Jette."

They hugged. "I was an ass," Alexandra wept. "I know you didn't mean to hurt anyone."

"No, you were right. I was stupid," Jette said, shaking her head. "Anyway, I should break it off with Nico, too, only I can't. I think I'm addicted to him."

—— ▶◀ ——

Alexandra waited several days to give Jette a chance to break up with Derek. Then she made arrangements to fly to Washington overnight, telling Richard she had promised to throw a $1,000-a-plate dinner for Derek and needed to finalize some plans.

She arranged to meet her brother for a late lunch at Duke Zeibert's, a D.C. restaurant patronized by high-powered politicians.

"So what brings you to the hub of the Western world?" Derek inquired over orange roughy. "Business? You're going to make a record with George and Barbara?" He snickered at his own joke, while nodding to Senator Howard Baker and Congressman Billy Ford.

Although her spinach salad was delicious, Alexandra

hadn't tasted much of it. She wanted to get this little talk over with.

"Derek, you're the reason I came to Washington."

"Me?" Derek raised a bushy blond eyebrow.

"Yes, you. Derek, you might be politically astute, but you are socially *dumb.*"

"Whaaaat?" He grinned at her. "Oh, gee, you mean I got caught? I thought nobody knew I was making it with Bella Abzug."

"Very funny. I can't believe you, Derek." Her eyes moistened. "You've got a lot of people's money and hopes riding on you, and number one on that list is our father. He loves thinking about you going to the White House one day, and damn it, I don't want you to spoil things for him!"

"Whoa, whoa, whoa," Derek said, laughing. "What are we talking about here?"

"It's your girlfriend, Jette. Maybe you don't know. She's also seeing Nico Provenzo . . . as in the Provenzo family of Chicago. As in *Mafia*, Derek."

Derek went white. "She's still seeing him?"

"Yes!" snapped Alexandra.

"Holy shit."

"What did you expect? She's a beautiful woman, a Hollywood star, and she's a little bit crazy. You know that, Derek. You know Jette is . . ." To her dismay, Alexandra's voice began to quiver.

"Will you stop with the waterworks?" Derek said, regaining his composure. "Anyway, it's a moot point, because she phoned me last night and said she doesn't want to see me anymore."

Alexandra felt her fear begin to subside. "Are you dating anyone else right now? I mean, besides Jette?"

He shrugged, lifting his water glass for a long swallow. "Oh, there is someone."

"Who?"

"Her name is Rita Sue Ashland; she's very Southern, gallons of blue blood, and she talks with so many 'y'alls' I can barely understand her. But very classy," he added. "Rich family, good table manners, knows how to throw a dinner party . . . you know."

"Pretty?"

"Very."

"Sexy?"

Derek pushed away his water glass uneasily. "Mmmmm.

She's actually pretty stuffy. Why? What's this leading up to?"

Alexandra hesitated. "I'm sorry, but someone's got to tell you. You'd better think about getting married to her, Derek, or to someone like her. If you really want to be President someday, you've got to be monogamous. And your sex life has to be very private and conventional."

"Jesus," he said. "You're telling me how to run my life? You, my baby sister? Do you know what you are? A rich man's wife! You couldn't make it on your own if you didn't have Daddy's and Hubby's money to buy you $3,000 Fred Hayman suits like the one you have on now."

Alexandra flinched as if she'd been slapped. "Let me tell you something," she cried. "If they took away everything except my piano, I could still make plenty to get by on. I made over $650,000 last year, Derek—that's a respectable income in anyone's book."

"Sissy—"

"And if no one wanted my songs, I'd find another job— probably right here in Washington. I've got the experience, I've got a degree from Vassar, and I don't appreciate you talking to me like that."

"Sorry, sorry," he said flippantly.

She tossed her napkin onto the table. "You just don't get it, do you, Derek?"

She walked out of the restaurant, leaving her brother looking dumbfounded.

As soon as Alexandra had disappeared, Derek threw some money on the table and stalked out, anger elevating his blood pressure. That little bitch, Jette Michaud. . . .

Instead of going back to his office, he drove straight to his posh Watergate apartment, where he slammed the door on the way in, went to the telephone, and told Mary Kathryn to cancel his three afternoon appointments.

His day cleared, Derek went to his large wet bar and poured himself a double vodka martini with a twist. He needed a drink.

Two hours later, Derek was still drinking and brooding about the iniquitous twist his fate had taken. Alexandra was right, of course. No more would the political climate allow a handsome President to bring beauteous "lady friends" into the White House for fun and games. Nowadays the press probed into a candidate's bedroom, and what they found had better be common, ordinary, missionary-position sex with a wedded wife.

Rita Sue Ashland, the most viable prospect on the horizon at the moment, was a sugar-and-spice Southern belle who refused to make love unless all the lights were out and they had a sheet over them. Of course, that did make her an ideal candidate for First Lady, right?

"Oh, fuck and double fuck," he said as he wondered if her sexual habits would ever improve.

His telephone rang, interrupting his reverie. Derek answered it curtly. It was Bo Donohue, now his administrative assistant, with word of the progress of a bill Derek had sponsored. They discussed it for twenty minutes, Derek becoming all business as he homed in on the issues.

He hung up feeling a little better, and then, while the mood was still good, he phoned Rita Sue.

"We still on for tonight, sugar?" he asked her, forcing his voice into honeyed tones.

"I thought you had a committee meetin'," Rita Sue said.

"Oh, that. I do have to go to that, baby, but I'm going to duck out early just to see you. About nine o'clock, all right? Maybe nine-thirty? I'll slip out of that meeting just as soon as I can."

"Nine-thirty?"

"I know it's late, doll, but we'll pick up something to eat, maybe some nice pasta at Lombardy's. Besides, I have a little, well, surprise for you."

"Oh, all right, hon. I'll be waitin'."

Whatever else her flaws, Rita Sue would make an ideal wife, Derek thought. Women's lib hadn't hit within five hundred miles of her. She would keep complaints about late hours to a minimum, going along with her husband's ideas and plans. And if the husband ever "fiddled" with another woman—well, she was the type to stiffen her spine and look the other way.

He went to the bar and fixed himself another double—his third or fourth, he had lost count. He savored the bite of liquor sliding down his throat.

Then he went to the phone and dialed again. This was his escape number, one he seldom used.

"Hello?" the voice on the other end of the line was soft.

"This is Derek. I have to see you."

"Tonight? It's not a good time, Derek. You should have given me some notice."

"Please, sweetie? Please. Baby, you know how I need you sometimes. I'll make it worth your while. Anyway, it's only an early date, I have to be gone by nine o'clock."

A soft, alluring laugh. "In that case . . ."

"I'm worth it," Derek said, laughing in relief. "I'll be over in half an hour."

"Make it forty-five minutes."

———— ▶◀ ————

It was a row house in Georgetown, not too different from the one in which Ingrid Hillstrom lived. Derek had often thought these side-by-side old houses would make a wonderful site for a President who wished to dally secretly with a mistress. All it required was the purchase of two homes in a row—under different names, of course. The mistress lived in one home, and the President would visit the one next door. A hidden doorway would be cut through the upstairs bedrooms, connecting the two units.

He fantasized about this as he vigorously rode a pair of rounded, white buttocks covered by skin that was velvet soft. Anal sex. One of his peccadillos—one that he seldom could indulge unless he paid for the privilege.

He threw himself into the effort, barely hearing the high, soft cries of his partner gradually intensify into sharp grunts. At last he came, shuddering, after receiving from his partner the hard squeeze of his balls that always intensified the pleasure.

Then he pulled out, wiped himself off, and both of them lay down in each other's arms. He had already brought Jackie to climax. He always liked to please his lover.

"You were very uptight tonight, you bad boy," Jackie Vanderpool murmured. A firm arm reached toward the bedside table, found a cigarette, and lit it. Jackie, a stylist at a prestigious Chevy Chase hair salon, had a hobby of gambling at Atlantic City. To support it, Jackie kept a very small after-hours clientele. A weekly medical checkup and a clean bill of health for AIDS were main attractions for men like Derek.

"Sorry," Derek muttered.

"Want to talk?"

"I don't know."

"Oh, poor baby, you really *are* unhappy, aren't you?" Jackie cooed, snuggling into him.

Derek sighed, looking deeply into the green eyes of his male partner. He didn't consider himself gay or even bi. This was just a forbidden interlude, something experimental that happened now and then, maybe every six months or so, when the pressures of life got too much for him. He'd met Jackie when he was an undergraduate at Harvard and got him the job at the salon. They'd been "friends" for more than twelve years now.

"Come on, Derie, spill it out. Tell daddy what's the matter," Jackie urged.

"Well, I'm going to have to get married," Derek sighed into his lover's chest. "Isn't it a bitch?"

"Have to? You mean like in 'I'm pregnant, honey'?"

"Not exactly. As in, 'You'd better settle down, son, if you want to get anywhere politically.' "

"Oh, I get it. Better not come back to me, then, Derek. I don't exactly fit into that picture, do I?"

"No, you don't."

Jackie considered his answer for a few minutes. "Of course, I would appreciate a nice monthly stipend, a sort of severance arrangement. Palimony for, say, two or three years. Nothing large."

Derek sat up, reaching for his clothes. "How much?"

"Oh, maybe three, four hundred a month. Cash, of course."

"Of course," Derek said wearily.

"I'm not one of those Washington bitches; I'll keep the faith, Derie," Jackie consoled him.

—— ◂▸ ——

That night, Derek proposed to Rita Sue Ashland. She accepted. She knew he was a rising star, and she wanted a shot at the White House along with him. They smiled and held hands, and they both knew it was more a business deal than an act of love.

He arrived home to find his answering machine blinking. There were five messages from Jette.

The last one was, "Derek . . . Derek, you're not there, are you, listening to me and not picking up? Derek, are you there? There's something . . . I really need to talk to you, so could you please, please return this call? Honest, I need to talk. There's something I didn't tell you yet."

He already knew what that was.

He considered. The thought of Jette Michaud, with her black hair and wild, sexy body was still tantalizing. Damn! He realized that he needed to talk with her, to find out about this

Nico Provenzo thing, how far it had gone, how much damage had been done.

He was going to be married to Rita Sue—a dull, incredibly boring woman. There would be no Jackie for de-stressing, no Jette for excitement. He would probably spend the rest of his life making love under sheets and quilts.

Maybe he'd tell Mary Kathryn to clear his schedule tomorrow, too, so he could fly out to L.A. for one last, mind-blowing fuck with Jette.

⸻ ◄► ⸻

The following night, Jette was dressing for a date with Nico, who had just phoned to say he was arriving in town for meetings with some people from a movie studio and wanted to see her. She shuffled anxiously through her largest closet, trying to decide what to wear.

Over the past four years, she'd acquired an amazing number of outfits, enough to stuff all the closets in her house. Print jumpsuits, wild, gypsy-looking outfits, leather, spandex, embroidered organza madras, cloth-of-gold . . . name it, and Jette probably had it crammed into one of her five closets. Because of her dark coloring, she could wear anything and usually did. One year she'd been on *People* magazine's "best dressed" list, the next on the "worst."

She finally settled on a sexy fuchsia cocktail suit by Bob Mackie and was just buttoning its gold buttons when she heard the buzzer for the driveway gate ring persistently. She went to the window and peered out, recognizing Derek in a rented Mercedes.

Oh, God!

She went to the wall panel and pressed the button that would open the gate. Then, looking out to make certain it had opened, she froze with horror. Nico had just pulled up, too.

Panic zapped her. She hurried out of the front door and trotted down the bricked walk, her three-inch heels clicking on the uneven stones. Derek had just pulled his Mercedes in, and Nico, in a gray BMW, was parked beside him. The handsome young Mafioso was glaring at Derek, the set of his jaw hard. Derek glared back. Oh, shit.

Both men got out of their cars.

"Hello," she improvised, speaking to Derek as if he were a

stranger. "I'll be with you in a minute if you wouldn't mind waiting." She met his eyes imploringly.

"Fine," he said curtly. "Am I supposed to wait in the car?"

"N-no," Jette stuttered, fighting the awful urge to break up in nervous laughter. "In the house. You can wait in the house. I'll be right with you, Mr. . . . ah . . ." She gave up.

She grabbed Nico's arm, but he wouldn't move. Jette began to feel desperate.

"This—this is my mother's financial manager," she explained to Nico, praying Derek would cover for her. "I took your advice, and I'm trying to find another business manager, and my mother suggested I talk to hers. He's very good," she rattled on. "He's made about a half-million dollars for my mother. Maybe two million."

"Is that so?" Nico stared at Derek with hard eyes. Jette knew, with a terrible sinking of her heart, that Nico didn't believe a word of her lie.

"Interesting," Nico remarked in a very soft voice to Derek. "You don't look much like a business manager. What you do look like is a certain Senator from Massachusetts. Amazing, how there can be such look-alikes." He stepped forward on the balls of his feet. "Now, if I thought you *weren't* her financial manager . . . if I thought another man was after my Jette, well, I might become a little peeved," he suggested menacingly.

Derek recoiled.

"Yes, I might be tempted to cut off that man's balls and shove them into his mouth, Chicago style. Yes, that's exactly what I might do."

He had said it so quietly that for a second Jette didn't even register what she'd heard. When it sunk in, she gasped. Derek, too, had turned white.

"I'm a Sicilian," Nico explained, his voice soft. "We *Sicilianos* don't look at the world the way others do. We feel very strongly about our women."

"I'll call you tomorrow, Jette," Derek said, returning to his car, backing it slowly out of the driveway.

Nico waited until the car was out of sight, then he turned to Jette, putting a hand on her arm. His touch did not hurt, but it was not loving. He had never touched her like that before.

"Derek Winthrop is *strónzo . . . pèzzo di merdo*," he said. It was the only time she had ever heard him swear in Italian. "I ought to kill you now for cheating on me."

She could only stare at him, her eyes wide with terror. She knew he meant every word of it.

"I'm really s-sorry," she whispered.

"Puttana," Nico snapped. "Maybe I have been treating you too kindly, eh? Maybe you don't like to listen when a man tells you something."

By the time they reached her bedroom, Jette was shaking all over. She'd known all along that Nico was like this. That had been part of the mystique. She'd been a fool . . . crazy . . . to play with fire.

Nico first took a small packet of cocaine out of his billfold and measured out two lines for each of them on a small mirror, taking his time. He tilted back his head and sniffed deeply, seeming to shudder all over as the coke took effect in his system.

Jette turned aside to take her lines, instinct telling her to blow the light powder away rather than ingest it.

"Take all your clothes off," Nico ordered.

Terrified, she fumbled at the suit, her fingers catching on the buttons. Underneath she wore only panty hose, and she stood exposed before him. She felt too lush, too ripe, too vulnerable.

"Everything," he said coldly.

She finished stripping. Her fingernails snagged her hose as she pulled them off. Humiliated and frightened, she started to cry.

"Please, Nico, baby," she burst out. "I—I know you're angry, but—but I really didn't . . . I just flirted a little. Just a little bit. He had kind of a crush on me. There's plenty of guys like that."

The cruel eyes seemed to soften slightly. "You're like cocaine to me, Jette. First-grade blow. Maybe that saved you." He began to pull off his clothes.

It was harsh and animalistic. He took her from behind, pumping savagely into her, and Jette knew it was because he did not want to see her face. She was dry, and his entrance hurt.

She endured the pain, uttering little sighing moans. She knew, as she offered herself to him, that he still loved her, that he was sexually hooked on her. Hadn't he admitted it? He would never hurt her. He would get over his anger.

She loved him so much.

Later, Nico pulled away in his BMW, arrowing the sleek car downward toward the lights of Los Angeles that twinkled in the distance. He felt drained and tired. He had come down from his cocaine high, and a headache had begun to pound in his temples.

The *puttana*. The whore.

And yet for him there was no more glorious moment than when he was plunging himself inside her. Maybe he did love Jette more than he even admitted to himself. She was beautiful and childishly free, did and said whatever she pleased, and Nico found that appealing.

Turning onto Hollywood Boulevard, he slowed the car, his eyes searching among the young girls wearing chains and leather over their baby fat. None of them was even an eighth as pretty as Jette. Damn. He'd hurt her, and he didn't want to.

In the morning he would call a florist and have them send Jette a huge bouquet of roses.

In the language of flowers, red roses meant deep, passionate love, but white meant the first stage of love, far more casual, less serious.

He would send white.

━━━ ►◄ ━━━

Bitsy returned to the apartment at 5:30 A.M., strung out from a night spent trying to sleep in her car. All night long, the nightmares had tortured her. Dreams in which the bullet hit her again, exploding into her face. Dreams where she was a witch. Or where people ran from her as if she were a leper. She hated to go to sleep anymore.

Anger always simmered in her these days, as if she were a pot of water just below the boiling point. It would almost be a relief to have the anger boil over, to give in to it.

She trudged up the stairs. Signs of the "big party" Ingrid had given hit her at once.

She opened the door to the apartment and stepped into a scene of littered chaos. Through a gray, smoky haze, ashtrays overflowed on every table, along with a mess of plastic cups, dirty plates, beer cans, wine bottles, drug paraphernalia, and pizza cartons. A pair of Ingrid's lacy bikini panties were flung on the coffee table.

The smell of the place was nauseating. Wearily Bitsy opened all the windows, then got a couple of large garbage bags and began filling them with trash. She doubted Ingrid would feel like cleaning up anytime soon.

It was while she was rummaging underneath the kitchen sink, searching for air freshener, that she stumbled upon an extra compartment way at the back, where no one would see it.

"Ingrid?" Bitsy said later that day, when Ingrid finally emerged from her room. "Ingrid, do you know anything about this?"

She showed her roommate the Gucci box she had found, with its odd collection of objects: a broken toy motorcycle and a Ken doll with its head twisted nearly off, together with an old newspaper clipping and a newspaper photograph of two people at a party.

"Where'd you get that?"

"Underneath the sink. There was a little hidey-hole."

Ingrid shrugged. "Oh, Giancarlo was helping me install my new garbage disposal once, and he got this idea. He wanted to build something for our stash."

Bitsy stared, remembering all the times she had begged Ingrid for information about Giancarlo. "Why didn't you tell me?"

Ingrid flopped into the couch. "I never thought of it. Why would I think of it? It was a stupid idea anyway. We never used it for that. Anyway, who cares? Dead is dead. I don't want to think about Giancarlo anymore."

Bitsy took the box into her room and laid the objects on her bed. She stared at them intently. The motorcycle. The doll. The clipping and photo.

Why had Giancarlo saved all this stuff? She studied the clipping, with its cryptic information about an accident in England. Then the photograph of Congressman Derek Winthrop and his sister, Alexandra Winthrop, the season's most prominent debutante.

What did it all mean?

Bitsy lay down on the bed and closed her eyes. She allowed her thoughts to flow. The doll with its head twisted off . . . the clippings . . . a death . . . two rich, society people . . .

Blackmail.

She snapped open her eyes, her heart pounding. What if Giancarlo was blackmailing someone, for instance, either Derek or Alexandra Winthrop? It made a crazy kind of sense. In fact, the more she thought about it, the more excited she became.

She got off the bed and went over to a cheval glass. She hardly ever looked in the mirror, but she did so now. Her own face stared back at her. It looked . . . wrong. Shuddering, she reached to touch the hairline scars around her right eye socket, the eye itself bulging forward.

She was hideous . . . permanently hideous.

And somehow, some way, this box of objects that Giancarlo had collected had something to do with it.

The library at Georgetown University was large and crowded with students at work. At the microfilm desk, Bitsy retrieved the film that covered the month in which the drug bust had occurred. Her heart was pounding so rapidly she thought she might vomit. In a dim part of her mind, she knew that she had gone over the edge.

She was an angry woman, she told herself. Colossally so.

She switched on the machine and flicked through the newspaper until she found what she was looking for, the article about the drug raid in which Giancarlo had died. She hadn't read it before, hadn't needed to.

Now her eyes devoured the print, and she found the name of the police officer who had shot Giancarlo. Byron McCafferty. There was a photograph of him, too, and she recognized him as the officer with the cold, empty eyes.

It all came flooding back . . . the sound of the explosions. Giancarlo jerking backward, red gushing from his head. Then the blow to her own head, the agonizing, incredible pain.

Wait a minute. If she had time to see Giancarlo being hit, then that meant the officer had fired more than once, as if to make sure he hit his target. Because she'd been hit on the second round, not the first . . .

"Hey, are you all right?" a woman asked from a nearby table. Bitsy realized that she was crying.

"I'm fine," she snapped. "Leave me alone. Please."

"I thought—I thought . . . well, I'm sorry," the woman said, returning to her book.

Bitsy sat staring at the screen, hatred forming a knot in her stomach.

— ◀▶ —

Byron "Bubba" McCafferty sucked in his stomach and stared at the girl at the far end of the bar. For the past twenty minutes, she'd been giving him the eye. She was a fox, with red, pouty lips and short auburn hair crimped into curls. She wore skintight denims and a red knit halter top that cupped small, very nice titties.

Young stuff—maybe too young for him. Hell, he had the Big Five-Oh coming up in three more days.

He was drinking boilermakers, and he snapped his fingers for the bartender to bring him more of the same.

The girl moved down the bar, smiling as if she knew him. "Hi. You come here often?" she asked in a soft voice.

"Oh, pretty regular. I kind of hang out here."

He inspected the girl. Lots of makeup, he noticed, but she was wearing no fingernail polish, and her nails were short and bitten. He wondered if the crimped auburn hair was a wig. It looked a little too perfect, and it caught the light with a polyester glimmer.

Shit, she was a hooker.

Well, so what? She was pretty, and he didn't see any tracks.

"Like what you see?" she asked him, smiling.

"I like it plenty."

"That's nice." She had brought her drink—white wine—with her. She lifted her glass and sipped, taking her time.

"I haven't seen you in here before," he commented. "You from this area?"

"Oh, yes. I'm . . . Bonnie," she said.

Prostitutes often used false names. He teased her. "Bonnie? You mean like Bonnie Bee honey? You got a lot of honey, Bonnie Bee?" he gave her his best flirtatious smile. "Want to share it? Show me how sweet it is?"

"I know it's sweet."

"I know *you* know, but do I know? I'd like to find out, Bonnie. Eighty dollars."

Her eyes widened momentarily. "Hundred," she said quickly.

"Ninety? Oh, shit, don't make me bargain. I'll get out of the mood for love. You won't be sorry, lady."

Once inside his apartment, he excused himself and went in the bathroom, where he took off his jacket and removed the .38 special he carried in a calf holster.

He found her in the bedroom. She had pulled down the navy blue comforter and was lying there naked, knees pulled up and splayed open, so that he could see the reddish-gold hair of her pussy and the pink, flower-like inner lips.

He felt a flood of immediate desire.

"Hi," she whispered in a soft, feminine voice. He started forward, then saw her eyes. They weren't soft. Jesus, they were as hard as a desk sergeant on Saturday night.

McCafferty hesitated. What had he got himself in for? He didn't know anything about this broad. Picked her up in a bar and brought her home like any damned fool suburban john.

"Come on," she urged, spreading her thighs a little more.

He was already hard, and he didn't want to worry anymore. He couldn't fuck and worry at the same time. "Hey, baby, I'm here."

Within two minutes he was in the saddle, thrusting in and out, now and then making circles. She was very tight—unusual in a whore. She had fantastic inner muscles and kept squeezing them, tightening herself around him until he nearly burst with excitement. Jesus . . . it had been years since he'd fucked a woman this tight. She was amazing—magnificent—

"Oh . . . God . . ." he groaned. "Faster . . . don't stop . . ."

He felt the premonitory ripples through his genitals, the swift rush of sweetness that meant he was due to explode. "I'm going to come!" he gasped. "I'm coming, I'm coming, I'm—"

It happened too quickly for him to prevent.

He sensed her hand moving underneath the pillow, and just as he erupted in a wild, bucking spasm, there was a sharp pain across his throat, just above his Adam's apple.

Warm liquid ran down his neck. Blood. Jesus, the bitch had a knife at his throat.

"If you move or even breathe, I'll slit your throat," she rasped.

"Please," he tried to beg, but he couldn't get the word out.

As if angered at his response, she pressed harder. She had him by the flat of the blade. Now she tipped it into his skin, drawing more blood.

"Tell me all about it," she ordered.

He choked, "All . . . w-what . . ."

"Tell me."

She repositioned the blade, aiming the tip straight into his jugular. It cut right into his skin, he didn't know how far. He didn't dare move or even breathe heavily.

"Can't talk," he gasped, his eyes filling with tears. "Move . . . that knife away."

She didn't oblige. *"You* shot me, didn't you?"

The question sent terror through him. God, who was she?

ent out of his past. And he didn't have a very good past.

"You didn't care, did you? You just aimed your gun and blasted it off."

He groaned.

"I was innocent," she grated. "I was innocent, you dumb fucking asshole!" She kept on. "Who told you to shoot Giancarlo Ferrari?"

He struggled to stay cool, didn't succeed. "Didn't . . ."

"I want to know it *all*, and I want to know *now*. I'll cut your throat," she threatened. "I *want* to cut your throat. Do you hear me? I want to see you bleed all over the room."

He saw her eyes. Shining, crazy. Dear Jesus God, she really meant it. He had had it. His only hope was to talk to her, get her to move the knife back a little so he could wrestle it away.

"Tell me, or I will cut your motherfucking head off."

He gasped it out, crying. She leaned forward, her weight pushing the knife all the way through his throat. He saw the red gush come out of him and couldn't quite believe it.

Dimly, he saw her red lips move as she said something. The last words he'd ever hear.

He choked and drowned in his own blood.

Twenty minutes later, out on the street, wrapped in a trench coat, the wig in her purse, Bitsy forced herself to walk away from the apartment building.

She was in shock. Weak, nauseated, sweat standing out on her body despite the forty-five-degree temperature of the April night. She'd showered in McCafferty's bathroom, but it hadn't made her feel better. Her skin still felt as if it crawled with him, with his come, sweat, and blood.

No one would remember her, especially in the nondescript trench coat. Also, McCafferty lived alone. It might be several days before he was found—more if she was lucky.

Her left hand involuntarily slipped into her purse, touching metal. The knife, nine inches long and purchased in the kitchen department of Foland's, was one of those Norwegian blades that could slice a telephone book in half. She'd washed it off in the shower. It was too perfect to throw away . . . not yet.

There was still work for it to do.

She would never forget the name that Bubba McCafferty had whispered to her. The person who had been the *real* cause of her scarring. Senator Derek Winthrop.

14

Chicago
1989

Senator Derek Winthrop and wife, Rita Sue, was neatly typed at the top of a sheet in the loose-leaf guest book that was turning out to be the bible for the party. Alexandra was in her study, scanning each page to see if new information about each guest should be added, and making notes for Judy, her secretary, on items that needed to be followed up.

She sighed and stretched her back, trying to work the kinks out of it. The day had been busy. She'd spent several hours this morning making a video that would be played in the guests' hotel rooms, welcoming them to Chicago and explaining all the plans she'd made for activities surrounding the gala.

There had been a conference call from Arista Records, finalizing arrangements for her *Sensuous Woman . . . Dionne Warwick* album.

Then she had a working lunch with Dolly and made more phone calls to resolve major and minor crises.

Twyla Tharp had agreed to bring her troupe to Chicago and to adapt several of her dance compositions for the occasion, but the dancers could not arrive until the afternoon of the gala. "Can't you arrive *any* sooner?" Alexandra pleaded. "We'll need rehearsal time."

"I really don't see that we can," said the choreographer. "We'll have to make do with a quick run-through before the party."

Alexandra had an idea. "Ms. Tharp, would the company come here the week *before* the party to rehearse, if we can get the sets built by then?"

"I don't see why not."

Another problem solved.

The designer for the decorative water fountains had done most of the waterworks at Busch Gardens in Florida. She had to meet tomorrow with him, and with the plumbing contractor who would do the actual pipe fitting.

And she had to supervise the creation of the ice sculptures, the Waleses' Royal Standard, flanked by a lion and a unicorn, both rampant.

There was so much to think of.

Alexandra was getting a little tense and decided to take a break. She turned on her stereo and lay on the couch with her eyes shut, giving herself up to the genius violin of Midori. As always, music relaxed her.

The phone trilled, shattering her mood.

"Alexandra? It's me, Di."

"Diana," she exclaimed, forgetting her annoyance at the interruption.

"I thought I'd ring you to see how the gala's shaping up," Diana said.

"Oh, wonderful," Alexandra said. "I mean, I'm busy with about ten thousand details, but they'll all get worked out. How are you? How is Charles?"

"Very chipper indeed," said the Princess with a giggle. Apparently their recent tiff had now been mended, at least partially amicably.

"Diana, what are you going to wear?" Alexandra asked. She still had to purchase her own gown.

"Well, I've gone to Bruce, and he's promised to do something smashing."

Bruce Oldfield, Alexandra knew, was one of Diana's designers. They settled down to a long discussion about which designer Alexandra should use. Valentino, both agreed, was too clashy this year, his colors too busy. Alexandra liked Mary McFadden's austere trademark pleating, but so many women were wearing her.

"Scaasi?" she pondered.

"Or Tarquin." Diana suggested. "I saw some wonderful silk georgette things in *W*, very filmy and glamorous."

Alexandra sighed. "I'd better get myself to New York. I've put it off far too long."

— ◄► —

Richard Cox strode through the lobby of the Fitz Executive Health Club, his jaw set grimly. He had just learned that the union had selected the Fitz chain as its strike target, and walkouts would begin the day of the gala. He was furious.

Media coverage over the past several years had glamorized Richard's wealth. Although the public pictured him as having endless amounts of cash at his disposal, in reality many of his assets were tied up in real estate or used as collateral. The union had done its homework and knew that the Fitz chain, in its present financial condition, could not handle a strike, at least not a long one. The banks would get too anxious. Damn. The Fitz was the ideal target.

Richard entered the men's locker-room. Swiftly he stripped, hanging up his suit, shirt, and tie on the padded hanger he kept in his locker. He put on navy shorts and a faded T-shirt, then he walked into the weight room.

"How you doing, Richard?" Arthur Green, paunchy and dripping with perspiration, greeted him from the bench press. Green, a former classmate of Richard's at Syracuse University, owned a nationwide chain of fast-food franchises and had been trying to buy into Richard's hotels for years. He and Richard played tennis together when their schedules permitted.

Richard waved at his old friend as he mounted a computerized exercise bicycle, his mind racing. His staff negotiators were in meetings now with Fraser, Marchek, and the others. Richard would step in only if they became deadlocked.

When the lights on the small screen of the bicycle blinked off, Richard moved to the bench press and set the weight bar at 160 pounds. Savagely he shoved the bar upward, his biceps quivering under the stress. Adrenaline pumped through his system as he did fifteen reps, grunting with effort.

He got up off the bench and increased the weights by thirty pounds.

The barbells slammed down with a crash. He hadn't been paying attention.

"Cox . . . Cox . . . Jesus." It was Green, his face anxious. "Are you OK? You've been really pushing it. Jeez, look at the weight you've got this mother set on. Almost 200 pounds? You're not a kid anymore."

"Fuck you," Richard said, sweat streaming off his face.

"Goddamn, you're bullheaded," Green said, returning to his own machine.

"You got that right."

"You're a damned fool is what you are, Richard. You have no fucking business pushing 200 pounds. I worry about you."

"Go play racquetball and worry about yourself," Richard snapped. "I'll be just fine."

By the time he had sat in a hot sauna, swum twenty-five laps of the Olympic-size pool, and sat in the whirlpool for ten minutes, Richard was feeling mellowed, drained of most of his aggression. His muscles were sore, but hell, a little extra today wasn't going to cause a problem.

He showered and dressed, his stomach beginning to growl pleasantly. Today he needed more than just his usual salad.

He decided to go out, and phoned for his driver to meet him in the hotel parking garage. However, as he was standing at the elevators, he was startled to see his ex-wife emerge from an upbound elevator.

"Dickey-bird!"

He groaned inwardly, his hard-earned good mood evaporating.

She started toward him, waving. "I thought you might be here. Your secretary said you were out, but I knew you always work out on Wednesdays."

She wore a violet leather jacket and pencil-slim skirt with a side slit that showed plenty of leg—a look she'd affected since recovering from her suicide attempt five years previously. It was a look Richard didn't find flattering.

"Darryl, I asked you never to contact me."

"I know, but I had to. This is important."

"Sorry," he began.

"What are you, the Pope?" she demanded. "Granting audiences only to a certain few? Dickey, we were married once. You can give me five minutes, can't you?"

Fortunately, a down elevator arrived. Hoping to get rid of her before any of his staff members spotted her, he took her with him down to the basement parking garage. His driver, Will, was waiting in the smoky gray limousine, the motor running.

He got in and slammed the door.

"Good-bye, Darryl."

"Please," Darryl begged. "Could you just take me to my hotel? I have a script I just have to show you."

"Darryl—"

"Dickey, it's just one little script I want you to look at, one tiny script. The Drake Hotel, driver," she instructed Will. Sighing, Richard opened the car door and nodded to his driver. He would just wait in the car while Darryl fetched the script, he decided glumly.

"Look at your face. You think I'm the same person I was, don't you?" Darryl began as they pulled out of the garage. "Well, I don't drink anymore; I haven't had anything but Perrier in two years. I don't even do coke. Now the only addiction I have is you-know-what."

He pretended he hadn't heard the innuendo. "Darryl, we've got 7-Up, Perrier, and ginger ale. What'll it be?"

She shrugged. "Perrier."

"Dickey," she said, taking the glass he handed her, "I really need you. There is a big, big favor you absolutely have to do for me."

He looked at his ex-wife. She was wearing violet contact lenses to match her outfit. Her skin was pulled tight by several unnecessary face-lifts so that she looked a beautiful but slightly plastic forty.

"You've made four movies in Hong Kong," he remarked. "And didn't I hear you're up for a couple more?"

"Oh, yes," she said, pouting. "But who cares about those? Dickey-bird, I want to come back to Hollywood."

He looked away. As far as he knew, her blacklisting was still in effect. Rusty Copa's star had risen, and he was even more powerful than before. And he still hated Darryl.

"Dickey, all it would take is one good picture to change things. You know that as well as I do. In Hollywood, money talks and bullshit walks."

He winced. "Interesting expression."

"You know what I mean! Money is what it's all about, and I know I'd be great box office if they would just give me a chance. I'm not a prima donna any more, Dickey. I had it all knocked out of me over there in Hong Kong." She spoke the name of the city with hatred. "I can't believe the way they treat their stars over there. I had to bow to the director, for God's sake."

"Get to the point," he said, noticing that she hadn't

changed a bit.

"Dickey-bird . . . Sidney B. Cohen is going to make a fabulous new movie, *Indigo Nights*. It's based on a romance novel, and women are going to flock to the theater to see it. I want that part; I *need* that part."

They had arrived at the Drake Hotel. "Come up to my room for just a second," Darryl begged.

"You know I can't."

"Why not? We're not going to *do* anything, Dickey-bird. Are you afraid of me? Afraid you might be tempted?

"Darryl—"

"Ten minutes," she said, her eyes filling with tears. "I just want to show you the script and go through one scene with you. One scene, and you'll know how right I am for this part. Richard, acting is my *life*. Maybe you don't know what that means. It means I don't want to do *anything else in this whole world*."

"All right," he said shortly. "But we have to make it fast. I have another appointment."

Richard entered the ornate lobby with Darryl, keeping a cautious distance from his beautiful ex-wife.

As they were entering an elevator, a well-dressed couple emerged. Richard's heart sank. It was Harry and Linnea Kremer, who owned the apartment on the floor below his own.

"Richard?" Linnea trilled, seeing him. "My goodness, I didn't know you liked the Drake Hotel—" Her husband nudged her in the ribs, and Linnea stopped, embarrassed.

"A script conference," Darryl explained helpfully. Richard winced, knowing how that must sound.

"*Indigo Nights,*" he said, giving the Kremers a self-confident smile. "Nice seeing you," he added, and the couple nodded and smiled.

"Well," Darryl remarked when they were in the elevator again. "I guess you didn't want to see *them.*"

"I'm a damned fool," Richard said heavily, glancing at his watch.

Her suite was strewn with clothes and opened suitcases, and it reeked of Giorgio perfume. Darryl rummaged until she found a script with a royal blue cover.

"Look," she said, handing it to him. "It's even well written, instead of the usual junk. Dickey . . . I have to tell you my problem. It isn't this script, it's Sid Cohen."

"Sid Cohen?"

"And the party you and Alexandra are giving."

Richard sighed. "Why all the cloak and dagger, Darryl? Can't you just call him on the phone like everyone else does?"

"It doesn't work that way. I've tried calling him about fifty times. He's been 'in a meeting' for the past three months. But he's coming to your party, and he can't avoid me then. I have to be there."

"Oh, shit, Darryl. You know I can't do it."

"Why? Why can't you?"

"My wife would never permit it. You caused enough trouble in my marriage when Andy was born. Alexandra was good about it then, we mended the rift, but I can't ask her to have you as her guest—it's asking too much."

Her eyes begged him, wet with tears. "Please. I won't even talk to her if that's what you're worried about. I just want to be there."

"No, Darryl."

She moved toward him, slid her arms around him, nudged her pelvis up close to his thigh.

"Don't try that. I'm not seduceable," he said, pulling away and starting toward the door. "And I think I overstayed my welcome—about ten minutes ago."

"Richard! Dickey!"

"Good-bye, Darryl."

"Damn you!" she screamed. "Asshole! Stupid fuck-head asshole! Well, let me tell you something. I'm coming to your party anyway, do you hear me? *I'm coming anyway!*"

"Darryl!"

"I'll find a way," she shrieked. "You just wait, Richard Cox, you just wait!"

—— ▶◀ ——

The jungle telegraph worked with brutal efficiency. Richard rushed home in order to explain to Alexandra what had happened, but he found his wife walking out of her study with a stunned look on her face.

"Richard," she said, in a voice that meant trouble. "Richard, I think we have to talk."

"Punkin—" he began.

"In here," she said, returning to her study and waiting for him to follow.

He sank into one of the soft chintz couches, pushing aside a stack of compact discs and a pile of sheet music written in Alexandra's own, precise hand.

"I don't like Linnea Kremer," Alexandra began. "She's a gossip who does nothing but buy clothes and go to lunch. And I guess she doesn't like me much, either, because she couldn't wait to phone me with the wonderful news that my husband was seen at the Drake Hotel, getting into an elevator with his ex-wife."

"Lexy, I can explain it all."

"Can you? I know why people sneak off to hotels together."

He flushed, knowing anything he said was going to come out wrong. "She had a script she wanted to show me—a new movie she wants a part in."

Alexandra nodded. "Oh! Oh, I see! So naturally you had to go up to her room with her, rather than having her bring it down to the lobby. And naturally, you just ran into her by accident, right?"

"Hey. That's exactly what did happen. I shouldn't have said I would go up to her room, but I felt sorry for her. She's not a happy woman, Alexandra, she—"

His wife's chin was lifted dangerously. "Well, I'm not a happy woman either . . . because I think you're lying to me, Richard. How could you? Do you really think I'd believe you went up to her room to look at a *script*?"

"I wasn't going to lie to you. I came right home afterward to tell you everything that happened."

She turned away, going to stand at the window. Her back was shaking slightly, and he knew she was crying. "I'll bet," she said bitterly. "If that bitch Linnea Kremer hadn't seen you two together, you wouldn't have said anything. I'd never have known. I'd have gone happily about my business, trusting my husband."

"Alexandra." He took her shoulders and pulled her around. She was rigid under his touch, her eyes glazed defiantly. "I'm not lying. I never lied to you, and I never will. I admit I never should have gone to her room. But I felt sorry for her. And guilty."

"Guilty!" She tore herself away from him.

"Baby, baby, don't be like this. I never touched Darryl. She did come on to me, but I said no."

"Richard, I think I need to be alone for a while," she said softly.

That night Richard made love to Alexandra, holding her tightly and stroking her, whispering over and over how much he loved and needed her. "There's been no other woman," he told her huskily. "No one. I swear it, Lexy. Please believe me. How could I love anyone else when I have you? It's impossible."

Alexandra clung to him, enjoying the tender lovemaking that culminated in a rare simultaneous climax. She wanted to believe him. She *had* to.

The next morning she rose early to leave for the airport. She had arranged to fly to New York to purchase a gown for the gala, and she was meeting Mary Lee for lunch.

—— ►◄ ——

Martha was a small and exclusive shop on Park Avenue, one of the few stores in the country that still used models to demonstrate clothing. Alexandra had shopped there for years.

Leaning back in her seat, watching the models glide past in a succession of haute couture gowns, Alexandra felt sudden hot tears. She couldn't muster any interest in these dresses. What did it matter what combination of silk, lace, and beading she put on her body for this party?

Another model glided out, clad in something silvery and clingy.

"This is a Calvin Klein strapless lace creation," said the saleswoman. "Very, very simple lines, Mrs. Cox, with nothing to break the flow of the material. It would be excellent to show off your jewelry."

"Mmmmm," Alexandra murmured, forcing herself to concentrate.

"And the next dress is a Mary McFadden, very stylish, with a strapless bodice embroidered in silver bugle beads . . ."

Alexandra recrossed her long legs restlessly. She wished she were home, in Richard's arms. Lovemaking would make her forget her troubled thoughts—the desperate fear that her marriage was falling apart.

Someone sank into the empty chair beside her. "Alexandra! God, look at these dresses; you are really going all out, aren't you?"

It was Mary Lee. Alexandra put aside her distress and greeted her friend with the usual cries, hugs, and you-look-wonderfuls.

Mary Lee did look wonderful, too, ever the stylish, confident woman-about-town. Today she had on a gray-and-silver Perry Ellis suit, decorated with huge sterling-silver buttons. Her narrow feet were elegantly shod in gray Charles Jourdan pumps. Her finger was still defiantly ringless.

The saleswoman discreetly excused herself to answer the telephone.

"Help me out of this mess," Alexandra said, laughing. "I can't decide which dress to buy. Everything they show me is very nice, but too fussy, or too lacy, or the stripes go the wrong way, or there's too much glitter, or—"

"Close your eyes," Mary Lee commanded.

Alexandra did so.

"Now picture yourself entering the ballroom, gliding beautifully forward, your head held high. Now tell me. What are you wearing?"

Alexandra snapped her eyes open. "If I knew, I wouldn't be sitting here in such a quandary. Mary Lee, you've seen the Fitzgerald Fifty. You know how overwhelming it is, how it can dominate an outfit. What would you choose?"

The prize-winning columnist and talk-show host frowned thoughtfully. But before she could answer, two women who had been looking at evening bags came up and asked for Mary Lee's autograph.

"I watch you all the time on TV," one woman gushed. "You can be so *wicked* sometimes! But I love it. The way you made Dan Quayle back down . . . amazing."

Mary Lee opened her gray Fred Eisen purse to find a pen. Alexandra noticed a tiny tape recorder in her bag. She scribbled two signatures, then thanked the women. "Now, where were we?" she said to Alexandra.

"The dress."

"Oh, yes—let's see. Very pale silver, straight, very plain. Strapless, so there's no fabric to impede the necklace or detract from it."

Alexandra considered. "She did show me one dress like that . . . it was a Bob Mackie, I think."

"Have her bring it out again. Stick with me, kid; I'll have you outshining even Princess Diana."

"I can't do that. She's my guest."

"Hon . . . you are too, too much."

An hour later, Alexandra had made her purchase, a slim

silver lamé gown that flared softly at the hem. On the hanger, it looked like a simple tube. On her body, it became distilled moonlight, gleaming and shimmering with every movement. It was the perfect foil for the Fitzgerald Fifty.

Mary Lee insisted on showing Alexandra L'Ecole restaurant attached to the French Culinary Institute, on Broadway down in the Village. Chefs-in-training prepared haute cuisine here, pulling out all the stops.

"Even most native New Yorkers don't know about L'Ecole," Mary Lee boasted. "I found this place when we did a feature on chefs."

Each of the five courses was a work of art. "Wonderful," sighed Alexandra. "This reminds me of the very first meal I shared with Richard."

"Romantic, huh?"

A stab of pain seemed to shoot straight through her. "Very."

They talked about the party. Mary Lee claimed that her invitation was the envy of everyone at NBC, and she had received fervent pleas from three or four anchors and studio execs who wanted to be her escort. Mary Lee laughed. "I said no, and they all hate me now. Of course, I'm bringing Jake. He deserves *some* perks for putting up with me. Sometimes I wonder why he does."

They exclaimed over a dessert cart of elaborate French pastries, but both declined them, settling instead for espresso served in delicate porcelain cups.

Finally Mary Lee said, "Now, let's get down to the nitty-gritty. I understand you've got a little problem on your hands. The American Service Workers Union is targeting Richard, and you've got a huge party to give. Doesn't that worry you?"

Alexandra frowned. "Richard assured me he would have everything settled by then—it's still three weeks away, Mary Lee. That's plenty of time to get it wrapped up. Their threats are empty anyway."

"What makes you so sure?"

Alexandra told Mary Lee about the tape she'd been shown in the elevator.

"My God. This is incredible stuff!"

"Mary Lee . . . please. Keep it confidential."

Mary Lee put down her coffee cup, her green eyes lit with the sharp intelligence that often terrorized guests on her program. "This is such great material. I've been wanting to do a series of articles, an exposé on that union, for months now," she said.

"A series?"

"Your party is a perfect example of the kind of pressure that is used by the unions. The whole thing stinks to high heaven."

"Mary Lee," Alexandra said warningly. "You aren't thinking of . . . I don't want to be part of any newspaper series!"

"You *are* a news item," Mary Lee said. "You can't deny it, Alexandra. A well-known pop composer. Wife of one of the country's richest men. One of the most famous and beautiful hostesses in the world. And now this party being threatened."

"Please—"

"I just want to cover it from a feature angle, that's all. Have you ever met Tank Marchek? What does Richard think of—"

"Wait a minute!" Alexandra said, stiffening. "I can't believe you would trade on our friendship like this." She fished in her purse for a bill and tossed it down on the table, enough to cover both of their meals and leave a generous tip. Tears burned in her eyes, and she could feel her face turn an angry red.

"Where are you going?" Mary Lee cried.

"Where do you think? I still have shopping to do."

Outside, the sky had turned white, and little rumbles of August thunder growled. Most of the taxis that cruised past were occupied. Alexandra started toward the curb, her hand up.

"Wait!" Mary Lee cried behind her. "Don't leave until we get this settled."

"What is there to settle?" Alexandra said without turning. "You have a lot of nerve, Mary Lee. You really do. There's nothing more to discuss."

"Please!" Mary Lee clutched at Alexandra's arm, preventing her from getting into the battered taxi that had just pulled up to the curb.

"OK. You just made me miss that taxi. What is it?"

Mary Lee's eyes burned. "I need this project, Alexandra! I need the dollars. My salary isn't enough."

Alexandra was repelled. "Oh, and you intend to use me to get it? My family, my husband, my party?"

She hurried along the sidewalk, tears flowing.

Mary Lee shrieked, "Alexandra! My mother really does have Alzheimer's! She's only fifty-five, and she's healthy as a horse. Do you realize what that *means*?"

Alexandra slowed her steps but continued to walk.

"It means she's going to need nursing home care for the *rest of her life*. That could be forty years, Alexandra. Have you any idea what nursing homes cost? Alexandra . . . please . . . listen to me!"

Alexandra stopped.

"I love my mother," Mary Lee said, weeping. "I . . . all these years I thought I hated her . . . part of me does hate her. But I can't just throw her in some welfare nursing home and leave her. It's going to cost about $80,000 a year to keep her. Can you believe that? Eighty thousand a year for forty years . . ." She was sobbing now.

A wave of pity washed away much of Alexandra's anger. She reached out to take Mary Lee's hand. "Oh, Mary Lee. I'll help you any way I can. But you can't use my family. I can't allow it."

Mary Lee looked at her friend. "All right. I guess I'm going to have to promise."

— ◄► —

Alexandra flew back early the following morning, arriving home by ten. Brownie had taken the children to the library, and the apartment, despite the presence of the staff, seemed oddly hollow. Stephanie had dropped her doll's shoe in the foyer. Alexandra picked it up, feeling a stab of emotion. God, she loved her children.

The day ahead would be a busy one, but she needed a few minutes to herself. She went to the white Steinway and sat down. As always, she could feel her body begin to relax as she began to move her fingers lightly across the keyboard.

Finally she began to sing, the rich phrases of "Ever-Loving Woman" filling the room. She sang it through once, then began to toy with it. She altered some of the lyrics, adding new verses and rhythms, variations on what she had already written. The song came alive for her again. Maybe she would use this variation in another album, build on it further.

Forty minutes later, Judy, her secretary, came in to tell her that Dana Chen, from the *Chicago Tribune*, had arrived to do an interview. Alexandra had decided to give several press interviews that focused on the hotel and the party, as publicity for the Fitz chain.

"I don't want to reveal everything now, but it's going to be very unusual and striking. Twyla Tharp's troupe will dance; Bruce Springsteen and Tony Bennett are scheduled to sing. We have a Hollywood set designer on retainer, prize-winning florists, and even our ice sculptor has won competitions."

"And what about the threatened union strike, Mrs. Cox?" the woman finally asked. "Do you see that as a danger to your party at all?"

"No, I don't," Alexandra said firmly. "I'm sure that the union issues will be settled to everyone's satisfaction in plenty of time for our gala."

"Well, what if that's not the case? What will you do then? Cancel the party, or just move it to a different spot?"

Alexandra smiled with a calmness she did not feel. "I really don't think it's even an issue, Miss Chen."

"Well, do you think that your husband's stubbornness might be a cause of this situation? As I understand it, he has not been willing to compromise on even one of the issues."

Alexandra rose. "I'm afraid I can't speak for my husband."

"But, Mrs. Cox, don't you think—"

"Thank you for coming today, Miss Chen. We've spent over an hour together, and now I'm afraid I have another appointment scheduled."

⸺ ◄► ⸺

Half an hour later, Dolly arrived, and they took the limousine over to the Fitz Hotel, where a security meeting was being held. The Secret Service, British advance security men, FBI agents, Illinois state police, Chicago police, and the Fitzgerald's own security team would all be present.

"All the top guns," Dolly joked.

"I know," Alexandra said. "And I'm not sure I like it. If we're not careful, it's going to feel more like a war zone than a party."

Jack Slattery conducted the meeting. The private ballroom entrance would be cordoned off and guarded by Chicago police and private security people. All hotel employees would be forced to submit to scrutiny of their background and a body search for weapons. The entire hotel would be thoroughly searched, and the guests would be asked to step through metal detectors.

As the three-hour meeting was winding down, Alexandra remarked, "Have we forgotten something?"

Sixteen heads swiveled in her direction.

"Helicopter surveillance? Bomb checks? This is a *party*," she stated. "Do what you have to behind the scenes; be very thorough. But I don't want the security measures to be obtrusive, nor do I want any of my guests to be embarrassed in any way."

———— ⋈ ————

Alexandra and Richard planned to meet at 6:30 P.M. in the executive offices. She arrived early and called home for her messages. One was from Mrs. Lockwood, the director at Trip's school.

Alexandra was able to get through to the woman, who was still in her office.

"Mrs. Cox, I just wanted you to know about an incident that happened at school today."

"Oh?" Alexandra said warily.

"A good incident," the director hastened to explain. "It seems that your son came to the rescue of another child who was being bullied by a larger youngster. He didn't fight, but he did pull the aggressor away."

"Trip was a hero?" Alexandra felt a warm smile spread across her face.

"Your son is a very unusual child, Mrs. Cox. Very altruistic. He seems to enjoy taking other children under his wing. You can be very proud of him."

"We are," Alexandra said, pleased.

Ten minutes later, she was seated in Richard's huge office suite, sipping a glass of chardonnay. The executive dining room was sending them up a light dinner so that Richard could go over some paperwork.

She told him what the school administrator had said, and for a minute they basked in parental pride. Finally Alexandra got up and went to the bank of windows. "Richard, everyone's been asking me if the union will wreck our party. I tell them it won't, but I don't really know what's going on. Should I be concerned?"

He leaned back in his chair, his expression preoccupied. "Punkie, didn't I tell you not to worry?"

"Yes, you did. But, Richard, I can't help it. I'm getting pressure from the press, and I need to have something solid to tell them. Rich, is there something wrong? Something you aren't telling me?"

He got up, walked around, and came to stand beside her, putting his hand lightly on her back. "Nothing that a little time won't fix."

"And what's that supposed to mean?" She saw the lines of tiredness etched beneath his eyes. "Is Diana going to arrive at the Fitz Hotel in her diamond tiara, only to find Tank Marchek and a bunch of union hooligans with signs telling her she can't come in?"

"Damn it, no! Of course not!"

"Then what, Richard? Tune me in to what's happening."

He hesitated. "OK. I'll tell you this much. The union threats are mostly hot air. The worst that can happen is that we get a ninety-day injunction from the federal district court that allows us a cooling-off period before resuming negotiations."

"Oh."

His smile was taut and made him look more tired than ever. "So you see, everything is just fine. I told you not to worry because there was really nothing to worry about. If you would just listen to me—"

She had begun to be mollified, but the last phrase seemed to add fuel to the fire that was already burning within her. Richard was pulling rank on her, and she hated it when he did that.

"Bullshit," she snapped. She saw Richard turn, startled by her use of the unaccustomed language. "I do listen to you very carefully, and do you know what I hear? I hear that you're being totally stubborn and unwilling to compromise. *That's* why we're being struck—because you won't give one goddamned inch, and that's what all the newspapers say, too!"

"Since when do you believe in the infallibility of the press? I think you're oversimplifying things—"

"I am not oversimplifying things! And I resent the implication!"

His voice rose. He hated being challenged. "You certainly are, and I don't know what implication you resent. I think you're getting hysterical."

She stared at her husband, feeling tears prick at the backs of her eyelids.

"God," she said, catching her breath with an anguished gulp of air. "Listen to you. Listen to us."

"Mr. Cox, Louie from the kitchen is here with your dinner," Richard's secretary interrupted them on the intercom.

He punched the button, snapping, "Tell him to wait."

"Richard," Alexandra pleaded. "Please, I know there must be issues at stake here, things you don't want to confide in me. But don't take it out on me. Please don't do that. And maybe you should try to compromise on some of the union issues, just a little bit. Can't you give them just a little, throw them a bone or something?"

He stared at her, his expression angry and offended. "What are you doing, going over to their side?"

"Their side? No! Richard . . . I didn't mean it that way. All I meant is that maybe you're being too stubborn."

"Alexandra," he sighed, interrupting her. "You know how complex my financial picture is. Our debt service requirements are over $10 million monthly. Complex? That's the understatement of the year."

"I know." She saw how tense he was, and her anger evaporated. She went over to him and slid her arms up underneath his shoulders, burying her face on his chest. "Oh, Richard, Rich, I do love you. I hate it when we quarrel like this—and we seem to be fighting more and more lately."

"We don't fight that much," he said in genuine surprise.

"Oh, God," she said, shaking her head and laughing a little. "We do. We do."

⸺ ►◄ ⸺

As soon as Alexandra left and Louie cleared away the remains of their dinner, Richard went to the phone and called his chief negotiator.

He waited impatiently while his staffer was paged.

"How's it going?" he asked Secchia without preamble as soon as he came on the line.

"They're stubborn SOBs. Hard-line all the way." Ray Secchia's voice was hoarse from long hours of talking and arguing. Negotiations involved twelve to fifteen lawyers and other parties for both sides spending as long as forty-eight straight hours in the bargaining room, with breaks only for food, bathroom needs, and intermittent alternate "snooze breaks" for each side. Tempers frayed, and there were often shouting matches and occasionally even threatened fistfights.

"Shit." Richard expelled his breath sharply.

"Emil Marchek is the problem; he's not listening to reason. They want all of their demands met, without compromise or exception, and half an hour ago, they added a new fucking wrinkle."

"What's that?"

"They want a profit participation program—get this—with a guaranteed minimum. Can you believe it? Can you fucking believe it? Whoever heard of anything in this fucking life being guaranteed, especially profits?"

"It's a throwaway," Richard said. "They don't want it; they're just bringing it up so they can sacrifice it."

"These mothers aren't sacrificing anything, Mr. Cox. They are loaded for bear."

"Where's Robbie Fraser? Isn't he there?"

"His wife got sick; she's in the hospital. He left to—"

"I'm coming over there, damn it," Richard said. "Give me twenty minutes."

He went into the large bathroom that adjoined his office and spent a crucial five minutes showering under a cold, needlepoint spray. He shaved, blow-dried his hair, and changed to a fresh white shirt. In the hectic and angry atmosphere of the negotiating room, he wanted to appear cool and controlled.

Ten minutes later, he was standing in an express elevator whizzing upward to the fortieth floor of the John Hancock Center.

"Mr. Cox? This way, please." Richard strode past the receptionist who attempted to show him into the meeting room, and he pushed open the door.

What he saw was chaos. The executive meeting room, with its deep-pile blue carpeting, leather-upholstered chairs, and long, gleaming oak conference table, was nearly obscured with a deep haze of blue cigarette smoke. As he entered, all heads turned toward him.

Eight men sat around the table in shirtsleeves. Four were union representatives, the rest were Richard's own staffers. They looked weary and somewhat relieved at Richard's entry.

"So, Cox?" muttered Tank Marchek. "You here to give us what's ours by right?" The union man's eyes were narrowed directly at Richard.

"I'm here to talk," Richard said curtly, as he took off his suit jacket, slung it over a chair, and sat down at the table.

— ◀▶ —

In the walled Provenzo compound in suburban Oak Park, only minutes from the Loop, four small boys squealed and

pushed each other as they fought over the controls of a motor-
ized toy car. They were curly-haired, handsome, and aggressive,
especially the youngest, Davy, who was only four.

Sam Provenzo, the *capo di tutti capi*, gazed out of the
window with paternal pride.

"That Davy," he boasted, turning to the six men assembled
in the long room, coffee cups and meeting agendas before them.
"Going to do the family proud someday. I think I might send
him to Harvard, too."

The godfather's tone changed abruptly. "Teach him to be
smart like our Nicolo, eh? Send him away for a fucking MBA,
and then let him tell us how to run things. He'll have all the
answers."

At these words, there was a little stir in the room that
extended to the door, where two bodyguards stood silently.

Sam's eyes focused on Nico. His son's blue eyes gazed back
at him, full of defiance. Goddamn, the boy never gave an inch,
did he? Still, Sam was inordinately proud of him. The only one
in the whole fucking family with an education. And not just *any*
education, but Harvard.

Sam knew he'd spoiled Nico and at the same time forced
him to compete with his three older brothers. Shit, how else
could the boy become a man? But he just didn't understand
Nico, and maybe he didn't want to.

Sam remembered he was in the middle of a meeting.
"Yeah," he finished. "I got myself quite a stable full of sons, eh?
Eight of them, and not one a pussy."

Sam had aged over the past six years, Nico thought, staring
coldly at his father. The wavy black hair was now more salt than
pepper, and the thick, bristly moustache had turned grayish
white. His father's cheeks sagged, and there were two age spots
on his right temple.

Once Sam had it all—he was smart, and he was brutal.
Now all that was gone, done. Now it was just a business they
were in. They'd just spent forty minutes discussing new ways to
launder all the money they earned, now that the Hollywood film
deals were coming under closer scrutiny by the feds.

Clearing his throat, Sam got back to business. "OK. Now
we got to talk about the next thing. Gotti."

A New York capo, John Gotti had requested assistance with
certain racketeering charges that were perilously close to putting
him in prison. The combined sentences would total hundreds
of years.

They argued about it for thirty more minutes. Nico made one suggestion, to "put a rocket in the pocket" of a certain federal judge.

"You got to be kidding," said Marco, who always opposed Nico, no matter what the topic was.

Nico said softly, "I never kid about anything like that. Ice him."

"With the feds sniffing around the way they are? Do you want us to end up in the slammer right along with Gotti? We can light his cigarettes," Marco said sarcastically. "Smuggle him in his dope. Bend over and open our cheeks for him."

"Up yours," Nico snapped. He looked around the room, disgusted. "You can't fight fire by having fucking meetings like we're some goddamned Fortune 500 company. A fucking tea party!"

A ripple went around the table, but it was Sam Provenzo who spoke, his gravelly voice deep with threat.

"You calling me a sissy? You saying tea party to me?"

No one spoke. The men seated at the table drew in quick, sharp breaths, and the guards at the door tensed.

"Yeah," said Nico. He repeated it. *"Yeah."*

Sam pushed back from his place at the head of the table and lunged toward his son. He raised a thick, gnarled hand and swung it toward Nico's face. The blow came within millimeters of touching him.

"Get the fuck out of here," Sam grated. "Go for a drive in that little sardine-can car of yours; go cool off. Don't talk to me like that again. Or next time my fist will land. *Capisce?*"

Nico stalked out of the room, pushing past the guards and slamming the door.

"Jesus," Marco muttered under his breath when the door had shut behind Nico. "No respect," he said softly. "No respect at all."

Nico's personal bodyguard, Raymond "Rambo" DiSicco, was waiting outside the meeting room.

Nico motioned to him. "Come on, Rambo, get off your butt."

Rambo jumped up and followed Nico outside to the four-car garage where he had parked his black Lamborghini.

The two men got in the car. Savage anger wrenched through Nico. The old man would pay for this—if not today, then soon enough. Sam was getting soft, weak, and senile. He would soon drag the rest of the family down with him into his decay.

As he squealed the car into the turnaround, the littlest Provenzo ran shouting up to the Lamborghini.

"My car! Don't run over my car!"

"What?"

"The fucking kiddie car," Rambo prompted.

Nico looked out of his window and saw the tiny vehicle only inches away from his rear tire. "So pick it up. Don't run your car where people back out, Davy-boy."

"I wanna! I can't run it on the grass!"

"Then watch it get crunched," Nico said. He reached in his pocket and pulled out a silver dollar, a leftover from Vegas. He flipped it to the child, who caught it deftly. "Stay out of the way, Davy-boy. Big cars are dangerous."

The child backed away, and Nico drove toward the gate. As soon as they were through, he floorboarded the accelerator. For a terrifying instant, tears sprang to his eyes, burning them. He had not cried since he was Davy's age. He blinked back the betraying wetness before Rambo saw.

Nico drove west, into River Forest and Maywood, then to Bellwood. He pulled into the parking lot of a tavern he knew, dark and quiet, with an old-fashioned, polished brass-and-mahogany bar. He and Jette came here sometimes, just to talk.

Jette. Shit, he'd forgotten she was in town today expecting to stay the night with him at his condo. That was the last thing he needed. On the way in, he stopped at a row of newspaper machines in front of the bar and purchased a copy of the *Tribune.*

"They fire Ditka yet?" Rambo wanted to know. Mike Ditka was the head coach for the Chicago Bears. "They should've for not taking the club all the way last year."

Without replying, Nico flipped him the sports pages.

They went inside, and each ordered a double Absolut on the rocks. The air-conditioned dimness of the bar had a slightly palliative effect on Nico's corrosive anger. He was still ready to kill, but it would be in his own time, in his own way. Meanwhile, the family needed to be taught a lesson.

The front page of the business section had a long article about the deadlocked hotel union negotiations. Nico studied the photograph of Cox. The photographer had caught him looking exceptionally bullish, his jaw squared aggressively.

Nico narrowed his eyes and read further, his interest growing. He knew Marchek from the Powerhouse Gym, where he and his brothers worked out.

Marchek was one of the toughest. Too bad he wasn't Mafia; he'd make a better "wise guy" than many others Nico could name.

"Hey," said Rambo, looking over his shoulder. "Hey, I know him. Martik?"

"Marchek."

"Yeah. Good ole Polack. I seen him at the gym; he can bench over 350." Rambo went on, "You know what those crazy fuckers did? I heard they put a real scare into Cox, made him wet his fancy silk drawers."

"What did they do?"

Rambo laughed expansively. "Why, he showed Cox's old lady a nice little TV show. Nice picture of her three kids lying on the floor dead, blood oozing out all over 'em. Scared the living shit out of her, too. They did it all with computers. Computers, now, it's amazing the stuff they can do with 'em. In fact—"

Nico tuned out the chatter of his bodyguard, his mind racing. A *lesson*. Maybe this was it, maybe he could accomplish something for the family and at the same time show them who *he* was.

"—I heard they got these machines, see, called scanners, and you feed the picture into 'em . . ."

"Shut up, will you?" Nico snapped.

Rambo's mouth closed immediately. Nico frowned, staring into his iced vodka as he thought about the ramifications of his plan.

The more he thought about it, the stronger the feeling in his gut became. He hadn't felt this excited in a long time. Fuck it. He would show them all. He shoved away his drink, got up, and went to the phone near the rest rooms.

He dialed the switchboard at the John Hancock Building.

—— ◄► ——

"Hey, Nico, mah man, what's up? What kind of emergency you got?" Tank Marchek was pissed at being called away from negotiations, but he did not dare let his voice give him away.

"Make up some excuse; get out of there for a half hour," Nico ordered over the phone. "I'll meet you at Mama Locricchio's on West Superior."

At 10:30 A.M., the small cafe was mostly empty. "I've got a proposition for you," Nico said in a low voice, after the waitress brought them big plates of eggs, hash browns, and sausage patties, with sides of thick-sliced toast.

"Yeah?"

"Look," Nico proposed. "Cox is a stubborn SOB. You're not going to break him around a conference table. I heard about the videotape you did. Great idea . . . only you could carry it a lot further."

Marchek stopped chewing his fried eggs. "We can't get involved with no stuff like that. Think we're crazy?"

"We do it, not you. You aren't involved at all. We won't ask for ransom money; we won't ask for anything. We'll just send the Coxes videotapes. They won't know who did it; they can assume any fucking thing they want to."

The sweat began to pour down Emil Marchek's back, dampening the seams of his already crumpled shirt. He smelled it all around him, sour. "Shit," he breathed. "And what do you get?"

"A sweet deal; we both profit," Nico explained reasonably. "*You* get a surefire way to break that strike, send Cox to his knees, get all the concessions you want . . . at absolutely no risk to you, because the feds can never prove anything on you, because you didn't do anything, you weren't involved at all."

"Jesus," Marchek said. "And what do you get? I assume this isn't charity; you got your own needs."

"Our needs are simple. We have money we want washed, more than $100 million over three years. We can do it through your pension funds, buddy boy. Millions, and we both profit. You get 20 percent of anything that comes out clean. How does that grab you, man?"

There was a silence while Marchek digested the offer. He felt his heartbeat speed up, hammering inside him at the thought of the huge amounts to be made, the dollars he could siphon off for his own use. He could retire. Be a wealthy man, go live anywhere he wanted to. Even buy his own gym, bankroll a fighter or two. Anything!

"Jesus Christ," he said slowly. "This for real? This come from the old man?"

"Yes," Nico said, his eyes hard.

"I don't know . . ."

"A hundred million over three years, Marchek. I don't know how you can even think about turning it down."

Marchek's entire chest felt tight. "Implicate any of us, any of my union men, or me, and you're done," he said hoarsely. "I personally will shoot both your balls off. I'll bust your whole leg off at the knee with an iron pipe. You'll be walking around three and a half feet high."

They gazed at each other across the table.

"We have a deal?" Nico said softly.

Marchek nodded.

———— ◄► ————

"Turn up the fucking TV, turn it up loud," Sam Provenzo barked that night, his face mottled with rage. Inside the Provenzo stronghold, the air conditioning hummed at a chilly sixty-two degrees.

D'Stefano, the banker, picked up the remote. The old man had been watching "Spenser: For Hire," and the sounds of a car chase blasted into the room. Marco looked up from the contracts he'd been examining.

"OK," said Sam in a hoarse voice. "Tell it again, Nico, boy. Just like you said before."

"I've arranged for us to launder some of that coke money."

"No shit," Marco said.

"Something *you* haven't accomplished," Nico pointed out to his older brother. "Marchek jumped right at it, and once we get him pulled in, we've got his ass. He'll jump through any hoops we hold out. He's got a fucking union in his pocket, sixty thousand members. And it won't be too long before he controls the international. That means heavy-duty shit coming down, like over three million members and hundreds of millions in dues alone."

There was an ominous silence.

Nico felt beads of perspiration gather under his arms and at his hairline. He did not move or drop his gaze. To show fear would be fatal.

"*Pezzo de merdo!*" Sam swore in sharp, gutter Italian.

"What the hell do you mean?" Nico snapped. "We can't pass this one up."

Sam Provenzo shook his head. "What are you, *stupido*? Where is your honor? I do not condone kidnapping or hurting *bambinos*." D'Stefano and Marco looked on, their satisfaction barely concealed.

"You have disgraced us," Sam went on in heavy, patriarchal tones.

Something snapped in Nico.

"No." He cracked out the word. *"You* disgrace *us.* I have given my word to Marchek now. My word is the family's word!"

"No longer," Sam said, and he lunged forward, smacking Nico across the left cheek with such force that the younger man reeled sideways from the blow.

In the Cosa Nostra, such a slap reduced its victim to child status, making him an outcast, no longer part of the family. The only thing worse was the infamous kiss of death on the lips of the victim.

Pain radiated through Nico's head and nose, and his cheek burned from the blow. Blood began to run from his nostrils onto his shirt. Slowly, he lifted his eyes to his father and smiled. It was a cruel, proud smile with teeth bared.

"No one hits me. Ever. Not even you."

"Go," Sam said in a stentorian voice.

For thirty seconds longer, Nico held his father's eyes and allowed the hatred in him, the terrible, simmering red hatred, contaminated with love, to find expression on his face. He knew with a white-hot sense of joy that he was the one with the real strength.

"Go, I said!" Sam shouted. "We will talk later. We will decide what to do with you; we will have a family meeting."

Nico laughed contemptuously. "Fuck the family meeting! And fuck you, *capo. Old man.*"

He turned and strode from the room.

— ▶◀ —

Jette had just arrived from a major bout of shopping on Michigan Avenue, after phoning up from the lobby to make certain Nico was back. He had never given her a key, nor had she asked for one. Nico's sense of privacy was fierce, and she knew he would never give a key to her.

"You're *so* late, Nico," she purred, tossing things as she entered, packages and shopping bags to the couch, her purse onto a black leather chair. The white linen jacket she wore went over the couch. She kicked her high heels onto the thick pile carpet. "So it's your fault I racked up my Gold Card. Aren't you sorry? Don't you feel guilty?"

Nico clicked off the TV set and stared at her, as if not quite registering what she'd said. Usually he was clean-shaven and immaculately dressed. Tonight, however, a slight stubble blued the skin on his chin and jaw. There was a tension about him, too. He looked as if he'd snorted a couple of lines of coke, she realized uneasily.

"We'll go in the bedroom," he said abruptly.

"I have to pee first." She padded barefoot toward the large bathroom, with its Jacuzzi where she had enjoyed her first orgasm and many subsequent ones.

"Now."

She stopped. "What's the matter, you're so horny you can't wait three minutes? I'm telling you I can't do a thing until I—"

He sprang toward her, grabbing her around the hips and pushing her in the direction of the bedroom.

"Hey!" she cried, trying to wrench away from him. "Hey!"

Then she saw the crazed look in his eyes and stopped struggling. She had seen that look before.

He took her from behind, jamming himself into her dryness with cruel, grunting force.

Afterward, she lay very still on the bed. Nico lay beside her, his face twisted. "Nico," she whispered. "I . . . I think maybe you're not in the mood to have me here tonight, so I'll go."

He didn't answer. Choking back a sob, she rose to scoop up her bra, panties, and dress, then fled with them out of the bedroom. She dressed in the living room and then let herself out of the condo.

After Jette left, Nico walked over to the eighth floor window. He watched the street until he saw a cab pull up in front of the building and the small figure of his mistress climb inside. The cab pulled away.

For a second he recalled the expression on Jette's face as he had pushed her onto the bed. He felt a brief spasm of regret.

Suddenly, violently, he turned and put his fist through the glass door of the breakfront. Blood and glass splattered all over the carpet. Drawing his fist back, he stared at it as if it belonged to a stranger.

The tears came on him suddenly. He staggered to the bathroom, wrapped up his bleeding hand, and then, leaning against the wall, surrendered to the sobs that racked his entire body.

Finally he was done, drained. He felt old and used. He returned to the bedroom and fumbled in the now-broken cabinet doors until he found the small box where he kept a supply of dime bags of cocaine. His hands shook as he got out the mirror and a $100 bill. He stood hunched over the mirror, drawing the white powder deeply into his nostrils.

Finally the coke took hold, mellowing his anger enough that he was no longer shaking. Nico hooked his hands under the front shelves of the cabinet and pulled it, so that it slid out from the wall on its casters.

Behind the breakfront was a jagged hole in the building, which Nico himself had carefully knocked out with a hammer and chisel. A rough two-foot step led upward, into the building that abutted his. It gave entrance into an efficiency apartment on which Nico secretly paid the rent.

This was his "extra exit"—a way to leave the building without the Provenzo-hired security or his brothers, who also lived in the building, knowing anything about it. No one knew about the exit, not even Rambo.

He used this exit now, pulling the breakfront carefully back behind him. He walked through the unfurnished second apartment, took the elevator to the first floor, and left the building. From the other building, there was good access to a municipal parking structure.

He walked into the parking garage, his footsteps echoing hollowly on the grease-spotted cement flooring. On the second level, he kept a spare car—a 1985 Lincoln. Another piece of insurance.

The Lincoln started up with a soft, powerful whisper of engine power. He had replaced the original engine, installing a V8 twin-turbocharged engine, fuel-injected with higher compression pistons and a hot cam. Sheer speed.

He peeled the Lincoln out of the garage, the car responding to his every touch like a restless stallion. It was a beautiful night, with gauzy clouds half hiding a silver coin of a moon. Car headlights and neon signs took on a sharp glitter.

Nico saw none of that.

He drove for hours, restlessly, angrily, stopping now and then to snort another line of cocaine.

— ◄► —

In Studio City, Darryl Boyer sat cross-legged on the floor of her bedroom, her Rolodex in front of her. She sighed and swore to herself as she flipped through the cards, many of which were yellowed with age or contained as many as four phone numbers, all crossed out.

"So this is what happens when you're blacklisted. None of your numbers are current anymore."

She was wearing pink running shorts and a white T-shirt emblazoned with *Sports Club LA.* Her body felt great. She had embarked on a new exercise program, and she looked tighter than she had in five years.

Finding another number that looked promising, she dialed. For a change, she got an answer. "Jeffie? Jeff, it's Darryl. Yeah, right, me! What have you been up to?"

Jeff Deemer was an actor she knew, gay but with tentacles that reached through most of Beverly Hills. She thought he might be able to tell her what she needed to know.

"Look, Jeffie, you hear anything about that party the Coxes are giving in Chicago?"

"Yeah . . . a lot of people are fighting for invites. She could only invite 650, and that's hardly a drop in the bucket."

"Do you know anyone who's been invited?"

"Of course, dear child, one or two."

"Like who?"

"Well, not me, sugar cakes, I don't think she's letting us campy guys in."

"Who, Jeffie?"

"Well, Kirk Douglas, I heard, and Tom Jones, and Burt Bacharach—he's an old friend of hers, everyone knows that. Clive Davis, from Arista Records, but he doesn't count because he's the boss; she had to invite him. Carly Simon. Olivia Newton-John. Linda Ronstadt. You know. A lot of Hollywood old-guard types. Oh, and Sid Cohen; I heard he's flying out there."

He listed a few other names. Darryl squeezed her eyes shut, wanting to scream from frustration. All the men Jeff named—other than Cohen—were either married or attached.

"Anyone else?"

"Hey, why you so interested, dearie? Could it possibly be that you are trying to wangle something? Like a nice hand-engraved vellum card with your name on it?"

"Me?" she said, forcing a laugh. Then she decided to admit the truth. "Well . . . look, Jeffie, I kind of would like to go. I thought—don't you know anyone else who's going?"

"Court Frank."

"Who?"

"You know . . . megabuck real estate developer. Hollywood star fucker."

"I don't suppose you have his phone number?"

"You're not going to call him?"

"I might."

"I wouldn't advise it, you know. He's not a fun date."

"Who is?" Darryl snapped.

"Oh, baby, are we getting hard up, or are we getting hard up?"

Darryl hung up and immediately dialed the number that Deemer had given her.

—— ⋈ ——

"Oh, God, you really know how to turn a guy on," Frank said four days later when he picked Darryl up in his Ferrari for dinner at Chasen's.

"You like?" Happily, she twirled for him, causing the scarf hemline of her gown to swirl sexily about her legs. She had allowed herself one small screwdriver in order to settle her nerves, her first drink in months. She needed it. This wasn't just any date, but had to be handled very, very carefully.

"I like," he said, leering. "I always have. How come you never came on to me before?"

"I was married before," she said, making her voice very smoky.

"That doesn't stop some people."

"Oh, you," she teased throatily.

Chasen's was packed, but Tommy Gallagher, the omniscient and suave maître d', escorted them to one of the choice tables. This did not escape Darryl's notice.

Unfortunately, dinner was long and boring. Frank was a notorious gossiper, and to hear him talk, it seemed that everyone else was working or had a sure shot for an Emmy or Oscar. She would never win any Oscars working on movies like *Aikido Hell* and *Shanghai Devil*, she thought bitterly.

She did her best, bantering, joking, making sure that she threw in plenty of compliments and double entendres. She didn't want Frank to be confused at all—she was definitely available for bed.

By eleven o'clock they were both slightly drunk, and Frank took the bait. Rather than driving toward Studio City, where she now had been forced to live, he turned toward his large home on Laurel Canyon Drive. Darryl could hardly hide her elation. She snuggled next to him, slipping her hand into Frank's crotch, which held a nice, firm erection.

At least he had a decent body, she comforted herself. He showed signs of being able to get it up, too. So far, all was going very well indeed.

His house, set back from the road behind the usual Hollywood barrier of hedges, wrought-iron fencing, and automated gate, was imposing,

"What do you think?" he wanted to know. "I designed this myself."

"Oh, it's a wonderful house. So marvelous," she raved.

Frank nodded, pleased, and escorted her inside, where he gave her a brief tour, allowing her only glimpses of a huge screening room, a big kitchen with two islands, and a living room that contained several large sculptures of museum quality.

"This is my real home," he told her proudly, opening the door to a bedroom that looked like a Hugh Hefner fantasy. There were mirrored ceilings, a water bed, a large TV screen with VCR hooked up—even a collection of vibrators, laid out on a table, along with various other sexual paraphernalia. But it was when Darryl saw the thick velvet ropes fastened to the wooden headboard, discreetly looped back as if they were decor, and two more ropes decorating the foot of the bed, that she realized what kind of a "not fun date" Court Frank was.

Oh, shit, she thought.

"I'm going to slip into the dressing room and get into something more comfortable," he informed her, winking. He motioned to a large adjoining bathroom and told her that she should do the same.

Gingerly Darryl walked into the bathroom, which was more of the same—plenty of marble, wallpaper featuring hundreds of black-and-white nude drawings, and a closet that contained a veritable Fredericks of Hollywood. She could still leave, of course, but it would be without the invitation. And she hadn't heard any rumors of women who had been actually *hurt* by Frank . . . His voice crooned to her from the bedroom . . .

"Baby? Baby? Are you ready yet?"

Hastily Darryl rummaged along the wisps of chiffon and silk, finding a black stretch teddy with openings for nipples and a split crotch. She took off her clothes and wriggled into its formfitting lace. Appraising herself in the mirror, she realized she'd been turned into a seventeen-year-old's wet dream.

"Baby . . . Darryl . . ."

She eyed herself one more time, and then stepped into the bedroom. "Hello, lovie."

The Beverly Hills real estate tycoon wore a minuscule black leather codpiece that barely held him. He was nearly nude, but it was not his muscles that drew her fascinated glance.

It was the whip. She guessed it was an antique buggy whip straight out of the 1880s, its leather handle well worn from years of use.

He was smiling, his eyes traveling over her body with lustful appreciation.

She smiled back, moistening her lips, aware that what she said now was crucial. "Court, the whip is fine, but I have three conditions. First, I don't want to get hurt too much. Second, I don't want the whip landing on any part of my body that might show in a strapless evening dress. And third—"

"Yes?"

"I want to go with you to the Cox party in Chicago."

He licked his lips. His eyes gleamed; somehow he had guessed. "I already have a date."

She kept the smile. "Then you're going to have to break it, aren't you? Or I go home right now."

It wasn't the best evening of her life, but neither was it actually painful. Which was a good thing, since he might expect this a couple more times before the big day.

He'd promised . . . and she intended to hold him to it.

— ►◄ —

They were staring at her again. Several girls studying in the Georgetown University library glanced up as Bitsy sat down at an adjoining table, dropping her purse on the floor with a thump.

"Bitches!" Bitsy hissed.

Scowling, she opened her textbook to a page of COBOL commands. She bent over it, forcing the formulas to enter her brain. It was getting harder and harder every day to concentrate.

Derek Winthrop. Over the past several years, she had tried to kill him three times.

The first time, she'd spotted him leaving the Jefferson Hotel near Sixteenth and K streets. Winthrop's men had grabbed her, but she'd managed to run to her car.

The second time, she had lurked near the entrance of the house he and his wife, Rita Sue, were renting on Dumbarton Avenue. She sprang out of the bushes as the couple left, in evening clothes, for some senatorial function. Rita Sue screamed, Derek shouted, and Bitsy fled down the street, criss-crossing through yards and again escaping.

On the third occasion, the Capitol police caught her loitering outside Senator Winthrop's office late in the evening. Suspicious, they led her through security and, after finding a knife on her, arrested her. The charge was carrying a concealed weapon.

Bitsy's grandfather flew up from Miami, bailed her out of jail, arranged for probation, and put her in a private mental clinic. For a while she started to feel good again, but after her release, she returned to Georgetown and stopped taking her medication.

She nursed her paranoia, brooding long hours each day. It was much harder than it appeared to shadow a man like Derek Winthrop.

"Miss?" A weedy-looking male student had approached her. "Miss, would you mind? You're making noises."

Noises? Bitsy stared at him. She hadn't been making noises.

The man returned to his table, and to get away from him, Bitsy went into the periodicals room. A copy of the *Washington Post* was lying on a chair, and she sat down with it.

She had read almost everything written about Derek Winthrop. He wielded real clout in Washington now. A heart attack and a cloakroom scandal had forced the premature retirement of two Southern Senators, and Winthrop had become a ranking member of the powerful Senate Foreign Relations Committee. Now, even acerbic and blasé columnists like Jack Anderson and Carl Rowan called him one of the most powerful men in the Capitol.

Bitsy had amassed a collection of Norwegian knives. Women's knives, each one shaped prettily. She loved their smooth steel finish, the handles that curved sweetly to the palm, the blades of surgical sharpness. She daydreamed about using each one of them on a different section of his anatomy.

He was, after all, the man who had ordered the hit on Giancarlo Ferrari that had ended up injuring and scarring her. Did he think he could just make one phone call and wreck people's lives? All the torture she went through. Didn't she have a right to nurse her revenge?

She unfolded the Style section, and immediately a headline jumped up to meet her eye. *Fitzgerald Jewels to Outsparkle Royal Gems.*

Jealousy consumed her as she inspected the photograph of Alexandra Winthrop Cox that accompanied the article. Alexandra's face held an almost cameo beauty.

And those diamonds. Even in newsprint, the effect was magnificent, and she could only imagine what the famous pink diamonds would look like in reality.

Then Bitsy froze. *He was Alexandra's brother. He would be attending the party.*

She'd have to figure out how to be there, too. Her mind raced. She knew someone who worked as assistant chef in the kitchen at the Chicago Fitz. At least, three years ago he had. She'd met Jorge Arrinda in Miami one time at a party. He'd remember her . . . she hoped.

She was excited in a sick, stomach-knotting sort of way. She grabbed up her frayed purse and hurried out of the room to a central lobby, where there was a bank of telephones.

Within seconds, she had been given the number of the Chicago Fitz and was being connected to the kitchen.

"Jorge," she said. "My God, it's been so long since we got together."

He had a fat man's voice, rich and friendly. "Who is this?"

"Bitsy. Bits. Remember me? Bitsy Lancombe. Only now I'm Dumbarton. I got married." She thought it best to have a different last name and impulsively chose the street Derek Winthrop lived on.

Jorge's voice rose with pleasure. "Bitsy! Jesus, where you calling from?"

"Well, it's Georgetown right now, but I'm moving out; my husband and I don't get along too good anymore. I'm coming to Chicago. Any chance of a job at the Fitz? I've got about two years' experience as a pantry assistant. And I can waitress."

"Sure, hey. We got a couple openings. 'Specially cocktail waitresses."

Payment, she thought giddily. It was time Senator Winthrop paid for what he had done.

◄►

"Another problem!" Dolly announced as she swept into Alexandra's office.

"What is it now?" Alexandra said, hanging up from a phone call to Ann Arbor and Twyla Tharp.

"The flowers," Dolly exclaimed. "Remember that big thunderstorm we had on Monday? Well, apparently it doused the power at our wholesale supplier's greenhouse, and they still haven't got it on yet. A frigging transformer part," she added bitterly. "Com Edison says they can't get the part for two days because so many homes were out of power."

"I thought it was sunshine that flowers needed, not electricity."

"Refrigerators," Dolly pointed out, sinking into a chair. "Roses, especially, have to be kept at forty-five degrees, or the blooms ripen too fast. And we've got all those humongous loads of white orchids being flown in. We'll end up with vases of overblown flowers dropping their petals."

"No, we won't," Alexandra said.

"Why won't we?"

"Because we'll call Lucci's in New York and arrange for them to send us what we need."

It was the last week before the party. Already scaffolding had been erected. Hordes of upholsterers and set workers had embarked on the time-consuming task of tenting, gathering, and bouffanting three huge ballrooms with thousands of yards of white silk moiré.

The union negotiations were still deadlocked, but Richard's attorneys were in communication with a federal judge. They were discussing the possibility of negotiating terms for a ninety-day reprieve, which he assured her would be completed by the end of the week, rescuing the party in plenty of time.

There could be no contingent location, not with the elaborate sets that had been constructed. Not this late.

"God," Dolly sighed, as she kicked her feet out of her Italian-made pumps. She wore a kelly green linen suit with wide, cropped pants. "My feet are killing me. Oh, and another thing. Those guest baskets, Alexandra. I've got two girls who're going to help me pack them, and we're going to spend all day tomorrow on it. The way things have been going, I don't want any mistakes."

Alexandra nodded. "And I have the dancers flying in tomorrow afternoon for the rehearsal, plus I've got to inspect the fountains. The plumber assures me they're in running order.

And the computer system we set up to run the spray pattern works perfectly, thank God. All we need now is the lights installed, to focus on the—"

"If nothing more goes wrong," Dolly interrupted, wriggling her toes.

"Will you stop being the voice of doom? Nothing will."

"I know. It's just—oh, hell," Dolly said, getting out of the chair and walking over to a small refrigerator. "I saw a bottle of Chablis in here, didn't I? Let's have a glass or two. Unwind a little. I don't know about you, but I could certainly use it."

Alexandra accepted the glass of wine that Dolly poured. "To the gala," Dolly toasted as Alexandra smiled, nodding.

—— ►◄ ——

Rambo sauntered up and down in front of the Fitzgerald Tower, pushing a wagon that contained bunches of cut flowers wrapped in green florist's paper. All around him Michigan Avenue shoppers jostled.

He moved slowly, bored. Shit, it was hot out here today, the first week in September. Anyone with any sense was in a nice, cool store, not out here on the walk frying their brains.

Still, these were his instructions. He'd been given photographs of all the Coxes and their servants. All he had to do was watch the entrance of the building and see who came and went.

A couple of old ladies passed him, one of them slowing up to examine the flowers he had in his cart—dahlias, lilies, and carnations, most of them a little brown around the edges—but rejected his wares.

Rambo sighed, wondering how long he was going to have to keep this up. Then, turning, he saw the English nanny and the oldest Cox kid emerge from the main door of the apartment building.

The long, smoke-colored Cox limousine had pulled up in front of the building, and the nanny took Trip's hand and walked him toward it. The woman was attractive and wore a navy blue shirtwaist dress, with no jewelry. But the boy was kind of cute. He walked beside the nanny, chattering away a mile a minute about the school he went to.

Rambo watched the nanny hurry ahead and pull open the door of the limo, lifting the kid in ahead of her. She got in herself and slammed the door. She always did it that way.

Again Rambo sighed. Nico had instructed him to be thinking of ways to get the kid. Shit, the kids were always in the limo, with a driver for protection, or upstairs in that apartment, which was wired so heavily for security that it would take an armored division to get in now. Even the damned school had security.

Then, just as the limo started away from the curb, another limousine turned the corner. It was gray, too, polished, classy-looking, identical down to the hood ornament. The only difference was the license plates. And that was when he had the idea.

He reached into his pocket for the small notepad he carried, and jotted down the license number of the Cox limo.

This job would be easier than they had thought.

———— ▶◀ ————

"Brownie, when I grow up, I'm gonna scuba dive!" Trip announced, as they left the Mattingly Day School. It was the usual after-class pandemonium. Mothers beeped car horns, limos jostled for position, and cabs waited in a line, blocking other traffic that was trying to get past in peak rush-hour time.

"I'm going to dive deep, deep in the water like on TV," Trip chattered on. "I'm going to go under and find sharks and big fish and whales, and I'm going to take pictures of them with my underwater camera."

Brownie smiled. Trip was her favorite of the Cox children.

The Cox limousine was just pulling up, its gray exterior glittering in the afternoon sun.

"Come now," she said, hurrying him along.

He resisted a little. "Brownie, that's not ours. It's not the same shiny."

"Oh, nonsense," she said, hustling him toward the car. "Come, do, or we'll be caught in the traffic crush, and we'll be forever getting home."

She strode across the curb and opened the door of the limousine. "In with you now," she said, giving Trip a little pat.

The little boy climbed in, and she followed him hastily, plumping down on the seat. She shut the door and immediately heard door locks click.

"Brownie," Trip said, his eyes riveted on the Plexiglas panel that separated them from the driver.

Brownie's eyes followed his gaze, across the spacious interior of the limousine with its drink and refrigerator bar in the wrong spot, to the back of the driver's head, which was longer and narrower, the hair blacker and curlier than Will's.

"Oh, goodness," she said in annoyance. By some mistake, they'd stepped into the wrong limo. She reached overhead for the panel and flipped the speak control.

"I'm afraid we are in the wrong vehicle," she informed the dark-haired driver, who had not even glanced around at them.

"No, you're not," came back his voice via intercom.

"I'm afraid you are going to have to stop and let us out at once. This next corner will be acceptable," she said in her best clipped, British voice.

There was no answer.

"At once!" Brownie repeated.

Still no answer. They did not even slow down at the corner, but swerved into the outer lane, making a swift, purring left. She looked at the door to her right, noticing then that the inner door handle had been removed. The door on the other side had been similarly prepared.

With horror it dawned on her. They were imprisoned.

"Brownie," Trip said, touching her arm, his eyes saucer-wide. "Brownie, we're not even going the right way. Brownie, Brownie, I think this man is taking us away!"

Of course, there was no way to signal for help. The windows of the limousine were opaque from the outside, so no one could see them if they waved, screamed, or cried.

Five blocks later, the limo pulled over briefly, and a second man got into the front seat.

She didn't get a good look at him. She didn't want to. Her brief spate of courage had already deserted her, and she rode huddled with Trip, their arms around each other, gazing out of the windows of the limousine in terror.

They first passed by office buildings, then crossed over the South Branch of the Chicago River. Heading along side streets, they saw weatherbeaten machine shops and small manufacturing plants, many of them vacant.

A sign said Provenzo Brothers Packing. They pulled up to a complex of one-story cinder-block buildings. At loading bays, several trucks were being filled with plastic-wrapped packages of meat. Brownie averted her eyes.

"Is this a factory?" Trip wanted to know, gripping Brownie's hand tighter.

"Yes."

"A factory for making meat?"

"Yes."

The limousine pulled up to a dingy building that looked

unused. Brownie stiffened, pulling the child close. Both men got out and came around to the back doors. The man on Brownie's right pulled open the door. The slaughterhouse smell came rushing in, odious, bloody, stifling. The nanny gasped. The man had pulled a section of panty hose over his face, and his features looked smashed and shapeless.

"Get out," he ordered in a low, husky voice.

Brownie huddled further back in the seat, pulling Trip with her, protecting him with her arms as best she could. She was shaking all over but had braced her feet, prepared for a struggle.

"Out, I said." The man in the mask bent down and grabbed Trip with both hands.

"Leave me alone!" the child shouted. He kicked at the man, his heel smashing down on Brownie's calf as well. Pain stabbed her leg. She held onto the boy, gripping him with all her strength.

"Let go of the kid, lady, or I'll pull him apart."

"No—no, please." She was crying now, too frightened to release Trip.

"Bitch," the masked man said. He motioned to the driver on the other side. The left door opened, and the driver reached in and grabbed Brownie by the shoulders, while the other man pulled Trip from her arms.

Trip fought his captor, windmilling his arms, kicking his legs, biting and scratching. The man held him out at arm's length and cracked him across the face. Trip's cry of pain was loud, but he did not stop kicking.

"Little bastard has fucking teeth," the man said. He slapped the child again and twisted Trip's arms behind him, pulling sharply upward.

As Trip cried out in pain, a dark wetness spread across his jeans. His captor started pushing him across the cement toward a large bay, beyond which stretched acres of cement flooring.

"Please," Brownie cried out, sobbing. "This is Richard Cox's son. Mr. Cox's son."

There was no response. The driver gave her a shove in the center of her back, pushing her after the boy.

———— ◄► ————

In the Cox apartment, Alexandra was glancing at her watch. "Four forty-five," she said to Dolly. "I'm going to call down and find out if Brownie's back with Tripper yet. Then I'm going to take a break. I promised to play some songs for the kids."

"All right," Dolly said. "Maybe I'll call home and tell my housekeeper I'll be a little late."

Alexandra punched the intercom button, calling through to her housekeeper. "Is Brownie back with Trip yet, Mrs. Abbott?"

"Not yet, Mrs. Cox. I expect them any minute," Mary answered.

"Would you buzz me when they come in?"

"I certainly will."

Alexandra stepped away from her desk, stretching catlike. She'd been hunched over the phone for two hours. She would go collect Andy and Stephanie, she decided, then head for the living room and warm up on the piano. She could use it to clear her thoughts just a little, until her oldest son arrived.

— ►◄ —

Their footsteps echoed in the old building, which in its heyday had packed more than a million sides of beef a year. Nico breathed in through the panty-hose mask, gripping the struggling child, who was still attempting to kick him despite the painful grip Nico had on the boy's arms. Behind him, Rambo was having no trouble with the nanny.

"Let go of me! I hate you! I hate you!" the child screamed, his voice echoing.

Just like Davy, feisty as hell.

"Calm down, little guy," Nico muttered, loosening his grip a fraction.

"I won't, I won't, I won't!"

Nico didn't bother to respond further but just kept dragging the kid across the floor of the main plant and then toward the meat lockers.

The third locker, the largest, was the one they had prepared. He pushed the child inside, shoving him so hard that Trip stumbled forward and fell on his knees.

"Ow! You hurt me!"

The kid was a pain in the ass, and now Nico wished they'd taken the little girl—except that a son, an oldest son, was far more valuable.

"Please, you've *got* to take us back," the Englishwoman begged. "This is the child of an important man."

"We know that, lady," Rambo said, grinning. "We ain't dumb." He gave the nanny a hard push. She struggled for balance, found it, and then stood looking around with wide, horrified eyes.

A portable carpenter's lamp provided the only illumination. The locker was approximately sixty by thirty feet, its white-painted bricks now peeling in places. It was in this very room that Nico had first been "made" by executing a Greek immigrant who had reneged on his debt to the family.

"You're not going to leave us here?" the nanny asked, her eyes shiny in the reflection of the lamplight.

"Why not?" Nico smiled at her. "You'll be fine."

He pointed toward the far end of the room, where a collection of supplies had been arranged. Two air mattresses, already inflated. A stack of blankets and pillows. Plastic coolers, one filled with food, the other with cans of soda. More paper bags of cookies, sugary cereal, crackers, and pretzels. A chemical toilet. Comic books. And a stack of new toys, still in their boxes, purchased from Toys "R" Us.

"Please." The sight seemed to stun the nanny. "You can't mean this. We can't stay here. The boy's mother is expecting us."

Rambo laughed. "Shit, lady, we know that."

Nico noticed that Rambo was eyeing the Englishwoman with new interest.

"Come on, let's do the video," he told his bodyguard shortly.

A camcorder was waiting outside the thick, insulated door, along with a copy of the day's *Chicago Tribune*. Nico retrieved them.

He ordered the two hostages to stand together. Trip refused to move, so Rambo slapped him across the face again, and the child squatted down, his cheek bright red.

Nico waved to the terrified nanny. "There, you, too. Sit down beside the kid, hold the newspaper in your hand, hold it up so people can read the headline. Yeah. Now look at the camera. We don't have any sound in this video, but I don't want you to talk; I don't want anyone reading your lips."

Carefully he aimed the viewfinder and zoomed in so that the picture took in only the woman and child, no background. It could be anywhere, a parking garage maybe. There were thousands of those in the Chicago area.

"Smile," he said sardonically, starting the film.

"My father is going to get you," the boy threatened as Nico shot the necessary one-minute footage.

"I hope so," Nico said, switching off the camcorder. He didn't care if Cox did read lips in that particular instance; in fact, he hoped he did. It would stir up the bastard.

"Please," the nanny begged. "Please, just let us go. The child is only a baby."

Nico stared at the kid, who was giving him a fierce look.

"Yeah?" he said softly. "Wait a few more years, lady. I think this one is going to be tougher than his old man."

———— ◄► ————

Alexandra sat at the piano bench with her two youngest children leaning against her, their hair fragrant with baby shampoo. She stopped playing and glanced at her watch again. Six o'clock.

She stood up, to the children's cries of disappointment. "I'll be back in a minute," she promised. "I'm just going to see about Tripper, that's all. He should be back by now."

A little tendril of anxiety attempted to uncurl itself in her. She pushed it back at once. Rush-hour traffic was always unpredictable.

She walked down the corridor and found her housekeeper, Mrs. Abbott, hurrying toward her, carrying a thick white envelope.

"Mrs. Cox? A man just delivered this."

"Oh, it's probably about the party. Haven't Trip and Brownie got home yet?"

"No, ma'am."

Alexandra frowned. "Well, please do call me when they get here. He's going to be late for his dinner. I'll be in the living room."

She returned to the living room, still carrying the package. Since sending out invitations, she'd been the recipient of a barrage of mailings from caterers, florists, and photographers who wanted her to use their services. This was probably from one of them. She'd look at it later.

She found her three-year-old daughter jumping on the chintz-covered couch, blonde curls bouncing. Andrew was curled on the floor, leafing through a book on African animals. She went forward and lifted the little girl down. "Stephanie! Steffie, we do not jump on the furniture."

"More piano, more piano!"

"More? I've played for forty minutes!"

"More, more, please, more, more . . ."

"OK, Steffie," she agreed. She played for another half hour, her heart not really in it. She kept looking over her shoulder toward the doorway, where Mrs. Abbott would surely emerge with the news that her son was safely home.

At six-thirty, she stopped playing and, over Stephanie's protests, went to the phone and dialed the school, asking to speak to the security guard, Mr. Fulton.

"This is Mrs. Cox, Trip's mother. Has my son been picked up yet? He's not still there at the school, is he?" she inquired, keeping her voice smooth for the sake of the children.

"They're all gone. I'm locking up."

"Did you see them get picked up? The nanny and my son?"

"Sure, Mrs. Cox. The limo was here right on schedule."

"I see."

She hung up, plagued by the feeling that something was wrong. She then dialed the car phone in the limousine, only to be told by a recording that the cellular customer she had called was not available or had traveled beyond the area.

Strange, she thought. Had they had car trouble?

She walked restlessly through the house, unable to relax. Something was definitely not right. Uneasily she remembered the incident in the elevator.

My God. The package. The shape inside the envelope was exactly that of a videotape. She hurried to the living room and retrieved the package, then ran into the library, her heart pounding.

She slit open the envelope carefully, and the tape fell into her hands, unlabeled, black, sinister.

She pushed the tape into the VCR.

Snow danced on the screen. She stood with her hands clenched to her chest, her lips pressed together, waiting for the tape to begin playing. Finally, with a static crackle, a picture appeared on the screen.

Brownie and Trip were sitting on some cement floor, huddled together like refugees. In one hand, the nanny held up the day's issue of the *Tribune*. The paper wavered and shook. Brownie stared into the camera with wild, frightened eyes. Trip's face was red. A swollen, cut lip and a bruise discolored the left side of his face.

"Oh, my God," she whispered aloud. "Oh, Jesus."

The tape ran through, then white snow once more appeared on the screen. Alexandra was breathing shallowly. This video hadn't been computer-augmented. It was real.

—— ▶◀ ——

Richard was in the midst of a phone call with Allan Gurrvitz, one of the younger attorneys in the firm handling the petition. His pulse rose as he digested the information the lawyer conveyed to him. The petition requesting a ninety-day delay of the strike would probably be denied. Someone had apparently got to the judge.

"What do you mean, they got to him?" Richard swore viciously. "If they've influenced him, then we've got to influence him even more, damn it!"

"I've been trying for the past eight days, Mr. Cox."

"Try harder then," Richard snapped, hanging up.

Fuck, he thought angrily. He was a sitting duck for them right now, all because of that damned party.

His buzzer sounded, scattering his thoughts.

"Yes?" he snapped.

"Mr. Cox, your wife is on the line. She sounds very upset."

"All right. Thanks." He waited while the call was transferred. "Alexandra? What's wrong?"

"It's Tripper," his wife sobbed into the telephone. "*He's gone!*"

A chill went through Richard. "What do you mean, gone?"

"They sent a video! Will you please, please come home?"

Richard telephoned for his driver but couldn't get through. He ran out to the elevator, stepped in, and smacked the door-shut button.

Another union prank; it had to be. Those fuckers. Those bastards.

As soon as the doors slid open to the lobby, Richard hurried out and headed at a half run toward the line of taxis that waited outside the main entrance of the Fitz.

There were fewer cabs than usual, but Richard found one and jumped in, thrusting a $50 bill into the driver's face. He barked out the address, 1500 North Lake Shore Drive. "Fast, man," he added. "As fast as you can."

Richard gripped the armrest anxiously. If Trip were hurt

... if they touched even one hair on his head ...

— ⊳⊲ —

In the library, Alexandra fought to control her emotions. She phoned down to the kitchen, steadying her voice, and told them to serve Andy and Stephanie their supper, explaining that Trip had stayed later at school. She kept seeing her son's face on the tape, his lower lip swollen and bloody, his cheek bruised.

She shut her eyes. *Trip, Tripper,* she vowed silently. *I'm going to find you. I'll do it; I'll do whatever I have to. I don't care. Just stay brave.*

Alexandra met Richard at the foyer elevator, her face ashen. "Punkin," he choked.

"It's in the library," she said, pulling at him.

They went into the library, closed and locked the door, and played the video four times. Richard tried to view it objectively.

"Where are they?" Alexandra whispered hoarsely. "Can you tell?"

He didn't hear her. He was studying the expression on his son's face. There were no tear streaks on Trip's cheeks.

"Richard?"

"Rewind," he told her, shaking his head.

She pushed the rewind button. "Richard, they have our baby ..."

"I'll handle this. Why don't you—"

"I'll stay here with you," she interrupted. Her eyes were wet, their blue darkened almost to black. "I'm not going anywhere. I'm a part of this. Are you going to call the police?"

"Not yet. Not until I hear what the demands are."

He picked up the telephone, punching out a number.

"Slattery? Over at my place, on the double." He hung up before the security man could ask any questions. Swiftly he dialed the number of Robbie Fraser.

"Fraser, your guys have kidnapped my kid."

"What? Come on, man ..."

"I've got the fucking videotape to prove it, and they've got today's *Trib* in it, with the headlines 'Union Negotiations Deadlocked.' If that doesn't point the finger, I don't know what does."

"No, damn it."

"Don't give me that. Where is my boy? Where the fuck are you keeping him?"

"We aren't involved," Fraser insisted.

"The hell you aren't!"

"Cox, you can't lay this at our door."

"Maybe not at your door. But how about at Marchek's door?" Richard rasped. "You don't know shit about what's going on in your organization, do you? You've lost control of it. Well, let me tell you something, and you listen good. *I want my son, and I want him now.*"

"Cox, listen . . ."

"Jesus Christ! Get control of your goddamned members, because if you don't, your name won't mean shit anymore. I promise you that, Fraser, on my life."

Richard slammed the phone down. He was shaking, anger and fear a poison in his gullet that he could not release.

Alexandra said, "Richard . . ."

He turned on her, unable to stop himself. "Alexandra, I've got this under control."

"Oh, really?" She narrowed her eyes at him. "This is all your fault," she whispered.

"What?"

"*You*, Richard Cox. You caused this. Your lifestyle, damn it. Always chasing around after more and more money. You never feel rich enough, do you? You always want more and more and then some more. You're going to win the whole damned Monopoly game, aren't you? Boardwalk and Park Avenue are next. Pass Go and collect $200. Is that all you care about?"

"Lexy, babe, please . . ."

" 'Lexy'!" she cried. "Oh, give me a break, Richard! Since when have I ever been a 'Lexy,' or a 'babe'? You always treat me like a doll. You only married me to beget a dynasty! I'm just like a brood mare."

He could not speak.

"Don't act so surprised," she snapped. "My father warned me, but I wouldn't listen. That's all I was to you, some kind of pretty breeding mare, someone to give you children. Someone to play a role for you while you spent more time making money than you did with your family. We're only secondary. Not important at all!"

He shook his head, his whole world coming apart. "You're wrong," he began. "So wrong. My world is nothing without you and the children."

"I am not wrong. If you hadn't tried to build the world's biggest conglomerate, none of this would have happened. We don't have a real marriage. We don't have anything except money."

He stared at her. "What are you saying?"

"I want a divorce, Richard. After we get Trip back." She was sobbing. "The kids are real human beings, Richard, and they deserve a real human being for a father."

"Oh, God," he groaned.

"If Trip dies . . . if they k-kill Tripper . . . I'll never forgive you—never!"

Her words filled the room, and Richard shook his head in bewilderment. "Lexy," he said, touching her arm. "Oh, God, baby, we'll get through this. I'll get him back, I swear it. Just . . . stop carrying on."

"I meant it," she said, sobbing hysterically.

He dropped her arm. "OK. We'll talk about that later. For now, you have to do two things. First, you are not going to tell a soul that Trip is missing. Not one other person unless I tell you it's OK."

Tears were rolling down her cheeks.

"Tell the staff Brownie took Trip down to visit your father and Felicia. And the gala goes on as planned."

———— ►◄ ————

Slattery and Richard were on their way to the Mattingly Day School. It was getting dark.

Richard had tried repeatedly to contact Will, his chauffeur, with no success. Was he in on it? Had he assisted in the abduction? It was a possibility, although Richard thought it fairly remote. Will Sabira had been with him for fifteen years and was fiercely loyal to the entire Cox family.

Slattery was saying, "Now, we've got to think through all the possibilities. Here's what could have happened. They pull the old switch. They get the chauffeur and kill him, or at least stow him in the trunk. Then they take his place, or maybe they pick the kid and the nanny up in another limo that's the exact same make and model."

Richard thought of his chauffeur, dead in some trunk. "Oh, Jesus. Those bastards."

"We'll report the vehicle stolen," Slattery said. "We have to—in case Sabira's still alive."

Richard sank into gloomy silence. He didn't want the police in on this—not yet, maybe not at all.

They pulled up in front of the school, on the Near North

Side. Established in 1925, it was a three-story brick building with window boxes of flowers and shrubbery in tubs that gave it a cheerful, British look.

"I told the security guy to be waiting for us," Slattery said. "There he is."

Ten minutes later, when they finished the interview, they knew little more than when they had started. The elderly guard insisted it was the Cox limousine that had picked up the woman and boy.

"Even the same license," he said. "I check stuff like that."

"You sure?" Slattery said.

"Yeah, I'm sure. Any problem here?"

"Not yet, and if I have my way, there won't be." Richard fished a $100 bill out of his money clip. "Keep quiet about this if you will."

The man looked at the bill, refusing it. "Hey, no thanks. It's my job."

They got back into Slattery's Ford Taurus. "Where to now?" Slattery asked.

"The Powerhouse."

"Where?"

"The gym where Marchek works out. I heard he's there almost every night. I want to talk to him."

—— ▶◀ ——

Powerhouse Gym was located in a former A&P super-market on Irving Park Road. A black man in a sleeveless T-shirt printed with the name *Powerhouse* was stationed in the minuscule lobby. His upper arms bulged, grotesquely muscular, and there were tattoos on his corded biceps.

"Five bucks a workout," he told them. "Towels a buck, and we got a boxing ring in the other room."

"I'm not going to work out. I just want to deliver a message," Richard said, slipping the man $50 and walking past the desk.

The man pocketed the bill, letting them pass.

"Great place," Slattery remarked. "Is Marchek here?"

They stood looking around. Almost every machine and bench was occupied. Richard pointed to a man at the far end of the gym.

"That's him," he said, striding ahead.

Tank Marchek was lying flat on a weight bench. He was a

big man with a barrel chest, wide all the way down. His thick legs were bent and spread, his body quivering with effort.

As Richard approached, Marchek was lowering the 250-pound barbells to the hooks above his head.

The weights never reached the supports. In four steps, Richard was beside the bench, and before the prone union official could react, Richard had forced the heavy bar so that it pinned Marchek by the throat.

The man uttered a strangled gurgle, gigantic muscles bulging with exertion as his feet thumped the floor.

"Where's my son?" Richard grated.

Marchek gagged, his face turning purple.

"*Where?*"

Despite his distress, Tank Marchek's eyes glinted with triumph.

A reckless fury came over Richard. Savagely he pressed down on the bar, jamming it into his victim's Adam's apple. "Emil! Fuck with my family, and you're dead."

Marchek made a choking sound.

Richard pressed down on the bar a bit harder. "I mean it, fucker. I want my boy back—tonight."

"Cox! Cox!" Slattery screamed. "Jesus Christ, you're going to kill the guy!"

Already others in the gym had gotten off benches and machines and were approaching them.

"Fuck it," Richard said, leaving the bar where it was.

Slattery hurried to keep up with Richard's long strides. "Jesus, Mr. Cox . . ."

A look from Richard silenced him.

— ▶◀ —

Back at the Cox penthouse, Slattery got on the phone to report the stolen limousine. Richard excused himself and went up to his own workout room. As he passed, Alexandra came running out of her study.

"Richard—what's happened? Have you heard anything?"

"Not much."

She looked tired, and he could tell she had been crying. "Please, Lexy, don't put any more pressure on me," he said. "I'm going back to the negotiations tonight. I've got to face those people."

Her eyes looked wide, apprehensive. "Oh, Richard—"

"I'm not going to let them jerk me around, Alexandra. I can't, and I won't."

She clutched his arm. "Just . . . please be careful."

"I'll do what I have to."

"I've had to tell Mrs. Abbott," Alexandra blurted. "She knew, Richard; she suspected something. I've sworn her to secrecy, though, and the rest of the staff have been told that Brownie took Trip down to Florida to visit his grandfather."

He nodded.

"Richard? God . . . what can I do to help? I'm going crazy; I have to do something."

"Right now you can just go on as if nothing happened," he said, seeing her face get that wounded expression again. For a moment he wanted to pull her to him, enfold her in his arms, feel her arms around him. But he resisted the impulse. Shit, if he even got started, he might fall apart, and he couldn't afford to do that. He had to keep himself tightly wrapped.

He went into the exercise room, where he changed into gym clothes and ran on the treadmill at the highest speed until he'd worked off some of his rage. He had really wanted to kill Marchek, and it frightened him.

He ran until sweat was pouring down him, and then he went into the shower and sluiced himself under the coldest water he could tolerate. The police. What if he did bring them in? What would it accomplish? The pressure might cause the kidnappers to panic and harm Trip even more. He needed to fight fire with fire. There had to be another way . . . another option.

By the time he turned the water off and stepped out, naked, onto the plush bath mat, a name floated in his head. A name from Palm Beach.

──── ►◄ ────

Alexandra sat in her office playing her stereo, restlessly switching from one tape to another, unable to settle on anything that would ease her painful thoughts. She badly needed to talk to a friend, even if she couldn't mention the kidnapping.

She dialed Jette's number in Los Angeles and waited while the phone rang three times. An answering machine picked up. "This is Jette, and I hate hangups, so don't hang up, but if you're a heavy breather stay on the line; I'm keeping a collection of obscene calls. At the beep, say something. Anything."

Alexandra smiled faintly. Jette was incorrigible. The beep sounded, and she hesitated, wondering what to say. She knew her voice would reveal her feelings, and she realized she couldn't afford to do that, not even with Jette. Not if it would endanger Tripper.

She hung up. *Sorry, Jette,* she muttered.

The phone rang, its sound nerve-racking, and she snatched it up.

"It's Mary Lee. Good grief, Alexandra, you must have been sitting right on the phone. I didn't even hear a ring."

"Oh," Alexandra said, trying to sound warm. "Hi, Mary Lee."

"You sound funny," her friend said. "Anything wrong?"

Alexandra stiffened. It was crucial that she not alert the reporter in Mary Lee. "Just this humongous party," she managed to say, keeping her voice light. "A lot of crises, you know. The usual stuff that seems terribly important to the hostess but is really very insignificant in the general scheme of things."

"Like what crises?" Mary Lee said.

Alexandra's mind went suddenly blank. All she could think of was Trip. She realized that more tears had filled her eyes and were trembling on her lashes, blurring her vision.

"Crises?" she said numbly.

"Hey. You sure everything's OK? You didn't have a fight with Richard, did you?"

"Kind of," Alexandra said, seizing this way out.

"Oh, great. Men," Mary Lee said. "I had a fight with Jake, too, isn't it the pits? His second ultimatum, or is it third, just fell due, and this time he says he means it."

Alexandra clung to the phone, feeling unable to banter. She knew this call from Mary Lee was an apology for the quarrel they'd had in New York, but she wasn't sure she was ready to make amends. She shivered. Maybe Mary Lee wasn't as much of a friend as she'd thought. You didn't have to censor your words with a true friend, did you?

"Alexandra? Are you there? Talk to me," Mary Lee said. "I guess I've got you at a bad time, huh?"

"I just—oh, Mary Lee," Alexandra said helplessly. "I just can't talk right now. Really. I've . . . I'll call you in a couple of days."

"That bad, huh?"

"Please, I'll call you next week. No, I'll see you before that, won't I? The party."

She hung up. This time she let the tears come, let them rack her body, bending her double with pain.

Afterward, she went to the living room, sat down at the piano, and began to play a Beethoven sonata. Crashing notes filled the room.

— ◄► —

In the huge locker, Brownie was helping Trip open the stack of toys from Toys "R" Us.

"I don't want to play," Trip said stubbornly.

"Trip," she said, steadying her voice. "You might as well play—till it's time to go home."

"I don't want to! I won't! You can't make me!" He stalked to the far side of the room, where he stood with his back to her.

Brownie sat on one of the air mattresses and watched him, feeling a twist of fear and pity. Were they going to die here in this terrible room with smears of animal blood on the walls? Maybe it was human blood. Brownie had discovered several spent bullets and shell caps lying on the floor.

They had been kidnapped, and often kidnap victims did not make it home alive. It was as simple as that.

She would have to protect the child somehow. But how?

— ◄► —

In the corridor outside the negotiating room at the John Hancock Center, Allan Gurrvitz was waiting for Richard.

"They think you're running scared. I overheard them in the john, something about Tank Marchek at the Powerhouse Gym. They said you attacked him with a weight bar. You didn't, did you?"

"That's exactly what I did."

"Oh, Christ, Richard. How could you do that?" Gurrvitz snapped.

Usually Richard's staff called him "Mr. Cox" and treated him deferentially. But the long days of arguments, tension, and hostility were getting to the lawyer. He was fed up, discouraged, and badly in need of a decent night's sleep and some kind of food besides sandwiches, pizza, and take-out Chinese.

"Don't worry about it," Richard said.

"God, no wonder they . . . You know what they're saying, don't you? They're saying that you freaked out because you're going to give in. That you can't handle the pressure."

I can't handle my son being taken, Richard thought. That's what I can't handle. Alexandra's attitude didn't help the situation. He said, "I'm not ready to give in yet."

"Also, we haven't got the ninety-day reprieve, and it doesn't look like we're going to. We're fucked. The judge wouldn't sign the petition."

"Fine. I'll manage another way," Richard said, wondering if he had made the right decision in keeping the kidnapping a secret.

He pushed open the door and stepped into the conference room. As before, the faces rotated toward him. Tank Marchek was at the end of the table, a dark bruise across his throat and a gloating look in his eyes.

Marchek believed Richard was ready to fold. The atmosphere in the room was alive with this conviction.

And was he now going to accede to the stiff union demands? It was a terrible moment. God, he wanted Trip back. There were no guarantees. If he acquiesced to the union demands on the table, he might get his son back within hours, or possibly tomorrow—or maybe never at all.

Richard walked to the head of the table, put his hands on the polished oak, leaned forward, and began to speak.

"Gentlemen, it's been a long battle." He drew in a sharp breath, steeling himself for the capitulation.

Just then the receptionist ran in, bearing a pink message slip. She walked around the table and handed it to Robbie Fraser, who looked at it and turned pale.

"Excuse me," he said, jumping up and hurrying out of the room.

The momentum for Richard's announcement had passed, and he wavered. If he gave in to the union, was he sure he'd get his boy back? He had another choice—but it was one he did not really wish to make.

The faces were turning to him again. Richard made an instantaneous decision. "Gentlemen, I'm afraid I'm going to have to leave, too. Something has come up. Something important."

He took the elevator down to the lobby, made a phone call, said what he had to say. Then he dialed another number and made arrangements for his jet to be fueled and waiting for him at Midway.

He was going to Florida, to Palm Beach. And it was not to visit his father-in-law.

———— ⋈ ————

In New York, Mary Lee hung up from her conversation with Alexandra, all her senses on code red. Something was very wrong with the Coxes, and it wasn't just a quarrel. She'd known Alexandra Cox for years, and there'd been more in her voice than just upset.

The more she thought about it, the more Mary Lee realized what she'd heard in her friend's voice. Terror.

She began pacing her two-bedroom apartment overlooking Park Avenue. It was carefully furnished, filled with porcelains, a collection of jewel-colored Cristal Lalique vases, gilt-embossed, terribly expensive clocks, rich Brunschwig & Fils chintzes. Luxuries she had bought before her mother became ill.

Somehow Marietta had spent most of her own money, leaving Mary Lee to finance her health crisis.

Money was the operative word, and Mary Lee knew only one way to earn sinfully large quantities of it: by writing a megabucks national series that could be spun off into a bestselling book.

The Coxes were larger-than-life people, Mary Lee reflected. Here was Richard, featured on the covers of *Fortune* and *Forbes*. Handsome, charismatic, powerful. And Alexandra, who looked like a movie star and had made her mark in the music world.

They were a golden couple, and now there was even the big gala coming up, which had already received more publicity than any other party in recent memory. There was a story here, a big one. A bestseller.

"Muggy? Muggy? Is it you?" A querulous voice interrupted her thoughts, and Marietta Wilde entered the room.

"Mother," Mary Lee said. "I thought you were napping."

"Muggy? Is it you? I can't remember if it's you or not; I thought it might be."

"It is me, Mother, but I'm going to be using the phone now, so why don't you go back in your room and watch TV? I think 'Roseanne' is on. You like 'Roseanne.'"

"I hope it's you," Marietta said, shaking her head angrily. "I sure as hell hope so, Muggy."

Mary Lee gazed at her mother. Marietta's deterioration had been rapid and severe. She no longer could be allowed to leave the apartment unaccompanied. She forgot her address and five times had been returned by the police in tears, a fifty-five-year-old lost child. Mary Lee had been told by Marietta's physician that her mother could be cared for at home for the time being. Eventually, however, she would grow even more helpless.

The thought made her shudder.

"Mother," she said, going forward and taking the rigid arm. "Please, go back into your bedroom, and I'll switch channels on the TV. I'll get 'Roseanne' for you. And I'll bring you some ice cream, would you like that?"

"I don't remember you," Marietta said suspiciously. "Do I? You're a stranger."

"Of course you remember me. I'm Mary Lee."

"I don't know any Mary Lees."

"Well, that's who I am. Your daughter. I'm Mary Lee."

She guided her mother into the bedroom, settled her on the bed, and raised the volume on the TV, which was always kept going, at Marietta's insistence, even when she slept. Marietta focused on the screen, where Ed McMahon was advertising some insurance plan.

Mary Lee fled into the living room, where she had been forced to crowd her office into one corner. She reached for the phone and began dialing.

"Lenny?" she said into the receiver when the phone was finally picked up.

"Mary Lee? Hey, long time no see, kiddo. You still as gorgeous as ever? Lady with the braidy, that's what I call you." Lenny Fulton laughed at his own joke. He was a staffer on the *Chicago Tribune*, and they had run into each other on various stories and become friends.

"I still have my braid," she said, smiling. "Lenny? I need a favor."

"I love to do favors for pretty ladies."

"What's going on in Chicago with the Fitz strike? What's happening there? Anything really interesting?"

"Still deadlocked. Judge Harlan Keith turned them down for a ninety-day cooling-off period, and they're due to walk by the end of the week."

"I see. Anything else? I don't care how small, any little detail."

She listened while he talked, covering negotiations, Robbie Fraser's wife's relapse, and other trivia connected with the meetings, some of which had made the press. She quizzed him for details on the Coxes, and Fulton told her he would call her back in half an hour.

She waited, pacing, listening to the sound of the TV from the other room mingling with traffic noises from the street. Once she heard her mother laugh. Finally Fulton called back, and she snatched up the phone eagerly.

"Yes? What have you got, Lenny?"

"Just a couple of things, not that much, really. The first thing is, Richard Cox apparently blew his cool today."

"Oh, how so?"

"Well, it seems he went over to Emil Marchek's gym and attacked him while he was lying on the bench press. Actually lowered a 250-pound barbell onto the guy's neck."

"That's interesting."

"Yeah, the union guys thought he'd lost it and expected him to throw in the towel today, but he didn't. He started a speech they thought was going to lead to it, and then he just quit and left the bargaining room. The other detail is, and this is really interesting, the British nanny and the oldest boy, Trip, I think his name is—what a god-awful blueblood name— they're supposed to have left for West Palm Beach, Florida, to visit the only grandfather, Jay Winthrop."

"Really? 'Supposed' to have left?"

"According to this source, it was a very sudden trip. The kid didn't even pack. Maybe they've received some threats."

Mary Lee felt a thrill of excitement, but she allowed none of it to show. If she alerted Lenny to her suspicion, he'd grab the story for himself.

"I doubt it," she said deprecatingly. "They make a lot of trips down there. The old man really, dotes on those kids. Anything else good? Any real dirt?"

"Sorry, that's about it."

"OK," she said. "Hey, Lenny . . . next time you're in the Big Apple, give me a holler. We'll go out and do something crazy."

"Right on," he said happily.

She hung up as quickly as she could, her mind spinning. Something *was* wrong, all right, and it had to do with Trip. She made another phone call, to Trip's school, reaching a night answering service. After much pleading, she was finally given the number of Hank Fulton, the security officer.

"What do you want at this hour, miss? Couldn't it wait until tomorrow morning? The office is open at eight."

"I'm from the Wilde Agency," she said, taking a chance. "I'm just calling for the Coxes about their son. Any further word?"

"Like I told Mr. Cox, I thought it was the same limo he always uses. I didn't see nothing wrong; it was the same license plate and everything. I got three hundred kids at this school, leaving and getting picked up every day. I . . ."

She hung up. The boy *was* missing!

What a story. Sympathy for Trip conflicted with her growing elation over a possible news coup. People loved to read about the rich and famous, and this had all the elements for drama. Mary Lee briefly considered the promise she had made to Alexandra, and with a spasm of guilt, she knew she wasn't going to live up to it. But how could she be expected to? There were syndicated writers all over the country who kept their eyes peeled for stories exactly like this one—and who would have no compunction about using every messy, sordid detail. If she didn't write about it, one of them would.

Swiftly Mary Lee dialed the number of a twenty-four-hour registered nursing service and arranged for a nurse to come in and take care of her mother for an unspecified number of days.

Then she phoned American Airlines.

— ▶◀ —

At 1:00 A.M. on Wednesday, September 6, a blue-and-white squad car pulled up alongside a gray limousine illegally parked in the Bridgeport neighborhood of Chicago. One of the officers radioed into Central for a make on the license plate, while the other left the police car to check out the vehicle. There was a noticeable stench coming from the trunk. Decaying flesh.

The officer pried open the trunk. The man stuffed inside wore a gray chauffeur's uniform, and his eyes were still open, glazed over and dry from prolonged exposure to air.

— ▶◀ —

Palm Beach at night was a diamond necklace of glittering hotel lights reflected in the waters of Lake Worth. The cab crossed the Flagler Bridge and turned left on North Ocean

Boulevard. A hurricane had recently touched the Caribbean, and the surf was still high, pounding the beach and sending up crystal prisms of spray. Richard gazed at the spectacle, his thoughts elsewhere.

Where was Trip now? Were he and Brownie still together?

"Think this is it, sir," said the cabdriver.

"Pull up to the driveway," Richard instructed. "And stop at the gate. The guard will have to announce me."

As they pulled parallel to the huge gate house, Richard scrutinized the building that loomed behind a wrought-iron barrier supplemented with electrically charged chain fencing. The house looked more like an embassy building in Washington than the home of the East Coast's most powerful Mafia godfather. A sweep of stone steps led up to the front. Four stone pillars dominated the main entrance, and on either side stretched long wings and endless rows of black-shuttered windows.

Richard gave his name to the guard and paced impatiently, wondering whether he should have come. He thought about Tripper, and fury resurrected itself. He suppressed it. He would need all his wits about him, and anger clouded the thinking.

"Mr. Cox?" A second guard appeared, and they walked up the sweeping circular driveway until they reached the front steps.

Richard was ushered into a huge 1930s-style library. Leather-bound books lined three walls. Incongruous next to the books was a row of gun cabinets, filled with shotguns, rifles, and handguns. No antiques. A few assault rifles and machine guns were interspersed among them.

Stranded in the middle of the huge room was a large and priceless oriental rug, on which were grouped a cherrywood desk and several chairs.

"Hello, Mr. Cox." A man was seated at the desk, a toast-colored springer spaniel curled up on the floor next to his feet. He was about fifty-five, with very black hair, an imposing forehead, and a square, hard-looking jaw.

"Bernstein," Richard said, walking over and extending his hand. Mo Bernstein's palm was warm, his grip powerful. He did not rise.

"Let's get to the bottom line," Bernstein said. "Hey, Cox, you think you can do that? Cut to the chase, so I can go upstairs and get back in bed with the pair of 36Ds I got stashed up there."

Bernstein was trying to get him off balance, of course. Richard looked around for a chair, found one, and sat down.

"All right," he said.

"Well? Spit it out."

Richard reddened. "I have a situation," he said.

"What kind of situation?"

Richard told him. The Mafioso listened intently. While Richard talked, the spaniel stretched itself and yawned, rubbing its nose against Bernstein's hand.

"So what you're saying, the ASWU took your kid, is that right?"

"Yes."

Bernstein frowned, and his eyes glittered with a street-smart kind of intelligence. "I don't know," he said. "Doesn't sound right somehow. I know most of them people. I gotta make some phone calls. You go in the other room and wait. Izzy!" He snapped his fingers loudly for the guard. "Izzy, you take Mr. Cox here into the TV room, turn him on a videotape. Make him feel at home. I'll be in there in a while, and we'll talk some more," he added.

— ◄► —

"Brownie?" Trip whispered. "Brownie, stop crying." His hands patted the nanny with loving, anxious strokes. "Talk, Brownie. Talk."

She uttered a little groan. She was huddled on the air mattress, a blanket rolled up over her face. "Come here, Trip. I was only having a bad dream."

They lay together on the air mattress, holding each other. The boy fell asleep, and Brownie snuggled him closer, taking some comfort from his presence. Maybe she dozed off, or at least entered a deeper state, because a sound startled her.

Brownie jumped a little and managed to glance at her watch without disturbing Trip. It was 6:30 A.M.

She heard the sound again and realized it was coming from outside the door. They were out there . . . on the other side. Both of them; she could hear their voices.

Her heart gave a sickening leap. She lay rigidly, waiting for the door to be flung open.

— ◄► —

At Highgrove, in England, the squeals of the two young princes, Wills and Harry, echoed among trees as they chased their latest puppy, a corgi named Spice. It was unseasonably hot for September. A breeze puffed over the top of the tall grasses and ruffled the petals of the wild Highgrove daisies.

Charles, just back from London, had come out to the garden to greet his wife. Still in his dark suit, Charles looked hot and irritable from his immersion in his duties in the city. London was stressful to him; he much preferred the country.

"Mrs. Thatcher's rung me up. Have you arranged all the people she wants to be at the Cox party?" he asked Diana after their greetings.

"Yes, they're all accounted for. I talked to Alexandra Cox' several days ago. All the important ones, the car people you wanted, will be there, as well as the Arabs and the Israeli ambassador."

Charles nodded. The red circles of color that usually stained his cheeks were darker than usual this afternoon. He had been in meetings all day. "She's assured you the hotel workers' strike is being settled this week?"

Charles was so involved in this project, so intense about it, Diana thought. "Actually I forgot to ask her, but I'll call her back. I'm sure they are settling it."

Even a year ago, Charles would have been annoyed at her forgetfulness, making some sardonic comment about her being "thick." Now he only nodded.

They looked at each other, an awkwardness between them. Last week the tabloids had intimated that she and Charles had quarreled again, showing photographs of Diana smiling at a young member of the House of Lords, taken while Charles was shooting in Scotland. The word *divorce* had been bandied about, the paper concluding that the Prince and Princess of Wales would "appear together whenever they must and stay apart whenever they can."

What did one do when one's own husband could pick up a newspaper and read material like that about himself and her?

"Charles?" Diana spoke softly, moving forward to slip her hand into his. They started walking along the mown path back toward the big, tea-colored house. "Have I told you how proud I am of what you're doing?"

He glanced at her, his eyes intent.

"If you can really get the Arabs and Israelis to talk, and if you can get the Americans to build auto plants over here . . . it will be a smashing accomplishment."

"More than architecture, you mean?"

Diana gave a little sigh. God, she had been infatuated with Charles since she was sixteen. She still loved him, despite her disappointments and no matter what the tabloids said.

"And, Charles?" Diana squeezed her husband's hand and began a speech she had been rehearsing for several weeks. "I have been thinking. After we finish in Chicago . . . America is so vast . . . I have heard that Yellowstone is lovely."

He stared at her. She had always been a city person. "What are you saying?"

"The wilderness. I would like to see it so much, and perhaps—perhaps we could hike? Perhaps ride into the canyon?"

Charles smiled. She never had suggested such a thing before.

— ◄► —

The door banged open, thudding against the brick. Brownie caught her breath, and Trip bolted up, startled from his sleep.

They had brought the video camera again.

"OK, OK, get over in the center again, the way you did before," Nico ordered. "Go on," he snapped impatiently, clapping his hands. "Move! Get going!"

Fearfully, the woman and child moved to the approximate spot where they had posed for the first videotape. Brownie's insides were rigid with horror. Today, Nico hadn't bothered with his panty-hose mask. Brownie saw his face, handsome, with a scar along one temple.

She shuddered. Why was he showing his face to them now, when he hadn't done so before? What did it mean?

"Kneel down, and get in close so we can get your picture," he ordered.

Trip, wide-eyed, dropped onto his knees as he was told, and Brownie lowered herself beside him.

"Yeah. Get closer together." Nico motioned to the other man, who walked behind him. Suddenly Brownie felt an arm snake around her forehead, yanking her head back. In front of her, a hand gripped a long, thin knife.

"Oh, God, no!" she sobbed.

The knife made a long, shallow cut on the side of her scalp, starting near the crown of her head and working down in front of her ear, stopping at the angle of her jawline. Blood spurted out, spilling hotly down her hair, face, and neck.

"Take your hand, dip it in the blood, and wipe the blood on the kid's face," Nico ordered.

She stared, stunned.

"Do it, bitch!"

"I can't . . . please . . ."

"Do it, or I'll kill you."

Slowly, shaking, Brownie raised her right hand to her bloody face.

"Now wipe it on him. His face. Go on, goddamn it . . . wipe!"

She looked down. Trip was staring at her with wide, appalled eyes, teeth biting down hard on his lower lip as he struggled not to cry.

"Brownie," he whispered.

"Go on," ordered Nico. "Put it on the kid's face. Smear it like paint."

Black dots spun in front of Brownie's eyes. Mrs. Cox was going to be watching this—would see her on the film, watch her smear the blood on her little son.

Grimly Brownie made a gory red handprint in the middle of Trip's left cheek. He flinched only a little. There were runnels of blood on the back of her hand, and she wiped that on him, too, as if he were a rag. As she did so, she stared straight at the camera. Her expression was desperate, intense.

"Meat locker!" she screamed.

Two seconds later, the blow hit her face, spinning her onto her side. Trip screamed, rushing at her assailant.

"You can't hurt my nanny! My nanny!"

"Pleeeease . . ." Brownie moaned from the abyss of her pain.

Trip kicked and bit.

"Fucking little bastard!" With one easy kick, Rambo sent Trip spinning outward. The child crashed, sobbing, onto the cement.

"Trip?" His anguished cries were heartrending. She tried to crawl toward her charge.

"Stupid bitch," snapped Rambo, and he hit her again with his tightly clenched fist. Her head snapped backward. Blood sprayed out of her nostrils this time.

"Shit," Nico swore. "For Christ's sake, don't kill the bitch.

I want to get this on tape for Mommy and Daddy. They'll wet their damned drawers when they see this stuff."

He stood over her with the video camera, pointing it practically in her face, capturing every detail.

"Motherfucker," Rambo said disgustedly as they left the meat locker, slamming the door behind them and padlocking it. He was thoroughly shaken by the scene but did not want Nico to know it. That little guy, scratching and clawing, reminded him of himself at that age. He'd been a fighter, too. Damned near got himself killed by his stepfather more than once. He went on, "Fuckin' bitch got blood all over me."

Nico did not respond. They walked through the echoing plant, exiting through a door that led across a loading area, and entered a section of the plant still in use. Men in coveralls identical to their own were carrying sides of beef into a cutting room. They sauntered past them, not bothering to hide any of the red stains. A meat-packing plant was one place in the world where bloodstains were normal.

"I'll take the tape home and edit it," Nico told Rambo as they changed and washed up in an employee rest room. "But even if they do catch her saying 'meat locker,' they won't recognize it. They'll probably think she's just screaming. It'll scare the shit out of them that much more."

"Shit, Nico . . . the Cox kid's just like Davy, practically the same age as your little brother."

Suddenly Rambo felt himself being flung around and shoved up against the rest room mirror so violently that his skull cracked the glass.

"Are you going soft on me?" Nico inquired in a quiet, chilling voice.

"Hey, man . . ." Rambo stared into the rigid face of his employer. Nico's blue eyes had darkened almost to black, their pupils doubled in size. The scar on his temple was silver-white, and a blood vessel near it throbbed. "Hey, man, don't worry; there ain't no pussy in me. Everything's cool, mah man. Real cool!"

"You sure?"

"For damn sure."

"All right." Nico stepped away, returning to the mirror to comb his hair. A thick crack now zagged crazily across the glass. "Look," Nico said in a more normal tone. "Don't question me, OK? I'm not going to hurt the kid unless Cox gets stubborn. I don't ice kids. I think Cox will fold like an accordion after he sees the nanny on tape."

"Sure," Rambo said, without great enthusiasm.

— ◄► —

The following morning, Mary Lee checked into her room at the Drake and got on the phone again, making several dozen calls, trying everyone she knew who was in any way remotely connected to the Coxes.

This took a fair amount of time, since each call had to include casual gossip and catching up. It was 3:00 P.M. when she finally came upon something useful. The oldest daughter of Alexandra's social secretary, Judy Wallis, had just been accepted at Yale Medical School.

Mary Lee put the phone down and contemplated that fact. As far as she knew, Judy was a single mother, and although the Coxes paid her well, it was going to require a small fortune to support a medical student through her internship. The woman just had to be strapped for cash.

Mary Lee dialed the Cox household line. "Judy Wallis, please," she said crisply when the housekeeper had answered.

Within minutes, she had Wallis on the line. "I'm calling from the Yale University admissions office," she told the woman. "There's been an irregularity. Could you meet me in half an hour at the Coq d'Or in the Drake Hotel?"

"But . . . my daughter has already been accepted," Judy said in bewilderment.

"I understand, but there is a problem that needs to be further discussed."

Now Judy was growing suspicious. "Who did you say this is? And why didn't you call my daughter?"

"This is Ms. Wilde. I couldn't reach your daughter, and I must discuss this right away."

"Well, all right. But I haven't much time."

"Plan half an hour," Mary Lee instructed coolly.

Five minutes before the appointed time, Mary Lee took the elevator downstairs and selected a table at the back of the elaborately appointed room, where shoppers were enjoying a late-afternoon snack: British-style tea with scones, imported cheeses, and profiteroles.

Judy Wallis hurried in ten minutes late. A diet-thin woman in her late forties, she had dark blonde hair pulled back from her patrician-looking face, which was marred by deep wrinkles. She looked both worried and puzzled.

A waitress came over to take their order, and Mary Lee ordered tea for both.

"Oh, not for me," Judy said. "I live by coffee." To Mary Lee, she added, "Could you tell me what this is all about? Aren't you one of Mrs. Cox's friends? I didn't know you worked for Yale."

"I didn't mean to alarm you by getting you here under false pretenses," Mary Lee confessed. "I know you've got heavy financial problems if you're sending a daughter to med school, and that's really why I'm here. I wanted to help."

"Help? How could you help?"

"I'm a professional writer." Mary Lee filled the woman in on her background.

"I need the assistance of someone like you," Mary Lee added, leaning forward and speaking in a confidential tone.

"My assistance?"

"Well, I'm working on a series of articles and a possible book about the Coxes, and I need some inside information about their household. Nothing heavy—nothing that would harm them in any way. If you could provide it, I would pay you a flat fee of $5,000—in cash, Mrs. Wallis, so it wouldn't have to be reported on your taxes. It might not make a huge difference in the overall picture, but it could be very helpful on a short-term basis."

"Oh. Gosh. I just don't know. I can't believe you'd want to talk to *me*."

"Well, I do. I can tell you have a talent for details, Mrs. Wallis, and that's exactly what I need. You'd be part of a large research staff."

"Research staff?" Judy digested the term. "What kind of information do you want?"

"Oh, nothing harmful. Nothing extraordinary. Just details on their household routine, little thumbnail sketches on each member of the household staff. Oh, yes, and details on the big party they're giving. Insider stuff, like any fights they might have had with their florist, that kind of thing. It's a real easy way to pick up a little extra to pay bills with. And it won't hurt anyone."

"I don't know—I don't want to lose my job."

"You won't lose your job, because your name will never be mentioned. I'll just use the phrase *inside sources*, or something to that effect. In fact, if you want, you can see the material before it's published."

That lie seemed to soften Judy Wallis. Wavering, she repeated, "I really don't know . . ."

Mary Lee smiled calmly, fully aware that the bait had been taken. If Wallis had been totally ethical, she already would have left. "And I promise, if you don't want to answer a question, you don't have to."

The woman's silence was consent. Mary Lee waved the waitress over and requested their check. "Look. I'll leave, and in five minutes, you take the elevator up to room 710. It'll all be very, very discreet."

Mary Lee closed the door behind Judy Wallis, who had left guiltily after spilling some *very* intimate details. She was well pleased. The woman had talked a lot—about everything from Alexandra's daily routine to several fights she had overheard between Richard and Alexandra.

She had even confided the rumors circulating among the Cox household staff—that Trip and his English nanny were not on a visit to West Palm Beach, as they had been officially told, but had turned up missing. Some said the nanny herself had kidnapped the boy.

Mary Lee felt a surge of elation. This verified everything she'd learned thus far.

"You swear you won't use my name?" Judy Wallis had begged as she was leaving.

"Why should I? Anyway, everything you told me is going to be a matter of public record soon, I'm sure. Now, Judy, if anything more should come up, anything just a little strange or different, no matter how small or insignificant it seems, will you call me? Here at this hotel room?"

"I . . . don't know if I should."

"How could it hurt anything? Especially when you've already talked to me? You're in this with me now, Judy; you're in for the duration, I'm afraid. Backing out wouldn't be good. And I'll pay you very well for any large piece of information I receive."

"Oh, my God, what have I done?" the woman choked, fiddling with the lock several times before she could pull the door open. She ran out into the hall, and with a shrug, Mary Lee closed the door behind her and drew the chain lock.

She stood toying with the chain, her brain already skipping

past the problem of Judy Wallis, who had been stupid and deserved whatever she got. Then she walked over to the bedside stand, where she had placed her partially opened purse with a small, pocket-sized tape recorder running inside it.

She pulled it out and removed the microcassette tape. These details were what would make her series zap readers with authenticity. And now she had an excellent inside source in the Cox home, someone right there at the scene.

She thought a moment longer. Maybe it was time to see Alexandra again. Lay her cards on the table. Yes, she could play it both ways.

——— ►◄ ———

Alexandra looked up as her secretary entered her office, Judy's face set in a curiously grim expression.

"Anything wrong, Judy?"

"Oh, no. There was just a little problem with Jessica's admission, but I got it cleared up. A misunderstanding."

Alexandra nodded, barely listening. She felt drained from lack of sleep and the severe tension she had been under. Richard had left on some mysterious trip, and, although he'd telephoned three times, he refused to tell her where he was. She was furious at him for running off in the midst of this tragedy. How could he do such a thing?

"I'll tell you about it sometime, Lexy, when we're both very old," he had said.

Now, what was that supposed to mean? Alexandra shook her head, giving in to her exhaustion. She'd spent all morning at the Fitz, conferring with the chefs and making a detailed inspection of the sets, decorations, and fountains. Only the flower arrangements were not yet in place; they would be arranged on the morning of the gala by a crew of florists.

She was being inundated with phone calls from invited guests and would-be attendees. Did the hotel have provisions for pets? Did Alexandra want to have a psychic circulate among her guests, doing personal readings? Would the hotel like the services of a medical doctor, veterinarian, or psychiatrist on a twenty-four-hour basis? Was Neil Diamond planning to attend, and, if so, would Alexandra be sure to arrange an introduction?

She sighed, rubbing her burning eyes. She was having Judy and Dolly field all the calls. How long could she be expected to act this ridiculous charade?

Even the household staff knew something was wrong. She could tell by the way the maids squeaked around the hallways on their work shoes, eyeing her sideways. The whole house seemed to vibrate with tension. Andrew and Stephanie also sensed it.

She heard the sound of tapping on her door and looked up. Mary Abbott stood there, sturdy in her gray uniform, her forehead creased with worry.

"Mrs. Cox? Another one of those packages has come."

Alexandra felt as if she'd been smacked right in the middle of her already queasy stomach. Perspiration sprang out on her forehead.

"I'll take it," she forced herself to say quietly.

The housekeeper handed over the package, which looked exactly like the last one. It seemed to ignite in her hands.

"Mrs. Cox?" The housekeeper hesitated.

"Yes?"

"There's rumors going on amongst the staff. They think that Brownie took Trip away—that she kidnapped him because she never had a baby of her own."

"What?" Alexandra's astonishment caused her mouth to fall open.

"People do talk when they don't have the facts."

"Oh . . . that's terrible." Tears filled Alexandra's eyes. "Oh, Mrs. Abbott, I can't stand this anymore. I simply can't."

Mary Abbott came forward and touched Alexandra's shoulder, then patted her like a kindly country aunt. Her voice shook. "Mrs. Cox, I'm praying for Tripper, for Brownie and you. Trip is such a good little boy."

The two women clung together for a few seconds, their positions temporarily forgotten. Then Mrs. Abbott pulled away and smoothed down the skirt of her uniform. "I'm sorry about the staff gossiping, ma'am, but people will talk when they don't understand things."

"I'll tell them," Alexandra sighed. "Meanwhile, I need to look at this tape."

The woman left, and Alexandra went to the library and quietly closed the door behind her.

She tore open the white envelope and removed the videotape, her hands shaking so violently that she dropped it. She picked it up, then inserted it in the VCR.

Within seconds she was staring at white snow, and then the faces of her son and her employee.

Oh, those bastards. Brownie was covered with blood, red all over her hair, blood matted in it and running down her cheek and neck. The woman looked wild-eyed, frantic with fear. Alexandra swallowed back nausea. What had they done to Brownie?

The camera pulled back a little. There was Trip, looking frightened. Brownie was rubbing the blood all over Trip's face.

Alexandra heard a strange noise, part scream, part cry, and realized it was herself.

The tape was still running. The nanny opened her mouth and cried out something that looked like "me." The camera bobbed and bounced, giving a brief flash of Trip again, bloodied. Then there was the snow again, and the brief, terrifying segment of film was over.

Alexandra was shaking violently. Was this the last glimpse she would ever have of her son, cringing as blood was smeared all over his face?

She was so angry. So scared.

Richard, she thought, struggling with the desire to burst into sobs. She longed for him, needed him desperately—just to blank out this horror, to be safe in his arms. Damn it! How could he have deserted her like this?

Then she did cry, her weeping brief, painful, and harsh. When it was over, she felt no better. She wiped her eyes, extracted the videotape, and put it back in its ominous envelope. She went upstairs again. A song croaked by Kermit the Frog drifted from the playroom, where Andrew and Stephanie were being supervised by a maid.

She ran into the playroom, knelt down, and pulled the two children into her arms, holding them too tightly. They were so beautiful.

"Mrs. Cox, Andrew had a little accident," the maid, Rafaela, was saying. "He wouldn't use the toilet."

"Andrew?" She gazed at her younger son, who wriggled closer to her, his face flushed with shame.

"I want Tripper," her son said. "I want Brownie. Where's my brother?"

His eyes pleaded with her. He knew something was terribly wrong. The little boys had never been separated from each other except for one night four years ago when Trip was hospitalized with croup.

Now her five-year-old son was looking to her with the hope she could make his world better. She felt such love for her family that it nearly paralyzed her.

"Andy," she responded, hugging the little body tighter. "They're coming back soon. They will. I just know it," she promised recklessly.

When she reentered her office, she found Judy Wallis waiting for her, a pink message slip in hand.

"Oh, there you are," her secretary said. She still looked pale. "Mary Lee Wilde called. She said it's urgent."

"Never mind that," Alexandra scolded impatiently. "I've got to get in touch with my husband right away. It's absolutely imperative. I want you to try to reach him. Do what you have to; call every number you can think of."

"Of course. I'll get started right away."

An hour later, Alexandra's and Judy Wallis's efforts had proved fruitless. Richard had taken his private jet, filing a flight plan for Florida. But none of his Florida hotels had seen him.

Alexandra swallowed back her desperation.

"I'm sorry," Judy said, reentering her office. "I managed to track his assistant, Gloria, down. She says he didn't tell her a thing about where he was going. None of his staff knows anything. It's very unlike him."

"I see."

"I'll start calling some more names and places he might be. Any kind of a lead might help."

"Good."

"Oh, and Mrs. Cox . . . Mary Lee Wilde called again. She says she wants to stop by here for just a few minutes. She has something to talk to you about."

"Oh, Judy, I just can't. Tell her I'm tied up. Make up some excuse."

Maybe she should call Jack Slattery, Richard's security chief, Alexandra was thinking. She could get his reactions to the tape. She didn't want to do that until Richard arrived, but if he didn't appear in the next few hours, she would have to do *something*.

"Mrs. Cox, did you hear me?" Judy said.

"What?"

"I said Miss Wilde is on her way over here. She said she knew you'd want to see her. I couldn't stop her, Mrs. Cox."

"Oh, Mary Lee, it's good to see you, but I wish you hadn't come. This really isn't a good time," Alexandra said when Mary Lee had been ushered into her study.

"I'm sorry to barge in." Mary Lee sank into one of the chintz-covered couches and stretched out her legs. She wore a severely cut navy trouser suit and little jewelry; her heavy braid was wound around her scalp. Her eyes were mirrored with emerald green contact lenses, the effect unnerving. "The thing is, I know."

Alexandra blinked. "You what?"

"I said I *know*, dear. I know what's been going on."

Alexandra's heart squeezed. She stared at Mary Lee incredulously. There was no way her friend could possibly know about Trip.

"You're going to have to be more specific than that, Mary Lee. Just exactly what's on your mind?"

Mary Lee fiddled with the large purse she carried, taking out a tissue, putting it back in again, leaving the mouth of the bag slightly ajar. "You can't hide it, Alexandra. Not from a person who knows you as well as I do. I heard in your voice that you had a big problem. And I found out what the problem was."

"What big problem?"

Mary Lee smiled. "You want me to say it, don't you? OK. I know about Trip and Brownie."

Alexandra gasped.

"I know they're missing. I know all about it. And, Alexandra," she went on, raising her hand as Alexandra started to speak, "I want in. I want in on the ground floor, because this is going to be a matter of public record within days. I'll do the story better than any other writer. I don't want anyone else getting hold of this."

Alexandra felt the blood leave her face. She stared at Mary Lee as if she were a stranger. "We're talking about a little boy here," she said slowly. "A six-year-old child. Not a news story."

"Hey, don't look at me that way. You and Richard are big, big news. With Trip missing, you're going to be in the public eye whether you like it or not. I only came here to help you."

"*Help*?" Alexandra began to laugh. "Very funny." She sat rocking back and forth, struck by the horrible humor of Mary Lee's words.

"Now you're getting hysterical," Mary Lee said, getting up to put her arms around Alexandra. "Please, don't take it so hard. I'm a reporter. I've got tons of experience; I can put it to use for you if you'll let me. I'll do—"

"You'll do absolutely nothing!" Alexandra twisted away from Mary Lee's arm. "Get away from me! Don't touch me!"

"Alexandra, now, calm down. If you fall apart, you'll just—"

"Get out of my house right now!" Alexandra screamed. "I can't believe you, Mary Lee. My God! What's happened to you? You've turned into someone every bit as despicable as your mother."

Mary Lee turned ashen. "What did you say?"

"Which word didn't you understand? I said you're acting just like your mother, damn it! You've turned into a cold, heartless bitch! Is that plain enough for you, Mary Lee? Oh, Jesus, please . . ." Alexandra sank down on the couch and began to cry, hands splayed over her face, her body shaking helplessly. She was aware that Mary Lee had sat down next to her, but she no longer cared.

"Alexandra?" The touch on her shoulder was tentative.

Alexandra did not respond.

"Look. I know I'm despicable. I know that."

Alexandra opened her eyes and saw Mary Lee's face, crumpled-looking now, eyes glazed with moisture.

"I . . . I can't seem to stop myself, sometimes, Alexandra. I've done some pretty shitty things in the past few years to get ahead. I've ridden roughshod over a lot of people. But I'm right about this. You *are* going to be the target of a lot of publicity, and if you'll let me in on it, I can help you. I'm good, Alexandra. I'm damned fucking good."

"I don't know," Alexandra began. She drew in a long, deep breath, and felt her anger recede. There was truth in what Mary Lee said. Anyway, what did a newspaper series matter? Doggone it, where were her own values? If Mary Lee's razor-sharp mind could help her, then she had to use it.

"All right," she said, capitulating. "The first problem is, I need to find my husband. Something has happened, and I need him—now."

An hour later, Mary Lee, with her gift for networking and genius for ferreting out information, had learned that Richard flew out of Midway to Palm Beach and had taken a taxi to the Ocean Boulevard mansion of Mo Bernstein.

"Mo Bernstein?" Alexandra said in bewilderment. "I don't even know who he is."

Mary Lee drew in a deep breath. "Maybe you don't want to know."

"Damn it, who is he?"

"Just the most powerful 'connected' man in the country.

He's big, Alexandra, he's at the top of the whole Mafia hierarchy. Bigger even than John Gotti."

Alexandra looked shocked. "How do you know all that?"

Mary Lee sighed. "I earn my living knowing things like that. As for Richard, did you ever stop to think, Alexandra, that he's really in a major bind? The Chicago police, *any* big-city police, have been so full of corruption in the past that you can't rely on them to handle a case like this. You really don't know the 'players,' like who's on whose payroll."

Alexandra shook her head. "But . . . Mafia?"

"I think he's just trying to fight fire with fire, that's all. Any way he can."

Alexandra's throat went dry, and she had to moisten her lips. "My God, Mary Lee," she exclaimed after reflecting for a few seconds. "He did it to get Trip back, didn't he?"

"I think that's highly possible."

Alexandra felt a rush of hope tinged with shame. "Do you think . . . do you think Bernstein can get our boy back?"

"If anyone can, it's him. And now I want to look at that videotape, Alexandra. Let's run it and see just what two smart women can pick up from it, if anything."

——— ◄► ———

Richard spent the entire night sitting up waiting for Mo Bernstein to complete his phone calls and collect his information. It was crazy, he thought, to be here. But he had to be realistic.

Several times, a guard brought him coffee. "Mr. Bernstein's still on the phone," he told Richard.

He thought about Alexandra and prayed he hadn't lost her. Still, it was Trip who occupied most of his thoughts.

At 7:00 A.M. Bernstein walked into the study, shaking his head. "I got some news, and it's gonna rock you right out of your socks."

"Yes?"

"Your kid didn't get snatched by the union. See, it was a deal with the Provenzos."

"*What?*"

"An exchange. The Provenzo family is using the union's pension fund to launder money. In return, they help the union bargain with you."

Richard stared. The Mafia had kidnapped his son?

Florida morning sunlight had begun to stream though the windows. Outdoors, gulls screamed and squawked, a gardener trimmed bushes, and a guard dog barked while on its rounds with one of the guards.

"You wanted the information; I got it for you. But the whole family isn't behind it. The youngest Provenzo son—some crazy-ass kid—got a wild hair up his butt." Bernstein had been up as many hours as Richard but didn't look tired at all.

"Jesus." Richard felt choked by anger, astonishment, and fear. This wasn't what he had expected at all.

"Look, Mo," he said. "I didn't come down here exactly empty-handed."

"I know," Bernstein said. "That's why I agreed to see you. I don't see anybody unless they've got something I want. Now, look, let's get some breakfast in here. Then maybe we'll go for a swim, eh? I swim two miles every day in the pool." Bernstein slapped his abdomen, which was rock-hard. "Keeps the gut from sagging, eh?"

Breakfast, served by bodyguards, featured everything from Belgian waffles with strawberries to a coffee cake studded with huge Georgia pecans. Richard ate little, however. He toyed with his eggs, ate a few bites of waffle, and drank a large glass of orange juice. The capo also ate lightly. Then immediately, without waiting for his food to settle, Bernstein led Richard through corridors to the back of the estate.

An Olympic-size turquoise pool shimmered on a jewel green lawn. Mermaids and sea horses had been frescoed on the bottom, where they seemed to move in the slight breeze off the Atlantic that ruffled the water. Richard expected the great god Pan to come bounding out of the water at any minute.

"You swim two miles with me, Richard, and I'll deal with you," Bernstein said.

"What?"

"You heard what I said. You want your boy back, you gotta humor me. Gets boring around here sometimes."

Richard's eyes widened. Shit, did he think this was some kind of macho competition? Apparently he did. Richard felt a chill. "If that's what you want, that's what you've got," he told Bernstein.

The man motioned to a large cabana. "Bathing suits in there."

When Richard emerged, Bernstein was waiting for him, still dressed and stretched in a lounge chair.

"Ready?" he inquired, grinning. Obviously he didn't intend to swim.

"Damned right I'm ready."

With the last bit of strength Richard possessed, he dragged himself out of the water. He sat on the edge of the pool, so exhausted he thought he might pass out.

"You did it, eh?" Mo Bernstein was holding a tall whiskey and water a guard had brought him. He looked at ease, relaxed, very pleased with himself.

"Yeah, I did it."

"Towel," Bernstein said, tossing him one.

Richard slung it over his back and shoulders, feeling too tired to dry himself off.

"Now I usually ride my bike," Bernstein said, smiling again as he pointed to a stationary bike positioned near the cabana. "You game?"

Richard stared at him, and Bernstein threw his head back and laughed uproariously, pleased with his joke. "Hey, I was just shittin' you. Can't you take a little joke, Richard? Come on over to the table; we'll have us a drink and do a little talking. Got to tell you something, Cox."

"What's that?"

"We could have talked the deal anyway. But you're the first one in three years that's been able to swim two miles with me. This new generation, they're weak, they're sissies. They ain't got no staying power. You got staying power, Richard. I like you."

Half an hour later, they had formulated the deal. The Florida legislature was on the verge of legalizing casino gambling, and Richard reluctantly agreed that if they passed the bill, he would open casinos in his six South Florida hotels. Bernstein would run them.

"OK," Mo said. "I'll take care of this thing with your boy; I'll get him back, no problem. Just let us do it our way."

"Please, nothing that would endanger my boy."

"Trust me. Now, there's just one more thing."

"Yes?" Richard was too tired to feel much elation.

"My wife's birthday is coming up. Got to keep the old lady happy, you know what I mean?"

"Yes . . ."

"She sure would like to go to that party of yours. Of course, we'll want to bring a couple of my boys who go everywhere with me. And Sam Provenzo."

Richard allowed himself to hesitate only infinitesimally. The Cosa Nostra invading their party, no doubt with bodyguards? Alexandra would kill him—just kill him. But what did that matter now? He would invite half the Eastern Seaboard to the Fitz Hotel on Saturday if that would bring Tripper running headlong into his arms. "You've got yourself a deal, Mo."

— ►◄ —

Alexandra was in the playroom with the two children, reading aloud to them from one of their favorite books. She couldn't concentrate, nor did the party seem important anymore. All that mattered was her missing child.

She heard a sound behind her and turned to see Richard enter the playroom.

"Daddy, Daddy, Daddy!" Stephanie cried out joyously, and ran to wrap her arms around Richard's thighs. Andy, too, ran forward.

"Hi, guys," Richard said. His voice was a husky croak. "I missed you. I missed your mother, too."

Their eyes met. Alexandra saw entreaty in her husband's eyes. She opened her mouth, but nothing would come out. Richard was a wreck. He was carrying his badly crumpled suit jacket, and his shirt was wrinkled and untidy. His tie was loosened, pulled down, and his collar was open. In the space of only a day, Richard had aged years.

"Rich—" she finally said, putting down the book and starting toward him.

"I had one hell of a day," Richard said, giving the children a hug. He held onto them tightly. "You'll never know how hellish."

"We have to talk. Andy, Stephanie, why don't you go and play now? Mommy and Daddy have to be alone for a minute."

As the children scampered to the other end of the long room, she said to Richard, "Nothing's happened, has it? Nothing—worse?"

His smile didn't touch his eyes. "My God, what could be worse?"

Alexandra called on the intercom for Rafaela to come and supervise the children. As she and Richard walked down the corridor to their bedroom, Richard began stripping off his shirt.

"What happened? I know you went to see Mo Bernstein.

He's Mafia, Richard, how could you?"

He shrugged, stripping off the rest of his clothes until he stood naked before her. His body was still youthfully lean and sinewy.

He still hadn't answered her.

"Richard!" she cried. "Damn it—!"

He walked into the bathroom, heading toward the large, glass-doored shower. "Do you want Tripper back?" he threw back to her over his shoulder.

"Of course I do!" She was almost hysterical. "Richard, Mo Bernstein! I can't believe you would expose us to a person like that. And something *has* happened. We got another videotape."

"What?" Poised to step under the shower, Richard turned. "What did you say?"

She felt herself slip over the edge of emotional control. "I said we got another video!" she shouted. "While you were out selling your soul to the Mafia, they delivered another tape. Brownie was all bloody, and they—they made her smear blood all over Tripper's face."

"Oh, Jesus, what next?" Richard said.

"Is that all you can say? 'Oh, Jesus'? They tortured Brownie, and they're going to do it to Trip, too. They're crazy, Richard; they'll do anything."

"Come on," he said quietly, reaching for a robe. "I want to see that tape. Now."

They were again locked in the library—a room Alexandra was beginning to hate. When this was finished, she decided, she would give away the VCR, purchase another television, redecorate, rip up the carpeting.

Richard watched the short film intensely. Alexandra saw the expressions pass over his face. Grief. Fear. Cold fury. He ran it five times, and when he flicked it off for the last time, she saw tears in his eyes.

"Those bastards," he said. "Alexandra, it's Mafia that took our boy. And Mafia who's going to get him back."

She stared at him, too stunned to speak.

"Punkin . . . Bernstein is the only one who has any possible hope of getting through to those fuckers. Mo has the network and the clout."

"But he's practically the biggest Mafia don in the country," she whispered.

"We're damned lucky he is. And we're even luckier I've got

something he wants, Alexandra. He asked me to give him a day or so. We cooked up kind of a war plan."

"A war plan! Oh, that's very nice, Richard. This is just a game to you, isn't it?" she exclaimed furiously. "A chess game this time, with you as the king and poor, innocent little Tripper as just another pawn!"

Alexandra knew instantly she had gone too far. Something flared in Richard's eyes. "Don't knock it," he snapped. "I made the decision, and it's one that's going to be difficult to live with, but I did it for Tripper. And if you don't like it, then you think of something better."

She felt lacerated by the coldness in his voice.

"Sorry," Richard muttered, but she knew he didn't mean it. He took the tape out of the VCR and slid it back into its envelope. "I'm going to have Slattery look at this, too. Go about your business, Alexandra; get everything ready for that fucking party you wanted so much. I'm really looking forward to it, and I just can't wait to see what kind of a dress Princess Diana has on. It's going to be the highlight of my whole week."

"Richard!"

But he was gone. Alexandra stood shaking, but this time she forced herself not to cry.

———— ▶◀ ————

That evening Richard carried out his part of the plan. It wasn't perfect—but it might save his ass, union-wise.

At 7:30 P.M. he walked into the meeting he had called with the union officials. He stood at the head of the table, gazing at their faces. Tank Marchek, sullen yet expectant. Robbie Fraser, noncommittal. Four other attorneys, negotiators, and lesser union officials in a state of bewilderment. Excitement stirred the air.

"I called you here tonight because I want you to hear a telephone conversation," he began without preamble.

There was an uneasy, startled movement.

"The call is to Arthur M. Green, the owner of the Green's restaurant franchise. I assume you've all eaten at one of his places before? He's got more than 650 of them all over the United States."

A telephone console Richard had had brought into the room suddenly lit up and began buzzing discreetly. Richard stepped forward and picked up the receiver. "I'm having this rung through on the speaker phone," he explained. "I want you all to hear this. Every word."

"Hey, Richard, what's doing?" The voice of Art Green suddenly filled the room, fresh, rested, cheerful. "Did you catch the Cubs on TV last night?"

"Art," Richard said. "I've got a proposition for you."

"Yeah? Like what?"

"You've always wanted a piece of my hotels, right? Well, how would you like to buy six of them? My five Hawaiian Fitzes and the one in Carmel. Subject to the lawyers hashing out the fine points, of course. A good price," Richard added. "Fair market value, something you can live with. We'll even manage them for you at a reduced fee."

A stir of surprise and anger sped around the conference table.

"Holy shit," came the amplified voice. "Richard Cox, you're not drunk, are you?"

"Cold sober and ready to do business, Arthur. One thing though—I want to sign a preliminary agreement tomorrow morning, nine sharp, in my office. Can you make that?"

"I had another meeting . . . but, sure, Richard, I'll cut it short and leave early. I'll call my law firm and have them get on it right away."

The murmurings in the room were growing angrier, and when Arthur Green clicked off, there were loud voices all talking at once. Richard gestured for silence.

"You heard what I just did. I've arranged to sell six of the hotels in my chain, and I'm going to arrange to sell six more tomorrow—to someone else. I'll break up my American chain, cut it in little pieces, six hotels at a time, until there isn't anything left to bargain over. There won't be any Fitz Hotel employees left to bargain with. In fact, I wouldn't be surprised if the new owners went nonunion. I could even make it a condition of the purchase that they do so. What do you think of that?"

"Hey, man," Tank Marchek burst out. "You can't do that. It ain't even legal. It's a violation of the Landrum-Griffin Act. Maybe even Taft-Hartley," he added as an afterthought.

Richard's eyes locked with Marchek's. "Is it? Don't be too sure. Nobody fucks with me, Marchek—and I mean nobody. Do you hear what I'm saying? And if you'll remember, I still own *thirty* hotels abroad, and they aren't unionized and never will be. I'll still be sitting pretty while your union loses a ton of jobs."

Marchek shook his head angrily, but Richard's voice was steel. "Either the contract is settled tomorrow, *and my son returned to me*, or I auction off more hotels. Oh, as a sweetener, I could offer 2 percent profit sharing . . . in two years, though, not immediately, and with escalators over two more years. It would eventually mean another $10,000 a year for each member. Could you buy that?"

There were mutters and stirs. Several negotiators could be heard asking what Richard meant about his son.

"And one more thing," Richard snapped. The heads turned to him again. "I've got excellent sources who can provide me with proof of wrongdoing on the union board. Proof that would stick and send a few bodies to the federal pen for, oh, maybe twenty to thirty years. Does that sound about right, Marchek?"

Marchek's face was turning a mottled shade of cranberry.

"I see I've made my point," Richard said, barely moving his lips.

"You bastard—!" Marchek jumped to his feet and came rushing around the table, fists raised. Three men jumped to hold Marchek back.

"I'll leave you gentlemen to think about my proposal," Richard finished. "I'm going home now. It should take me, oh, say, about twenty minutes to get there. When I walk in the door, I expect my phone to be ringing with your decision to settle this matter. No strike, and compromises on two of the four issues as recently suggested. The whole contract to be worked out within the week. Ratification by the membership just as soon as the vote can be called."

"That's a tough one, Cox," Fraser began.

"I don't think it's so tough. I've got a couple other buyers lined up besides Green. David Kwan in Hong Kong and Jay Pritzker here in Chicago. Go ahead and test me. Good night, gentlemen," Richard said, and walked out of the room.

In the cab he took back to his office, Richard leaned against the seat back, succumbing to his weariness. Jesus, if he didn't sleep soon, he'd collapse. He had probably saved his hotels—most of them. But it seemed small satisfaction now.

——— ◉ ———

"What? *Ti rompo il culo,*" Sam Provenzo swore. He stared at his unexpected guest with genuine shock and horror. "It can't be true."

"It is, man. Every fucking word of it. Your son did a snatch on the Cox kid," Mo Bernstein said in his soft but authoritative voice. He had flown from Palm Beach to Chicago, an unusual and ominous act, since Mo loathed traveling, especially by air. "Cox is my friend, and it's an embarrassment."

They were in Sam's study, a large tray of antipasto spread out before them, along with iced glasses of Sambucco. Sam swallowed down a lump of bile. Shit—was it never going to end? He hadn't slept soundly since he'd been forced to slap his son's face in front of everyone.

Why had Nico done this? The answer was only too clear. It was his way of making a big statement. A direct strike at Sam, a blow to his self-respect.

Bernstein fixed him with cold, fishy eyes. "Sam, you let your son get out of control."

It was the ultimate insult. Sam started to say something but, with difficulty, shut his mouth.

"I didn't come up here to Chicago to crap around," Bernstein went on. "I came up here to tell you that if the Cox kid and the Englishwoman aren't back, unharmed, in twenty-four hours—well, I am going to hold you personally responsible. *Capisce?*"

Sam's face reddened, and he felt a brief, stabbing pain under his breastbone, an indigestion that seemed to be cropping up more and more often these days.

"*Capisce?*" Mo repeated, eyes hard.

"Right," Sam said heavily. "I'll take care of it."

As soon as Mo left, Sam got on the phone and called a meeting, family only.

Within fifteen minutes, they had arrived. Joey, who had been on the treadmill at the Powerhouse Gym, was still dressed in workout shorts and T-shirt. Marco and Lenny were in business suits, and all three had brought their personal bodyguards.

Nico's absence felt awkward. Marco was scowling, tapping his fingers nervously on the top of a small occasional table. Despite their frequent quarrels, he had been closest to Nico.

"Jesus!" Sam snapped at Marco. "You sound like Gene Krupa. It's a bad habit you have, Marco."

Marco stopped.

Sam gestured impatiently, indicating that the troops should

wait in the living room out of earshot. As soon as the body-guards were gone, the capo shut his study door and stuck a videotape in the VCR. *Rambo: First Blood Part II.* He turned up the sound to full volume.

"OK," he said to his sons, now that he was convinced they wouldn't be overheard. The pain under his breastbone had gone away, replaced by a deep, heavy anger and grief. Quickly he described Mo's visit, repeating their conversation word for word.

When he was finished, there was a brief silence. Then all three brothers began to talk at once.

"Shit!" Joey cried. "He doesn't belong to this family. He works alone, does anything he damn' well wants to."

"I told you," Marco exclaimed. "Damn it, I told you he was unstable. He's dangerous. To do something like that without us even knowing? Crazy man. What got into him? I can't believe this shit."

"I'll tell you what's going down. He wants to run things," Lenny said. "That's what got into him. He wants to be top banana, *numero uno.* Better watch your ass," he added, speaking to Sam.

"I heard there's rumors going around," Joey whispered. "Crazy ones, sick ones. Some people say Nico, he gets fits. Crazy in the head! You know? They said he keeps it a secret, he takes out people that find out about it."

"That ain't true," Sam interjected in his gravelly voice. "Nico don't have fits; that's just damn' lies, and whoever said it is fucking full of bullshit. I want their names; I want to talk to them." He cleared his throat. "Meanwhile, we got ourselves a major problem."

He fixed his sons with reddened, steely eyes. "We don't have no choice now. There's no fucking way out, and it hurts me in the heart to say it. We got to do two things. We got to get that Cox kid back, or Bernstein is going to be on our asses. The other thing, and the one that hurts . . ."

"No," Marco said.

"Yes, damn it! He's a danger, a goddamn' liability to this family!" With each syllable, Sam pounded his fist on the desktop.

Joey's face was impassive, but Lenny and Marco were visibly upset. "Pa—" began Marco.

"Shut up!" Sam roared. "You got a rotten spot, you cut it out. Just like cancer. You don't let it eat away at you; you don't let it kill you. I been getting phone calls from L.A. and New York. They told me to cover my ass. I have to cover my ass from my own son?"

Lenny and Joey were nodding.

Sam started to sweat under his armpits and felt the angina in his chest squeezing him like steel pincers. "I don't have to spell it out, do I? I don't have to say the words."

The younger men murmured among themselves.

"OK," Sam said in an unrecognizable voice. "Now get the hell out of here. All of you. Get out. I don't want to see your faces again until we've cleaned up our own shit. There ain't no other way."

Within seconds they were gone, their faces somber. Sam knew they had expected this but were still shocked. It would be the first contract he had put out in five years—and on his own son.

He weaved his way to the bathroom and vomited again and again into the toilet bowl until there was nothing left to heave. Emerging from the bathroom, he stalked toward the TV set, leaning over to pick it up. The cord snapped out of the socket, and the screen went blank.

With all of his still-formidable muscles, Sam threw the television across the room. It landed with a smash of glass and metal, and Sam growled as he attacked the set again. He kicked at it and battered it, picked it up and hurled it down again. In seconds the TV was demolished, and he snatched up a lamp and began swinging it wildly, smashing out the windows in his study.

Several minutes later, the room was a shambles of broken glass, overturned furniture, and wildly strewn papers. Sam stood in the wreckage breathing heavily, red-hot pains shooting through his chest. Tears rolled down his cheeks, and his mouth suddenly twisted awry in a violent sob.

God, who would he celebrate his birthday with next year?

— ▶◀ —

"Brownie?" Trip said. "Talk, Brownie. Please say something to me."

Elizabeth Clifford-Brown had been lying in a huddle on the air mattress, a strip from the hem of her slip wrapped around her head in lieu of a bandage. She stirred slowly.

"Brownie!" the boy entreated, pummeling her gently with

his small, hard fists. "You're making funny noises. Wake up, Brownie!"

Her eyes, dull with pain, fluttered open. She blinked several times to clear them. Her scalp and face throbbed, feeling hot to the touch.

Groggily she glanced at her watch and saw that it was 8:30 A.M. They had been here two days now. She knew she was seriously ill but was determined to hide this from Trip. He must live out his last hours in relative peace—that was her job, to see to that.

"I'm hungry," he announced now. "Is there any break- fast?"

Brownie sighed weakly and sat up. "There's still some Sara Lee. And some tinned juice."

"Tomato juice?" Trip pouted.

"I'll drink that," she said. "You can have the 7-Up."

"For breakfast? I want a candy bar, too. And Lucky Charms."

Brownie moved about, laying out their meal. She noticed there were only four soft-drink cans left. The men had not been back since they had cut her face, and she wondered whether she should begin rationing their food. What if they were just left here to die of thirst?

They sat eating. Brownie tasted a little dry cereal, forcing it down. The tomato juice tasted too thick and salty, and she set the can down, half finished. She touched her throbbing face and wondered whether the scar would be noticeable.

Then she remembered it wasn't going to heal. It would not be given a chance. How could they let her live when she had clearly seen both their faces and had heard one calling the other "Nico"?

"Brownie?" Trip was tugging at her again. "Brownie, look up there at those holes."

"What?"

"Those holes. Are those tunnels up there? Like in the comic books?"

"What?" she said again, shaking her head.

"Like Spider-Man," Trip explained. "I could crawl out of the holes if you could lift me up there. I'm little enough."

"Oh, Trip. I don't think you can. And even if you could . . ." Her voice trailed off.

"Lift me up," the boy commanded.

Brownie did so, but the ceiling in the room was too high for the child to reach. He struggled in her arms, arching himself to reach higher, but his arms were far too short.

She set him down again.

"Trip, go and play with your Transformers now," she said, patting his shoulder gently.

He stood for several minutes, staring at the ceiling. She could see his hope gradually fade. Then, obediently, he did as she asked him. Soon the boy was involved in an imaginary game with the metal robots. A game in which one robot beat and pushed the other.

— ►◄ —

The cab pulled up to the banquet entrance of the Fitz Hotel. Alexandra paid the driver and stepped out. She felt drained by the events of the past two days. Word that their chauffeur, Will, had been found dead in the trunk of their limousine had shocked her, intensifying the considerable fear she already felt.

Still, Mo Bernstein had promised to help, and Richard had told her to go about her normal routine. She now carried a beeper in her purse so that Mrs. Abbott could contact her immediately with any news. Meanwhile, working on the gala was going to keep her sanity intact.

She and Mary Lee had reached a truce of sorts. Mary Lee had viewed the tape eight times, and her theory was that the cement in the background was not an ordinary parking lot, but some sort of factory or shop setting. The cement was pitted, which meant it was old. There were traces of pebbles visible that Mary Lee thought might be significant. She was now making phone calls to try to track down that cement flooring.

Please, God, Alexandra prayed. Let someone find something, I don't care who. Even Mafia, if they can get Tripper back. Richard was right. What does it matter who finds him?

One of the set designer's assistants, Marian Baum, greeted her and began to take her through. Alexandra inspected the two stages where the dancers would perform, and she had the fountains turned on to make certain the water sprays were working properly. The water would be regulated by computer, and the possible combinations of spray patterns were mind-boggling.

Already in place was a Steinway piano where Sammy Fain

would perform a medley from the more than forty platinum records he had made popular. Tables were being set up for hors d'oeuvres and for dining.

As Alexandra was gazing at the long head table, wondering about its placement, a kitchen worker passed her, pushing a cart stacked with folded-up table linen. The woman paused, eyeing Alexandra curiously. She was about thirty, thin, with a face that might have been attractive if it hadn't looked so intense. The name tag she wore identified her as Elizabeth Dumbarton.

"Are you Mrs. Cox?"

Alexandra was startled out of her musings. "Why . . . yes, I am."

"I read about you, and I've seen your picture. You're very beautiful."

"Why, thank you." Alexandra smiled and moved on, feeling the woman's stare in the center of her back.

The head chef, Georges Taxier, had spotted her from the kitchen, where he must have been waiting. He came hurrying up. His face looked flushed and annoyed, and she had no doubt that another kitchen disagreement had flared up again.

"Mrs. Cox—Mrs. Cox—"

"Yes, Georges," she sighed, preparing herself for another session as mediator.

An hour's discussion about the menu left her exhausted. There would be sole veronique over flame, followed by brambleberry sorbet in pony glasses with demitasse spoons. A princess salad of bibb lettuce, Belgian endive, white asparagus, and sliced tomatoes Polonaise, served with Dijon vinaigrette dressing made with walnut oil. Guests would be offered a choice of entrées: sea bass stuffed with pike and smoked salmon with a truffle sauce; rack of lamb Provençale; grilled, boned quail with juniper berry sauce; or chicken *en croute.*

The discussion about the potato baskets alone took twenty minutes, as Taxier detailed how he would create a crispy, delicate-looking basket of deep-fried, shredded potatoes to showcase various petite vegetables.

"Oh, Georges," she was finally forced to say. "I'm just going to have to trust your expertise."

She left the hotel and walked two blocks to the bank where she kept a large safe-deposit box. Over the lake, storm clouds were rolling in, darkening the street.

The attendant at the bank vault recognized her, greeting her with a smile, but still insisted on every signature and procedure. They each inserted a key into the lock of the safe-deposit box. Alexandra took the large metal tray into one of the small rooms provided for customers to examine their valuables.

She sat down and opened the lid. Inside were stacks of stock certificates, manila envelopes containing various papers and trust agreements, and boxes containing the most valuable of her mother's jewelry, plus the necklace and earrings that Richard had given her. Even the replica of the Fitzgerald Fifty was there, as it was worth over $10,000. Such a shame to keep these treasures hidden away.

She took out the pearlized box in which she kept the real Fifty. Slowly she undid the clasp and opened its lid. The overhead light in the small room caught and refracted the spill of diamonds, creating rainbows of crystal light. The pink diamonds, especially, glowed as if lit from within by fire.

Irresistibly, her mind took her back to the day when Richard had given her the necklace. Her eyes filled. She touched one of the glittering pink stones, seeing it through a filter of tears.

Dully she closed the box that held the necklace, secured its clasp, and thrust the whole thing into the tote bag she carried. It seemed to burn a hole there, to be far too heavy.

On an afterthought, she took the box containing the replica and put that in her bag, too. Then she turned and left the booth.

15

End Game

Wind mixed with heavy raindrops rattled the windows of Nico's eighth-floor condominium. Beyond the prism of rain, the city lights seemed blurred and softened.

Nico and Jette were in his black-and-white kitchen, naked except for aprons. The aroma of crushed garlic and oregano filled the room, along with the less pleasant odor of newly cooked shrimp.

"The whole place is going to smell," Nico told her, his tone less than gracious.

"Oh, you, complaining when we are going to have such marvelous shrimp marinara. I found the recipe in an old cook-book. They used to make it at Mama Leone's, in New York. You are so *cross* recently, Nico, I really don't know what is the matter with you."

Nico looked at his girlfriend of seven years. She was so beautiful. The tiny apron barely covered her flat tummy and pubic area, leaving everything else to spill out lushly.

"Here," Jette said, pushing an onion toward him. "Chop that. Why don't you buy a food processor, maybe one of those mini-choppers? Then you won't have to get onion and garlic smells all over your fingers."

Ordinarily, Nico would have nudged her and teased, "I want to get *you* all over my fingers," but today the quip froze in his throat. In the three days since his father had slapped him across the face, he had been unable to eat. Even the smell of food was making him nauseated.

He shoved away the onion. "This stuff stinks. I'm going in the other room. You cook if you want to—I'm not hungry."

"For crying out loud, Nico, you didn't eat any breakfast either," she said.

"Just cook and eat. Don't worry about me. I'm going to play some music."

He was sorting through his compact discs when the telephone rang. He picked it up on the first ring. Rambo was supposed to come over in an hour, so they could go to the meat locker and work on the English nanny again. This time they planned to bleed her good, cover the boy with blood.

"Yeah?" he said into the receiver.

It wasn't Rambo; it was Marco. By the traffic sounds in the background, Nico guessed that his brother was calling from an outdoor phone booth.

"Listen, kid, you're in deep shit," Marco said hurriedly.

"What?"

"That's all I can tell you. Good-bye." The phone clicked in Nico's ear, and then he heard a dial tone.

He put down the receiver and shivered. There was only one "deep shit" he could be in now.

"Nico." Jette was beside him. She slid her arms around him, enveloping him in the faint odor of Jette perfume. "Baby, are you mad or something? What's wrong? We don't have to eat shrimp if you don't want. I'll just wrap this in foil, and we'll go out. Or if you'd rather—"

"Shut the fuck up, will you?" he said viciously. He shook her off, his head buzzing with the rapid pump of his blood.

"Fine." Jette's feelings were hurt. She pulled away, smoothing down the ruffles of the provocative apron.

"Get out of here," he added. "Get dressed and shove off."

"What?"

"I'm in some kind of family trouble, I don't want you around. I'm—" To his horror, he saw a watery flickering at the outside of his vision. The aura. Grimly he fought it.

"Nico?" Anxiously she touched him.

If they were to hit him here in the apartment, she would be caught in it. Shit! This was what happened when you became weak and cared for a woman too much.

He snapped, "Get away, I told you. Just find your clothes and leave. I don't want you around anymore."

"OK," she said, her eyes filling with tears. "I'll be staying here a couple days, until after Alexandra's party. You *are* coming to that with me, aren't you? I'm staying at the Fitz. I'm in room—"

"Who the fuck cares?"

As soon as Jette was out of the door, Nico shoved a CD in the player. It was an album of Nepalese Buddhist monks' chants that often helped him to clear his mind. He threw himself on the couch and shut his eyes, fighting the tension that tightened every one of his nerves and muscles.

The monks' chanting was melodic and eerily pure, but it did nothing to relieve Nico's anxiety. He wondered when they would do it, how they would kill him. Would it be here in the apartment? Maybe they would put a bomb in the Ferrari. He would have to start driving the Lincoln he kept in the public parking garage.

What should he do? Maybe he would just let it happen. Yeah. Without family, what was a man? Nothing.

The apartment buzzer roused him. Rambo. He stumbled up and went to the door to let his bodyguard in.

"Nico—Nico . . . shit, did you hear?"

"Hear what?" Nico asked dully.

"Hey, they're all sayin' it; I heard it from Angelo. The Don went crazy and busted up his study, broke all the windows and shit. They could hear him in there, yellin' and screamin' and carryin' on."

Nico felt spears of glass puncture his chest. "What else?" he said.

"They said there was a big meeting, too," Rambo went on, his unease apparent. "Uh, with just Lenny, Marco, and Joey, though. I hope that ain't bad news. Maybe it means they found out we took the Cox kid, eh? Maybe it means we gotta move him."

"Yeah, right," Nico said automatically.

"Question is where. We gotta have a place to put him, right? And we got the kid's nanny to think of. You gonna ice her?"

Perspiration began to run down Nico's cheeks, and he saw the flashing lights at the corners of his eyes again, wobbling just past his vision.

Jesus, no, he thought, begging God for mercy. Not now!

"Nico! Jesus, man!" From a distance, Nico heard his bodyguard's voice. He felt hands slap his face. "Wake up! You OK? Geez, you fell on the floor and got all funny, just staring."

Nico moaned thickly. He was lying on the white carpet. He could see Rambo and hear him, but everything was fuzzy. He hated being out of control, at the mercy of his body.

"Here," Rambo said, pushing something at his mouth. It was a bottle. "This is brandy; I got it in the kitchen. Drink it; it'll settle you."

Nico turned his head away, but Rambo forced the brandy in. "That's it . . . drink . . . shit, you're spilling it all over yourself. I bet you had a fit, right? I bet that's what that was. I heard you had them."

He'd heard? Did they all know? Marco? Lenny? But worst of all, most horrible of all, his father? Nico's thoughts were scattered by hate and fear. People were talking.

"Jesus Christ, you are really spaced out," Rambo was saying. "Maybe I oughta call a doctor, huh? Maybe I ought—"

Rambo didn't get any more words out. His neck was suddenly gripped in the vise of Nico's hands—hands that at first didn't possess full strength, but kept on squeezing until they did. There were the sounds of choking . . . then gurgling.

When Rambo's body had gone limp, Nico finally took his hands away. He stared down at his spread fingers, flexing them as if in surprise. They were shaking.

Twenty minutes later, still weak and sweating, Nico had wrapped Rambo's body in several large plastic bags, strapped the bundle with duct tape, and pushed it into the building's incinerator chute. Within hours, it would be burned.

He then returned to his apartment and left through his secret exit.

It was still raining, water slanting down at a forty-five-degree angle. It washed along the gutters, creating puddles that came halfway up to his hubcaps.

The Lincoln plowed through the water with a satisfying sound as spray battered the underbody of the car. Nico remembered that he had stuffed a bottle full of 'Ludes in the glove compartment, along with a plastic "gun" for snorting cocaine.

He leaned over and opened the glove compartment, taking out the coke "gun." He pulled the trigger and squeezed the coke up his nostrils. It exploded directly into his brain.

Almost instantly he felt a sweet, rolling surge of energy. The powerful high that careened through his head placed him on top of a world of power. He was tough. Even tougher than

Richard Cox, with his blonde wife and that diamond necklace they bragged about.

The necklace. An idea entered his cocaine-pumped brain. It was brilliant, and it might still save him from his family.

——— ►◄ ———

Brownie, seated on an air mattress with her arm around Trip, was reading aloud again from the comic books. They were engrossed in a story about "Spidey" and a cat-villain, when she heard the sound of the chain being unlocked on the other side of the door.

She paled. Her fingers clenched the brightly colored page, tearing it.

The one called Nico entered the locker. He stood still for a moment, legs planted wide in an arrogant stance.

"Stand up," Nico ordered, speaking to Brownie. Laser eyes impaled her. "Let go of the kid, and stand up."

"Brownie?" Trip whispered, his hands clutching her.

"Now!"

Fear swallowed her up. This was it, she knew, the end of her. She'd been expecting this for the past two days. She could see the knife glitter in his hand. He was going to kill her now, stab her to death in front of Trip. Then maybe he would kill Trip, too.

"Stand up, or do you want to take it lying down? Is that what you want?"

Slowly she got to her feet. Trip was standing, too, looking at Nico with puzzlement growing to horror.

"My nanny!" he cried in a high, scared voice. "Don't hurt my Brownie!"

She felt very far away from what was happening, her emotions blunted and cool. She was dying now, would be dead in seconds. She leaned down and whispered to the little boy.

"Trip . . . you have to run, honey."

"No!" Trip screamed, grabbing her around the waist. "No, Brownie, no!"

The man lunged forward and shoved the child, sending him stumbling away. Brownie screamed, running toward the boy. She saw movement, felt a tear in her side, a hard, ripping pain.

"NO NO NO NO NO!" bellowed Trip, who came charging at Nico, all flailing arms, kicking legs, and teeth that snapped and gouged like a vicious, small animal.

Brownie sank to her knees, watching this with astonishment. Blood streamed out of her, spattering the floor. So red. She watched it, dazed.

"Don't you hurt my Brownie!" Trip screamed.

Brownie continued to fold to the floor, landing in a vivid red splash of her own blood. Was this how it felt to die?

"My Brownie! I hate you!" Trip had gone wild, struggling with the man in frenzied, small-boy rage. He was no match at all for Nico, who gripped him from behind, holding him out like a puppy.

Brownie was looking at cement, pitted with holes, stains, and roughened chunks of gravel. So gray and gritty.

She watched as the gray of cement changed to a steely blackness. Her vision was going. Or maybe she was passing out. The pain was gone.

Rain battered the loading dock, washing off it in sheets and drumming on the automatic bay doors. Nico came out, wincing as the torrential downpour instantly soaked him. He threw the boy into his car. He had trussed Trip in a pair of white coveralls, tying the sleeves in a knot, like a straitjacket.

The kid, he couldn't believe it, wasn't even blubbering or crying. He just kept struggling, trying to wiggle his way out of the tight-binding cloth. Nico couldn't help admiring the boy. That Cox had been damned lucky in a son. Nico ejected the thought from his mind. He drove away from the packing plant, tires squealing on wet pavement. He had started to come down from the coke high, so he blew another two lines to keep his shit together.

He needed to get back into his condo again for a minute or two, to get the guns he kept there, the stash of weaponry he'd been collecting for years. Also he needed to make a phone call.

His plan was simple, but it would be effective, and then he'd have something to bargain with. Wouldn't he? He felt a twinge of doubt that slid away as the additional cocaine took hold.

It was his father who had ordered the hit, not his brothers. Hell, Marco had actually warned him. As soon as this was over, he'd reverse matters. The old man had lived too long, was weak and stupid with age. His brain was going soft. Even thinking about this made Nico's heart pound with anticipation. Shit, he was king, or would be; Chicago was *his* world, not Sam's.

His nerves thrumming like supercharged wires, he switched on the radio. A rock song by Guns N' Roses jumped into the car, and Nico turned it up, moving his shoulders to the rhythm.

As he drove, he formulated his escape plan. He decided to drive to Detroit, where a boyhood friend, Al Licavoli, from the Licavoli family, owed him a big personal favor. Al could be convinced to help him for three or four days.

Yeah, Detroit. Who would think of looking for him there? But first he needed to make a phone call to beautiful, blonde, rich-bitch Alexandra Cox.

— ◄► —

Alexandra had returned home and was on the phone to Jette, who was crying. It was something about Nico suddenly turning on her and throwing her out of his condo for no apparent reason.

"I don't understand him," Jette wept bitterly.

Alexandra closed her eyes. She didn't need this. She hadn't told Jette yet about Tripper, and now, with Jette acting so hysterical, she didn't feel she could. Maybe there *was* something wrong with Jette, but she didn't have the strength to think about it now. She wished her friend would hang up. Mary Lee was due here soon. She wanted to find out what new information there was.

"I mean, do you think I ought to see a shrink?" Jette wanted to know.

"A shrink?"

"Aren't you even listening? Alexandra, I have allowed this man to treat me like total shit. Smack me around, abuse me . . . Do you know something? When he's really pissed at me, he likes to fuck me from behind. I think it's so he won't have to look at my face. That prick!" Jette babbled on. "Now, thanks to him, I have two days to kill until your party. I don't suppose you want some company? Maybe I could help."

"What?"

"I could write out place cards or something."

"Oh, my dear," gasped Alexandra, "650 place cards? That was done weeks ago, by a professional calligrapher."

"I'll do something else, then. Arrange flowers. Yeah, I could do that." Jette subsided into snuffling sobs. "Oh, you have florists to do that. You're probably so busy you don't want anyone. Maybe I'll just go shopping . . ."

Jette sounded so pathetic, Alexandra didn't know what to say. The instant Jette stepped into her apartment and asked for the children, she would know that Trip was missing. She'd be horrified.

The click of call waiting saved her. As had been the case for the past two days every time the phone rang, she felt a stabbing sensation in her stomach. "Just a minute, Jette," she said, switching to the other line. "Yes, this is Alexandra Cox."

"Hello, Mrs. Cox." The voice on the other end of the line was male, well modulated, quiet. Something about it chilled her.

"Who is this?"

"I have your boy. If you want him back, you'd better listen carefully."

Alexandra clutched the telephone, listening to the voice as it gave her instructions on bringing the Fitzgerald Fifty to an apartment building near State Street. She was to enter the building wearing the necklace under her clothing. Go straight up to the eighth floor, to apartment 808. He would meet her there and take her through.

"Through?" she asked, her voice shaking.

"You'll see when you get here. Now don't tell anyone you're coming—not *anyone*," he emphasized. "Especially your husband. If you do, I'll cut the kid's throat." There was a pause, and then she heard a high-pitched, childish cry.

"Trip!" she cried.

"Mommy!" her son could be heard calling, and then the sound was muffled again, as if a hand had been put over his mouth.

"I'm not kidding around, Mrs. Cox. Believe me, I'm not."

She did believe him.

"Mrs. Cox? Are you there?"

"Yes, I'm here. I . . . I'll be over in twenty minutes," she said.

"Make it fast."

He clicked off, leaving nothing but a dial tone.

Forgetting about Jette, Alexandra rose, her thoughts racing. Maybe she should call Richard. She pressed the phone button to get an open line. But the man had said not to tell anyone. If she disobeyed him, Trip could be killed. She hesitated, her heart pounding violently.

"Alexandra? Alexandra? Is that you?" Jette's voice came over the wire. Alexandra realized that she had punched in the other line. "Say something, girl!"

"I . . . I don't . . ."

"You sound so funny. There's something the matter, isn't there?" Jette said anxiously, putting her own problems aside.

Alexandra stood swaying.

"Alexandra," Jette urged. "I *know* something's wrong. I knew it a few days ago when I called you, and I can sure tell it today. Even if I have been crying on your shoulder like a fool."

"It's Trip," Alexandra heard herself say. She blurted out the essential details, not wanting to waste the twenty minutes Nico had given her. Jette was astounded.

"*Mafia?*"

"Yes. Jette, I've got to hang up. I have to go—"

"Mafia," Jette repeated, a quiver in her voice. "What's the address the guy gave you?"

Alexandra repeated it.

Jette's shock was genuine. "Oh, my God. That must be the building next to Nico's."

Nico. Alexandra felt her heart slam, her stomach clenching.

"I *really* have to go now," she said, and hung up.

Alexandra hurried upstairs. In her bedroom, she threw off the Bill Blass suit she'd been wearing, ran into her walk-in closet, and grabbed a pair of jeans, pulling them on. Then a cotton T-shirt with a neck high enough to hide the necklace.

Calm, she told herself. *Just be calm.*

The admonition seemed to work. She began to feel as she often did before playing and singing her music in front of an audience. Nervous yet contained. She was a strong person, she knew, raised by her mother to face problems head-on. She would do what had to be done.

She walked over to a painting on the wall and lifted it off its hooks, revealing the small wall safe where she kept jewelry. She worked the combination, pulled out the box, and opened its lid. Her heart contracted as she stared down at the blazing gems. This was what Nico wanted—these diamonds that stood for her and Richard's love. He would pull the stones out of their settings and peddle them in New York or Amsterdam like so much booty.

Her eyes watered. No, she *wasn't* letting him do that. Quickly she grabbed the plain box that held the fake necklace.

Alexandra fastened the clasp of the replica and adjusted it so that it hung underneath the T-shirt. He had not asked for the earrings, so she did not include them. She moved to a mirror.

Did a lump show? Not enough to make a difference.

She walked downstairs and told her secretary that she was going over to the Fitz to double-check some of the menu arrangements with the night chef.

— ►◄ —

In her hotel room, Jette replaced the telephone receiver. Numbly she stared at its beige plastic, feeling sick to her stomach. Nico, kidnapping Tripper! It couldn't be true.

And yet . . . She thought back over the past few days. Nico's refusal to eat. The several times he'd made a lame excuse and left, returning edgy and in a black mood. That awful bodyguard, Rambo, who acted as if he and Nico had a secret.

She rubbed her suddenly throbbing head. Nico a kidnapper and killer?

Impulsively she reached for the phone and dialed Nico's number. The phone rang twice.

"Yes?" Nico snapped.

Jette's heart drummed as she held onto the phone, not daring to say a word. Then she heard a sound in the background. Was it a child? Or just a TV set?

Nico slammed the phone down before she could decide what she'd heard. Jette sat rubbing her face, her temples aching with a dull throb.

Damn! Her eyes filled with tears.

She got up off the king-size bed and reached for her snakeskin purse. Tears blurred her vision. There was only one thing to do now. She had to go over to Nico's apartment and find out the truth.

— ►◄ —

Alexandra stepped out of the elevator and had just started across the lobby when she saw Richard. He was entering the double doors and wore an expression of intense preoccupation. New worry lines radiated from his eyes.

She stared at him, thunderstruck.

He, too, looked startled as he recognized her. His eyes went downward, taking in the outfit she wore, the T-shirt carelessly stuffed into jeans, the worn Reeboks.

"Lexy? Where are you going at this time of night?"

"Over to the hotel," she told him. "There's a problem in

the kitchen. I have to talk to the night chef now. It's the only time we can get together," she added.

"Dressed like that?"

Her voice unexpectedly trembled. "What's wrong with jeans?"

"Nothing. Alexandra, come upstairs, will you? There's something I've got to tell you."

She was frantic to get moving, to reach Nico during the time limit he had set. "What is it, Richard?" she said impatiently.

He eyed her strangely. "Do you want me to tell you now? Down here in the lobby?"

Her eyes pleaded with him to understand. "Yes. There's nobody here. Just the security man, and he's watching TV. Please, Richard, what is it?"

He hesitated, then spoke quietly. "It's just this, Lexy. Our son—the Mafia are fighting over him."

"What?"

"I've been on the phone with Mo Bernstein. It seems that Sam Provenzo's son has gone crazy. He's the one who took Tripper, with some screwed-up idea of proving something to his father. Now Bernstein's got the father in on it, Sam Provenzo. He's going to be working with us to get Tripper back."

"Oh," Alexandra said.

"Is that all you can say? 'Oh'?" Richard fell into step beside her.

They were outside the door now. Rain poured down on the awning of the building, splattering against the canvas and streaming down in mini-waterfalls from its corners. Several cabs waited in line in front of the building. Alexandra raised an arm toward the first one, catching the driver's eye.

"Lexy!" Richard caught her arm. "Jesus, you didn't listen to a word I said, did you? You haven't even got a jacket. Or an umbrella."

"*Please*, Richard," she said, shaking his hand away.

"No!" he cried, gripping both of his arms around her waist. To her shock, she saw that his eyes were wet with tears. "Please, Alexandra . . ."

"I'm not—it's not—" She struggled against him.

"Lexy, I love you! Don't wall me out like this; don't do this to me. I'm begging you!"

"If Tripper dies . . ." She was sobbing now. "I don't know what's going to happen then."

"Alexandra, you really do blame me for this, don't you? You're so wrong."

She ran toward the cab.

"Lexy!" he shouted.

As the cab started down the street, she looked back to see Richard standing in the rain.

———— ◄► ————

Bitsy was in the room she'd rented on North Broadway, mending a rip in the underarm of the uniform she would wear to serve hors d'oeuvres at the Cox party. The rain, rattling against the six-foot-high sash window, had been getting on her nerves all night.

In fact, everything was getting on her nerves lately. The closer it got to the gala, the more sharply Bitsy felt the burden of what she hoped to accomplish. Not that she was afraid to kill. She'd already done that, and it hadn't been bad.

But killing Derek Winthrop wouldn't be like killing the crooked police officer. This was going to be an assassination in the middle of a large crowd. And not just any crowd, either, but rich people, famous people, several Presidents, and the Prince and Princess of Wales.

There would also be several dozen Secret Service men, other security teams, and police officers circulating through the party guests—even hovering above the hotel in helicopters, according to Jorge, who'd been only too happy to fill Bitsy in on the juicy details.

She had thought it over, long and carefully. She wasn't a fool. She knew this could be a suicide mission.

She busied herself taking tiny, perfect stitches, the act curiously soothing. Maybe, Bitsy thought, adjusting the gray rayon as she sewed, maybe she was ready to have her life be over. She hated her life now. When people stared at her, she wanted to die.

Suddenly her hands were shaking so hard she could scarcely hold the needle.

She remembered being shot—the pain beyond agony. But dying would take her past all that, wouldn't it? To a flat nothingness, where nothing would bother her anymore.

Finished, she held up the repaired uniform. It was made of silver-gray rayon, its cut fashionable. A white, lace-trimmed apron went with it, and there was lace on the collar as well. The printed name tag, giving her name as Elizabeth Dumbarton, would let her pass freely.

Satisfied with her handiwork, she replaced the uniform on its hanger. Everything was set. She'd hidden her small, beautiful Norwegian knife in a drawer in the kitchen, since Jorge had told her that on the day of the gala, all staff members would be given body searches and would have to walk through a metal detector.

Tomorrow would be a hectic day. Big as the Fitzgerald Hotel kitchen was, it would be strained to handle all the preparations.

Good, Bitsy thought. She needed the hubbub. It would occupy her mind, get her through the hours until she could act.

To test herself, she reached for the *U.S. News & World Report* she had bought at a drugstore near her room. It featured a big article on Senator Derek Winthrop's efforts to pass a bill to cut off foreign aid to South Africa. A picture showed Winthrop seated casually on the edge of his desk in the Senate Office Building, a flag on the wall behind him.

She forced herself to stare at the picture. Waited while her pulse went through a wild spate of pounding, then dropped back to her normal heart rate. She had been doing this all week, forcing back the fear she believed could weaken her, maybe even stop her.

He wouldn't notice when she edged close to him. There would be 110 women in uniforms exactly like hers. Deft, invisible servants who wouldn't really be seen by the thronging guests. If she was very careful, very swift, she might even be able to step away afterward. Pick up a tray, and fade into the crowd.

Derek Winthrop did deserve to die.

—— ◄► ——

Sam Provenzo, Marco, Lenny, and Joey were in the parking garage of Marco Towers, across the street from the Provenzo Building. The four men were seated in the back of a van. In the front sat the driver and a Provenzo soldier. More men occupied another van, parked behind them, and both vehicles were loaded with automatic weaponry.

Sam owned Marco Towers. The occupant of one of the apartments, Hank Monastero, the plant manager at the Provenzo Packing Plant, had been called and ordered to leave his place immediately without locking the door.

"Shit," Marco said impatiently. "How come we're sitting

around here with our thumbs up our asses? We got the weapons, we know he's up there. What more do you want, the key to the city?"

"I told you," Sam growled. What was it with these sons of his? Did they see only four steps ahead of themselves? "There's the kid involved, the *bambino*."

"So?"

"So, I told you, Marco, I don't hit babies. Will you get that through your thick skull? Now, I want to handle this good," Sam said. "No fuck-ups. Bernstein wants the kid back unharmed."

"Well, hey, let's just call Nico on the phone," Lenny said.

"Oh, sure, sure," Marco said. "Oh, great. We'll just phone him up and say, 'Hey, little bro, how's about coming up close to the window so we can really pick you off nice and easy without any fuss?' "

"Yeah," Sam snapped. He had aged ten years in the space of only a few hours. "Maybe we'll do it like that." Stepping out of the van, he directed several men to take up positions in cars on the street, two others to stand in the lobby of the Provenzo Building, and several more to stand in the lobby of Marco Towers. "Joey," Sam continued, "you stand on the street to supervise this. And Dominic and Jimmy, they'll go up to the apartment with the rest of us. *Capisce?*"

"It's raining out there," Joey said, shaking his glossy head of hair. "Shit, I hate rain."

Sam stared at his fashion-plate son. He shook his head, his jowls wobbling with the force of the motion. Then he swung his right arm, his wounded hand striking Joey's face. As the blow landed, pain shot up Sam's fingers and into his wrist.

Joey put a hand up to touch his cheek, opened his mouth to say something, then thought better of it.

"Don't you never complain about nothin' again!" Sam shouted. "Now, move your ass—all of you, goddamn it!"

—— ◄► ——

Richard watched Alexandra's cab take off down the street, its tires spitting water as it turned the corner.

"Richard! Richard, is that you standing there soaking wet?" He turned to see Mary Lee Wilde getting out of a second cab, unfolding a small umbrella. She wore a sea green suit with white piping and collar, the cut emphasizing her lean, rangy figure.

He swore to himself. The last thing he needed tonight was Mary Lee.

"Richard—Richard, I saw Alexandra in that cab. Where was she going? I've heard about Trip; I know, she told me. I was helping her on it. What's happening?"

He stared at the prize-winning author and journalist—a beautiful, cold woman who, even in the rain, managed to look in command of herself.

"Richard," Mary Lee coaxed, taking his arm. "I know you hate my being involved, but I am. I only want to help."

"I don't need your help," he said wearily, turning to go back into the building.

"Don't you? Where did Alexandra say she was going, anyway?"

"The hotel. Something about the party."

"Or something about the kidnapping," Mary Lee snapped.

He looked at her, groaning. "Oh, Jesus. Where were my brains? The way she kept trying to pull away from me—so anxious to leave . . . Why didn't I follow that cab?"

"There's still a way," Mary Lee said. "Come on, let's go up to your apartment. Maybe she left some kind of clue."

They took the elevator to the fifty-ninth floor. Inside the apartment, everything was as always, tabletops lustrous with polish, vases of pink roses perfuming the air. Richard led the way toward Alexandra's office but found only his wife's secretary switching off her computer.

"Do you know where my wife went?" Richard asked.

Judy seemed to shrink away from him. "Why, to the hotel. Something about the menu."

The main staircase that connected the two levels of the apartment was a curved work of art, once photographed in *Architectural Digest* with bouquets of flowers on its risers. Richard took the steps two at a time, leaving Mary Lee to hurry after him.

He hurried into their bedroom and stopped dead. Alexandra's suit lay flung over a chair, half on the floor. A floral painting lay face down on the carpet, and the safe door stood open. The contents looked as if they'd been hastily ransacked.

"What do you think she took out?" Mary Lee asked.

Richard was already at the safe. Reaching in, he pulled out the pearlized box he had bought in Paris. He jerked it open. Pink and white diamonds glittered in the light. He checked the clasp for the engraved initials that marked this as the original.

They were there.

Then on the floor he spotted the plainer box for the replica. It was empty.

He swore. "Why would she take out the fake one?" he said, more to himself than to Mary Lee.

"Because *they* want it, of course," Mary Lee said. "They told her to get the real one; she gave them the duplicate. Very clever, I'd say."

"Clever?" He stared at his wife's friend. Fear for Alexandra caused his voice to thicken. "She's a goddamned fool. Why didn't she tell me? I could have gone with her. How can we find out where she went?"

"Try this," Mary Lee said, picking up a scrap of paper from the floor. "Maybe subconsciously she did want us to know where she went."

Richard snatched it from her. There was an address scrawled in ballpoint pen.

——— ►◄ ———

The minute Jette's cab pulled up across from the Provenzo Building, she realized that something was very wrong. She could see through the glass doors that at least three men were guarding the lobby, not the usual bored security guard. There seemed to be more men lurking across the street, and another man sat in a car double-parked along the street. Also, she was almost positive that the man she saw walking toward the building was Nico's brother Joey.

She stepped from the cab into the rain, which had temporarily abated to a light drizzle.

"Joey!" she cried out impulsively. She forced a smile. "Joey, how are you? Don't you remember me? I'm Jette Michaud."

Dapper Joey Provenzo didn't even answer her, just gave her a fishy stare. She noticed there was a red mark on the left side of his face, as if someone had hit him hard.

Fingers of fear tightened on her esophagus. "Joey? Joey, I'm just a little worried about Nico. He—"

"Get out of here. Go home, cunt," Joey snapped. "Before you get in trouble." He disappeared into Marco Towers.

Jette stopped on the walk, stunned and frightened. She choked on a sob, unconsciously brushing rain off her hair. Then she got an odd feeling—as if someone were watching her.

She was on the opposite walk, which gave her an excellent

view of the Provenzo Building. She lifted her eyes to the eighth floor. To her shock, the living room window of Nico's apartment had been opened, and Nico stood looking down at her. Because of the interior lights, she could see him silhouetted clearly.

Out of the corner of her eye, she noticed the men across the street stiffen, their attention riveted on him, too. And then her mind made the necessary connections, and she realized the truth. They were planning to kill him.

She found herself backing up on the walk again, cupping her hands to her mouth. She called out his name. "Nico!"

He reappeared at the window. No, loomed there, his shape surprisingly black and solid.

She was crying now, because she didn't know what to say to him and knew she shouldn't be there in the street at all. The rain kept drizzling down, water reflecting in the street.

Please, she thought, *don't let them hurt my Nico.*

"Nico!" she called out again. "They're out here. They're in the lobby, and—and I saw your brother. I saw Joey!"

He looked down at her again. Maybe he hadn't heard. Rain fell on her upturned face.

"*Nico!*" she yelled despairingly.

— ◄► —

Up in the room, Nico stood at the window, boldly silhouetting himself for anyone who cared to look and not giving a flying fuck. He'd kept himself steadily coked up and was rocketing in the stratosphere, high on power. Standing on the eighth floor put him above everything, like an eagle on some rocky crag.

He looked down at the small, gesticulating figure of Jette. How stupid she looked, a *puttana* in her high heels and short skirt. Gusts of wind in the canyon between the buildings swept away most of her words. *Nico.* He heard that several times. He couldn't hear the rest.

Behind him on the couch, the child uttered a muffled, angry whimper. He was still straitjacketed in the white uniform, and Nico had added tape over his mouth to shut him up.

"Mmmmmmmm," the boy grunted.

"Hush," Nico snapped. He looked out of the window again, his anger now focusing on the small, forlorn, quixotic figure standing down there in the rain. What the hell was she saying?

Then the wind changed, and he heard a couple of the

words. Something about . . . yeah, *Joey*. And *brother*.

He couldn't believe what he heard. She was down there talking about *his family* like she was *on their side*. Hey, what was this? At his core, he felt frozen, like dry ice. He wasn't even aware that he had raised the rifle he held loosely in his hands.

The little shit. How could she do that to him?

"Nico!" Her voice rose in the rain.

The sound irritated him. She was a fly buzzing in his ear. He lifted the rifle and aimed, intending just to scatter a few bullets, make her dance a little, scare the living shit out of her.

He squeezed off a bullet and saw her jump and scream and nearly lose her balance.

"Nico!" she screamed at him. It was funny to see her stumbling like that, so he squeezed off another one. He didn't bother to aim much, just pulled the trigger.

Let her dance, yeah.

—— ▸◂ ——

Jette heard the first bullet land with an explosive ricocheting pop only a few feet away from her. At first she thought Nico had thrown a stone at her. Then she heard the echoing report of the rifle. *He had shot at her.*

There was another shot.

"No!" she screamed, and she tried to dodge, twisting her right ankle in her high heels, stumbling to her knees.

Several more bullets whipped past her, one only inches away from her outstretched hand. Jette screamed and tried to roll away from the explosions, but they were suddenly all around her. This was crazy—things like this just did not happen.

"Nico! For God's sake! Please!" she screamed at the building, at the senseless hail of bullets. "Help!"

She started to get to her feet when she felt a sudden pain in her right foot, white-hot. She fell to the pavement as blood welled out of her foot, gushing through her patterned panty hose.

"Oh, shit!" Jette cried, and began crawling toward the entrance of Marco Towers.

Another bullet. Holy shit! Even crawling, the pain in her foot was unbearable. *Please, God*, she prayed.

She was almost to the door. She glanced back and saw Nico leaning out of the window, either aiming or throwing something at her with deliberate precision. Maybe her picture, in its beautiful pewter frame.

Jette tried to crawl faster, but her body wouldn't oblige. Then something landed on her back with such force that it was like a whole-body explosion. The pain was a dimension beyond agony.

Jette passed out.

—— ▶◀ ——

The cabdriver had slowed, searching for the right address, a difficult feat in the gray, misty curtains of rain that kept falling.

Oddly, Alexandra didn't feel frightened. Her mind had gone into some sort of protective mode, insulating her from her fear. She was dimly aware of this, and glad for it. She wanted all her energy for getting her son back.

The cab pulled up to the building with a jerk and screech of tires, and she paid the driver and jumped out.

Alexandra entered the lobby of the ten-story apartment building for which Nico had given her the address. It was new and modern but not nearly as nice as the Provenzo Building next to it, or even the Marco Towers across the street. In the lobby were a commissary store and two maddeningly slow elevators.

She rode to the eighth floor. Exiting the elevator, she stepped into a cheaply carpeted corridor lined with doors. Behind one of them she could hear a small dog yapping. As Nico instructed her, she went to apartment 808 and rang the buzzer.

Within seconds, the door opened. Nico pulled her inside and reached behind her to snap the arrangement of deadbolts and chain locks that secured the door.

What a handsome man he was, with his chiseled features and blue eyes set under thick, straight brows. No wonder Jette had been so smitten with him.

However, his cheeks seemed flushed, and there was a shiny gloss to his dilated eyes. He was breathing fast and seemed terribly excited. She wondered what he was on. Speed? Cocaine?

He was wearing a shoulder holster, she saw, and carried a rifle.

He asked her, "Did you bring the necklace?"

"Yes." She clutched at her neck, terrified he would snatch the necklace and shove her out the door again. "I want to see my son."

"You'll see him if you've been straight with me. Give me the necklace."

She faced him angrily. "Not until I see my little boy."

He didn't bother to reply but just grabbed the neck of her T-shirt, ripping downward. It was an act as violent as a slap.

"All right," she said, her eyes filling with angry tears. "Take it, but I'll have to unfasten the clasp myself."

He took it from her almost before she had it off her neck, grabbing it greedily. She watched the sparkling zircons swing from his hand, feeling a spurt of terror. What if he recognized they weren't diamonds?

But he didn't seem to notice. He examined the necklace briefly, then thrust it into a pocket.

Her eyes slid away from him, and for the first time she looked at the apartment. There was no furniture except for an old twin bed that didn't even have sheets and a huge cabinet that had been pulled partially away from the wall. He couldn't live here. No one lived here; the place smelled unused, and, she saw, the kitchenette was stacked with cardboard boxes and junk.

"Come on," he said, grabbing her arm again. Bewildered, Alexandra allowed herself to be pulled toward the ugly cabinet.

He gave her a shove, and Alexandra stumbled forward, managing to catch herself before she fell through the open space. She had to take a large step down. Suddenly she was standing in a fully decorated, high-tech bedroom with white carpeting and a geometric, black-and-white spread.

My God. She was in the building next door. She stopped where she was, startled and even more frightened.

Then she heard a muffled sound coming from the adjoining room—the noise a child might make with his face in a pillow.

"Trip?" Her voice quivered.

The sound again.

"*Tripper?*"

Another smothered cry.

She tore loose from Nico's grip and ran toward the sound. She saw a flash in front of her—Nico's foot thrust out. She fell sprawling.

"Not until *I* tell you, bitch," Nico said, hitting her in her left side with the stock of the rifle.

"Here we are—this is the right number," Mary Lee said, squinting to read building numbers through the layer of water that blurred the windshield of the limousine.

"Son of a bitch," she added. "Isn't this supposed to be Mafia territory? I hear they own several apartment buildings in this area, and none of the residents will call the police, no matter what they see or hear."

Richard was on the car phone, dialing the number he had been given by Mo Bernstein. It was picked up on the second ring.

"Yeah?" a man said curtly.

"This is Richard Cox. Mo Bernstein told me to call. I want to talk to Sam Provenzo."

There was the rattle of the phone being tossed down, a pause, and then the deep, gravelly voice. "This is Sam Provenzo."

"Richard Cox here. My wife got a phone call, and she left. I would like some assistance in dealing with this. Here's where I am now." Richard gave the address.

"We know," Provenzo said. "We can see you from here."

Richard felt his heart pound. "Where are you?"

"In an apartment. Across the street. Park the limousine on the street, and enter through the lobby. Ninth floor, first apartment on the left."

"I have someone with me," Richard said, and Mary Lee, who had been listening intently, gave a startled movement.

"Yeah, we saw. Leave her in the car."

"Fine. As long as she'll be safe down here."

"No!" Mary Lee grabbed Richard's arm. "I won't stay here, if that's what you're talking about. I'm coming up with you."

"Shit," Richard said. "You would. OK, then, damn it, but I want you to keep your mouth shut and act invisible. These are Mafia, and they've got a lot on their mind. They're only helping me because Bernstein forced them to."

A few minutes later, they were in the elevator on their way up to the apartment occupied by the Provenzos, the cab jiggling slightly as it moved upward.

"This is just so incredible," Mary Lee said, digging into her purse and bringing out a small microcassette tape recorder. "Thank God I've got extra tapes. I'm going to get all of this down for—"

"Are you fucking crazy?" He knocked the recorder and tiny tape out of her hand. "They don't really give a damn about my little boy, or Alexandra. They're only doing this because they have to. Do you get that? Do you comprehend?"

"Oh, I get it, all right. But I've got a great memory, and they can't stop me from using that, can they?"

The elevator was almost to their floor. Richard gazed at the woman Alexandra had loved as a friend for years. "Listen to me, Mary Lee Wilde, and listen good. You keep your mouth shut and stay the hell out of the way. You are no friend of Alexandra's, lady, and after this is over, I want you out of her life. For good! Get the picture?"

———— ◄► ————

In the meat locker, Brownie stirred, groaning. She had heard sounds. There were voices, and the echo of footsteps along the cement flooring of the outer part of the packing plant.

She fought to open her eyelids, but they felt heavy, gritty, weighted down by the blood that had dried on her face. She felt weak, as if her arms and legs were not quite attached to her body. And every time she breathed, she heard a horrible gurgling sound.

She was dying. She felt it quite clearly. Where was Trip? Was he dead, lying crumpled and bloody beside her? Was that why she heard no sound from him? Brownie sucked with difficulty at the air, struggling to breathe. *She had to know.*

Torturously, fighting off unconsciousness, Brownie managed to raise her head a few inches. The room was empty.

Trip might not be dead. Maybe they had taken him somewhere else. Brownie collapsed on the cement, sobbing her gratitude. Her breath caught, and she started to choke. She lay there gasping, trying to breathe.

"*Caramba! Hijo de puta!*" said a voice. "*Mira, amigo, una mujer aparece muerta!*"

Brownie did not hear.

———— ◄► ————

Half-lying on the floor, her side stinging from the blow, Alexandra looked up at Nico. He stood above her, legs braced, grinning. He no longer looked handsome. The wave of anger she felt was so intense that she almost threw up.

OK, she thought. She could play his game, and play it even better.

"Please," she begged in as humble a tone as she could force. "I plead with you, I just want to hold my son. For a minute. I will do anything you say. *Anything*," she added.

He reached down and yanked her up with such force that she thought her arms were going to tear out of their sockets.

In the living room, he let go and gave her a push. Alexandra looked around the large room.

Guns were everywhere—lying on the couch, stacked on the floor, their sinister barrels sticking out of cardboard boxes. Her eyes traveled to the couch, where she saw a white bundle that looked like a stack of towels. Until it moved.

Her heart stopped.

"Trip!" she screamed, and rushed to him. She was sobbing with joy and fear. "Oh, God, Tripper—!"

He was so little, pitifully trussed in the rough cotton cloth like a bundle of laundry. There was even tape wound across his face, nearly covering his nose as well as his mouth. His huge eyes, the only part of him that was visible, beseeched her.

Alexandra was sobbing as she found the knots in the fabric and tore at them with her fingernails. As the knots came loose, the child gave an urgent moan and tried to pull the tape from his own mouth.

"How *could* you?" she cried to Nico. She found an edge of the tape and gave it a tug. It was caught in Trip's hair. His eyes widened, and tears rolled down his cheeks, but he didn't utter a sound.

He collapsed against her, his eyes filled with tears. Alexandra held him, kissing his eyes, his nose, again and again.

"Mommy, they hurt my nanny; they killed my nanny," Trip finally cried. He clutched her with more strength than she believed a six-year-old could possess.

"They what? Oh, baby, oh, no!"

"They put a knife inside her and made her bleed. *He* did," Trip said, pointing to Nico.

Alexandra's heart froze. She looked up. Nico stood over them.

Panic burned in her chest.

"I'm thirsty," Trip said.

"Oh, baby . . ."

"Want a drink."

"Keep him quiet, lady, or I'll shut him up for you," Nico growled, his voice a whiplash.

Trip was instantly silent, and Alexandra's heart ached for what he must have gone through to be so quick to obey.

Nico said, "Now I'll tell you what we're going to do. I've got a car in the—"

The phone rang.

Alexandra saw the color slowly drain from Nico's face until it was ashen. He seemed to know unconsciously that it was bad news.

The telephone rang again. Uttering a curse, Nico reached for it.

———— ►◄ ————

The door of the apartment was opened by an Italian man with discolored teeth.

"You Cox?"

"Yes."

The place was full of men ranged at the window near curtains that would partially shield them from view, pacing the floor, or standing in the kitchen, loading high-powered rifles. One was at the telephone, speaking in a low voice.

Seeing them, Richard's heart sank. Jesus—all they needed were flak jackets.

"Sam Provenzo," said an older man, coming forward. Richard recognized him; he had seen Provenzo's picture in the paper in articles about organized crime. In person, Provenzo had a curiously flat, dangerous face that would have been impassive except for the eyes. These were red-rimmed, alive with smoldering anger.

"Richard Cox." The two men shook hands. Despite a bandage on his right hand, Provenzo had one of those steel-vise handshakes. Richard squeezed harder.

"This is Mary Lee Wilde," Richard added.

"She can wait in the bedroom," Provenzo said. "Down the hall. Door shut. Curtains drawn. *Capisce*? There's something in there she can do. A woman's touch."

Richard didn't know what the man was talking about, but he said, "Go on," giving the unwilling Mary Lee a push.

To her credit, she went quietly. Fighting his fear, Richard

turned to Provenzo. "What is going on? Please, fill me in."

The man spoke dispassionately, as if Nico were a total stranger. "First, his apartment—across there, one floor down, to the left—is an arsenal. Automatic machine guns, you name it. His hobby."

"My God," Richard said, paling.

"He could hole up in there for years if he wanted to. I don't think he wants to."

Richard swallowed. "Is my wife in there? My son?"

"We think they are. My son, Nico, *stupido*," Provenzo's lips curled. "He has moved back and forth in front of the window several times, and we think we saw her, too. Somehow he got her in without passing her up through the lobby. We don't know how."

A guilty sickness filled Richard. Jesus, what kind of a bargain had he made with Bernstein? "Your plans?" Richard said, looking toward the window, where a man was attaching a silencer onto a rifle. "You're not planning to—Jesus, you *are*."

"When he walks in front of the window again, we take him out," Provenzo said. "This neighborhood, it belongs to my family, eh? We own much property around here; these people know it, and they are loyal to us."

"But you can't shoot in there!" he cried desperately. "For Christ's sake, Provenzo—my wife is in there! My little boy!"

Heavily, Provenzo said, "We know this. But I have two men who were in Vietnam, and one was certified as a sharpshooter. All we need is a clear shot at my son. He has become a mad dog. He is endangering others."

Richard was silent, realizing what he was being told. He had stepped into a world he knew little about, and now Alexandra and his son might have to pay for his error. "Provenzo, can't you call over there? Talk to Nico?"

"Yes, we can. We are on the phone to him now. He is refusing to turn over the *bambino*."

"Make him put Alexandra on the line."

"What?"

"Yes," Richard improvised desperately. "Tell him . . . tell him I have to talk to her about the ransom we're willing to pay. Say anything, but get her on the phone. I want to tell her to stay away from the windows. I want to give her some instructions. I want to tell her how to protect herself so she doesn't get hit."

◄►

Angry at being pushed aside, Mary Lee stalked down the hall toward the bedroom where she had been told to wait.

She stepped into the room and decided not to flick on the light. She didn't want the room to be a target.

A haunting moan filled the air. Mary Lee looked down. A sliver of light from the hallway fell across someone lying on the floor. Mary Lee stared, her eyes adjusting to the dim light.

Jette.

Horrified surprise flooded through Mary Lee, followed by panic.

"Please," Jette muttered, only half-conscious. "Don't, Nico. Don't . . ." Her voice slid into unintelligible pleadings.

Mary Lee knelt beside her friend, feeling something damp and sticky cling to the bent knee of her hose. There was blood on the carpet.

She looked around the room, which evidently was used as an office. Eventually she was able to make out a small desk lamp. She grabbed it, placed it on the floor, and cautiously flicked on the switch.

A cone of light illuminated Jette's prone body. She lay on her stomach, her peach-colored silk blouse spattered with blood. It was ripped apart at the shoulder blade in tatters that revealed a huge laceration beneath. Jette wore no shoes, and her legs were scratched and bloody; more red was pooled around her right foot.

There was another moan.

"Jette?" Mary Lee reached under her fashionable skirt for her ecru half-slip, trimmed with delicate lace. She pulled it off and, with difficulty, managed to tear one of the seams apart, creating a long strip of material. She yanked at it, ripping it in two.

She managed to get one makeshift bandage on Jette's back, but as soon as she pressed it in, Jette uttered such a howl of pain that Mary Lee jumped back.

"Jette? What *happened* to you?"

"Shot me," Jette croaked. Her voice sounded weaker than before. "Nico. Then d-dropped something on me. God . . . it hurts."

"But why? Why would he have done that?" Mary Lee said, realizing to her shame that she was a reporter first and foremost.

"On . . . the walk . . . wouldn't listen . . ." Jette gave a little sigh and passed out again.

Shaken, Mary Lee left the bedroom and walked down the

hall. The men were arguing, grouped around Sam Provenzo. A thickset man of about forty was standing near the hallway. "Please," Mary Lee begged. "The woman in there . . . she needs a doctor."

The man turned. "She'll get one when we're done here."

"But she needs help now! She's bleeding! I can't stop it."

He shrugged. His look became menacing. "She'll last. We brought her up here, didn't we? She's a *puttana*; they always make it. Now get back there with her, bitch, and *you* take care of her."

Unwillingly, Mary Lee returned to the bedroom. Jette's condition frightened her because she didn't know what to do. There was a telephone on the desk, and it occurred to her that she could call the police herself. Why hadn't she thought of it before?

Decisively she stepped over Jette and picked up the black princess-style phone. But someone was already on the line. She hung on to the receiver, listening intently.

—— ◄► ——

"Nico," Sam Provenzo said into the phone. "Son, you must put the *bambino* and the woman in the elevator and send them downstairs. Then all will be well."

Richard, standing nearby, didn't hear Nico's reply. But it wasn't hard to guess it from the thwarted, angry expression that crossed the elder Provenzo's face.

"The necklace is fine. If you give back the child and the woman, we will talk about it," Provenzo went on. "We need to talk, Nicolo. You have gone too far."

"*Fuck you, old man!*" Nico screamed into the phone. Richard could hear him, even from where he stood.

Provenzo's eyes darkened, his mouth tightening. He looked heavy and very dangerous. "Never talk to me like that, Nicolo."

"*You're weak, old man! You're over, done, finished!*"

"Nothing is over until it is over. Nico, put the woman on the line."

Nico's voice became less loud, and Richard didn't hear the response.

Provenzo said thickly, "Why? Because her husband wishes to tell her about a ransom payment. She has brought the necklace, but he has decided to pay more than that. Yes. He will talk to you. But her first. That is his condition."

There was a long, nerve-racking pause.

Numbly Richard realized that Provenzo had handed over the telephone to him.

"Lexy?" He spoke into the receiver. His voice shook. "Punkie, are you there?"

"Richard." Her response was low, husky, infinitely dear. He hung onto the phone, averting his face from the Mafia *padrone* so as not to reveal the naked emotion that swept through him.

"Is Tripper OK?"

Her voice was tight, on the verge of a sob, but still controlled. "Yes . . . oh, yes . . ."

"Lexy, you have to do everything I tell you," he said urgently. "You have to get yourself and Tripper as far away from the windows as you can. Do you understand me? *As far away from the windows as possible.*"

"Yes, I—" Then there was a sound as the phone was snatched away.

"Fuck you, Cox," came the harsh, low voice of Nico. "You're as bad as my old man, do you hear? He's got no balls. Just like you!"

Richard silently handed the telephone to Provenzo.

— ◄► —

In the other room, Mary Lee was just dialing 911 when the door burst open and Sam Provenzo appeared, his face reddened with fury. "I heard a click. A goddamn' fucking click!"

The Mafioso lunged toward her and snatched the telephone out of her hand.

"You do one thing to ruin this, *one thing*," he rasped, "and I'm gonna ruin that fuckin' pretty face of yours. Did ya hear me, you dumb broad? I ain't forgot how to throw acid, and it does the job, if you know what I mean. And for sure you won't be doing any more TV shows. Understand?" he bellowed.

She stared at him, her blood curdled.

"Take care of *her*," he added, gesturing toward Jette. Then he was gone, slamming the door behind him.

On the floor, Jette moaned deeply. Mary Lee lowered herself to the floor, her body shaking. Hot tears stung her eyes. There was a blanket flung over a day bed in the room, and after a long moment, Mary Lee remembered that a warm blanket was an antidote for shock.

She got up, folded the blanket over double, and arranged it around Jette. Then she sat down again. She reached out and took Jette's hand in hers. It felt cool and clammy.

Mary Lee bit back a sob. She was going to miss out on the best damned story of her life.

—— ▶◀ ——

Nico was snorting two lines of cocaine, using a clean $50 bill. He sniffed deeply, his nostrils flaring. Alexandra could see his chest expand as the cocaine locked into his system.

"Aren't you thirsty?" Alexandra whispered to Trip, hoping Nico couldn't hear. Richard's warning over the phone had terrified her, but she fought back her hysteria. If she allowed any weakness at all, she and Trip could both die.

"Want a drink," she quietly prompted her son, nudging the little boy in his ribs, from her hunched-over position on the couch.

But he was definitely bright, and she saw his eyes light up, acknowledging her instructions. "I'm thirsty," he wailed loudly. "Mommy . . . I want some water!"

"He wants water," she said to Nico, pulling herself up. "I just want to get him a drink. And maybe some food. I'll cook something."

"No, you won't cook."

Her heart dropped down to her knees. He was probably afraid she'd grab a knife or something and use it against him. How long did she have to get them away from the front of the apartment? Minutes? Seconds? She pictured bullets bursting in, exploding all around them, blood spurting.

She spoke with rapid desperation. "I promise, I swear I won't touch anything; I'll just find a glass. My little boy hasn't had anything to drink in hours. He's only a baby, Nico; he is just a first-grader. For God's sake, have a little compassion!"

She waited tensely. He seemed to think this over.

"Get me a beer," he said finally.

"What?"

"A beer!" he snapped. "Are you deaf? The kid can have a can of pop."

She scooped up Trip, carrying him to the kitchen with her, and she placed him flat on the floor behind the refrigerator, which she hoped might afford him some protection. She patted her son, indicating he was to stay there. It was an eerie moment. She sensed Nico watching her, and she realized he knew why she was doing this.

Trip watched her with alert eyes. He looked exactly like Richard, with the same wide forehead and strong chin, even the same chin cleft she loved so much.

"Get the fucking beer," Nico told her.

"If any shooting starts, I want you to run out of here," she told Trip in a fast whisper.

"Without you, Mommy?"

"Trip, you can. You have to. Daddy—"

Machine-gun bullets sprayed through the window, stitching the couch where, only seconds before, Trip and Alexandra had been sitting.

Nico staggered backward, blood gushing from his right thigh to soak his black houndstooth check pants. As Trip and Alexandra watched in horror, he lunged toward the kitchen, lurching on his injured leg. His eyes looked shocked, glazed. He was carrying one of the guns and still wore his shoulder holster, the butt of a .45 protruding from it.

"To the bedroom," he instructed her hoarsely. "The hole— the exit. We'll leave by the other building."

More bullets smashed behind them.

"Mommy," Trip sobbed in terror.

Dragging her son by the arm, Alexandra started toward the hall, then felt herself being violently grabbed.

"Help me walk," Nico ordered. He was breathing so fast she thought he was having a heart attack. "Help me, goddamn it! Or I'll kill you right here."

She did as she was ordered.

They left through the hacked-away hole, took the elevator in the adjoining building, and entered the municipal parking structure.

The garage, between cement pillars partly open to the elements, gleamed with a wet sheen. The space echoed unpleasantly with Nico's jagged, wheezing breaths. He must have taken too much cocaine. He seemed on the edge of physical as well as mental collapse.

"Faster!" he screamed at her, pounding on her. "My car's on the next level!"

She struggled on, her son at her side, Nico's weight pushing her down. Her heart was hammering from the exertion. But then they were at the top of the ramp, and he pointed to a car about thirty feet away.

"Mine," he gasped. "Different . . . they won't recognize it."

They reached the car. Nico, groaning and swearing with pain, bent over and scooped up Trip. He pressed the boy to his chest, so Trip's legs dangled in the air.

"Mommy! Mommy!" Trip kicked wildly.

Nico smacked him.

"In the car, lady. I hold the kid; you drive."

He yanked open the car door and shoved her into the driver's seat.

Nico staggered around to the other side of the car, supporting himself on its roof. He climbed in and clamped a whimpering Trip in his arms. He jammed the barrel of the gun into the child's side.

"*Drive*," Nico ordered. "I don't care anymore, do you know that? I don't fucking care. Just get me the hell out of here. And if we get caught, I'm going to shoot this kid. Do you get it, sweetheart?"

Alexandra looked at her little boy, took the key Nico handed her, shoved it in the ignition, and started the car.

The motor revved up immediately, and she could tell by the feel that it was far more powerful than it looked.

She decided to exit from the parking structure in a slow and normal manner, so they would not attract any attention.

Alexandra pulled onto the street and turned right. But as she did so, a man sitting in a van along the street rolled down the window and began shooting at them.

"The other way!" Nico screamed at her. "Back through the garage! Out the other side!"

Desperately she executed a U-turn, heading back into the parking structure, squealing her tires through the crowded lower level.

"Oh, shit!" Nico kept screaming, jamming the gun tighter into Trip.

She pulled out of the other exit. The rain had faded to mere mist, and the street looked clear. She allowed herself a tinge of relief. Quickly she turned left, deciding to head toward the nearest expressway. That was when she saw the headlights behind her. High ones, as if from a van. Another set of headlights was behind that.

"Drive, for Christ's sake!" Nico screamed at her. "Drive,

goddamn it!''

She didn't need urging. She floorboarded the Lincoln.

— ⋈ —

"What the *hell?*" Sam Provenzo cried out, banging his fist on Marco's shoulder as Marco drove hunched over the wheel of the Chevy van. "Where the *hell* is she going?"

"Shit, *I* don't know," Marco muttered, swinging the wheel wildly left to follow the old Lincoln.

"She's a goddamned woman!" Sam screamed. "A woman driver, for Christ's sake! Catch up with her, Marco, so we can shoot her tires out."

"I can't," he yelled.

Sam barked out orders. "Come on! Jesus H. Christ, Marco, come on, come on, before the state police spot her. She's in the outside lane now, pull up, pull up!"

"I am, but that car's been souped up, and we're in a cruddy van."

"I don't give a son-of-a-bitchin' fuck. Catch up to her!"

A car length behind them was the other van, carrying Cox, Joey, Lenny, and some of the others. Shit, it should be easy to shoot a set of tires out, especially when the driver was a broad. Marco narrowed his eyes, seeing Alexandra zip in and out of traffic, her speed at least 100.

Shit—a truck was switching lanes ahead of them. Marco swerved into the center lane just in time to avoid being crunched by a Mobil 10-wheel oil tanker.

— ⋈ —

The taillights of the cars were oddly hypnotic, blinking and red. Nico could hear his own breath, deep, full, and strong. On his left knee, the child sat rigidly, his hair smelling very familiar, a little-boy odor. Nico smelled him and thought of himself. Too long ago, too young.

"Get away from them, or it's all over for baby boy here," he growled at the woman who handled the wheel. "I can. I'll shoot him in the stomach, and it won't be pretty."

She flashed him a look—not terrified as he expected, but almost calm. Her profile was dimly etched, the night creating pools of shadows along the curve of her cheekbone.

━━━ ►◄ ━━━

You feel the car, Giancarlo had once said. *You feel it with your body. Then you must allow your instinct to direct you . . .*

Alexandra had never been so terrified in her life, but she had gone into a strange, icy calm. She was at one with the car, the steering wheel an extension of her body. She barely heard Nico's shouts or Trip's frightened cries.

How long could she keep up this nightmarish ride without killing all of them?

Oh, God. Brake lights blinked on ahead, dozens of them. She reacted instantly. There was an exit sign on the right, and she swerved into the next lane, cutting off a Toyota, whose driver blasted his horn at her. She nearly overcut the exit but managed to compensate, making it on the shoulder. The wet road caused the tires to skid and shimmy.

"Shit, motherfucker!" Nico shrieked as the two vans followed them off the ramp.

A huge Bekins moving van exited just ahead of them and was taking up the whole exit ramp, creeping along at twenty-five miles per hour. Alexandra braced herself and pumped the brakes, feeling the shudder as the car fought gravity. The big truck body blocked them as effectively as a wall.

"Go around it!" Nico yelled. "Go around it, goddamn it!"

She yanked on the wheel and spun past the big truck, perilously close to the asphalt wall. The van behind her did the same thing. Its yellow headlights filled the car, reflecting off her rearview mirror like a laser beam.

Suddenly the Lincoln jerked violently. The steering wheel grabbed, pulling wildly to the right.

"The tire!" Nico wailed. "Fuck, they shot out the tire!"

━━━ ►◄ ━━━

Richard sat in the back of the second van, watching in horror and a kind of terrible pride as his wife did the best job of driving he'd ever seen outside of the movies.

Now he saw the Lincoln pop and jump on its springs, still moving but sagging to one side as someone in the first van shot out its right tire. He knew it was all over. He realized that tears were running down his face and had been for the past five or ten minutes.

Nico Provenzo was suicidal. And these Mafia assholes were forcing his hand. How could Alexandra and Trip survive this?

As soon as the van jerked to a stop, Richard lunged forward, pushed the door handle, and jumped out. He was crying as he went running toward the Lincoln. The driver of the moving van had gotten out of his truck, too. As Richard ran, he heard a distant, high-pitched siren.

The police. Too damned late.

— ►◄ —

Alexandra heard the police sirens, but they registered only as extraneous sound.

What else was there to do but brake? She did so, her mind still disconnected, still in that fearless racing mode. Every muscle in her body hurt from being so tightly clenched for so long.

"No, no, no, no, no," Nico moaned in her ear. "Don't stop now; don't stop! I told you, *don't stop!*"

"We've only got three tires. I can't drive on the rim."

She bumped to a halt but left the car in drive. It was over now, she thought.

Nico was hyperventilating, and her child was trapped in his tight, spasmodic grip. He twisted to peer out of the rear window.

Behind them, the vans had pulled cautiously up, sheltering themselves behind the bulk of the Bekins truck. Men jumped out, carrying Uzis. A man ran toward them—Richard? Nico had seen them, too. His eyes got even wilder, and he clutched at the gun he held, raising it.

Alexandra's mind spun. He was going to do it. Maybe he had intended to do so all along.

"Nicolo!" a voice called, full of pain and heavy grief.

"Stop! Get away! I'll blow the kid!"

"Nicolo, listen. Don't murder a baby."

"Get away, old man, or I'll blow your fucking head off!"

Sam Provenzo stepped back and sheltered himself behind the moving van.

Alexandra watched Nico's head swivel back and forth, his eyes glazed, his hands twitchy. He was about to explode, probably within a second or two. He would kill first Trip, then her, then himself.

"Get ready!" Nico screamed, she did not know at whom.

"No!" she screamed back.

He raised the gun, trying to position it in the narrow confines of the car.

Alexandra screamed again. Then, in a seizure of fear, her body reacted. She rammed her foot down on the accelerator, putting her entire weight on it.

Anything, anything, her mind shouted.

The Lincoln shot forward. Into the cement wall. A shot rang out.

16

The Party

The *Chicago Tribune*'s Dana Chen pushed her way through the crowds that had gathered outside the Fitzgerald Hotel, her photographer, Al Cole, following in her wake.

It was bedlam, the year's biggest story. All the networks were here, and tempers frayed as news crews jockeyed to get as close as possible to the silk-canopied banquet entrance of the hotel.

Shit, thought Dana, she had to get closer than this. She couldn't see anything here but the tops of the limousines that had pulled up through the mounted police cordon. Big, tall Fred Manfra, from ABC network radio, was standing directly in front of her with Byron McGregor of CBS Radio News and J. P. McCarthy of ABC Television.

"Lady—lady—watch your damned elbow!" a fat man snapped at her. Dana slipped past him, making a space for Al. She might be tiny, but she was determined, and this was her town.

Fighting to the front of the crowd, Dana felt a lilt of excitement. She had covered plenty of society events but nothing like this.

Gruesome scenes from the five o'clock newscasts flashed before her eyes. The stretcher covered with a blood-soaked sheet; Richard Cox, his face taut with a soundless cry of rage and anguish.

Overhead a helicopter hovered, blades chopping air.

"OK, OK," Al said behind her, two cameras hanging from him. "What shot do you want now? Who's this arriving?"

Dana peered ahead. "I think . . . yeah, it's Farrah Fawcett." The actress, dressed in clinging white crepe, stepped from her white limousine. Her famous mane of hair reflected the popping flashbulbs. Ryan O'Neal was instantly at her side.

Two security guards hustled a protester carrying a placard saying *Feed Children, Not Rich People,* to the periphery of the crowd. Another sign read, *We Didn't Strike This Time—Wait 4 Years.*

Two handsome couples stepped out of a silver Rolls-Royce. The women, luxuriant hair flowing, were dressed in elaborate Scaasi gowns, one black, the other midnight blue, diamonds and sapphires gleaming at their throats.

"That's Donald and Ivana," Dana nudged Al. "With Mercedes and Sid."

The cars continued to disgorge passengers. Malcolm Forbes back with Elizabeth Taylor, ravishing in violet silk. Jay Winthrop and Felicia Revson. Clint Eastwood with his new girlfriend. At the sight of the stone-faced star, women in the crowd began to scream. A phalanx of police officers and security men surged together, forming a protective cordon.

"I can't believe they got Clint Eastwood here," Al said.

"Al, they got anybody they wanted to. Jeez, if a bomb fell on the Fitz Hotel tonight, *People* magazine would have to go out of business."

Another limo approached, deep, lustrous, shining black. Shrieks greeted it.

"Jette!" someone screamed. "It's Jette!"

"Move it, Al," Dana snapped. "I want to get up close, damn it."

"So she's here. I was worried when I heard about her on the news."

The small figure of Jette Michaud emerged from the black limousine. She wore a bright emerald formfitting Fred Hayman gown. Her escort, Cliff Alsburg, came around from the other side to assist her and handed Jette a pair of crutches.

They weren't ordinary crutches. These were covered with the same emerald fabric as her gown, with rhinestones embedded in its design.

Leaning on them, Jette pulled herself to a standing position. All around her, the crowd cheered wildly. Jette waved at her fans, her face a megawatt smile.

"You gotta admit, she's got the looks," said Al, snapping away.

—— ▶◀ ——

In a conference room set off the main ballroom area, 110 cocktail waitresses were being briefed by the maître d'.

Bitsy sighed tensely. Tomorrow at this hour, it would all be over. Derek Winthrop would lie in state in some Brookline funeral home. Newspapers would eulogize what a wonderful Senator he'd been. He would be compared to Bobby, Teddy, and Martin. Whoever.

She was going to be more than a footnote in a history book, it occurred to Bitsy for the first time. Actually, Winthrop's death would even change history a little bit.

From the ballroom came the sweet sound of an orchestra beginning to tune its instruments. A collective ripple passed through the assembled women.

Bitsy felt a stab of fear. Unconsciously her hand went to her face, to her right eye, where the orbit had been shattered by the bullet and laboriously repaired by plastic surgeons.

For years she had lived a fantasy about what would happen now, embroidering every detail in her mind. Now it would be reality.

—— ▶◀ ——

Dolly Rutledge hurried into the ballroom, lifting the skirt of her coral Mary McFadden gown with its fluid crepe pleats.

For better or for worse, the evening was under way. Even now, Prince Charles and Princess Diana were in the Green Room, the VIP lounge. President Bush had just arrived by Presidential helicopter and would be joining them shortly.

Guests had begun to arrive and were waiting in the reception area until the Prince and Princess were ready to make their entrance.

Now Dolly drew a deep breath and looked almost astonished at what she and Alexandra had wrought. The enormous ballroom had been transformed into a moonlit bower. Thousands of yards of cream silk had been looped up and tented to the chandeliers. The fabric shone with thousands of winking Italian lights and more thousands of Austrian crystals, tiny sparkles of light that shot fire whenever a breeze shifted the fabric.

Flowers were everywhere, from clear, almost blue-white to richest ivory. There were lush white roses and Princess Di roses tinged with the faintest blush. Orchids, large and small, in magnificent sprays.

Dolly walked further in, making a thorough inspection. In the first two ballrooms, tables for ten had been set up, with a head table that seated thirty. The tables were draped with ivory moiré, a gossamer cloth laid over that, the sides shirred in Austrian swags pulled up with "love knots" of satin ribbons.

Dolly was especially proud of the stunning centerpieces. They varied slightly from table to table, but each contained lush white roses and orchids, strung with more of the winking little lights.

She gazed upward at the two stages, now filled with undulating bodies. The dancers' limbs twined together, spines arched, their bodies an arabesque of light.

"Oh," sighed Dolly, entranced.

— ▶◀ —

Darryl Boyer was wearing a splash of fuchsia by Bob Mackie. Strapless, it barely kissed her breasts. At her side was Court Frank.

She heaved a sigh of relief. Finally! She was here! She glanced around, awed.

"Smashing, huh, babe?" Court took her arm in a proprietary manner. "But where's the receiving line, huh? Where's our Lady Di?"

"Probably putting on her tiara," Darryl said. "More to the point, where's Sid Cohen?"

They peered around the gathering crowd. As at Academy Awards night, every female was dressed to outdo every other one. A photographer from *Women's Wear Daily* was already at work, snapping the good, the bad, and the ugly. Darryl spotted David Kwan moving through the crowd, a Eurasian beauty on his arm—Mei Lee, a star from one of his karate films.

"Oh, there's Kwan," Court said. "Who's the little pretty with him?"

"Who cares?" Darryl snapped, moving out of his grasp. She was annoyed when Court slid his arm through hers again.

"You're my date, cutie, and you're not giving me the slip. I'm sticking to you like glue. What do you mean, who cares? Kwan gave you a comeback, babe, when you were cat piss in

Hollywood. But you always were ungrateful, Darryl, baby."

Ungrateful? When she had screwed his brains out for the past week? Darryl narrowed her eyes, methodically searching the crowd. Where was Sid, damn it?

She spotted Kenneth Jay Lane, very British looking, talking to Kirk and Anne Douglas and Betsy Bloomingdale.

"There he is," Court suddenly said. "He's just walking in."

Darryl watched the short, pot-bellied man stroll into the room.

"Let's go over," Darryl urged.

"Wait a minute."

"What?"

Court Frank grinned. A malicious excitement danced in his eyes. "I know Sid; he's one of my closest friends, Darryl. I've got influence with him. You didn't know that, did you?"

"No." Darryl stared at her escort.

"Well, pussycat, it's this way. You aren't going near him—not unless you promise to move in with me."

"Whaaat?"

"I drive a hard bargain, girlie-girl. I like your style, if you know what I mean. So what do you say?"

Darryl hesitated only a few brief seconds. She could always renege on her deal with Court Frank later. Sid Cohen was here, and she'd had no idea Frank was so influential with him.

"Sure," she promised without missing a beat. She smiled brilliantly, swaying her hips in languorous, practiced movement as she and Court approached the studio head.

— ▶◀ —

Peter Duchin's orchestra finished the last notes of Bill Conti's theme from the James Bond movie *For Your Eyes Only* and launched into "I'll Be Seeing You," by Sammy Fain. The air rang with laughter and conversation.

Sam Provenzo glanced at his watch, wondering when the Prince and Princess were going to get their asses out here so they could meet the people and he could go home. He wanted to be here about as much as he needed a second asshole.

"Goddamn," said Mo Bernstein. He moved closer to Sam, holding a scotch. Two bodyguards in rented evening wear hovered awkwardly a few yards away, as uncomfortable as their bosses. Mo added, "Ever seen anything like this before, man? In-fucking-credible."

The two men and their wives stood with their backs to the wall, trying to pretend they hadn't noticed that none of the other party guests had spoken to them but had, in fact, been giving them startled, incredulous glances all night.

Muori, maledette, Sam had muttered only an hour ago over the sheet-draped form in the bed in the intensive care unit of Michael Reese Hospital. *Traditore. Fucking traitor.*

The only response had been the dry whistle of Nico's respirator as it moved air in and out of him. His son was brain-dead, and Sam was at the party only because he had to prove something: that Nico had not been the son of his heart, his favorite, whose death was going to leave him bereft, bitter, and lonely.

◄►

The Meyer Davis Orchestra took over, playing a medley of Alexandra Winthrop ballads—"Easy Woman," "Forgiving Woman," "Ever-Loving Woman," and her latest, "Lonesome Woman." The tunes drifted across the crowded room with the rhythmic, bluesy harmony that was Alexandra's trademark.

Bitsy circulated among the guests, balancing her tray of fluted champagne glasses. Senator Winthrop had not yet arrived.

Everyone seemed to be talking about the kidnapping of the Cox child. *Can you believe the Mafia was involved? And did you hear . . .*

Bitsy shut her ears to it. All that mattered to her was the fact that the entrance of the Royals would focus attention elsewhere so that she could carry out her execution.

She couldn't resist lightly brushing her uniform pocket. Through the fabric, the knife made a neat, smooth bulge. No one had even noticed when she retrieved it from the pantry area, where extra silverware was kept.

Bitsy went back to the bar to refill her tray of champagne glasses. The scene was getting hectic, with more than six hundred people attempting to position themselves so that they would have a good view when the Prince and Princess of Wales entered the ballroom.

Then Bitsy saw him.

He strode into the reception area like a blond Kennedy, all wide, toothy smile and confidence, looking fabulous in his black tuxedo jacket and black tie. On his arm was his wife, Rita Sue,

Little Miss Southern Comfort, in romantic mauve.

Bitsy froze, chunks of ice replacing the blood in her veins and arteries. She barely noticed when a man walked past and took a glass from her tray. She felt as if she hadn't breathed for five minutes, as if she were about to explode from lack of oxygen. Every fantasy she'd ever had for the past four years, every nightmare, nearly every waking thought . . .

"Elizabeth," hissed one of the other waitresses, whisking past her with a tray of champagne glasses. "Move it, will you? Walter wants us to move these drinks. Charles and Di are about to come in."

Bitsy didn't even hear her. She didn't hear the orchestra, now finishing a second chorus of "Easy Woman." She didn't notice the flutter and stir among the guests, the security men trying to clear a space in the crowd.

All she knew was that *her* drama was starting. Within minutes, Senator Derek Winthrop would be dead.

— ►◄ —

In the Green Room there was a hubbub of voices. The room was full of security personnel in formal attire: Royal bodyguards, Secret Service agents, and Chicago police. Most wore earpieces and carried small walkie-talkies. All wore intent expressions. When word had been received of the Cox child's kidnapping, Charles decided they would still attend the party; however, security forces were to be doubled. President Bush and his secretary of state were both nervous over the decision but recognized the magnitude of the occasion and concurred with the rationale of Prince Charles.

The strict security made for close quarters and the annoyance of being surrounded at all times by grim faces.

Princess Diana emerged from the changing area that had been allocated for her use. Her lady-in-waiting, Anne Beckwith-Smith, had been standing outside the door to guard her from intrusion.

"Only a few moments," said Beckwith-Smith.

Diana felt a pull in the roots of her hair and reached up to discover that her tiara, borrowed from the Queen's own jewels, was slipping. She tugged at it. It was called the Lover's Knot tiara and had teardrop pearl pendants topped by delicate diamond bows. It was stunning, but tiaras were notoriously difficult to wear.

"There," the lady-in-waiting said, doing magic with a pin she removed from a tote bag. Diana carried no purse.

Diana looked around the long room. President Bush, his wife, Barbara, the Quayles, Reagans, Fords, and governors Jim Thompson of Illinois and James Blanchard from Michigan were sipping champagne and swapping political war stories.

At the far end of the room, Charles was in deep conversation with Lee Iacocca, Roger Smith, and the other auto executives.

Diana sighed. Absorbed in the magnitude of his discussions for the United Kingdom, Charles's cheeks had taken on a bright flush. She was so pleased for him. His diplomatic mission was going to be so successful. Mrs. Thatcher would be elated. The Queen would probably share their enthusiasm.

If only . . .

—— ⋈ ——

"But you *have* to let me in!" Mary Lee Wilde cried frantically to the security guard who stood inside the silk-canopied entrance to the hotel.

"Sorry, ma'am, you are not on the list."

"But—of course, I am! Look! I have an invitation!" She reached into her beaded evening bag and extracted the invitation. She thrust it into the guard's face. Already others were in line behind her, and she flushed bright red with embarrassment.

The guard examined the proffered invitation. He ran down the Ws again with his finger. "Sorry," he repeated.

"Please," she pleaded. "Can't you call somewhere? This is just a clerical error!"

"You're going to have to step back, ma'am," the guard insisted.

Mary Lee looked around desperately. A woman in a Mary McFadden gown had walked over to the guard and began to confer with him in a low voice. Mary Lee struggled to remember her name. Dolly Rutledge! Yes, Alexandra's party planner.

Mary Lee rushed forward. "Dolly, it's so embarrassing, but I think there's been a mistake of some kind. I know I was on your guest list; I've got my invitation, and I'm Alexandra's best friend."

Of course, Dolly recognized her at once—who wouldn't?

Within seconds, Mary Lee was on her way through the security gate.

Once inside, she paused for a minute, trying to adjust the hammering of her heart to more normal levels. She was, as always, prepared for anything with another of her microcassette tape recorders tucked into her larger than usual evening bag. But that was just a reflex. Tonight wasn't about a newspaper series. She had to straighten things out between herself and Alexandra.

She strode through the crowds, six feet tall in her high heels, attracting more than a few looks in her lettuce green silk georgette gown. She was unescorted because she and Jake had had another one of their quarrels.

Now a woman CEO she had once interviewed on her show looked up, saw Mary Lee, and then spoke to her escort. "Bitch," Mary Lee lip-read.

She took a few more strides, her bearing still confident, but inside she was shaken to the core. Was that how people thought of her?

She wended her way through the crowded hall. ". . . don't you think Diana's rather simplistic in the way she dresses?" a woman was saying. "I mean, British design." Another woman said, "She wears a size ten shoe."

Mary Lee grabbed a fluted glass from a waitress's tray and gulped half of it, hoping it would settle her nerves.

At the door of the VIP room, she encountered a phalanx of hard-eyed men in tuxedos.

"Press," she said briskly. "NBC." She flashed her NBC press card at one of the men and waited for him to recognize her. She flattered herself that she was nearly as recognizable as Barbara Walters, and this time her calculations proved right.

She walked into the Green Room. Beautifully decorated with Laura Ashley wallpaper and huge urns of mixed roses, orchids, and lilies, it was crowded with people, half of them security personnel. Diana wasn't in sight at all, but Charles stood huddled with a group of auto men, all of them talking intently.

"Mary Lee . . . damn it," Richard Cox said, coming up to her. In his evening wear he looked suave, handsome. Every detail was perfect, from the impeccable black silk tie to the black onyx-and-diamond stud set, to the matching silk cummerbund that made his lean stomach look even leaner.

"Hello, Richard. A lovely party," she said, but her smile trembled.

He didn't look thrilled at seeing her. "What the hell are you doing here? I thought I took you off the list. I told you, Mary Lee, I want you out of Alexandra's life."

"That's being awfully blunt," she said, her eyes filling with tears that she hadn't planned on. "Richard—I know I've been shitty—please. At least let me talk to her. Let me explain things to her. I want to straighten everything out between us."

He looked at her doubtfully. "Alexandra will be coming out in a minute to circulate among the guests, but she's very fragile tonight."

"I know." Her eyes filled. "Richard, I love her. I do love her! I tried to use her. I know that, and I wouldn't blame you for cutting me out of her life, but . . . I hope you won't. I hope you'll let her make that decision. I haven't got very many friends," she heard herself blurt. Now the tears were running down her cheeks.

She couldn't say anything more. She just looked at him, letting her eyes plead for her.

"All right," Richard said reluctantly. "I'll let you see her now."

"Thank you," Mary Lee said, clasping one of his hands in hers. It was her first warm and sincere act in years.

Richard led Mary Lee into one of the several conference rooms that adjoined the Green Room. Crouched on the rug in front of a TV watching *The Rescuers* were Stephanie and Andy Cox. The three-year-old girl wore a long, pale pink, ruffled dress, the boy a tiny tuxedo jacket.

Mary Lee's eyes traveled to the long couch, where Alexandra was seated. She wore a beautiful silver lamé gown, a filmy shawl pulled over her shoulders, her cloud of blonde hair gleaming. Around her neck the Fitzgerald Fifty was a blaze of light. Alexandra herself looked pale, her beauty ethereal. Her sprained right arm was in a sling.

Cuddled up to his mother, his small body inched so close to hers that he was almost on her lap, was Trip. The six-year-old's face was discolored with bruises, and there was a bulky bandage on his forehead.

On Alexandra's right, also sitting close, was Jette.

Mary Lee's eyes filled with tears.

"Alexandra. Jette." She choked up, not knowing whether she would be accepted.

"Mary Lee?" Alexandra's face looked wan, growing momentarily even paler. A tremulous smile touched her lips.

Mary Lee's bag dropped to the floor as she rushed forward and knelt down on the floor in front of Alexandra.

She put her head on Alexandra's lap and started sobbing. She was crying for so much.

"I know I'm not perfect, but I do love you, Alexandra," Mary Lee wept. "I do!"

"I know," Alexandra said, crying.

"Both of us do," Jette sobbed, joining in.

The three women clung to each other, tears streaming down their cheeks.

"Mrs. Cox?" a security man said, entering the room. "Mrs. Cox, they're ready to make their entrance. It should be only five more minutes now."

"Oh!" Alexandra straightened up. Her hand flew to her tear-streaked face. "Oh, my makeup!"

"We all look like trolls," Jette exclaimed. "But never to fear—I'm a makeup genius, remember? I brought a big bag full of stuff . . . tons and tons of lip gloss and mascara wands."

Mary Lee laughed, remembering a day, so long ago in London, when Jette had made them up. "Let's go for it," she said huskily. "Let's party."

—— ▶◀ ——

Dolly Rutledge stood in the crowd that ringed the door of the Green Room, her husband, Manny, at her side. All around her, the guests were standing on tiptoes, anxiously awaiting the entrance of the Prince and Princess of Wales.

Dolly clutched at Manny's arm.

"My God, the door's opening!" she said to him. "We really did it. A future King of England's going to come through that door. And a future Queen. I wonder what Di will be wearing."

"You always think about clothes," Manny teased good-naturedly, but she could tell he was as excited as she was.

—— ▶◀ ——

Bitsy, hearing the music, quickly set down her tray on a nearby chair.

Derek Winthrop and his wife stood only three feet from her, engrossed in the spectacle. Rita Sue was saying something about how Daddy had once taken her to Buckingham Palace.

Bitsy heard only a few words of it. Her entire being concentrated on what she had to do. She was a machine, programmed to step forward, her right hand reaching across her body to remove the knife from her apron pocket.

Swift movements. Smooth ones. Step around to Derek Winthrop's right. Step forward two steps and turn. That placed her within perfect striking distance. Then there was nothing between them, nothing to stop her or change what had been inevitable since the bullets were fired that night in Georgetown.

She sensed rather than saw the knife blade flash through a perfect arc . . .

Then strong hands gripped her arm, dragging her away.

It had all happened in a matter of seconds, without drawing attention. Bitsy couldn't even scream or struggle—she just looked around wildly, stunned.

"*Puttana*," growled a deep, angry male voice. It was Sam Provenzo, Mafia *padrone*.

Bitsy still couldn't cry. Derek Winthrop had turned around to stare at her, his face white. *He didn't even know who she was.*

She moaned helplessly as Sam Provenzo walked her over to the nearest security guard.

— ▸◂ —

"Charles?" said Diana in the VIP room, waiting as her husband approached her. He was shining in his full-dress uniform, and his face looked as it did in hundreds of photographs in dozens of magazines—handsome, sensitive, a bit aloof. He had talked to everyone else but her.

"Do you like my dress?" she asked shyly. The question, both knew, meant so much more.

She was ravishing in a deep blue Bruce Oldfield gown, the flowing chiffon skirt accenting her tall grace. A beautiful, blue-sequinned tiny jacket just barely hugged her shoulders, revealing the strapless bodice beneath. The Lover's Knot tiara glittered in her blonde hair, and around her neck she wore the magnificent Sri Lankan sapphire, a huge, dark, glowing gem fixed to the center of a seven-strand pearl choker.

The music was playing, their signal to move into the big

ballroom. Inspector Graham Smith, their security chief, motioned them to step forward.

"Do you like it? My dress?" she repeated, her voice a bare whisper. He looked so regal tonight, he awed even her.

Their eyes met.

"I like it. It's rather smashing," he said, and a slight smile touched his lips. "Definitely."

He lifted her hand and kissed it gently, his breath a soft puff on her skin. All the security men, the ladies-in-waiting, the reporters, the staff members, Richard, and Alexandra . . . all of them saw.

As they stepped forward, Diana smiled a smile that was utterly radiant.

—— ►◄ ——

"Alexandra," Richard said, gently taking her arm and helping her to her feet. Jette and Mary Lee had already gone to stand with the children. "Are you feeling all right? Are you ready for this?"

"I'm ready," she said steadily.

"I'll be with you every minute. If you start to feel tired, I want you to tell me right away. Everyone will understand."

"I created this party, and I'm not going to get tired," she said. "Richard . . . do you like what I've done?"

His eyes locked with hers, and she could see a glitter of pride in them, mingled with the outpouring of unrestrained love she had seen ever since, in total disregard of his own life, he had pulled Trip and her out of that crashed Lincoln.

Nico could have murdered all three of them, mowing them down with the automatic weapon he carried. But he hadn't. Some shred of kindness had held him back at the last second, and he'd let them escape behind the safety of the truck.

There'd been the sound of shots as Nico had turned wildly on the Mafia soldiers who converged on the car. The ensuing carnage ended with two dead, Nico himself slumped over in a wild barrage of bullets.

"Lexy," her husband now whispered. "I love what you've done. I love *everything* you've done—and you know it's much, much more than just a party. You saved our baby. And you got yourself back."

"I love you," she whispered, leaning into his strength.

He held her, and through the fabric of his shirtfront, she could hear his steady, strong heartbeat. "I love you, too, honey. More than you'll know." With his right forefinger, he touched one of the glorious diamonds that nestled at her throat. "Remember what I told you about these? Each one stands for a year? I'm still holding you to that, darling."

"Rich—" Her voice was choked. She gazed at him through crystal prisms of tears.

"Hey," he said, wiping away a full droplet. "Don't cry any more of them, punkie. Not until later, when all of this is over and we can go home. Then you can cry all you want."

"I'm never going to cry again," she promised him, smiling.

—— ►◄ ——

Dolly Rutledge's sigh mingled with every other sigh in the huge ballroom, the air humming with a soft, collective murmur. The guests strained to get closer, pressing their bodies tightly together.

Dolly caught her breath and forgot to breathe again. The orchestra struck up "Rule Brittania." Emerging from the door of the VIP room were the Prince and Princess of Wales.

Behind Charles and Diana came President Bush and Barbara, the First Lady in powder blue satin. Then former President Ronald Reagan, suntanned and smiling, waving to the crowd. Nancy was in deep burgundy red. Former President Gerald Ford and his wife, Betty, were behind them, Betty in light peach. The Jimmy Carters followed, both looking younger than when in office. Then came Richard and Alexandra. The evening had begun.

Party voices, a hubbub of talk, laughter, carried along on a wave of orchestra music, fizzing and bubbling like the Cristal Roederer champagne being served. Bare white shoulders gleamed in the muted light, as diamonds glittered from necks, ears, and wrists.

Richard and Alexandra escorted Charles and Diana to the head table, where they took their seats. After they had been seated, the rest of the head table filed in. President and Mrs. Bush, the mayor of Chicago, and the governor of Illinois were also at the first tier, while at the second tier were ex-Presidents, ambassadors, and other Royalty. The third tier of the head table held the automakers, senators, congressmen, and other honored guests.

When all guests had been seated amid murmurings of suppressed excitement, and after the invocation, Richard rose and offered the first toast. The room grew still as he welcomed Charles and Diana as their guests.

"To international peace . . . a superb peace ambassador, Prince Charles," he finished, to the sound of loud applause.

Later, as Charles rose for a speech of his own, Alexandra leaned close to Richard and whispered, "I know we have the protocol right, but more important—is the chemistry right? I mean, is it really happening? All the political things that Charles wanted?"

Richard smiled. "Lexy, it is happening like nothing else ever happened before. Have you taken a good look at him? Charles looks like a man who's just taken his country for a tie-breaking touchdown. Babe," he reached out to take her hand, "I'd say there's more than one person responsible for this winner. You made this party. It's you, honey." His voice broke a little. "Always you, Alexandra. I mean that."

Unashamed, they held hands, looking into each other's eyes.

17

Bouquets

The following day, Sunday, was bright and clear, a day on which all things seemed possible.

At the Fitzgerald Hotel, cleaning crews swept through the huge triple ballroom in which 650 people had eaten, danced, gawked at Royalty, initiated deals, gossiped, shown off, and been shown off—in short, had a good time.

A cleaning woman bent down and picked up a silk flower dusted with glitter that had come off one of the dancer's costumes as she left at 2:30 A.M. The woman held it in her hands, a tiny souvenir of Royalty, the closest she would probably ever get. She decided to take it home and slip it in the mirror of her dresser.

— ◄► —

In the Royals' private jet, Charles and Diana were on their way to the Grand Canyon. Diana, surprising her staff and amazing Charles, had decided to hike alongside her husband.

While Diana dozed, Charles was on the telephone to Margaret Thatcher, giving her the good news. Talks were begun to bring five auto plants to England. And Charles would begin a peacekeeping mission to the Middle East in three weeks.

— ◄► —

Darryl Boyer woke up to find herself in Court Frank's hotel room at the Fitz. God—her feet were still cramping from all the dancing she'd done with Sid Cohen, who had taken an astonishing shine to her.

Cohen wanted her for a new ten-hour miniseries based on the latest Judith Krantz bestseller. Incredible! She couldn't believe her marvelous good luck.

— ◄► —

At Michael Reese Hospital, a pale woman occupied a bed in a room filled with roses.

Trip dropped his mother's hand and rushed to the bed, throwing his arms around his nanny.

"Brownie-Brownie-Brownie!" he cried jubilantly. He snuggled into the grip of the weak arm that nonetheless managed to clasp him tightly. "I love you, Brownie. I just love you."

"I love you, too, Trip," Brownie said, her voice stronger than it had been in three days.

— ◄► —

David Kwan was having breakfast with Sid Cohen on the hotel's Garden Terrace, wrapping up a purchase deal for Omni Studios and rights to all the pictures being made there, including the projected Krantz miniseries.

Mei Lee, Kwan's mistress, sat at the table, too, toying with a papaya half. She wore a red cheongsam embroidered with dragons and chrysanthemums.

"David, darling," Mei Lee finally interrupted in her soft Hong Kong accent. "David, if you buy this studio, will there be a part for me? I want the part that Darryl Boyer is testing for. Please?"

She rubbed her knee against Kwan's thigh under the table and gazed at him with her beautiful almond-shaped eyes. She knew he would say yes.

— ◄► —

Derek Winthrop was just waking up with his wife. He got out of bed, unable to sleep anymore.

What a party! There had never been one like it. An assassination attempt, which would turn out to be a huge publicity advantage, giving him nationwide coverage.

But best of all, he had been approached. The word was that if he minded his p's and q's and won the Senate reelection with a big margin, he just might get the rest of the alphabet.

Starting with a Vice Presidential nomination.

—— ►◄ ——

In the hospital's intensive-care unit, Sam Provenzo took his dying son's hand. "Nicolo," he whispered to the silent body. "Nicolo."

There was no response but the sound of machines. Silent tears began to run down Sam's face, and he brushed them back with his free hand.

"Nicolo," Sam said. "I got to tell you. I think I'm gonna take little Davy, I think I'm gonna send him to Harvard like you. What do you think of that, Nico? I . . ."

And then Sam broke down. He leaned forward on the bed, burying his face against the prone, silent body, his hands splayed on Nico's chest, and he cried. It was hard to outlive your son.

—— ►◄ ——

Mo Bernstein had hurried his girlfriend out of bed at 6:30 A.M. Now they were in a cab on their way to the American Airlines terminal at O'Hare.

He flipped open a copy of the Sunday *Chicago Tribune*. The headlines were full of the party and the assassination attempt on Senator Derek Winthrop. However, two smaller lines of print on an inside page hit him in the face like a sharp slap.

FLORIDA LEGISLATURE REJECTS CASINO GAMBLING.

Oh, shit, Mo thought. It looked as though the casinos in the Florida Fitz Hotels were not going to materialize . . . this year, anyway.

—— ►◄ ——

Later that day, Alexandra and Richard stood in the hallway outside the children's playroom. Alexandra was holding something in her arms, something small, furry, and wiggly, with huge brown eyes.

"Isn't it wonderful of Diana to have sent this puppy? She wanted to send a corgi from England, but it would have had to wait to go through quarantine, so she sent this little spaniel instead."

Alexandra bent over and set down the puppy. He wiggled and lurched forward on his little fat legs, heading into the playroom, where he was greeted with squeals of delight.

Alexandra and Richard stood back and, grinning, watched the melee. As the children held and petted the dog, Richard slid his arm around Alexandra.

"Babe . . . Lexy . . . I have something for you, too."

"For me?"

He pulled her face up to meet his, giving her a kiss that was as long and lingering as it was passionate.

"Well, for us. You were right. I'd become so involved in building our future that I was losing touch with our here-and-now, so I've bought a château in Switzerland. Our hideaway. The union contract is signed and there's no pressing business. It's time for us to be together as a family and let the corporation run itself for a while. We can leave next week and stay for a month . . . you, me, the kids . . . what do you say?"

"Oh, darling," tears filled Alexandra's eyes.